LESSONS

from the

CLASSROOM

DEVOTIONS FOR TEACHERS

Alton Royer Ph.D.

ISBN 979-8-88851-295-1 (Paperback)
ISBN 979-8-88851-296-8 (Digital)

Covenant Books
11661 Hwy 707
Murrells Inlet, SC 29576
www.covenantbooks.com

These devotionals are presented to encourage educators who give their lives to young people. As a teacher, you will have many opportunities to be a positive influence for Christ through your kind words and actions.

Keep in mind that in most cases, parent perceptions of teachers are formed through the eyes of their children. Teachers may gain great reputations or somewhat negative reputations entirely through their positive or negative interactions with their students. Listening to parents' conversations about school while they are in the school building, at the grocery store, or at the ballpark will confirm that their child's teacher has formed a reputation of some kind.

Comments such as "He/She is a nice teacher" or "That teacher won't listen to you" or "That teacher is unfair" or "That teacher won't help if your child has problems" and "We just love Mr./Mrs. Jones" are heard all the time, particularly at the beginning of another school year. Whether or not these perceptions are deserved is beside the point. Take it for granted that they will be formed about you as well. View each day as an opportunity to be "salt and light" in a manner that represents Christ to a lost world.

DEDICATION

To my wife, Pam, who encouraged me all along this journey. God blessed me with a wife who has strength, dignity, and wisdom (Proverbs 31:25–26).

To my two children, Camille and Michael, who, along with the Holy Spirit, provided inspiration for several of these devotionals.

To the Christian teacher, who has the privilege of working in the profession God chose for his Son and who is the "salt and light" in today's challenging environment of education.

ACKNOWLEDGMENTS

My sincerest thanks and appreciation to Carol Zembower, MEd, who assisted with the initial edit of this manuscript.

DAY 1

First Impressions

You are the salt of the earth, but if salt has lost its taste, how shall its saltiness be restored? It is no longer good for anything except to be thrown out and trampled under people's feet. You are the light of the world. A city set on a hill cannot be hidden. Nor do people light a lamp and put it under a basket, but on a stand, and it gives light to all in the house. In the same way, let your light shine before others, so that they may see your good works and give glory to your Father who is in Heaven.
—Matthew 5:13–16

So also faith by itself, if it does not have works, is dead.
—James 2:17

Jesus said that "you are the salt of the earth and the light of the world." Notice that while using these two metaphors, Jesus didn't give an option of whether we wish to be salt and light! Being a Christian means that we *are* salt and light! It is our responsibility to be that Christian example every day for our students. We also must be extremely careful not to lose the saltiness that was given to us when we were saved.

How can our "salt" or influence be lost? Our saltiness can be lost through a thoughtless action, an unkind comment, or even a subtle negative facial expression. I heard a student say, "I will never respect Mrs. B. again because of what she said to J. about her paper." Thoughtless comments, unkind words, and even facial expressions can change the positive perception people have toward us to a negative perception.

Know that each day you arrive at school, every action, facial expression, and word said are continually being scrutinized by your colleagues, students, their parents, caretakers, or guardians. Understand that parents' perceptions about you will be formed through the lens of their child.

In verse 16, Jesus commands us to let our good works be seen so that God may be glorified. How is this accomplished? By allowing Jesus to be himself in us every moment of every day. James puts it very succinctly, "Faith without works is dead."

Are you ready for the day? Ask Jesus to be himself in you at every moment.

DAY 2

Ready for Evaluation

> Not many of you should become teachers, my brothers, for you
> know that we who teach will be judged with greater strictness.
> —James 3:1

James, the brother of Jesus, was speaking through experience, "We who teach will be judged with greater strictness," and his audience understood the scrutiny that teachers endured: "for you know that we who teach will be judged with greater strictness." Our words and actions will be continually judged just as Jesus's actions were judged and critiqued.

We are reminded of this judgment by others when incidents at school are recorded on social media and then reported on the nightly news. In this current educational environment, we must assume that every action and every comment we make may be recorded, posted on social media, and critiqued! The capabilities of portable electronic devices now make it possible to record, edit, and post a different version of the incident from what really happened.

Unfortunately, people will record and edit events, and their version of that event will not be what really happened. Assume that in any meeting that you attend, particularly with an irate parent or disgruntled student, this meeting may be recorded. Keep in mind that your words in the classroom may be recorded without your knowledge.

I was in a parent meeting one time, and the parent requested to record the meeting. I had to pause the meeting to get my own recording device! During this meeting, the parent continually tried to get me to say things that would enforce their position. For my protection, I needed the recording of this conversation in case items that we discussed were taken out of context and put on social media.

Are you ready to have your actions or comments judged? Ask God for wisdom in everything that you say and do today as well as taking the critique of your practice by others in a kind spirit.

DAY 3

Consider Our Calling

Ponder the path of your feet; then all your ways will be sure.
—Proverbs 4:26

"Ponder the path of your feet." *Ponder*—to consider deeply and thoroughly, even to meditate regarding the way we should go. We need to ask the Holy Spirit to help us make wise decisions regarding our chosen profession, finances, marriage, church affiliation—in other words, everything. If the decision *we* make is not part of God's will for our lives, we may not be as effective in our witness and will certainly be miserable.

For example, I know of a great pastor who used to be an exceptionally effective salesman but was miserable because he wasn't in the profession in which God had called him. This man has a God-given talent for persuasion. As a salesman, he was particularly good at getting people to buy big-ticket items. He was in a profession that utilized this talent, and he was successful by the world's standards; but it was not the profession chosen for him by God, and he knew it. He made the bold decision to leave that profession with its monetary perks and get the necessary education to become a pastor.

Many people have a talent for numbers, but they chose the wrong profession, accounting over engineering. Others may have a great aptitude for medical science but not a good physician because they lack empathy and people skills; however, they may make a great researcher. Then there are those with great people skills and do well with children but are not effective educators because they cannot teach the subject with the depth needed to adequately educate young people. In other words, this person may not possess the math skills needed to be an effective algebra teacher but has the necessary math skills needed to effectively teach middle school math.

A few years back, one day, on the drive to the airport with my then eleventh-grade son, we became engaged in a discussion regarding his choice of majors when he went to college. He said he wanted to be a band director and to major in music education. Having been a former band director and now a principal, I was strongly discouraging him from being an educator, particularly in this current environment. He looked at me and said, "Dad, what if I am being called to be a music educator?"

I looked at him and said, "Son, if you genuinely feel that God has called you to do this, then I would never stand in your way and proudly support you in your endeavor." At that point, our discussion ended. He majored in music education, then went on and received his master's degree in percussion performance and is now a successful teacher.

Are you sure of your calling? Ask God for reassurance or for wisdom to make right decisions regarding your chosen profession.

DAY 4

Sound Practice

The fear of the LORD is the beginning of wisdom; all
those who practice it have a good understanding.
—Psalm 111:10

The fear of the Lord is the beginning of wisdom,
and the knowledge of the Holy One is insight.
—Proverbs 9:10

The fear of the Lord means having an attitude of reverence, respect, and awe of Almighty God. Having this attitude toward God puts us in the right frame of mind toward him and gives us a willingness to accept good teaching and new knowledge.

Those that love the Lord are more open to knowing more about him. In addition, they possess the characteristic of inquisitiveness enabling them to ask questions and to discern right and wrong.

Take note of the second half of the verse, "all those who practice." Practice requires an intentional effort made by the individual. The amount, intensity, and method of practice explains why some students succeed and others fail and explains why some students with greater ability may not achieve to the level as students of lesser ability. The amount and intensity of practice is a significantly important variable in learning.

Satan has propagated the myth that all students are able to achieve equally. He has worked into our vocabulary the confusion of the word *opportunity* with the word *equally*. C. S. Lewis describes the "opportunity versus equality" issue in his book *The Screwtape Letters*.

In the chapter "Screwtape Proposes a Toast," Screwtape discusses an idea heard often today that says, "I am as good as you." Lewis states, "No man says, 'I'm as good as you,' believes it. The claim of equality...is made only by those who feel themselves to be in some way inferior." To further quote Lewis, "The basic principle of the new education is to be that dunces and idlers must not be made to feel inferior to intelligent and industrious pupils—for they are obviously and nakedly individual differences—must be disguised." Lewis demonstrates in this chapter that these ideas of "self-esteem" and "not hurting a student's feelings" are vocabulary that, over the years, have been twisted by Satan, and we now live in a society that embraces these lies which are straight out of hell.

Screwtape continues, "Let them, for example, make mud-pies and call it modelling. But all the time there must be no faintest hint that they are inferior to the children who are at work. Whatever nonsense they are engaged in must have—I believe the English already use the phrase—'parity of esteem.'"

The equal achievement myth does not take the variable of proper practice by the learner into consideration. "Good teaching" does not necessarily make the subject "easy" for all learners as some parents will assert to you when their child is not making the highest grade. The *learner* must embrace the struggle for learning the subject matter. Some subjects are easier for some students than for others.

The second verse states that knowledge of Christ is insight. Remember that as Christians, we have the Holy Spirit to guide us, thus knowledge is insight, or as *Webster's Dictionary* defines, "penetrating mental vision or discernment." We have all that is needed to make good decisions with the Holy Spirit. Putting these verses together, we see that with the fear of the Lord, we can have understanding and insight.

What do you do when students have difficulty learning a concept that you taught? Ask God for patience, wisdom, and the initiative to diagnose the issue and work with that student and their parents.

DAY 5

Testing the Boundaries

The fear of the LORD is the beginning of knowledge;
fools despise wisdom and instruction.
—Proverbs 1:7

Johnny was a sixth-grade student and was large for his age. He encountered issues with multiple teachers as he was sent to my office different times by different teachers. His problems were that he was constantly leaving his seat without permission, distracting other students by touching them, not following the teachers' directives regarding stopping inappropriate behavior, or making inappropriate noises to see if the teacher noticed. I counseled with him several times, but the behavior persisted. I called home and spoke to his mother, and she stated that she would "talk to Johnny about this." The behavior would stop for a few days and then begin again. After each incident, I would call home and receive the same response.

One day, while in the computer lab, Johnny decided to get under the desk. The teacher requested that he come out from under his desk, and he refused. He then put a paperclip into a wall socket, and the socket made a pop and a spark. The teacher, totally frightened, finally got him to get out from under the desk and sent him to me. I called home and explained the incident to his mother. She stated that we were being overly concerned and that this was the behavior of a twelve-year-old boy. I stated, "Let me see if I understand what you are saying. Your twelve-year-old son went to a computer class, got under a desk, refused to come out from under the desk when asked, put a paperclip into a wall socket so that it popped and sparked, which endangered his life, and you are saying that these are the behaviors of a twelve-year-old boy?" I didn't receive a response to that question. The mother advised me to talk to his father.

I called his father, explained the context of the incident, and Johnny's father's response was that they encouraged Johnny to "test the boundaries." I explained to the father that the "boundaries" had been tested and that if this behavior didn't cease, Johnny would have to be placed in "in-school suspension." The father said that he didn't agree with this and that I should send Johnny to the coach and make him run laps. I stated that the school did not follow this practice, that there were protocols set by our board of education that we were to follow. I explained that the first step was to inform the parent; the second step was to place a child in "in school suspension," where he/she would attend school, but be isolated from all other students; and the third step would be to suspend the child at home for three days.

Dad said that the three-day home suspension couldn't happen because he and Johnny's mother had to work, and there was no one that could care for Johnny. I stated that we would work as much as we could with Johnny here at school and that the three-day home suspension would be a last resort. Dad still asserted that Johnny was encouraged to "test the boundaries" and that we should not "break his spirit." At the conclusion of this conversation, Dad said that he would discuss this behavior with Johnny, that they were "buddies," and that the behavior would stop.

The same pattern continued. Johnny's behavior would improve for a few days, and then the behavior would begin again. Johnny had to spend three days at home several times that school year.

Johnny didn't want to learn. He was focused on making a scene in the classroom, and his father encouraged the behavior by counseling him to "test the boundaries." In this case, the fool was the father who was teaching his son wrong behavior.

This verse serves as an excellent reminder that there will be times that we will be at odds with students who just do not want to learn. We handle this by pressing on, continuing to offer positive encouragement, and when needed, using the discipline process. Touching base with the parents to see if there is something occurring outside of school is always a good strategy. You may gain some insight, as I did with Johnny's father, as to why there is pushback toward learning by the student. Reminding ourselves that we, too, were once "fools" regarding the knowledge of Jesus and the Way is a good spiritual checkpoint for us.

How are you handling that student who just doesn't want to learn? What insights have you discovered as to why this is happening?

DAY 6

Wisdom and Insight

Get wisdom; get insight; do not forget, and do not
turn away from the words of my mouth.
—Proverbs 4:5

The beginning of wisdom is this: Get wisdom,
and whatever you get, get insight.
—Proverbs 4:7

Websters Dictionary defines *wisdom* as "knowledge of what is true or right coupled with just judgement." From a *spiritual standpoint, wisdom* is being able to see and perceive things from God's perspective or point of view. *Insight* is defined as "apprehending the true nature of issues through intuitive understanding."

God gives us a command, "Get wisdom, get insight." How do we follow this command of God? First, we must recognize that gaining wisdom and insight implies a conscious and a willful decision, just as the way we come to Christ, after listening and heeding the promptings of the Holy Spirit.

"Do not forget" implies a conscious effort through constant repetition to remember what has been taught. How do we not forget something important? We do not forget what was taught by making it a priority and through repetition.

The daily reading, study, and memorization of the Bible enable us to gain proper wisdom (knowledge of what is true and right, seeing issues from God's perspective) and insight (apprehension of the true nature of an issue). This repetitive process helps us to know God better and prepares us to make decisions and judgments that agree with God's perspective. Remember, God sent his Holy Spirit to help us pass the test!

Have you studied the subject that you teach to the extent that you can teach it with the depth of knowledge needed by your students? Ask God for insight, an awareness of the true nature of your students' learning difficulties when they occur.

DAY 7

How Wisdom Looks

Who is wise and understanding among you? By his good
conduct let him show his works in the meekness of wisdom.
But if you have bitter jealousy and selfish ambition in your
hearts, do not boast and be false to the truth. This is not the
wisdom that comes down from above, but is earthly, unspiritual,
demonic. For where jealousy and selfish ambition exist, there
will be disorder and every vile practice. But the wisdom from
above is first pure, then peaceable, gentle, open to reason, full
of mercy and good fruits, impartial and sincere. And a harvest
of righteousness is sown in peace by those who make peace.

—James 3:13–18

Seeing things from God's perspective is one thing, but how does this
inward perception translate so that others can evaluate whether we
have wisdom? James contrasts earthly wisdom and heavenly wisdom
by listing some characteristics of both. Interestingly, Jesus, James's
half brother, lists some of these same characteristics in the Sermon
on the Mount and calls these people blessed.

My prayer is that people will see me as pure, peaceable, gentle,
open to reason, full of mercy and good fruits, impartial, and sincere.
When others speak of you, can they describe you in one or more of
the traits that James lists? How would your students describe you?

DAY 8

Repetition

You shall teach them diligently to your children, and shall
talk of them when you sit in your house, and when you
walk by the way, and when you lie down, and when you
rise. You shall bind them as a sign on your hand, and they
shall be as frontlets between your eyes. You shall write them
on the doorposts of your house and on your gates.

—Deuteronomy 6:7–9

Moses discusses the repetition of God's commands and statutes. Notice his emphasis on repetition. Repetition may be boring, but it is necessary.

When we were in school, to pass a math test, countless hours were spent studying to memorize formulas or to practice the process of solving a problem. When we prepared for tests in the social sciences, we memorized the words of a sonnet or studied and memorized the lecture notes so that the proper application could be made to arrive at the correct answer on the test.

In our profession as teachers, we constantly remind our students to study for the upcoming test. We encourage them to practice problems so that they remember processes. We continually cycle learned material back through our lessons to ensure that our students remember important concepts. We encourage them to be the best that they can be today. Repetition, repetition, repetition!

Have you included enough lesson activities so that important concepts are recycled and used by your students?

DAY 9

Engaging in Apologetics

And I tell you, for everyone who acknowledges me before men,
the Son of Man also will acknowledge before the angels of God.

—Luke 12:8

For the Holy Spirit will teach you in that
very hour what you ought to say.

—Luke 12:12

Be prepared because at some point, you will be questioned about your faith by students or colleagues. Issues such as evolution in biology, a required reading in English, or a discussion of current events in social studies will occur during the school year. Your colleagues may inquire about your church affiliation and beliefs at the lunch table.

When I taught beginning band and introduced the concept of playing in tune, I would demonstrate by asking two students playing the same instrument to play the same note. I would ask the students to listen for a "wha wha" sound in their ears. I explained that the faster this sensation was, the more out of tune they were with each other. The object was to get that "wha wha" sensation to stop.

At this point, I would say, "When God made us, he put our brain directly between our ears so that we could hear and think very fast." In that one statement, I made it known that I believed in God and that we are wonderfully made by him.

Several times in my career, I was asked, "Do you believe in evolution?"

My short answer: "Evolution is just a theory, not yet proven, and I believe that God created us." I promptly returned to our lesson.

Know that at some point in time, students will ask what your beliefs are. Why will they question you? Because like it or not, at this point, *you* are the authority on whatever subject that is being studied. Use these moments as opportunities to acknowledge your faith in Jesus and engage in apologetics. You don't have to be "preachy." The Holy Spirit will provide wisdom on how to witness within whatever context you may find yourself. Remember that even Jesus was tested by his enemies, the Pharisees, in their attempts to catch him in some way so that they could discredit his ministry.

Have you thought about your Christian beliefs in your subject so that when asked, you can speak a word in defense of your faith in Christ? Ask the Holy Spirit to give you good insight so that when questioned, you will be ready to speak on Christ's behalf.

DAY 10

STOP

If any of you lacks wisdom, let him ask God, who gives
generously to all without reproach, and it will be given him.

—James 1:5

Get ready it is going to happen. You are going to receive an ugly
email, an irate phone message, or be called into a parent conference.
As a principal, I regularly received such emails, irate phone messages,
and parents who "dropped by" demanding my attention.

As a teacher, when these events occurred, my mind would be
preoccupied because I would not have time to immediately respond.
Why? I was too busy with my students. My stomach would be wound
in knots until the issue could be resolved. How do we handle such
events? *S-T-O-P!* Summarize the issue in your mind; *t*hink about
your response; *o*rganize your thoughts; *p*ray for wisdom.

Attempt to respond within 24 hours to parent inquiries. Your
response may be that you want them to know that you have received
their question and that you will be getting back to them. This may
give you a little extra time to formulate a proper response.

Summarize the issue. Do a summary of the issue in your mind
remembering what happened in your classroom before and after.
Summarize in your mind the entire context of the incident.

Think about your response. Think about how your response will
be received and what the consequences of your response may be. Be
prepared to give the context of the situation and be prepared to offer
an apology if you find yourself in the wrong.

Organize your thoughts. Take some time to write down your
thoughts because when you write them, you may see that you are

making the situation worse. Depending on the situation, you may want to talk through the issue with your supervisor and get some advice before you respond. A conversation with your supervisor is helpful because you may get the question from the parent or guardian, "Who else may I discuss this with?" If needed, your supervisor will be informed and ready to respond.

Pray for wisdom. Pray for God to keep you calm and for your thoughts to be organized. Before making a phone call to an irate parent, or before going into a meeting that looks to be potentially contentious, put James 1:5 into practice and ask God for wisdom.

Are you prepared for the inevitable email, phone call, or conference? Ask God for wisdom as you work through parent and student issues.

DAY 11

A Clear Conscience

So I always take pains to have a clear conscience
toward both God and man.

—Acts 24:16

What a wonderful example Paul gives! He makes this statement during his defense before Felix against accusations from the Jews regarding his ministry. Paul, being a great teacher, took great pains to make sure that he was not a hindrance to anyone coming to Christ.

How can we keep a clear conscience? By following the directions of God and by maintaining an intimate fellowship with him by engaging in daily quiet time. Paul took great pains to practice this; in other words, he made this a priority in his life.

Reading further in this account reveals that Felix had an accurate knowledge of Christianity, was married to a Jew, and even conversed more with Paul regarding coming to Christ. All we know is that Paul's testimony alarmed Felix, and he sent Paul away. To our knowledge, Felix never made that important decision to follow Christ.

Paul's example reminds us to treat all students fairly and with the dignity they deserve, even when they are ugly and disrespectful, so that our conscience is always clear. When our conscience is clear before God, and we are right with him, the odds are that the professional decisions that need to be made will be correct.

Even when your students are not cooperative, do you "take pains" to treat all your students fairly and with the dignity they deserve?

DAY 12

It Is Well

Though a sinner does evil a hundred times and prolongs
his life, yet I know that it will be well with those
who fear God, because they fear before him.
—Ecclesiastes 8:12

But the Lord laughs at the wicked, for
he sees that his day is coming.
—Psalm 37:13

There will be times when we will wish that an unruly student or difficult parent "get his/hers," yet they seem to go unpunished. When we send students to the office, and there seems to be no discipline given, it is difficult for us to understand.

As a principal, I had two "thou shalts" when administering discipline. The first was to never let the student return to the classroom the same period that they were sent. The second was to follow up with the teacher and explain the discipline decision.

In the Christian context, to fear God means to have an awe and a healthy respect for him. As Christians, we have no issues with this because we're so grateful for what God did for us when he sent Jesus to save us from our sins. This concept is foolish to the non-Christian. So remember that when we see evil being done and sometimes rewarded, time tells much.

After being in this profession any length of time, we see former students reaping what they sowed in earlier years. We are saddened when we hear of them living unhappy lives, in bondage to possessions, in debt, in bad relationships, not having a clear conscience about anything, and always in turmoil.

In contrast, we who fear God when life's troubles come are much more capable of dealing with them. Horatio Spafford, a devout Christian could say, "Whatever my lot, thou hast taught me to say it is well; it is well with my soul." May this be our disposition also.

Ask God to give you the disposition of "it is well," even when you do not agree with the decisions of your colleagues and supervisors.

DAY 13

First Things First

But first make me a little cake of it and bring it to me, and
afterward make something for yourself and your son.

—1 Kings 17:13b

Wealth gained hastily will dwindle, but whoever
gathers little by little will increase it.

—Proverbs 13:11

You cannot serve God and money.

—Matthew 6:24b

"But first," Elijah asked on behalf of the Lord for the first portion of
what the widow was baking. Note that the widow obeyed. Honoring
God with our tithe, and with the first portion (or first check that is
written after payday) is an excellent way of prioritizing God in our
lives. Writing the first check each month helps us to say, "Lord, I
honor you with the first fruits of what I have earned." It is a wonderful way to manage the money that God has allowed us to earn. We
tithe out of obedience and should do this willingly and cheerfully,
"God loves a cheerful giver."

By the world's standards, we as educators do not make much
money, but that does not excuse us from the tithe to the Lord because
"the tithe is the Lord's." We must develop habits of being more frugal
with our finances than in other professions.

A useful principle in managing our finances is to give a tenth
and save a tenth. In addition, using debt sparingly and wisely will
enable us to navigate challenging financial times. Tithing also helps

to keep the perspective of stewardship. All we "have" is really God's, and we should be good managers of what he has graciously allowed us the privilege of managing.

Are you putting God first in your finances? Ask God for wisdom in managing your money.

DAY 14

Keeping Up with the Jones

And he said to them, "Take care, and be on your
guard against all covetousness, for one's life does not
consist in the abundance of his possessions."

—Luke 12:15

Covetousness is defined as a desire to possess something, typically something that belongs to someone else. Covetousness is an enemy to be avoided at all costs because it can poison our minds and cause us to become ineffective teachers. Remember, we did not become teachers to become rich but to enrich the lives of young people!

I personally know several teachers who started their teaching career satisfied with their lifestyle. As their acquaintances who graduated in other professions began to have more disposable income and accumulating possessions, their disposition toward their career choice became more negative. As I overheard conversations these teachers had regarding their acquaintances, it became obvious that they desired what their acquaintances now possessed. Those once effective teachers became disgruntled and began to lose their effectiveness with their students.

We must be careful of developing the attitude of "I'm not paid enough to do this or to put up with that!" This attitude becomes a slippery slope where our professional standards lapse into compromise, and we can become more and more ineffective and negative with our students.

It is sorrowful to see veteran teachers who have become ineffective, know it, and are miserable. These teachers feel that it has become too much of a chore to change their practice by tightening their classroom procedures and routines to be the teachers they once were.

Has your attitude toward teaching been negatively affected by your income? Ask God to help you be content with what you have and to be a good steward of the income with which he has blessed you.

DAY 15

Think on These Things

Finally, brothers, whatever is true, whatever is honorable,
whatever is just, whatever is pure, whatever is lovely,
whatever is commendable, if there is any excellence, if there
is anything worthy of praise, think about these things.
—Philippians 4:8

Possessing a disposition toward students that is true, honorable, just, pure, lovely, and commendable will increase our effectiveness as teachers because we will approach the needs of our students with greater love and care. We will make better educational decisions that benefit our students.

Try this exercise: think of your most challenging student and reflect on that person putting a "not" in front of all the characteristics Paul outlines. See how toxic this thinking is? We all have experience with persons who have this toxic way of thinking. Out of their mouths come sarcasm as well as negative and derogatory words about children. On one occasion, I listened as a colleague spoke negatively about his students, and I asked, "Do you like children?"

Following Paul's directions will take conscious effort on our part until with the assistance of the Holy Spirit, our minds are trained to view challenging students through the lens of God.

Are you thinking good thoughts about even the unlikable child? Ask God to give you a positive disposition toward that unlikable child.

DAY 16

Think before Speaking

Do you see a man who is hasty in his words?
There is more hope for a fool than for him.
—Proverbs 29:20

But avoid irreverent babble, for it will lead people into more and
more ungodliness, and their talk will spread like gangrene.
—2 Timothy 4:16–17

This verse from Proverbs is self-explanatory. We must take care to choose words wisely as there will always be somebody, whether student, parent, or colleague who will be listening. Practice becoming an excellent listener, and then you can carefully evaluate your listening; this will become an invaluable tool. By being slow to speak, we choose our words more carefully; and they may have more meaning to others. I remember that it was said of a colleague of mine that he never says anything in meetings; but when he does, you better listen! That is a good reputation to have.

Additionally, Paul reminds us to "avoid irreverent babble, for it will lead people into more and more ungodliness, and their talk will spread like gangrene." Idle gossip and talk lead to ugly rumors. As teachers, we have witnessed many student issues caused by "irreverent babble" as Paul puts it. One student starts a rumor about another, and the rumor is repeated and spread. Irreverent babble is now more prevalent due to social media. In fact, issues that arise between students are now brought to school from the home and through social media more than ever before.

One observation that I have made is that for the most part, adolescents have the same maturity levels as in previous generations, but today, the social media aspect makes this lack of maturity potentially more dangerous. Before social media, adolescents passed notes regarding others. Remember the days when notes were passed such as "Let's not play with Anna during recess" or people would put a note on someone's back that read "I'm stupid." Now they text, put it on Facebook or Twitter, and a wider audience becomes involved.

At our school, a student left her desk to turn in an assignment and left her Facebook page open on her phone. While she was away from her desk, a young man picked up the phone and, as a prank, stated an untruth. He wrote on her Facebook page, "I feel so liberated now that I have come out." The young lady's parents discovered this post when the mother's sister, who lived in another state, called them. The parents were at school less than one hour after the post.

We must remember that every student now possesses a camera and recording device. What we say in the classroom can be immediately put out there for the world to see. Be wary of creating issues for yourself through unprofessional talk regarding your students. Think before you say it!

Do you weigh your words before you speak? Ask God to guard your speech.

DAY 17

Perception Is Reality

My brothers, show no partiality as you hold the faith
in our Lord Jesus Christ, the Lord of glory.
—James 2:1

As educators, we must constantly be aware of how our actions are perceived by others. Students, colleagues, and parents are constantly aware of our mannerisms, sayings, and nonverbal behaviors. Teachers can execute some simple practices in the classroom to avoid the appearance of partiality.

Make it a practice to change seating periodically throughout the year, and make sure that Johnny doesn't get called on more than Jane. Be cognizant of nonverbal actions, facial expressions, and the tone of your voice. Keep a mental record of your classroom wanderings. Do you tend to gravitate more to certain places in the classroom? How do you use proximity to students to your advantage? As much as the lesson permits, individually engage as many students as possible during the class period. Learn names quickly and use them, calling students by name sends a powerful message that they are important.

Your tone of voice and facial expressions are two behaviors that parents pick up on quickly as they observe you working with their child. Remember that most parents will form their conceptions of your "fairness" through the lens of their children. Being perceived as "fair" is beneficial to you in working with your students.

Have you established the reputation of being a "fair" teacher? Ask God to show areas in your practice that may be perceived by others as showing partiality to certain students or student groups.

DAY 18

Honoring God in Our Work

Whatever your hand finds to do, do it with your might.
—Ecclesiastes 9:10

Commit your work to the Lord, and your plans will be established.
—Proverbs 16:3

Whatever you do, work heartily, as for the Lord and not for men.
—Colossians 3:23

Teaching is not a "half in" profession. We find greater fulfillment in our jobs when we put our whole heart into it. The day goes by faster when our minds and hearts are not idle. I have noted some interesting contrasts of attitude people bring to this profession.

Some teachers are seeking routine and hoping to teach the same lesson year after year in the same way. During my first year of teaching, a social studies teacher told me, "You have to work hard the first three years, and after that, you just take your folder and go." That social studies teacher left the profession after about eight years in the classroom.

Others are the last ones to arrive in the morning and the first to leave in the afternoon. I was on bus duty one morning, standing with the principal, engaged in light conversation. I witnessed a teacher at this school who literally pulled into the parking lot five minutes before the first bell rang every day. You could set your watch by his arrival. The principal quipped, "We can start school now. Burt's here." Your habits will be noticed by your colleagues and supervisors.

On the contrary, there are those teachers who are constantly striving to improve their methodology and discover new ways to reach their students. These persons have a much happier disposition, an infectious personality, and students are happy to come to their classroom. Dedicated teachers discover that they are occupied preparing their lessons and/or engaged in professional development during the "down" times of summer and holidays. With the right motivation, the long hours and low pay are not noticed when we are doing the Lord's work in the profession that God has called us to do.

Are you dedicating yourself to be the best you can be to honor God in your work?

DAY 19

How It's Said Matters

Let your speech always be gracious, seasoned with salt, so
that you may know how you ought to answer each person.
—Colossians 4:6

Whoever guards his mouth preserves his life; he
who opens wide his lips comes to ruin.
—Proverbs 13:3

Put away from you crooked speech, and
put devious talk far from you.
—Proverbs 4:24

For out of the abundance of the heart the mouth speaks.
—Matthew 12:34b

First impressions are everything. People will make their own personal evaluation about us by our speech. How we say things offers a distinct impression whether we are a positive or negative person, "for out of the abundance of the heart the mouth speaks."

We must establish positive relationships. Experience tells us that when we establish positive relationships with our students and their parents/caregivers, half of the battle has been won. Students who respect their teachers are more likely not to cause classroom disturbances and are eager to please their teacher. Parents who feel their child's teacher likes their child will be much more supportive and cooperative.

The adolescent years bring with them many relationship challenges. These verses are helpful when we counsel young people who thrive on drama. Young people sometimes have a difficult time removing themselves from the social drama and to not "have the last word." Several times, I have encouraged young people to step back, close their mouths, and not contribute to the ongoing verbal back and forth in which they are engaged.

Social media has made this issue even more challenging because students will take the opportunity to say hurtful comments about others with the advantage of anonymity or delayed repercussions. Words spoken or written in anger or coarse jesting cannot be retrieved.

Before social media, students had a "cooling off period" because when they left school, they didn't see the person that they were having a conflict with until the next day. Not true with social media now on the scene. Many times, the use of social media exacerbates the issue, and when the two conflicting parties arrive at school the following day, the issue has become much larger and involves more people.

Our wise choices of words will help establish our credibility when difficulties come and will help avoid needless conflicts with others. Our example of using positive word choices will allow us to be the role model Christ intended.

What does your speech reflect about you? Are you a "cup half full" person or a "cup half empty" person? Ask God to give you a positive outlook and to give you wisdom in your speech.

DAY 20

Don't Do It

If you turn at my reproof, behold, I will pour out my
spirit to you; I will make my words known to you.
—Proverbs 1:23

For the simple are killed by their turning away, and the
complacency of fools destroys them; 33 but whoever listens to me
will dwell secure and will be at ease, without dread of disaster.
—Proverbs 1:32–33

Whoever heeds instruction is on the path to life,
but he who rejects reproof leads others astray.
—Proverbs 10:17

Whoever causes one of these little ones who believe in me
to sin, it would be better for him if a great millstone were
hung around his neck and he were thrown into the sea.
—Mark 9:42

"If you turn at my reproof" or if you turn at my expression of disapproval are powerful words from the Holy Spirit. When we are about to do something or partake in an activity, and we hear the whisper of "Don't," it is important to heed that warning. When we do not heed that warning, our senses to the promptings of the Holy Spirit are dulled and poor decisions will follow. Note the promise that follows: "I will pour out my spirit to you; I will make my words known to you." To be an effective educator, we must obey all promptings of the Holy Spirit. Verse 33 also offers a promise: "but whoever listens to me will dwell secure and will be at ease, without dread of disaster."

Rejecting God's reproof will eventually have a negative effect on others. "Whoever heeds instruction is on the path to life, but he who rejects reproof leads others astray."

Jesus stated, "Whoever causes one of these little ones who believe in me to sin, it would be better for him if a great millstone were hung around his neck and he were thrown into the sea." We must be sensitive to the Holy Spirit's promptings for the sake of our students.

I have had several experiences of dealing with hurt students and their disappointed parents after a teacher was arrested. Invariably, in my conversation with the arrested teacher would be the comment, "I knew it was wrong when I started, but I didn't think I was hurting anybody when I was doing this. I always thought I could stop when I wanted to." The beginning of that statement, "I knew it was wrong," lies the confession of receiving reproof and not heeding the voice of God and turning from the practice. Accepting reproof from the Holy Spirit guards our witness and maintains our positive influence on our students.

Do you listen to the whisper of "Don't"? Ask God for sensitivity and the discipline to follow the Holy Spirit's promptings.

DAY 21

Invitation to Learn

> My son, if you receive my words and treasure up my commandments with you, making your ear attentive to wisdom and inclining your heart to understanding; yes, if you call out for insight and raise your voice for understanding, if you seek it like silver and search for it as for hidden treasures, then you will understand the fear of the LORD and find the knowledge of God.
>
> —Proverbs 2:1–5

Notice the word *if* in the first verse. *If* is a very powerful word because when it is used, there will follow implication. Usually, after *if,* there follows *then.* For example, "If you put your hand too close to the fire, then you will get burned!" The greatest *if-then* statement written is found in 2 Chronicles 7:14: "If my people who are called by my name will humble themselves and pray and seek my face and turn from their wicked ways, then I will hear from heaven and will forgive their sin and heal their land."

These verses contain many important words after *if.* Look at them: *receive, treasure,* "making your ear attentive," "inclining your heart to understanding," "call out for insight," *seek,* and finally, *search.* All these words imply the engagement of our will.

Self-will is the attribute that God gave man that is different from every other part of his creation because it involves free choice. Free choice gives us the opportunity to fellowship with God, which is why we are created. All these verbs and phrases require the use of our self-will as well as concerted effort on our part.

We sometimes forget that learning is work, and learning is intentional. So many times, the focus is on what the teacher does when there actually must be hearing, receiving, and application by the student. We cannot make our students learn. We invite our students to learn, and we gladly accept the challenge to arouse the "want to" in them to learn. Ultimately, though, there must be "buy-in" on the part of the student.

Are you designing lessons that invite your students to learn? Ask God for wisdom in devising that learning "hook" that brings them to the table to learn from you.

DAY 22

Pure Motives

Whoever walks in integrity walks securely, but he
who makes his ways crooked will be found out.

—Proverbs 10:9

We are encouraged to walk in integrity and to keep our ways and
motives pure. Included is a warning that those who make their ways
crooked will eventually be exposed.

There will always be those that practice wickedness, such as the
student who cheats on a paper or test and denies it, the parent that
completes their child's homework, or the colleague that takes your
work and passes it off as his/her own.

Many times, during ninth-grade parent conferences, we discovered that the parent had been "helping" their child so much in middle school that the child did not develop the work ethic to complete
homework on his/her own. When the student reached ninth grade,
the amount of homework increased, and the parent would confess
that he/she couldn't do it. We would discover the type of "help" given
to the child at an earlier time made the child overly dependent on the
guidance provided by his/her parent.

Sometimes I was asked to examine the attendance records of
students and found that there was an unmistakable pattern of them
being "checked out" from school by their parents before a period
where there was a major exam. In many cases, the students did not
perform well on the makeup exam.

Are the motives for all your actions pure? Keep your peace and
perspective and know that eventually, the student will eventually pay
a price for not completing homework, passing others' work off as

their own, or being habitually absent the day of an exam. Ask God for a pure heart and mind as well as for wisdom should you need to address wrongdoing by your students. Ask God for the ability to keep your perspective when others do not tell you the truth.

DAY 23

Examining Our Motives

Do nothing from selfish ambition or conceit, but in humility count others more significant than yourselves.
—Philippians 2:5

Bondservants, obey in everything those who are your earthly masters, not by way of eye-service, as people-pleasers, but with sincerity of heart, fearing the Lord.
—Colossians 3:22

While examining ourselves (2 Corinthians 13:5) and keeping watch over ourselves (Galatians 6:1b; Malachi 2:16b; Proverbs 4:23), it is also important to consistently examine our motives. We all have witnessed people in this profession who do things to "look good" or to "get ahead."

Remember that Jesus stated in the sixth chapter of Matthew:

> Beware of practicing your righteousness before other people in order to be seen by them, for then you will have no reward from your Father who is in heaven. Thus, when you give to the needy, sound no trumpet before you, as the hypocrites do in the synagogues and in the streets, that they may be praised by others. Truly, I say to you, they have received their reward. But when you give to the needy, do not let your left hand know what your right hand is doing, so that your

giving may be in secret. And your Father who sees in secret will reward you. (Matthew 6:1–4)

Are your motives pure?

DAY 24

Listen

Even a fool who keeps silent is considered wise; when
he closes his lips, he is deemed intelligent.
—Proverbs 17:27–28

If one gives an answer before he hears, it is his folly and shame.
—Proverbs 18:13

Whoever restrains his words has knowledge, and he
who has a cool spirit is a man of understanding.
—Proverbs 17:27

How well do you listen? Taken together, these verses remind us to be considerably careful not to speak too quickly, particularly when dealing with an emotional parent, student, or colleague. In parent conferences, I have seen teachers get immensely defensive of their practice, even to the point of "cutting the speaker off" before their thought is completed. It only exacerbates the situation.

A good strategy to use during these times is simply to listen, repeat what was said, and then ask, "And what else?" Give that parent or colleague an opportunity to completely vent. The real root of the problem is sometimes discovered after the second or third "what else," and it is found that the parent is angrier at their child or circumstance in which they find themselves. After you listen, they will feel they have "been heard" and, hopefully, a fruitful conversation may ensue. Your reputation of being a good listener is genuinely helpful.

Are you a good listener? Ask God for patience and restraint when dealing with an emotional parent or colleague.

DAY 25

Present a Good Presence

A good name is to be chosen rather than great
riches, and favor is better than silver or gold.
—Proverbs 22:1

One of the young men answered, "Behold, I have seen a
son of Jesse the Bethlehemite, who is skillful in playing,
a man of valor, a man of war, prudent in speech, and a
man of good presence, and the LORD is with him."
—1 Samuel 16:18

Our reputation is continually being made. Students and parents talk, and they will discuss their perceptions about you to others. I remember having to tell a teacher that the reason many parents asked for a schedule change when they discovered that their child was in her class was because she had built a reputation as an unfair, difficult teacher who treated her students like they were not very bright by her condescending remarks when they asked questions of her in class. I reminded her of incidents that happened previously in her classroom as well as comments she made that were overheard. All these incidents built her reputation, and the only way this could be remedied was for her to change how she dealt with students.

David built a good reputation during his time as a shepherd. He was characterized as a man prudent in speech and of good presence. In addition, people knew that he was a man of God; they could tell that "the Lord was with him."

We create a presence about us by the things we do and the manner we speak. We have had experiences with people in the workplace who laugh at the dirty joke. In contrast, there are people whose presence will change a misguided conversation when they approach. We as believers bear the name of Christ, and we should be seriously careful not to do or say anything to tarnish his name. In this instance, we can use David as our model and strive to be a person of good speech and presence so that people know that we have been with Jesus.

What kind of "presence" do you present? Ask God to give you the distinct reputation that people will know that you have been with Jesus.

DAY 26

Training and Discipline

Train up a child in the way he should go; even
when he is old he will not depart from it.
—Proverbs 22:6

The rod and reproof give wisdom, but a child left
to himself brings shame to his mother.
—Proverbs 29:15

Discipline your son, and he will give you rest;
he will give delight to your heart.
—Proverbs 29:17

These three verses provide enormous keys for the success of students. Have you ever been in a conversation with a parent regarding their child, and you notice many of the characteristics of the child are possessed by the parent? I have heard many teachers say after such a conversation with one of their students' parents, "Well, now I know where he/she got that from!" In many cases, we can assess some characteristics of a parent we are dealing with by the actions of their children.

Today, many children are "left to themselves" at a young age because both parents are at their workplace. These "latch-key children" may not receive the parental guidance that is needed during their formative years. Conversations reveal that students are "trusted" to take care of their school business when they arrive to an empty home with no supervision. Other conversations reveal students are left alone in their rooms with a computer with unfiltered access to the internet. Both practices are recipes for disaster in the rearing of children.

Notice the word *train* in the first verse. Training implies rigor in raising children. Training requires discipline of parents to guide the child in the right way. Training has no place to allow the child to "wear the parent down." Parents who continually take the path of least resistance when the child is young reap unwanted benefits when the child reaches their preteen and teenage years. Remind yourself of these verses when you are attempting to work with that undisciplined student and their parents.

Do you see students that are left to themselves? Pray for them and for their parents to gain wisdom in raising them. Pray for guidance as you work with these students.

DAY 27

Professional Development

Iron sharpens iron, and one man sharpens another.

—Proverbs 27:17

This single verse provides the biblical basis and our motivation for professional development. The effective teacher knows that there is always more to learn and that this is done through watching others teach, attending seminars, reading professional journals, etc. None of us wishes to have a surgeon who uses outdated surgical practices and procedures. We want someone that knows and practices all the new researched-based methods and procedures.

What have you done to sharpen your skills lately? Seek opportunities that will sharpen your skills professionally and spiritually.

DAY 28

Preparing for Unpleasant Experiences

Better is the end of a thing than its beginning, and the
patient in spirit is better than the proud in spirit.
—Ecclesiastes 7:8

You know that the upcoming parent conference is not going to be
a pleasant experience. How do you know? Because being the con-
scientious teacher who you are, you have called home and have sent
emails, and the responses have been terse, hateful, and have placed
blame on you for their child's lack of success. Either you, the parent, or your supervisor has decided that it is time for a face-to-face
meeting.

Be patient with the parent and do not give the feeling that you
are trying to appease them so that you can leave and "go to the next
item on your list." Be an active listener and ask questions for clari-
fication. Make sure that you come across as humble and not proud
or arrogant. Arrogance is a trait that will make more enemies and
hinder your efforts to be a positive influence. Remember also that
patience is one of the gifts of the Holy Spirit, and remember that the
Holy Spirit, if you let him, will help you in your responses.

Just prior to a conference you know is going to be difficult, pray
a short prayer, asking for calmness, wisdom, and patience.

DAY 29

Qualities of the "All-Star" Teacher

For this very reason, make every effort to supplement your faith
with virtue, and virtue with knowledge, and knowledge with
self-control, and self-control with steadfastness, and steadfastness
with godliness, and godliness with brotherly affection, and
brotherly affection with love. For if these qualities are yours
and are increasing, they keep you from being ineffective or
unfruitful in the knowledge of our Lord Jesus Christ. For whoever
lacks these qualities is so nearsighted that he is blind, having
forgotten that he was cleansed from his former sins. Therefore,
brothers, be all the more diligent to confirm your calling and
election, for if you practice these qualities you will never fall.
—2 Peter 1:5–10

Our practice of the qualities Peter outlines will give us a much greater
chance to be successful both professionally and personally. Not only
will the practice of these qualities draw us closer to Christ but will
enable us to be a positive influence on impressionable young people
as well as colleagues and parents.

Look at it this way: everyone wants the "all-star" teacher who
is "fair" (virtuous), who knows their subject (knowledge), who is in
total control of their emotions (self-control), who doesn't give up
on a student (steadfastness), is a good role model (godliness), and
friendly (brotherly affection and love). Applying these qualities to
our professional and personal lives will make our career exciting and
purposeful.

Are you the "all-star teacher"? Ask God to remind you of these
qualities and practice them each day.

DAY 30

Avoiding Desensitization

Behold, the days are coming, declares the Lord God, when I
will send a famine on the land—not a famine of bread, nor
a thirst for water, but of hearing the words of the Lord.
—Amos 8:11

We live in a time where the Gospel is readily available through many forms of media. A general desensitization to the true Gospel has occurred, and we encounter many individuals in our society who have reached this threshold.

An example of this famine of hearing the words of God is desensitization to sin. Many students today have no issue with the sin of plagiarism. With the assistance of the world wide web, they easily take copies of the work of others and use it as their own. Our English department, as well as many colleges, now require students to submit papers via programs that detect plagiarism.

Other examples of this desensitization we see in our teaching profession include parents completing homework for their children, parents allowing their child to miss school on the date of a big assignment or test, even students stealing food out of the cafeteria and justifying it, saying that they were hungry.

To successfully navigate through these issues, we must first examine ourselves each day and "take up our cross and follow Jesus." Second, we must accept the fact that we will have encounters with colleagues, parents, and students who have reached this threshold of desensitization.

The words of the hymn are appropriate here, and the repetition of the two phrases is hugely important. "*I have decided to follow Jesus,*

I have decided to follow Jesus, I have decided to follow Jesus, no turning back, no turning back."

Ask God to reveal sin in your life that may be keeping you from intimate fellowship with him. Pray for those students, colleagues, and parents who you will encounter who have reached the threshold of desensitization to the things of God.

Could there be areas in your life where you have become desensitized to the spirit of God? Ask God to reveal these areas to you.

DAY 31

Remove the Gray

For all the peoples walk each in the name of its god, but we will walk in the name of the Lord our God forever and ever.
—Micah 4:5

And if it is evil in your eyes to serve the Lord, choose this day whom you will serve, whether the gods your fathers served in the region beyond the River, or the gods of the Amorites in whose land you dwell. But as for me and my house, we will serve the Lord.
—Joshua 24:15

But Daniel resolved that he would not defile himself with the king's food, or with the wine that he drank.
—Daniel 1:8a

The words *will* and *resolve* assist us in preplanning good decisions before a negative situation occurs. God granted us the power of choice to make decisions that reflect Christ in our personal and professional lives. At our school, we have a program called PALS (Peer Assistant Leadership Students) where students from our high school first receive training and then travel during the school day to mentor students at our elementary schools. These students are chosen to be in this program based on teacher recommendation as well as through an intensive interview process.

During the interview, "situation" questions are asked of the students. One question used quite often is, "What if you and your friends are at a movie and someone decides to sneak in a bottle of beer?" You didn't know they had it before you sat down in the theater. What would you do?

I have been pleased to hear many of these students begin their response with "I am a Christian" and proceed to outline how they would remove themselves from the situation and report it. Many students voluntarily state that they have preplanned to not drink, smoke, do drugs, and to refrain from sexual encounters.

Are there some areas in your personal or professional life that you classify as "gray"? Ask God to show you some decisions you can make to remove the "gray."

DAY 32

Making Good Decisions

No one can serve two masters, for either he will hate the one and love the other, or he will be devoted to the one and despise the other. You cannot serve God and money.
—Matthew 6:24

But if not, be it known to you, O king, that we will not serve your gods or worship the golden image that you have set up.
—Daniel 3:18

But seek first the kingdom of God and his righteousness, and all these things will be added to you. Therefore do not be anxious about tomorrow, for tomorrow will be anxious for itself. Sufficient for the day is its own trouble.
—Matthew 6:33–34

Do not be anxious about anything, but in everything by prayer and supplication with thanksgiving let your requests be made known to God.
—Philippians 4:6

Preplanning decisions in alignment with God's Word is helpful because when temptations come, we can rest on our decisions. Still another example of preplanning appropriate decisions is the example of Shadrach, Meshach, and Abednego informing the king that they would not worship his golden image. Their decision regarding this issue had already been made; therefore, they courageously informed the king that they would not worship his golden image.

As teachers, we may experience unneeded anxiety because we have not preplanned decisions regarding situations in which we may find ourselves. We feel pressure sometimes from parents to change a grade so that their child will be eligible to participate in a sport or to compete in an extracurricular activity. Does the grade that you assign properly reflect the students' progress in your class? Establish to yourself that your standards are fair and are in line with the grading policy. If you have done this, and you have followed the correct procedures on grading established by the district, then you don't have to be anxious when a grade is challenged.

Taken together, these passages give the reality that only one master is dominant. By choosing the right Master, we can derive a godly perspective in decision-making, and our anxiety will be limited. Notice the second sentence. *"Therefore do not be anxious,"* is a command from Jesus. Finally, Paul in his letter to the Philippians reminds us, *"Do not be anxious about anything, but in everything by prayer and supplication with thanksgiving let your requests be made known to God."*

What anxieties do you have regarding decisions that need to be made? Seek God's guidance, make the decision, and "get on with it."

DAY 33

Provide Parental Support

For the son treats the father with contempt, the daughter rises up against her mother, the daughter-in-law against her mother-in-law; a man's enemies are the men of his own house.

—Micah 7:6

Because the days are evil.

—Ephesians 5:16b

Children, obey your parents in the Lord, for this is right.

—Ephesians 6:1

If possible, so far as it depends on you, live peaceably with all.

—Romans 12:18

I was in a parent/teacher/student conference, and the student was being extremely belligerent toward her mother. After several minutes of listening to this young lady speak to her mother in a horrible manner, including a few choice profanities directed at her, I stopped the conference and said, "Excuse me, but I cannot sit by and allow you to speak to your mother like this. You will refrain from this behavior, or you will be asked to leave."

The student was surprised at my directness and immediately ceased the barrage of comments. The mother looked at me and said, "Thank you. Nobody in our house takes up for me."

I felt sorry for this mom who had lost all aspects of her office as *parent* in this household. In further conversation in this conference, we discovered that the mom and dad were not on the same page as far as rules and discipline in the home. The mother would abdicate to the dad regarding rules, and when Mom tried to enforce rules, she did not get support from Dad. We further found that the child spoke to Mom in this way in front of Dad and was not disciplined.

After we finished the conference, I dismissed the teacher and student and spent some time with the mother. I encouraged her to speak to her husband privately regarding their differing approaches toward the discipline of their child. I stressed the importance of them coming to an agreement on how they were going to parent the child as well as the importance of them being united in front of their child.

Do not be surprised when speaking with students and their parents when the scenario described in Micah is witnessed. We are living in a time when broken homes are almost the norm. Many families are experiencing constant strife and discord among their family members, and this discord is often found in their extended family such as aunts, uncles, and cousins.

Remember that these situations are products of Satan as he continues his onslaught on the family. Paul reminds us in Ephesians 5:16b that "the days are evil." As teachers, we must encourage our students to *obey their parents in the Lord for this is right.* Encourage the adults to try to live peaceably as much as possible for the sake of the children. *"If possible, so far as it depends on you, live peaceably with all."*

Do you see children showing disrespect to their parents? Ask God for boldness in calling students out when they do this. Do not be afraid to tactfully speak up in a conference when you hear a student disrespect their parents.

DAY 34

Don't Rush to Judgment

In fact, I do not even judge myself. For I am not aware of anything against myself, but I am not thereby acquitted. It is the Lord who judges me. Therefore do not pronounce judgment before the time, before the Lord comes, who will bring to light the things now hidden in darkness and will disclose the purposes of the heart.

—1 Corinthians 4:3b–5

Often we are quickly judged by students and their parents. We are sometimes quick to judge our students and their parents.

Paul reminds us that it is the Lord that judges. Paul approached all things with a clean conscience as can be seen in this scripture. Let us take our example from Paul and stay in a state of constant confession of our shortcomings to Christ as well as of our shortcomings to others.

When a student begins to act differently to not turn in work or to have periods of lapses in judgment, give that student a short amount of time to change. Ask the student questions as to why their work habits have changed. You may say something like, "James, I've noticed that you are not completing assignments like you were doing for this class. Are you having less time out of class to get work done for me or have you needed to spend more time on another class lately?"

This type of open-ended question isn't accusatory and gives James some room to respond. Speak with other professionals who have interactions with the student. They may be experiencing the same behaviors or have knowledge of situations that may be going on at home or with others at school. Do not rush to judgment.

Students today encounter more significant issues outside of school than in years past. Unfortunately, some of these issues are of such magnitude that the average adolescent has not yet developed the social or intellectual coping skills needed to navigate the issue. Give issues time to sort out, ask good questions, remain watchful, and eventually, the Lord will "*bring to light the things now hidden in darkness.*"

Do you take notice when one of your students has a sudden change in either their behavior or work habits? Ask God for sensitivity to these types of changes and refrain from making judgments until you have enough data.

DAY 35

Guard Your Heart

So guard yourselves in your spirit, and do not be faithless.
—Malachi 2:16b

Keep your heart with all vigilance, for from it
flow the springs of life. Above all else, guard your
heart, for everything you do flows from it.
—Proverbs 4:23 (NIV)

Keep watch on yourself, lest you too be tempted.
—Galatians 6:1b

We must place a twenty-four-hour guard on our hearts where our thoughts are harbored. When we accepted Jesus as our Savior, he gave us the Holy Spirit to be our help for this. He will guard our hearts if we let him.

Taken together, these verses emphasize the importance of guarding our hearts, keeping godly thoughts and not allowing our inner being to harbor evil. It is possible to evaluate a person's heart by observing his/her actions, deeds, and speech. A person's heart is exposed by his/her speech when times of stress and trouble occur.

I am reminded of the first part of Proverbs 23:7 in the King James Version, *"For as he thinketh in his heart, so is he."* There is much truth in the saying, "We become what we think about." The NIV emphasizes the importance, "Above all else." Preplanned decisions can be made in matters of the mind and heart. The saying in millennial language, "Garbage in, garbage out," certainly applies.

We must pay attention to this important aspect of our spiritual life so that when times of trouble arise, our speech will be *"gracious, seasoned with salt"* (Colossians 4:6a); *"for out of the abundance of the heart the mouth speaks"* (Matthew 12:34b); *"so that you may know how you ought to answer each person"* (Colossians 4:6b).

Are you guarding your heart?

DAY 36

Using Our Time Wisely

Look carefully then how you walk, not as unwise but as wise,
making the best use of the time, because the days are evil.
—Ephesians 5:15–16

The school day seems to fly by. We teach our classes, and suddenly, the day is over. We are always pressed for time during the school day.

The question really becomes a question of how time is prioritized. Be the person who uses time wisely. Be your own worst critic in this issue. "Look carefully."

Colleagues will notice when you have time for idle gossip in the workroom, are repeatedly at the copier at the last minute, or arriving at work with insufficient time to adequately prepare for class. Students will notice and take advantage of your tendency to be lax in your reporting of their "tardies," not getting class started in a timely manner, and not having them engaged in meaningful class activities for the full period. Administrators and colleagues will notice when you are not at an assigned duty station on time and actively engaged in monitoring student conduct, choosing instead to text on your phone, surf the Internet, or even engage in preparation for another class instead of moving about the room helping students as needed.

Notice what Paul says in the first part of the verse, "Not as unwise but as wise." Examine your perceptions of people who are chronically late and/or consistently make poor use of their time. Many times, we don't hold them with the same esteem as we do for colleagues who do not waste time. Build the reputation of one that's "got it together" by making wise use of your time.

Do you make wise use of your time while at school? Ask God for self-discipline with your time.

DAY 37

Remaining Humble

Have this mind among yourselves, which is yours in Christ
Jesus, who, though he was in the form of God, did not count
equality with God a thing to be grasped, but emptied himself,
by taking the form of a servant, being born in the likeness of
men. And being found in human form, he humbled himself by
becoming obedient to the point of death, even death on a cross.

—Philippians 2:5–8

I know a teacher who was a significantly gifted Algebra I teacher and
he knew it. He was also an extremely good wrestling assistant coach.
This teacher was doing a fantastic job. He had the gift of being able
to get the poor math student to at least pass. If you looked at the
grades of his students and their performance on their standardized
tests, he was what you would call a "rock star" teacher.

But he did not accept advice or constructive criticism because
he thought he was invincible. He really believed that he had all the
answers. Even his colleagues would say sarcastically, "Ask Andrew
because he knows it all."

One day, he was dealing with an unruly student in the hallway. The talking turned into an argument as the student continued
to disrespect this teacher. Finally, the student took a swing at him.
This teacher completely lost his composure and body slammed the
student to the floor. Simply put, his teaching career ended that day.

Remember that we are practicing the very profession that God
assigned to his Son, Jesus, that of a teacher. We must always *"put on
Christ"* (Romans 13:14) and be the humble servant. When we have
that fleeting thought of exalting ourselves or having too much pride,

remember the extent Jesus humbled himself for us. Paul challenges us to have this mind, which is ours in Christ. The Holy Spirit will help us remember.

How humble are you? Ask God to show you areas in your life where you tend to exalt yourself.

DAY 38

Being a Good Example

Brothers, join in imitating me, and keep your eyes on those
who walk according to the example you have in us.
—Philippians 3:17

You, however, have followed my teaching, my conduct, my aim
in life, my faith, my patience, my love, my steadfastness.
—2 Timothy 3:10

Think about what bold statements Paul makes! It has been said that
character is who you are when no one is looking. As teachers, we
constantly find ourselves inside the fishbowl being observed from all
angles. Many times, we do not know that we are being observed. A
colleague of mine related an encounter while on a cruise for spring
break. About three days into the cruise, this teacher encountered a
student and his family. He mentioned that this family could have
seen him the first couple of days, and he didn't even know that they
were around. This remark caused me to wonder if there were some
actions that he now regretted.

Get ready because you will have at least one student who will
look up to you so much that they will want to imitate your lifestyle.
You yourself probably chose to enter this profession because of the
influence that a teacher had on you.

Our goal should be to always set the Christian example so that
we, like Paul, can be examples to others. Strive to be as Paul who was
so secure in his actions that he was able to invite all to imitate him
and follow his example.

Do all the places you go, the events you attend (and your conduct at these events and places), as well as items and pictures that you post on social media honor Christ? Ask God to show you areas in your life that need to be addressed.

DAY 39

Your Credentials and Mentors

The next few readings contain instructions from Paul to Timothy. In 1 and 2 Timothy, Paul, the seasoned veteran teacher, is giving instructions to Timothy, the young colleague. What credentials does Paul have to be giving this wisdom? We find these credentials in Acts 22:3. *"I am a Jew, born in Tarsus in Cilicia, but brought up in this city, educated at the feet of Gamaliel according to the strict manner of the law of our fathers, being zealous for God as all of you are this day"* (Acts 22:3).

Gamaliel is celebrated as a Pharisee doctor of Jewish Law. In Acts 5:34, Gamaliel is viewed as a man of great respect and his advice was followed. *"But a Pharisee in the council named Gamaliel, a teacher of the law held in honor by all the people, stood up and gave orders to put the men outside for a little while"* (Acts 5:34). Notice what he said to the council regarding Paul.

> And he said to them, "Men of Israel, take care what you are about to do with these men. For before these days Theudas rose up, claiming to be somebody, and a number of men, about four hundred, joined him. He was killed, and all who followed him were dispersed and came to nothing. After him Judas the Galilean rose up in the days of the census and drew away some of the people after him. He too perished, and all who followed him were scattered. So in the present case I tell you, keep away from these men and let them alone, for if this plan or this undertaking is

of man, it will fail; but if it is of God, you will not be able to overthrow them. You might even be found opposing God!" So they took his advice. (Acts 5:35–39)

His advice turned out to be prophetic because this gospel is still being proclaimed.

So it is established that Paul studied under one of the great teachers of the day. He knew the formal Jewish law and he spelled out why this law was inadequate for salvation in the book of Romans. He was converted to Christ on the way to Damascus, and the rest is history. In the following readings, a closer look is taken at Paul's advice to the young teacher, Timothy.

Do you have a mentor in your subject area? Ask God to place a godly mentor in your life.

DAY 40

Censor Everything

Desiring to be teachers of the law, without understanding
either what they are saying or the things about
which they make confident assertions.
—1 Timothy 1:7

Watch out for false teachers! I was a junior in college, and I had the privilege of taking a private French Horn lesson with a professor at a prominent university. This man is a devout Christian, and during the lesson, and hence many times after that initial time, he has given me solid advice both personally and professionally. One of the matters he mentioned to me in that lesson that I have never forgotten is a statement regarding the teaching profession. He said, "Remember this: there are a lot of quacks in this business. The problem is that they don't teach, they write books." Since that time, I censure everything that I read and hear from the so-called "experts."

Knowing Timothy's deep abiding faith, Paul nevertheless felt it necessary to warn him of false teachers. Knowing Timothy to be young and possibly impressionable, Paul tells him that there are going to be many "quacks" in the business. Notice that Paul puts this warning at the very front of the letter. Why? Because at every turn, Paul found himself correcting the false teachings of others. He wanted Timothy to be on guard regarding this issue.

This advice holds true in our profession. Many educators espouse teaching methods, pedagogy, and philosophies that are contrary to Christianity. We need to be constantly on guard against such practices. Allow the Holy Spirit to guide and to be the sifter of the many sands of philosophy that come your way. Examples of such philosophies contrary to our Christian faith include the teaching of transgender, the rewriting of history books such as the 1619 project and critical race theory, and some of the literature studied in the English class. Seize these teachable moments to give a good word regarding your faith.

Are you allowing the Holy Spirit to guide your thinking when you are presented with "new" methodology and philosophy?

DAY 41

Stop and Pray

First of all, then, I urge that supplications, prayers, intercessions, and thanksgivings be made for all people, for kings and all who are in high positions, that we may lead a peaceful and quiet life, godly and dignified in every way.
—1 Timothy 2:1–2

Paul reminds Timothy to pray for all people. Do you pray for the students under your care, their parents, and the leadership in your school? *"Pray without ceasing"* (1 Thessalonians 5:17). When you are in the hall or at your duty station, pray for that student passing by. Pray for those students you supervise, pray over your classes that they go well, and pray for wisdom to assist every student do his/her best.

Stop to take a few moments to pray for your department chair, your school leaders, and for those making decisions that affect you.

DAY 42

Dress Appropriately and Professionally

Likewise also that women should adorn themselves in
respectable apparel, with modesty and self-control, not
with braided hair and gold or pearls or costly attire.
—1 Timothy 2:9

One of our best volunteer parents stopped by my office and asked to speak with me. This mom enjoyed a reputation among our staff as being supportive and not "meddling" in the affairs of the school.

By her composure, I could tell that she was unsettled about something. She profusely apologized for what she was about to say, stating, "I don't want to be one of those parents that complain." I assured her that she did not have that reputation and asked her what was troubling her. She stated that one of our teachers was wearing a leopard bra under her white blouse, and it was a topic of conversation among our eighth-grade boys! I thanked her for this information and asked our female assistant principal to please pass by the classroom and verify.

Unfortunately, it was true. As soon as that period ended and the students had left the room, and before the students arrived for the next period, our wonderful assistant principal addressed this issue with the teacher. She held up a mirror to the teacher and asked her if she felt something was not quite right. The teacher looked in the mirror, immediately saw what the problem was, and put her jacket back on. She explained that the room had become hot, she had taken the jacket off, and didn't think about what she was wearing underneath. Fortunately, this never happened again.

Another time, one of our male coaches came inside the building with coaching shorts that were too tight. Several of our female teachers were uncomfortable and mentioned it. I reminded the coach of the district policy that stated that coaches, band directors, etc. must change into street clothes when coming inside the building and teaching in the classroom.

Although Paul says "women" in this passage, it is equally applicable to men. We are reminded to dress modestly, appropriately, and professionally for work with impressionable young people. Remember that, often, opinions are formed first by appearances. Don't let your dress be the topic of negative conversation among your students, their parents, or your colleagues.

Check your wardrobe. Are you dressed appropriately and modestly for your work with impressionable young people?

DAY 43

Personal Training

Have nothing to do with irreverent, silly myths.
Rather train yourself for godliness.

—1 Timothy 4:7

Paul reminds Timothy not to get caught up in issues that are not important but, instead, train himself for godliness. Consider the implication of the word *train*. Training implies much work, repetition, and refinement of a certain skill. The track athlete trains his/her body for many months, sometimes years for a short race. The football player spends an entire offseason in training to make his body fit for a season that only lasts for a few months. The musician trains his/her body and refines skills to be able to meet the demands of the music literature.

A wise saying in music states, "If I don't practice one day, I know it, if I don't practice two days, my teacher knows it, and if I don't practice three days, the whole world knows it."

Are you training your spiritual muscles by reading God's Word and praying each day?

DAY 44

Sound Advice

Let no one despise you for your youth, but set the believers an example in speech, in conduct, in love, in faith, in purity.
—1 Timothy 4:12

Keep a close watch on yourself and on the teaching. Persist in this, for by so doing you will save both yourself and your hearers.
—1 Timothy 4:16

Do not rebuke an older man but encourage him as you would a father, younger men as brothers.
—1 Timothy 5:1

A new teacher at our school was fresh out of college and in her first teaching position. This teacher wanted to be "hip" with her students and be their buddy. Since she was not very far away in age from the age of our seniors, she experienced many discipline issues with them in her classroom. The pictures she chose to post on her social media were not appropriate for her students to see. She thought that it was "cool" to allow students to "friend" her on social media despite my advice to the contrary. By Christmas break, she had lost control of her classes, and parents were upset about her communication with their children via social media. We tried several times to help her, but she didn't take our advice. She had a horrible spring and chose not to return.

Taken together, these words of wisdom are sound advice. You will gain the respect and confidence of your colleagues, students, and their parents by your speech and conduct.

Are you setting a good example by your conduct with students and your posts on social media?

DAY 45

Associations and Places

Nor take part in the sins of others; keep yourself pure.
—1 Timothy 5:22b

Our department chair came to me one Monday morning, upset with one of our teachers. The previous weekend, this young lady had gone to several bars in the downtown area of our city. She evidently had considered the type of activity that she would be engaged in (drinking heavily) because she elected to take public transportation. On her way home, she passed out on the tram and missed her stop. Our department chair found out because this teacher came to school and shared this experience with her colleagues and posted this incident on her social media.

Be cautious of associations with colleagues, particularly after work hours. Do not get caught "in the moment" regarding your social associations and places that you frequent. If you do, you may find yourself in the wrong place and at the wrong time. Don't ever be "guilty by association." An administrative colleague of mine, when invited to "happy hour" by a teacher, responded, "I cannot come because I never take a drink with someone I might have to fire."

Like it or not, the kinds of associations that you have with your colleagues outside of school hours will have an effect, either positively or negatively, on your working relationship at school.

Are you cautious about your associations and places you frequent after school hours?

DAY 46

Secret Sin Can Appear Later

The sins of some people are conspicuous, going before
them to judgment, but the sins of others appear later.
—1 Timothy 5:24

At our school, there was a teacher couple who appeared to be happily married with a beautiful daughter. Both were highly esteemed by their colleagues as well as their students.

We learned that this art teacher had engaged in an affair with a student three years ago while doing a senior portrait shoot in a downtown park. The young lady was underage at the time of the affair. Now in college, she had held this secret for three years and finally confessed to her parents what had been troubling her. The parents informed the police and pressed charges against the teacher.

When this happened, the teacher was in Europe with a group of students. The tour company immediately brought him home to face these charges. The teacher confessed to the charges and lost his position. I felt sorry for his wife who had to face the humiliation of this incident at school with her colleagues. This action by her husband caught her completely off guard because she never expected that he would partake in such an incident.

Unfortunately, these situations happen all too often in our schools. We read about colleagues who were caught driving while intoxicated or see their picture on the news, busted in a pornography sting operation. One of the items we now must address with our teachers at our in-service meetings before school begins is "Don't sleep with your students!"

Keep in mind that all sin is harmful and that the "secret" sin you commit may eventually affect others, particularly those closest to you. Confess, ask for forgiveness, and stop!

DAY 47

Decisions Made from Fear

For God gave us a spirit not of fear but of
power and love and self-control.
—2 Timothy 1:7

My secretary received an urgent call from one of our teachers, saying a student suddenly became ill, vomited, and passed out. I instructed our campus secretary to call the ambulance, and we rushed to the classroom. The teacher had removed the other students to the hallway, and they were escorted to the library to remain for the rest of the period.

The assistant principal said, "We need to put the school on lockdown right now."

I said, "No, we still have about five minutes before the bell. I hear the ambulance coming. The paramedics should be able to remove the student before the bell rings to change classes."

"No, I'm calling for a lockdown," said the assistant principal, and he instructed the secretary to place the campus on lockdown.

Sure enough, the ambulance arrived, the paramedics removed the student, and all was well before the bell rang to change classes. We immediately canceled the lockdown, the bell rang, and the students changed classes. I looked at the assistant principal and said, "Now you have to deal with the teacher inquiries and parent phone calls because you created this situation."

The rest of his day was spent explaining his decision to many people. As for the student, we discovered that he had mixed a potent alcoholic beverage he brought from home into his orange juice at breakfast. After receiving the necessary care at the hospital, the student continued his recovery at home. His parents, though upset with their child, were grateful for the quick action of the school and for the care given by the medical professionals. For this action, the young man also received three more days of "rest" as he was suspended from school.

That decision by the assistant principal was made from fear and not reason. He failed to think through how much time we really had (even though I tried to tell him) and needlessly disrupted our school routines.

People often make quick decisions out of fear as part of their reaction to a sudden negative event. Events such as the one just mentioned, threatening parent phone calls or emails or sudden confrontations with colleagues or parents put pressure on us. Beware of making a quick decision out of fear. Fear is Satan's playground. Have you taken the time to properly assess the situation with the help of the Holy Spirit?

Think about your decision-making when sudden negative events come your way. Do you make your decisions out of fear or with the guidance of the Holy Spirit?

DAY 48

Difficulties Will Come

But understand this, that in the last days
there will come times of difficulty.
—2 Timothy 3:1

Paul, the seasoned teacher, was reminding Timothy that he will encounter difficulties and trials. We, too, will encounter difficult students, their parents, colleagues, and administrators. Don't necessarily be convinced that a better job is to be found on another campus. I have served in poor schools and in wealthy schools, and each brings its own set of difficulties.

Pray each day for wisdom from the Holy Spirit and remember that Jesus said, *"When the Spirit of truth comes, he will guide you into all the truth, for he will not speak on his own authority, but whatever he hears he will speak, and he will declare to you the things that are to come"* (John 16:13). As Christians, we have a wonderful privilege to be the voice of reason when times of difficulty arise. When we are controlled by the Holy Spirit, we are in the normal state that God intended for man.

Are you ready and willing to face the difficulties that come with your job?

DAY 49

Making a Statement

Follow the pattern of the sound words that you have heard
from me, in the faith and love that are in Christ Jesus.
—2 Timothy 1:13

What a bold statement Paul makes! Can we, like Paul, be so in tuned to what Christ wants, and our example be such that we would be able to give this advice to our mentees? Accept the challenge to be all that you can be through Christ so that you can say, like Paul, "Follow my example."

Are you following the pattern of Christ so that you are an example to others?

DAY 50

Unappeasable People

For people will be lovers of self, lovers of money, proud, arrogant, abusive, disobedient to their parents, ungrateful, unholy, heartless, unappeasable, slanderous, without self-control, brutal, not loving good, treacherous, reckless, swollen with conceit, lovers of pleasure rather than lovers of God, having the appearance of godliness, but denying its power. Avoid such people.

—2 Timothy 3:2–5

Paul is giving some sound advice. We need to have our spiritual eyes open and avoid continuous associations with people who display these characteristics Paul described. From time to time, however, we as teachers will be confronted by people like this and not be able to avoid them. Such situations present an excellent opportunity for us to respond in a manner that is pleasing to Christ.

One day, an argument ensued in the school cafeteria between two young ladies who got exceptionally heated and animated. The duty teacher walked over and attempted to calm them down. I saw this incident unfolding and approached the group. The young ladies refused to lower their voices and spoke extremely unkindly to the teacher who then looked helplessly at me. I asked the young ladies to come to the office where I hoped this could be settled.

The uniformed school resource officer also came to our aid because he noticed the commotion from across the room. We took the young ladies to the office where they calmed down and agreed to disagree with each other. I instructed them to choose different places to sit the next day so they would not have to confront each other.

The mother of one of the young ladies called me and stated that I had singled her daughter out and embarrassed her in front of her friends in the cafeteria. I calmly attempted to explain the circumstances surrounding the incident but to no avail. The parent stated that we were rude to her daughter and demanded an apology. We were now having one of those conversations where we were going to have to agree to disagree! This parent is a good example of a person who was unappeasable!

The Holy Spirit helps us recognize unappeasable characteristics in people and guides us in dealing with them in a thoughtful, Christlike manner.

Are you ready to put on Christ when faced with an impossible parent or colleague?

DAY 51

Collegial Development

And I pray that the sharing of your faith may become
effective for the full knowledge of every good thing that
is in us for the sake of Christ. For I have derived much
joy and comfort from your love, my brother, because the
hearts of the saints have been refreshed through you.

—Philemon 1:6–7

Paul, the teacher, is writing words of encouragement to his protege. One of the most gratifying aspects for us is to see our former students successful in a career path or choose to become a teacher because of our influence. More importantly, it is gratifying to see a former student positively influencing young lives for the sake of Christ and knowing you had a part in it. Further, what a privilege it is to pray for their effectiveness in their ministry!

Our primary purpose in this profession is not necessarily to "turn out good students" as the intelligentsia might say but instead to develop colleagues. How are you doing with preparing your students so well that one day you may be able to trust their work as colleagues?

On a spiritual level, remember that we are the method that Christ chose to carry the good news to the next generation. Jesus developed eleven colleagues who obeyed his Great Commission and began a work that we are called to continue. Don't let this generation be the generation that does not carry Christ's Great Commission forward.

How are you developing colleagues?

DAY 52

Review the Fundamentals

Therefore we must pay much closer attention to what
we have heard, lest we drift away from it.
—Hebrews 2:1

This passage is a warning to Christians to not neglect their salvation. In the busyness of life, we can easily neglect to be grateful for the simplicity of the gospel.

Musicians warm up with scales, arpeggios, and material to awaken their senses. Athletes go through a strict regimen of warmups specific to their sport each day to awaken muscle memory. Likewise, we as Christians need to review the fundamentals of our faith to be effective in our witnessing and living for Christ. Remember the formula: salvation equals grace through faith plus nothing (Ephesians 2:8–9).

Remember that today, the students you teach have been exposed to many false doctrines regarding coming to Christ. In our nation today, 80 percent of the population professes to be Christian, yet many cannot articulate the basic truth of the Gospel. Many, in fact, will profess to only believe the parts of the Bible in which they agree. Much of this is due to a lack of review of the fundamentals of salvation and lack of discipleship once people are saved. Be ready in season and out of season to gently correct and steer people to the truth regarding Christ! Also remember that this message will be met with resistance because Jesus said that it would.

Have you reviewed the fundamentals regarding your faith? Can you articulate your faith to others?

DAY 53

Hardened

But exhort one another every day, as long as it is called "today,"
that none of you may be hardened by the deceitfulness of sin.
—Hebrews 3:13

Have you become hardened to sin? Unfortunately, we all have been hardened somewhat in twenty-first-century America. It's common to turn on the local news and hear of murders and not be horrified. We have become desensitized to sin in this world.

I remember during my first year of teaching, a band instrument was stolen out of the band hall while I was on bus duty. Fortunately, I was able to find the instrument in a local pawn shop. The trumpet had been pawned for $30. I felt guilty because this happened on my watch, and I had to relay the incident to my principal. He advised me that bad things happen, that this is the society that we live in, and to not look at the world through rose-colored glasses. He, at the time, was more hardened than I.

We become hardened over time, getting used to disrespect by students, filthy language in the halls, and improper attire in what used to be a school dress code. We see students cheating on papers, stealing belongings from one another, drug use, and even sexual sin. We have "gotten used to it," in a manner of speaking. Hopefully, we have not become so accustomed to these behaviors that we ignore them.

The *deceitfulness* word is important in this verse. Sin is dishonest and deceptive. We become deceived by sin when we "get used to it" or dismiss it by thinking, *There are larger battles to fight* or *This is the way society is*. This type of thinking condones sin. Don't turn a blind eye to sin. Deal with it in your classroom; and when appropriate, report it.

It is significantly important that we maintain relationships with fellow Christians, encouraging one another to wage war on the battlefront of our minds to refrain from being dulled by the onslaught of culture. Do you have a trusted Christian colleague who you can share and pray? Seek out such a person so that you may encourage one another.

In what areas of your life have you become hardened to sin? Continually ask God to give you discernment and a tender heart not to be hardened by the deceitfulness of sin.

DAY 54

Exasperation with Our Students

And he said, "Are you also still without understanding?"
—Matthew 15:16

About this we have much to say, and it is hard to explain, since you
have become dull of hearing. For though by this time you ought
to be teachers, you need someone to teach you again the basic
principles of the oracles of God. You need milk not solid food.
—Hebrews 5:11–12

In these two passages, two of the greatest teachers the world has ever
seen became exasperated with their students because they failed to
grasp concepts that had been taught again and again.

In Jesus's case, the teaching was regarding the reality of a person being defiled from within and giving evidence of this defilement
by their speech. In Paul's example, he was trying to get his listeners
to leave the elementary teachings of the faith and move on to more
deeper concepts so that they could enjoy an even closer relationship
with God. Notice that in both cases, after the expression of exasperation, both teachers retaught the lesson. Jesus explained the parable
again in verses 16–20 of chapter 15. Paul, in Hebrews 6, states that
they are to leave the elementary principles of "laying a foundation of
repentance and faith toward God."

It encourages me to see that these great teachers were at times
not happy with the progress of their students. Their exasperation
with their learners can be an encouragement to us when we teach
lessons that the students don't get, and we try even more to break
the lesson material down, simplify, and try new strategies to get our

students to a deeper understanding. Why do we do this? Because the students must understand the basics of any subject to be able to move to more complicated ideas.

Learning is not always easy, but the first step any person must take to learn anything is to decide to learn. Sometimes, students (especially adolescents) do not want to leave the basic concepts because leaving the basic concepts places added responsibilities of learning.

The same holds true in our spiritual life. In our daily Bible study, do we sometimes not want to make application of truths we read because there are sins that we wish to hold on to? Have you ever skipped over a passage because when it is read, God calls attention to sin?

To really be an effective teacher, we must keep our own house in order spiritually so that in every way, the students see Jesus. They need to see him in our speech, mannerisms, and how we react to their remarks and questions. Both Jesus and Paul never gave up on their students. They may have left the concept for a time but always returned to it so that their students finally understood! We need to make every effort to follow their example.

When your students "don't get it," how do you respond?

DAY 55

Proper Practice and Training

For everyone who lives on milk is unskilled in the word of righteousness, since he is a child. But solid food is for the mature, for those who have their powers of discernment trained by constant practice to distinguish good from evil.
—Hebrews 5:13–14

Continuing the thought from the last verses, Paul gives an important phrase on how to move on to deeper ideas spiritually and to more complicated concepts in learning. "Trained by constant practice." Think about what the word *trained* implies. Training requires that we set a goal, decide what steps need to be taken to achieve that goal, and then repeat the activity over and over until proficiency is acquired. It requires daily discipline to continue working, even when the results are not apparent. This is "constant practice."

In addition, we must be careful not to practice the wrong way. One of the biggest lies is the phrase "Practice makes perfect," because if we practice the wrong method, we will have to go back to unlearn bad habits.

Likewise, we need to make sure that our spiritual practice is accurate. To ensure this spiritual accuracy, it is important to always refer to the original source, our Bible. The daily discipline of the study of God's Word will ensure that we are progressing toward a deeper knowledge of our Lord. Progress may not always be apparent to us, and we may continue to struggle with certain sins, but we continually ask for forgiveness and repent, striving to be like Christ.

On the surface, this may sound like the "works oriented" manner of doing things, but repentance is when we realize that we cannot, and God can! Major Ian Thomas defines repentance:

> Facing the facts of life, recognizing how God made you, how you were intended to function, and then being restored to that relationship of mutual inter availability that the Lord Jesus enjoyed between Himself and the Father, a mutual inter availability in which you are prepared to let Him be God. That is true repentance. (Excerpt from Major Ian Thomas, *The Indwelling Life of Christ*, iBooks, https://itun.es/us/i3-ez.l)

This idea relates to us professionally because as we develop personal discipline, we model that for our students. When a new concept is difficult for your students, share with them a time you experienced difficulty learning something and how the application of constant practice enabled you to become proficient. Encourage them to be diligent in their daily practice of their lessons. Remind them that it is never a good idea to wait until the last minute to try to master all the concepts at once. Break ideas or concepts down for them and give them concrete, daily items to accomplish, and tell them that you have their best interests at heart and that the assignment is not to give them "busywork" but to keep them from becoming frustrated as concepts build. Remind them also that they must continue to "use it or lose it!"

Are you training yourself by "constant practice" spiritually by engaging in daily Bible study and prayer as well as professionally by participation in appropriate professional development activities? Make the choice daily to put your faith into practice.

DAY 56

Learning Contentment

But godliness with contentment is great gain.
—1 Timothy 6:6 (NIV)

For I have learned in whatever situation I am to be content.
—Philippians 4:11b

Keep your life free from the love of money, and
be content with what you have, for he has said,
"I will never leave you nor forsake you."
—Hebrews 13:5

Contentment is a state not often achieved by most people. Contentment is defined as to be in acceptance of and in an emotional state of ease with your situation. Contentment is a learned skill as Paul said that he had learned to be content. Being totally in step with Christ as we walk this earth, doing exactly as he says when he says to do it—that is a life of quiet confidence we have with the Holy Spirit as our guide.

As we do our work of educating young people, confident of our calling, we can be accepting of our situation materialistically. Guided by the Holy Spirit, we can make monetary decisions in a manner that keeps us free from the bondage of debt, for we have that wonderful whisper in our hearts that "I will never leave you nor forsake you."

Like Paul, have you learned to be content?

DAY 57

Guard My Speech

For out of the abundance of the heart the mouth speaks. "I
tell you, on the day of judgment people will give account for
every careless word they speak, for by your words you will
be justified, and by your words you will be condemned."
—Matthew 12:34b, 36–37

It is not what goes into the mouth that defiles a person,
but what comes out of the mouth; this defiles a person.
—Matthew 15:11

But what comes out of the mouth proceeds from the heart, and
this defiles a person. For out of the heart come evil thoughts,
murder, adultery, sexual immorality, theft, false witness, slander.
—Matthew 15:18–19

Set a guard, O Lord, over my mouth; keep
watch over the door of my lips!
—Psalm 141:3

Surprises sometimes bring out the worst in us. Sometimes, in a fit of
rage or surprise, a person will say something that does not reflect the
witness that he/she should be.

One of our talented young teachers was pregnant with her first
child. A student placed a pin in her chair, and she sat on it. She
screamed and dropped the F-bomb twice toward the student. The
student, of course, reported her conduct, and we had to do an investigation into the matter. In the teacher's explanation regarding the

incident, she reminded us that she was pregnant and was afraid of what disease could have been transmitted by a sharp object breaking her skin. Unfortunately for this teacher, she had to be reprimanded because of her language. Yes, the student was wrong to do this and was appropriately disciplined.

The teacher, however, immediately uttered what was in her heart. This is what Jesus meant when he said that what comes out of the heart defiles a person. Listen to your colleagues as well as to people in general. Listen to their speech when they are just being themselves. What kind of language do they use? How does their speech reflect their attitude toward students? Is the attitude that they display positive or negative? These are "heart words" and can give a good clue as to what is going on inside a person's mind.

In today's world, incidents like these can get on social media and utterly ruin a person's career. A daily walk with God will help with the "heart attitude," and when issues occur, the language will be much more in line with how God wishes for his children to talk. David addresses this issue in Psalm 141:3 when he asks God to "set a guard over my mouth; keep watch over the door of my lips." May this be our daily prayer.

Are you guarding the words that come out of your mouth?

DAY 58

Preformed Opinions

Seeing they do not see, and hearing they do not hear, nor
do they understand. Indeed, in their case the prophecy of
Isaiah is fulfilled that says: "You will indeed hear but never
understand, and you will indeed see but never perceive."
For this people's heart has grown dull, "and with their ears
they can barely hear, and their eyes they have closed, lest
they should see with their eyes and hear with their ears and
understand with their heart and turn, and I would heal them.
—Matthew 13:13b–15

First they led him to Annas, for he was the father-in-
law of Caiaphas, who was high priest that year.
It was Caiaphas who had advised the Jews that it would
be expedient that one man should die for the people.
—John 18:12, 14

Then those who had seized Jesus led him to Caiaphas the
high priest, where the scribes and the elders had gathered.
—Matthew 26:57

With Annas the high priest and Caiaphas and John and
Alexander, and all who were of the high-priestly family.
—Acts 4:6

Annas and Caiaphas are perfect examples of the type of person Jesus
was speaking about as he explained why he spoke in parables. These
men serve as examples of people that close their minds to the reality

of a situation, and no matter how hard one attempts to convince them of a certain reality, they will not hear it. Annas and Caiaphas had many opportunities to accept Jesus. They were even eyewitnesses to Jesus's miracles, yet they did not accept him but condemned him.

After Jesus's resurrection, they tried to cover it up. Then in the Acts account, they are threatening Peter and John, telling them to stop speaking of Jesus, even when there was physical evidence of a crippled man healed.

Remember that during your career, you also will encounter such people, whether it be a student or parent who will deny clear evidence of a situation because of a preformed opinion or notion. Pray for them and ask God for patience and strength when dealing with them.

Do you pray for your challenging students each day?

DAY 59

Change of Personality

Simon Peter followed Jesus, and so did another disciple. Since that disciple was known to the high priest, he entered with Jesus into the courtyard of the high priest, but Peter stood outside at the door. So the other disciple, who was known to the high priest, went out and spoke to the servant girl who kept watch at the door, and brought Peter in. The servant girl at the door said to Peter, "You also are not one of this man's disciples, are you?" He said, "I am not."
—John 18:15–17

Then Peter, filled with the Holy Spirit, said to them, "Rulers of the people and elders, if we are being examined today concerning a good deed done to a crippled man, by what means this man has been healed, let it be known to all of you and to all the people of Israel that by the name of Jesus Christ of Nazareth, whom you crucified, whom God raised from the dead—by him this man is standing before you well. This Jesus is the stone that was rejected by you, the builders, which has become the cornerstone. And there is salvation in no one else, for there is no other name under heaven given among men by which we must be saved." Now when they saw the boldness of Peter and John, and perceived that they were uneducated, common men, they were astonished. And they recognized that they had been with Jesus.
—Acts 4:8–13

Peter changed from the coward who denied Jesus to the brave man that confronted Annas and Caiaphas regarding the resurrection of

Jesus. This change in Peter is an example of the difference between a heart that will not hear and a heart that is willing to hear.

Read the account from John and from Acts and notice the changed personality of Peter due to the presence of the Holy Spirit that Jesus had promised. Note: the "other disciple" is known to be John.

The last sentence of this passage is extremely telling. "And they recognized that they had been with Jesus." The change in Peter and John was so apparent that unbelievers noticed a marked difference in their speech and boldness. This is a good question to ask ourselves. Do our students, parents, and colleagues recognize that we have been with Jesus by our actions and deeds? Let us continually ask God for a willing heart that is teachable and moldable so that we will be the best witness for him every day.

Can others tell that you have been with Jesus?

DAY 60

Proper Perspective Influences
Daily Decisions

And Eli said, "What was it that he told you? Do not
hide it from me. May God do so to you and more also if
you hide anything from me of all that he told you."
—1 Samuel 3:17

This statement from Eli the prophet to young Samuel reveals much
about his state of mind and where he was in his relationship to God.
Eli already knew that bad news was coming. In chapter 2, beginning in verse 27, a man of God came to Eli and told him that God
had rejected him because of the treachery of his sons. Eli was told
that his house would be punished, his sons would die on the same
day, and a new priest would take his place. Eli was "out of sorts"
with God. This caused him to make bad decisions, and he didn't
discipline his sons who were described as "worthless" and "did not
know the Lord."

This account is a valuable lesson that we must learn. Eli knew
he had been rejected as priest, and his mental state was affected.
When we sin, it puts a barrier between us and God, grieves the Holy
Spirit, our decision making becomes flawed.

Do not be fooled; being "out of sorts" with God affects our
judgment in the classroom and how we deal with students and colleagues. We must always put God in his rightful place in our lives or
it is at our peril if we do not. If you read further in 1 Samuel, the ark
of God was captured and taken to the Philistines, and everywhere
it went while in that country, the people were cursed with sickness.
Why? Because God was not in his rightful place. Only when the ark

was returned to Israel did these pestilences cease. If we remember to acknowledge God as first in our lives, everything else will be put in the proper perspective.

Are you putting God first in your life each day?

DAY 61

Knowing Our Students

But the LORD said to Samuel, "Do not look on his appearance
or on the height of his stature, because I have rejected
him. For the LORD sees not as man sees: man looks on the
outward appearance, but the LORD looks on the heart."
—1 Samuel 16:7

One of the toughest things we as teachers must do is to avoid making judgments of students by their appearance or demeanor. Teachers must get to know their students so that they can know their hearts; truly "knowing" your students proves to be vital to success in the classroom. How many times have we witnessed the "tough" kid that really has a tender heart but spends more time trying to cover it by acting out? Some of these children have had their hearts broken many times and don't want to get "burned" again. Beware of that absent-minded young man who is smart! Also be aware of that student who works to not appear intelligent because that is not "cool" in the circle of people who he/she associates with.

See students as God sees them, and your relationship with them will be changed for the better. If that student is unruly, the relationship may improve over time. If that student is bright and well-mannered, the already good relationship that you enjoy will get even better!

Ask God to give you a discerning spirit so that you get to really know how to approach each student who comes into your classroom.

DAY 62

Follow the Rubric

Now go and strike Amalek and devote to destruction all
that they have. Do not spare them, but kill both man and
woman, child and infant, ox and sheep, camel and donkey.

—1 Samuel 15:3

One of the biggest challenges teachers face is in grading projects that
have extensive written instructions. Most often, these projects are
assigned, and a rubric is given for how the project will be graded.
Students will invariably follow most of the directions but not all the
directions. In many cases, the first direction of the project is "Follow
all instructions given completely!" When the grade is assigned and it
is not the grade the student felt he/she should have received, the point
is often made "I did most of it correctly"; and an attempt is made to
bargain for a higher grade. Often the teacher is put on a guilt trip by
either the student or his/her advocate (parent) as to not being fair and
understanding of this student's particular situation.

In this reading, we see that Saul did not follow the instructions
completely!

But Saul and the people spared Agag and
the best of the sheep and of the oxen and of the
fattened calves and the lambs, and all that was
good, and would not utterly destroy them. All
that was despised and worthless they devoted to
destruction. (1 Samuel 15:9)

Now Saul is called out by Samuel the prophet. Notice in this exchange, Saul first states that he followed the instructions, then Samuel calls him out, and Saul attempts to deflect the blame and put it on the people, much like Adam did to Eve! He also tells Samuel that these things were going to be sacrificed to God…a convenient excuse!

> And Samuel came to Saul, and Saul said to him, "Blessed be you to the LORD. I have performed the commandment of the LORD." And Samuel said, "What then is this bleating of the sheep in my ears and the lowing of the oxen that I hear?" Saul said, "They have brought them from the Amalekites, for the people spared the best of the sheep and of the oxen to sacrifice to the LORD your God, and the rest we have devoted to destruction." (1 Samuel 15:13–15)

Samuel then, like teachers or administrators, had heard enough.

> Then Samuel said to Saul, "Stop! I will tell you what the LORD said to me this night." And he said to him, "Speak." And Samuel said, "Though you are little in your own eyes, are you not the head of the tribes of Israel? The LORD anointed you king over Israel. And the LORD sent you on a mission and said, "Go, devote to destruction the sinners, the Amalekites, and fight against them until they are consumed. Why then did you not obey the voice of the LORD? Why did you pounce on the spoil and do what was evil in the sight of the LORD?" And Saul said to Samuel, "I have obeyed the voice of the Lord. I have gone on the mission on which the LORD sent me. I have brought Agag the king of Amalek, and I have devoted the Amalekites to destruction. But the

people took the spoil, sheep and oxen, the best of the things devoted to destruction, to sacrifice to the LORD your God in Gilgal. And Samuel said, "Has the LORD as great delight in burnt offerings and sacrifices, as in obeying the voice of the LORD? Behold, to obey is better than sacrifice, and to listen than the fat of rams. For rebellion is as the sin of divination, and presumption is as iniquity and idolatry. Because you have rejected the word of the LORD, He has also rejected you from being king." (1 Samuel 15:16–23)

Not following God's instructions completely cost Saul his kingdom and his fellowship with God. From this passage forward, the Bible depicts Saul as a tormented man, exhibiting manic depressive behavior, jealousy, and even making several attempts to kill David, God's anointed successor. His mind is divided, and he makes poor decisions as a leader. Instead of consolidating Israel, he makes it weak so that the Philistines gain the courage to attack again. He finally commits suicide.

When we choose not to follow God's entire instruction, we do so at our peril. Granted, we may not lose a kingdom, but we may lose the blessings of good things, events, and people that God would have placed in our path. Make it a conscious choice to always follow God's instructions completely in the daily decisions that are made, and when you answer to the student (and parent) regarding the grade, remember this passage to enable you to be resolute in your defense!

Are you following God's rubric for your life?

DAY 63

Awareness of Surroundings

Now Joseph was handsome in form and appearance. And after a time his master's wife cast her eyes on Joseph and said, "Lie with me." But he refused and said to his master's wife, "Behold, because of me my master has no concern about anything in the house, and he has put everything that he has in my charge. He is not greater in this house than I am, nor has he kept back anything from me except you, because you are his wife. How then can I do this great wickedness and sin against God?" And as she spoke to Joseph day after day, he would not listen to her, to lie beside her or to be with her. But one day, when he went into the house to do his work and none of the men of the house was there in the house, she caught him by his garment, saying, "Lie with me." But he left his garment in her hand and fled and got out of the house. And as soon as she saw that he had left his garment in her hand and had fled out of the house, she called to the men of her household and said to them, "See, he has brought among us a Hebrew to laugh at us. He came in to me to lie with me, and I cried out with a loud voice. And as soon as he heard that I lifted up my voice and cried out, he left his garment beside me and fled and got out of the house." Then she laid up his garment by her until his master came home, and she told him the same story, saying, "The Hebrew servant, whom you have brought among us, came in to me to laugh at me. But as soon as I lifted up my voice and cried, he left his garment beside me and fled out of the house." As soon as his master heard the words that his wife spoke to him, "This is the way your servant treated me," his anger was kindled. And Joseph's master took him and put him into the prison, the place where the king's prisoners were confined, and he was there in prison.

—Genesis 39:6b–20

Beware of compromising situations with students. As I read this incident that happened to Joseph, I am reminded of several issues where fine educators' careers were ruined because of compromising their morals and engaging in inappropriate relationships with students. Many times, these relationships began innocently with the teacher providing one-on-one assistance outside of school hours, then entertaining advances from the student, and finally engaging in an inappropriate relationship.

Although Joseph was completely innocent and reacted in the appropriate manner, he still was put in prison. Examine the actions of Potiphar's wife. She trapped Joseph in a situation where it would be her word against his. When Joseph didn't respond to her advances, she accused Joseph of trying to sleep with her. This situation underscores that in these types of situations, the accused is presumed guilty until proven innocent.

The world in which we work is no different from the world Joseph encountered. Like Joseph, we as teachers may innocently find ourselves during the workday in a compromising position with students. If/When this occurs, change the situation or setting immediately if it is humanly possible. You might say something like, "Let's move into this area where we can see better" or "Let's move to where we have the benefit of the board or computer" or "Let's move to where I can be closer to these other students who are working so that if they need help, I can give it to them."

In all circumstances, avoid one-on-one associations with the opposite sex. If students need to stay after school for assistance, make sure this occurs in an open setting. Avoid one-on-one situations in the music practice room, black box theatre, in the dark room of the photography class, or out at the agriculture barn, caring for animals. Avoid the situation of students asking to come to your room to eat lunch, particularly if it is a one-on-one situation. Plan tutorial activities so that a compromising situation is not created.

I remember hearing that when the Billy Graham team traveled, they were careful not to have one member ever get into an automobile with one member of the opposite sex. They always traveled as a group of three or more. This is a good practice to adopt when working with students before or after school hours or during lunch. Make sure to always be in the presence of mixed company, preferably where other adults are nearby.

Are you constantly aware of your surroundings when working one-on-one with a student?

DAY 64

Love for the Unlovely

Love one another earnestly from a pure heart, since you have
been born again, not of perishable seed, but imperishable,
through the living and abiding word of God.
—1 Peter 22b, 23

Abide in me and I in you. As the branch cannot bear fruit by itself,
unless it abides in the vine, neither can you unless you abide in me.
—John 15:4

How can we love all our students? How can we love even the "bad
ones"?

Yes, sometimes it is difficult but possible when we look through
the lens of Christ all the time. We love all people because of who we
are. We have been born from above and are part of Christ's body, so
we love because of who we are and because of who we serve.

Remember Jesus's command and promise, "Abide in me and
I in you." We can love the unlovely because Christ is in us. In our
abiding, we give Christlike responses which will bear fruit. We may
not see this fruit in our career, but the positive memory of you by
your students will be the fruit. They will someday remember what
you said or did in that tense moment where they were on your last
nerve!

How are you showing love for that student that is on your last
nerve?

DAY 65

Choosing Words Wisely

For whenever the Israelites planted crops, the Midianites and the Amalekites and the people of the East would come up against them. They would encamp against them and devour the produce of the land, as far as Gaza, and leave no sustenance in Israel and no sheep or ox or donkey. For they would come up with their livestock and their tents; they would come like locusts in number—both they and their camels could not be counted—so that they laid waste the land as they came in. And Israel was brought very low because of Midian. And the people of Israel cried out for help to the Lord. Now the angel of the Lord came and sat under the terebinth at Ophrah, which belonged to Joash the Abiezrite, while his son Gideon was beating out wheat in the winepress to hide it from the Midianites. And the angel of the Lord appeared to him and said to him, "The Lord is with you, O mighty man of valor."

—Judges 6:3–6, 11–12

"The Lord is with you, O mighty man of valor." The way students are addressed by adults can be either extremely helpful or harmful to their self-esteem. Specifically, the way students are addressed by their parents shapes their personality and character. As I have listened to parents speak about their children, I have heard them say things like, "He's my smart one" or "I must be realistic about my son's/daughter's ability to pass." Children receive these positive and negative messages that shape their personalities.

On the flipside, parents are sometimes guilty of rearing children who think they can do no wrong. Both extremes in parenting can be potentially harmful to the child as he/she matures and must interact with others. The communication the child receives from the time he/she can understand words is significantly important; parents should choose their words wisely.

As teachers, we should also choose our words wisely! How we positively communicate our expectations to our students is greatly important. If a student is treated as not being smart, he/she will respond by meeting those expectations! Conversely, if we hold our expectations high, students will also respond. Some students may take a while to respond depending on the type of messages they are receiving from their parents and friends outside of school.

Examine how the angel of the Lord addressed Gideon. Remember, Gideon was in the wrong place to beat out wheat. A person beats wheat in the open where there is a breeze to carry away the chaff and stubble. Gideon was in the winepress, nowhere near the proper place to do this chore, and he was there out of fear of the Midianites. The angel completely redefined who Gideon was and gave him a new self-image…"mighty man of valor!"

We should strive to do the same with our students. Communicate your positive expectations and positive opinion of them in your communication. For many, this may be the first time anyone believed in them.

Are you that teacher who is consistently finding the "good" things to talk about, even with your most challenging students?

DAY 66

Positive Messaging through Actions and Speech

So that even if some do not obey the word, they may be
won without a word by the conduct...when they see your
respectful and pure conduct...imperishable beauty of a gentle
and quiet spirit, which in God's sight is very precious.
—1 Peter 3:1–4

Show me your faith apart from your works,
and I will show you faith by my works.
—James 2:18

As a principal working with teachers and students, I have noticed that the teachers who experience the most success are the ones who genuinely care about the welfare of their students and display this care by their manner of speech. A caring "tone" of positive communication works best. Conversely, I have noticed the teachers who use a sarcastic, disrespectful tone have more difficulty with their classroom management as well as with the overall success of their students. Something interesting to note is the difference in overall grade distributions between the caring teacher and the sarcastic teacher.

"Actions speak louder than words." One of the ways that we can be a positive witness for Christ is by our conduct. Students notice how you treat their friends. They will watch how you interact with your colleagues. They will remember what you said when that sarcastic, disrespectful tone comes out of your mouth.

Likewise, they will notice your loving spirit, your acceptance of them for who they are, and your genuine tone that displays your care for them and their well-being. Though Peter is primarily speaking to wives regarding their husbands in this passage, it is good advice on how to witness by our conduct. Examine the Christlike traits Peter speaks of in this passage—respectful, pure, gentle, and quiet spirit. Are these traits exhibited in your life before your students and colleagues? Remember that James said that he would show his faith by his works.

What message do your speech and actions communicate to your students and colleagues?

DAY 67

Spiritual Truths in Daily Routines

If my people who are called by my name humble themselves, and pray and seek my face and turn from their wicked ways, then I will hear from heaven and will forgive their sin and heal their land.

—2 Chronicles 7:14

He will bring to remembrance all that I have said to you.

—John 14:26

Isn't it amazing and wonderful how the Holy Spirit brings to our memory verses in the Bible as we go about our daily work! Remember what Jesus said regarding the Holy Spirit: "He will bring to your remembrance all that I have said to you." The following occurred as I was observing a geometry class:

This class was beginning a new unit which was proofs, not the most popular unit in this course! The teacher was explaining to the class that the purpose of a proof was to be able to formulate an "if-then" statement regarding phenomena. In this lesson, the teacher was speaking regarding deductive reasoning, moving from general to specific. He went on to explain that the part of the sentence after the "if" is called a hypothesis, and the part of the sentence after the "then" is called the conclusion.

Thinking about what this teacher was saying in the context of my own educational research coursework from graduate studies, I remembered that one of the basic tenets of hypothesis testing was the ability to formulate an "if-then" statement. The hypothesis followed by the conclusion is called an "if-then" statement or a conditional statement.

Suddenly, the greatest "if-then" statement ever written came to my mind: "If my people who are called by my name humble themselves, and pray and seek my face and turn from their wicked ways, then I will hear from heaven and will forgive their sins and heal their land."

As we draw closer to God, we will notice more and more the Holy Spirit directing our thoughts toward God as well as to the things of God. We will also begin to lose our appetite for some of the worldly aspects that we thought we could not do without! Our thought process will change. Why does this happen? Because we are beginning to learn how to fulfill the conditions of the hypothesis, seek his face, and turn from our wicked ways.

These requirements of God require an act of our will as well as directed constant practice. The more we practice "seeking his face," the more aligned our spirit becomes with him. Pray today that in everything that you do, you will seek his face. Doing so will make the rough times easier to bear, and we will begin to experience the "reckless abandon," as Oswald Chambers stated, to the will of God.

Take a moment to reflect how God has brought to your attention appropriate passages in the Bible as you encounter different situations.

DAY 68

Meet All of the Conditions

If my people who are called by my name humble themselves and
pray and seek my face and turn from their wicked ways, then I will
hear from heaven and will forgive their sin and heal their land.
—2 Chronicles 7:14

If we confess our sins, he is faithful and just to forgive us
our sins and to cleanse us from all unrighteousness.
—1 John 1:9

Let us examine more closely the greatest conditional statement ever
written. There are four equally important parts to the hypothesis: (1)
humble themselves, (2) pray, (3) seek my face, and (4) turn from their
wicked ways.

Many times, I have heard well-meaning Christians quote this
verse when discussing the moral decline of our country and their sincere wish for genuine revival. Interestingly, their quote of this verse
goes something like this: "If my people who are called by my name
will humble themselves and pray, then I will hear from heaven and
heal their land." What is the problem? For the hypothesis to be true,
all the conditions must be met! The two conditions that get left out
happen to be the ones that require daily discipline and willful acts on
our part; "seek my face," aligning our wants and desires with his, and
"turn from their wicked ways," the daily act of repentance followed
by willful action on our part.

Perhaps our unanswered prayer and subsequent frustration with
God are misplaced because we have not met conditions 3 (seek my
face) and 4 (turn from their wicked ways) of the hypotheses! We must

not be so quick to claim the conclusion if all the conditions have not been met.

Speaking of the conclusion, notice that God gives three promises: (1) he will hear from heaven, (2) he will forgive sin (individual), (3) heal their land (corporate). In the "cliff note quotation" of this verse, people forget about the individual component, the forgiveness of our sins.

Also notice that in this verse, there contains all the necessary components of one coming to Christ initially, recognizing sin and the need for forgiveness, humbly coming to God and requesting forgiveness, repentance, and salvation. To the Christian who stumbles (which will happen often!), this verse offers the same, recognizing our sin, humbly seeking forgiveness, and restoration.

Let us never forget that we serve a loving God who is willing to help us, forgive us, prop us up, and sustain us if we fulfill the conditions given in the hypothesis. The Holy Spirit will assist us to humble ourselves, pray, and seek God's face.

First John 1:9 sums up this idea well: "*If we confess our sins, he is faithful and just to forgive us our sins and cleanse us from all unrighteousness.*" This process may be viewed as the teacher reminding the students to read the rubric carefully as to how to complete the assignment as well as to understand the standards of how the assignment will be graded. Let this be our challenge to work on conditions 3 and 4 daily!

Reflect on how you are seeking God's face and turning from sin.

DAY 69

Remind and Practice

For this very reason, make every effort to supplement your
faith with virtue, and virtue with knowledge, and knowledge
with self-control and self-control with steadfastness, and
steadfastness with godliness, and godliness with brotherly
affection, and brotherly affection with love. For if these qualities
are yours and increasing, they keep you from being ineffective
or unfruitful in the knowledge of our Lord Jesus Christ.
—2 Peter 1:5–8

Therefore I intend always to remind you of these qualities.
—2 Peter 1:12

For if you practice these qualities you will never fall.
—2 Peter 1:10

When I had the responsibility of hiring teachers, I tried to make
mental observations of their personal qualities. When conducting
their interview, I tried to determine if they were kind and patient as
well as possessing the technical knowledge required to successfully
teach the subject. I wanted to find people who possessed the technical knowledge to teach the subject, who would be a positive influence
on students, and be a good "fit" with our current staff. These personal qualities are exceedingly important because that person must
be trusted with the shaping of impressionable young people's minds.
In a sense, I felt like the shepherd of the flock (my staff and students),
and it was my responsibility to keep the wolves out!

Peter is speaking to Christians because he assumes they already believe and have faith. These qualities supplement and are vital nutrients to our faith. Peter lists these qualities of Christians: virtue, knowledge, self-control, steadfastness, godliness, brotherly affection, and love. Perhaps more importantly, Peter implies that these qualities do not necessarily come naturally. He specifically states that one must *practice* these qualities!

Examining the life of Peter, we can see that when he was part of the inner circle of Jesus, he didn't possess any of these qualities! Reading this passage, we see that there was a great change in Peter evidenced by his great sermon at Pentecost.

How did Peter change? Through the work of the Holy Spirit. See, the Holy Spirit gives us the "want to" to obtain these qualities, but the believer must make a willful decision to *practice* these qualities.

Peter also states that he has the intent to continually *remind* us of these qualities; *remind and practice!*

Keeping the qualities of virtue, knowledge, self-control, steadfastness, godliness, brotherly affection, and love at the forefront of our minds will enable us to be truly successful in our dealings with difficult students, parents, bosses, and colleagues. More importantly, practicing these qualities will open opportunities to "let your light shine before others so that they may see your good works and give glory to your Father who is in heaven."

Are you practicing these qualities?

DAY 70

Intense Conversation

When they had finished breakfast, Jesus said to Simon Peter, "Simon, son of John, do you love me more than these?" He said to him, "Yes Lord; you know that I love you." He said to him, "Feed my lambs." He said to him a second time, "Simon son of John, do you love me?" He said to him, "Yes, Lord; you know that I love you." He said to him, "Tend my sheep." He said to him the third time, "Simon son of John, do you love me?" Peter was grieved because he said to him the third time, "Do you love me?" and he said to him, "Lord, you know everything; you know that I love you." Jesus said to him, "Feed my sheep."

—John 21:15–17

And the Lord turned and looked at Peter. And Peter remembered the saying of the Lord, how he had said to him, "Before the rooster crows today, you will deny me three times."

—Luke 22:61

Therefore I intend always to remind you of these qualities, though you know them and are established in the truth that you have. I think it right, as long as I am in this body, to stir you up by way of reminder... And I will make every effort so that after my departure you may be able at any time to recall these things.

—2 Peter 1:12–13, 15

The conversation Jesus had with Peter undoubtedly had a lifelong effect to the extent that Peter probably vowed to himself that he would never forsake his Lord again. How could Peter ever forget looking into the eyes of Jesus, his (and our) Savior, and Jesus asking him three times, corresponding to the three times he had betrayed him, if he loved him? That penetrating look of Jesus at him during this conversation, like the penetrating look he received from Jesus after his third betrayal, was imprinted on his consciousness, seared upon his memory to the extent that he would never forget it.

When we read the verses in 2 Peter 1:12–13, 15, Peter's sense of determination is evident. Examine closely the text in 2 Peter, *"Therefore, I intend to always remind you of these qualities"*; "Feed my lambs"; *"I think it right as long as I am in this body to stir you up by way of reminder"*; "Tend my sheep"; *"And I will make every effort that after my departure you may be able at any time to recall these things"*; "Feed my sheep."

Jesus says the same to us; how are we doing?

DAY 71

Primary Sources

For we did not follow cleverly devised myths when we made
known to you the power and coming of our Lord Jesus Christ,
but we were eyewitnesses of his majesty. For when he received
honor and glory from God the Father, and the voice was borne
to him by the Majestic Glory, "This is my beloved Son, with
whom I am well pleased," we ourselves heard this very voice borne
from heaven, for we were with him on the holy mountain.
—2 Peter 1:16–18

[A]nd they recognized that they had been with Jesus.
—Acts 4:13b

I was observing a US history class, and in this lesson, the teacher was
discussing the importance of primary sources. Primary sources provide firsthand accounts of events. Firsthand information is important because, usually, the details of that event are the most accurate.

Listening to this teacher instruct the class on the importance
of primary sources, I realized the importance of 2 Peter 1:16–18 and
its implications. Peter reminds us that he was a primary source of
the good news of the gospel! As he states, he was present at Jesus's
transfiguration, Jesus's betrayal, Jesus's denial (he did it), and Jesus's
resurrection. He had a direct relationship with Jesus that qualified
him as a primary source of information regarding who Jesus was.

Interestingly, we too are primary sources of information if we
have accepted Christ. We have a unique testimony regarding our personal relationship with Jesus. It may not be that flashy, hellfire testimony where one was addicted to drugs, almost died, and turned to

Jesus. It may be a quiet, unflashy testimony (as is mine) of your childhood experience of asking Jesus to be your Savior when you prayed at bedtime. Some people may not remember the exact time of the event, but how they live their lives bear out their dedication to Jesus. *"And they recognized that they had been with Jesus."* As Christians, we are the primary source because we serve a living Savior! *We* are his witnesses!

Are you a primary source? When the opportunity arises, can you tell someone how you came to know Christ?

DAY 72

Accurate Proper Citations

And we have the prophetic word more fully confirmed, to which
you will do well to pay attention as to a lamp shining in a dark
place, until the day dawns and the morning star rises in your
hearts, knowing this first of all, that no prophecy of Scripture
comes from someone's own interpretation. For no prophecy
was ever produced by the will of man, but men spoke from
God as they were being carried along by the Holy Spirit.
—2 Peter 1:19–21

Let us carry this idea of being a primary source forward. Verse 19
of today's passage begins with a significantly important word: *and*.
"*And we have the prophetic word more fully confirmed.*" The prophetic
word is more fully confirmed because Jesus came and did everything
the prophets said he would do. Read the gospels and note the many
instances that the writer stated that Jesus did what he did to fulfill the scripture. "*No prophecy of Scripture comes from someone's own
interpretation.*"

"*For no prophecy was ever produced by the will of man, but man
spoke from God as they were carried along by the Holy Spirit.*"

Peter gives us a wonderful example of confirmation of the prophetic word in his very first public sermon. What was Peter's text?
The text for his Pentecost sermon came from the book of Joel (Acts
2:16–21; Joel 2:28–32). So, Peter, the primary source referring to
the primary source—rather interesting, wouldn't you say? Part of our
responsibility of being a primary source is to be able to direct others
to *the primary source, Jesus*! One way that we do this is by using our
Bible to show others scripture and how the scriptures point to Jesus.

To effectively use our Bible, we must know our Bible. We must be able to cite and show others passages that point them to Jesus.

As we live out our Christian life, we will inevitably receive comments and/or inquiries from those who observe our actions and our demeanor regarding what makes us like we are. Be ready to offer not only your personal testimony, but also be able to direct individuals to the answers that the Bible gives regarding salvation as well as to principles regarding other life issues.

Are you able to cite as well as show others scripture to point them to Christ?

DAY 73

Meeting Deadlines

The Lord is not slow to fulfill his promise as some count slowness,
but is patient towards you, not wishing that any should perish,
but that all should reach repentance. But the day of the Lord
will come like a thief, and then the heavens will pass away with
a roar, and the heavenly bodies will be burned up and dissolved,
and the earth and the works done on it will be exposed.
—2 Peter 3:9–10

Unfortunately, many deadlines that are given are no longer real. Perhaps one of the greatest disservices to all of us has been the implementation of "soft deadlines" or "grace periods." In the classroom, for example, the teacher assigns dates that a paper, project, test, or assignment is due. Many times, the teacher will then state that should the assignment not be turned in on the "due date," he/she will still accept the assignment for less credit. The consequence is that students are trained to believe that no real deadlines exist or, in a larger sense, absolutes. The teacher has now established an "everything is negotiable mentality" which unfortunately is currently pervading our society.

Many everyday examples of this mentality exist. On every bill that we receive, there are two amounts, one for "on time" and one for "after due date." Interestingly, this vocabulary has changed because it used to read "late payments!" In the workplace, deadlines for projects are extended, people are late to meetings, and startups of new projects or businesses are delayed due to construction overages. In our court system, sentencing of criminals is delayed, and continuances are granted. Even at the highest levels of our country, ultimatums are given and rescinded.

Operating within this culture makes the teachers' job more difficult. One of the toughest conversations any teacher has is having to say that the deadline has passed for the completion of assignments, making up a test, or turning in a paper. Students and parents request leniency and offer the reason that they were very busy. Parents will go as far as to say that they are to blame for the assignment not being completed as they had their child involved in other activities. They will request the teacher not "punish" their child due to their negligence. If that doesn't work, they then invoke accusations of the impatience of the teacher! The poor teacher says, "I've been patient the entire grading period, and I must submit the grade!" Interestingly, the deadlines in question are most always *known deadlines*!

Peter addresses this issue by stating that there is going to be an absolute deadline one day. This deadline is *unknown* to us! God himself is the only one who knows what it is. Today we are living in a period of grace, and God is showing his patience so that all can make the decision to accept Jesus.

Soft deadlines or grace periods may be viewed as a lesson from God given to us about his benevolence, giving all an opportunity to come to Jesus. The lesson of absolute deadlines is equally, if not more so, important because it teaches the reality that one day, the ultimate deadline will occur.

When you give a deadline and then extend it, view it as a mini lesson on the greatest grace period ever known, the period of grace that we are living in today!

DAY 74

The Look

And the Lord turned and looked at Peter. And Peter remembered the saying of the Lord and how he had said to him, "Before the rooster crows today, you will deny me three times." And he went out and wept bitterly.

—Luke 22:61–62

Effective teachers develop the "teacher voice" and "the look." The "teacher voice" is that special tone used so that students know that when they hear this tone, they need to cease the activity in which they are engaged or are beginning to be engaged. "The look" essentially does the same thing. For "the look" and/or the "teacher voice" to be effective, the relationship between teacher and student must be so well established that the student knows the expectations of the teacher and has developed a healthy respect for the office of the teacher. Most students have an innate desire to please their parents or someone in authority.

Let us focus on "the look." For effective teachers who have built a relationship with their students based on mutual respect, "the look" is all that is needed to change the atmosphere in a classroom. The disciple Peter had that kind of relationship with his teacher Jesus.

I am reminded of a high school friend relating an incident that occurred in the locker room during halftime of a football game. He was asked, "What did the coach say that made you all play so much better and come back to win the game?"

His response was, "It's not what he said, it's what he didn't say. He just looked at us and went into his office."

Peter got "the look" and remembered Jesus's prediction that he would deny him three times. That look, seared on his brain forever, changed his life, and he later went and followed Jesus's command of spreading the Gospel!

A "healthy fear" or respect is one of the most important tools that a teacher *must* have in his/her toolbox. Have you developed that type of loving relationship with your students that "the look" matters to them?

DAY 75

Informed Indifference

And assembling all the chief priests and scribes of the people,
he inquired of them where the Christ was to be born. They told
him, "In Bethlehem of Judea, for so it is written by the prophet.
—Matthew 2:4–5

It was the Sunday before Christmas, and the sermon of course had a
Christmas theme. As our pastor read the account of the magi from
Matthew 2, he stopped at this portion of the account. I was thoroughly familiar with the account of the magi but had glossed over
this part in my many readings. He called this portion of the passage
"informed indifference." Herod asked the chief priests and scribes
for information regarding the birth of Jesus. They gave it to him
by quoting Micah 5:2 where the birthplace of Jesus was prophesied.
Our pastor's emphasis was that the chief priests and scribes knew the
right information but failed to do anything with it other than report
it. They didn't act on the information by going to Bethlehem, unlike
the Magi who did, to worship the Savior. They were well-informed
but indifferent to the fact that what was prophesied had taken place.
Interestingly, these were the very people Jesus would confront again
and again during his earthly ministry. So they missed it from the
beginning.

    This revelation caused me to think about this fact on a couple
of levels, spiritually and professionally. Spiritually, I read my Bible,
pray, and attend Bible study and worship. But have I grown numb
to the promptings of the Holy Spirit due to my familiarity with the
Scriptures? My first prayer was one asking forgiveness of this. I now
more fully understand that one of Satan's best weapons of destruc-

tion is the weapon of complacency, a feeling of satisfaction with the status quo.

Professionally, how do we as teachers treat students that are not achieving? Are they treated with an attitude of indifference? We see the data constantly pouring in—65 on a quiz, missing homework assignments, 61 on a major test. The question will be asked, "At any time during the semester, did you reach out personally to the student, parent, or guardian?"

Instead of answering the question, answers are given, such as, "I teach 150 students and can't help all of them"; or "He/She never asked for any assistance." Do we soothe our conscience by giving these kinds of answers or thinking these thoughts?

Make the decision to not be complacent spiritually or professionally. Decide to nourish your spirit by studying the Word and hanging on to *all* the text and professionally, to look at student performance and personally reach out to those who are not achieving.

Are you reaching out to students who are underperforming in your classes?

DAY 76

Discerning Methodologies

His winnowing fork is in his hand, and he will clear
his threshing floor and gather his wheat into the barn,
but the chaff he will burn with unquenchable fire.
—Matthew 3:12

In this passage, Matthew quotes John the Baptist. John uses an interesting metaphor in using the word *chaff*—the husk or waste material that surrounds the part of the plant that is eaten. The word has a long history as a metaphor meaning objects and/or ideas that possess little or no value.

We live in an age of competing philosophies and ideologies. The Internet is full of varying philosophies and half-truths. During Donald Trump's first campaign for president, we became familiar with a term called "fake news," false stories that are perpetuated through the Internet and through some news outlets. "Fake news" or false ideas may "take legs" for a period, but John the Baptist assures us that eventually, they will be exposed and demolished.

Jesus himself addresses this issue of competing philosophies in the parable of the weeds.

> But he said, No, lest in gathering the weeds you root up the wheat along with them. Let both grow together until the harvest, and at harvest time I will tell the reapers, Gather the weeds first and bind them in bundles to be burned, but gather the wheat into my barn. (Matthew 13:29–30)

Finally, John the apostle encourages us to test the spirits:

> Beloved, do not believe every spirit, but test the spirits to see whether they are from God, for many false prophets have gone out into the world. (1 John 4:1)

In education, many false ideas regarding learning have been presented, tried, and failed. We as teachers many times come under pressure to teach using unsound practice because of the influence of the liberal education intelligentsia that now permeates higher education.

Take John's advice to "test" these notions regarding your teaching practice. Rely on the Holy Spirit to assist you as you navigate through the ideological land mines that are so pervasive in our education system. Do not be afraid to speak out against unsound practices and expose them for what they are. Remember that, eventually, they will be "burned." It may take a while as the weeds grow with the wheat, but take heart that eventually, they will be destroyed.

Are you discerning in your approach to the use of teaching methodology in your subject?

DAY 77

Preparing for Success

And if it is evil in your eyes to serve the Lord, choose this day
whom you will serve, whether the gods your fathers served in the
region beyond the River, or the gods of the Amorites in whose land
you dwell. But as for me and my house we will serve the Lord.
—Joshua 24:15

When a person has in place a values system and a set of beliefs
regarding how he/she acts, where he/she goes, what influences will
become part of his/her thinking, right decisions are easier to make
when tempting events occur. Many call this one's moral compass.
Joshua shows us that personal decisions regarding issues of morality
need to be made prior to tempting events: "as for me and my house
we *will* serve the Lord." Note the emphasis on the word *will*.

Have for yourself a set of absolutes regarding moral behavior
both at the workplace and in your private life. Hint: they should
be the same! Be honest with yourself and with God regarding certain "bents" to sin with which you may struggle. Prepare yourself
spiritually how you will react when temptation occurs. Decisions
made regarding your conduct *before* temptations occur will make
your decisions easier *when they do* occur. Remember the promise of
James 4:7, "*Resist the devil and he will flee from you.*" Let all decisions
be made against the standard of serving the Lord. This will be a true
litmus test for each decision, both spiritually and professionally, that
you will make.

Joshua 24:17 also has profound applications for how we set students up for success in our subject area. Good teachers will set their
students up for success by providing and enforcing specific expec-

tations for behavior and performance prior to events or situations. Successful coaches review game situations and practice them with the players so that when they occur in games, the athlete is prepared to react in a certain way. Spell out to your students the learning objective as well as the specific performance standard so that they will know by their performance whether they have mastered your expectations for their learning. Break learning tasks into small measurable performance standards so that when these tasks are combined, the student will have mastered the learning objective.

Are you setting your students up for success?

DAY 78

Weeding and Cultivating

Other seeds fell among thorns, and the
thorns grew up and choked them.
As for what was sown among thorns, this is the one who hears
the word, but the cares of the world and the deceitfulness
of riches choke the word, and it proves unfruitful.
—Matthew 13:7, 22

To routinely examine ourselves proves to be spiritually profitable to see where our heart is in relation to God. The parable of the soils and Jesus's explanation of it is a wonderful tool for the Christian to use to do this periodic "heart check" to remain close to God. God is always communicating with us, and we need to examine ourselves (1 Corinthians 11:28) and determine if the condition of our heart presently is a path, rocky ground, thorns, or good soil.

Christians find themselves choked by the thorns of schedules, work, raising children, money, keeping up with the Joneses, and other "cares of the world." Notice that some items on this short list are good items to be doing but may have become idols because they have not been placed in the proper perspective relative to God, *You shall have no other gods before me.* Closer examination of this text reveals that the thorns will come, but it is important not to let them grow! "The thorns grew up"; therefore, cultivating the soil of our heart is extremely important to keep the "bad stuff" out!

Just as Jesus the Teacher recognized that he was teaching basically to four levels of receptivity, (path, rocky ground, thorns, good soil), the classroom teacher must recognize that he/she will also be teaching to different levels of student receptivity. Students today deal with "thorns" of all types, such as the thorn of not having proactive parents, the thorn of social media, the thorn of apathy, and the thorn of peer pressure to name a few. Be ready to review and revise for individuals when needed. Understand that just because you "taught it" doesn't necessarily mean that learning has taken place.

The late John Wooden wrote a book titled *You Haven't Taught Until They Have Learned*. Keep that idea at the forefront of your thinking when working with students who may be hard to reach.

Are you weeding out the "thorns" in your spiritual life or are you cultivating them? Do you recognize the "thorns" in your students' lives? And are you being an influence in assisting them to weed them out?

DAY 79

Varied Opportunities to Learn

You shall love the LORD your God with all your heart and with all your soul and with all your might. And these words that I command you today shall be on your heart. You shall teach them diligently to your children, and shall talk of them when you sit in your house, and when you walk by the way, and when you lie down, and when you rise. You shall bind them as a sign on your hand, and they shall be as frontlets between your eyes. You shall write them on the doorposts of your house and on your gates.

—Deuteronomy 6:5–9

This passage is referring to the commandment of loving God with all our heart, soul, and might. As Christians, we take this commandment as our challenge to study God's Word and to keep it at the forefront of our thoughts.

Professionally, this passage gives good guidance to our teaching pedagogy. Notice in verses 7–9, Moses is considerably specific about how God's Word is to be taught. To teach diligently implies consistency of effort, persistence, and perseverance as well as painstaking attention. To talk of them constantly implies much repetition. "Bind them as a sign, write them on the doorposts of your house and on your gate" implies making visible reminders. In today's language, use a sticky note and put it in your phone! In other words, review constantly, stay focused, teach in many ways, provide different contexts to the information.

Remember that the God who created us created each of us "unique and wonderfully made." God understands that each of us learns in different ways and at different speeds. Remember this as you go about your day working with students. Many times, the reason students are not successful is because of their exasperation in their failed attempts to learn. Remain persistent, and give them multiple ways to learn the material.

Are you providing different opportunities for your students to learn?

DAY 80

Genuineness

Let not steadfast love and faithfulness forsake you; bind them
around your neck; write them on the tablet of your heart.
—Proverbs 3:3

Effective teachers love their students and are dedicated to them by
showing them faithfulness. Faithfulness is demonstrated by the
teachers' attendance, timeliness, follow through, patience, kindness,
perseverance, and persistence. Love is the one constant in this profession that makes teachers successful regardless of socioeconomic
status of the students. *"But the greatest of these is love"* (1 Corinthians
13:13).

Students in prosperous economic settings want to be loved as
much as students in poor economic settings. They may demonstrate
their need for love and affection differently but know that the need is
there. Once they know that you love them and are faithful to them,
they will make a much greater effort to perform for you. In fact,
some teachers may not be as academically proficient as their peers but
are better teachers because their love is evident to their students *"since
love covers a multitude of sins"* (1 Peter 4:8).

Teachers who genuinely care for their students have a much better chance to "win them over" and instill a love of learning. Think
back to a subject that you enjoyed as a student. Probably the first
reason that you began to enjoy the subject was because of the personality of that teacher who inspired you. In reflection on your experience with this person, you probably described that person as "nice"
or "tough but fair" or "he/she liked me." Students will do the work

because they "like and respect" the teacher just as that teacher gives this respect to them.

When I was involved in the selection of teachers, the one trait that I always looked for was the potential candidate's love of children. Genuine love of children will indeed carry you when your students encounter difficulties with the subject matter. Your love, patience, and encouragement may help to keep them from becoming exasperated. Take the challenge of this verse and bind the attributes of love and faithfulness to your personality.

Do your students know that you genuinely care for them? This is *all* they really want to know: do you love/care about them enough to teach them what they need to know?

DAY 81

Be Careful

Be careful to obey all these words that I command you…
Take care that you will not be ensnared to follow them.
—Deuteronomy 12:28, 30

Be careful… Take care. One of the last words I remember my parents saying when I departed from their presence was "Be careful!" What were they really saying? In those two words, they were reminding me not to get into trouble and that if I got into trouble, I would be into more trouble when they found out! They were also reminding me that I was going into situations where I would be free to make choices and that those choices carried with them consequences, good consequences for good choices, bad consequences for bad choices.

They were also reminding me that I had been taught the right principles in life, and I had a good moral compass to make right decisions. As I examine these words more carefully now, I realize they also imply that we must be watchful, be attentive, and be wary of enticements that lead to entanglement in sin.

Sin affects both the personal and professional areas of our lives. I knew a teacher who succumbed to the enticement of the sin of adultery with one of his female students. He wrote a note to her, stating that after she graduated, he would like to be with her intimately. Interestingly, this person had not yet physically committed the sin. The note was shared, this good teacher lost his job, his wife divorced him, he lost his home and his family, and ultimately, he committed suicide. This fine teacher succumbed to the personal enticement of sex, followed by an unwise professional decision which took away his livelihood, his reputation, and ultimately, his life. Heed the voice of God. Be careful...take care!

How careful are you regarding your thoughts, motivations, and actions?

DAY 82

Responsibility to Be Proactive

You have heard that it was said, "An eye for an eye and a tooth for a tooth." But I say to you, do not resist the one who is evil. But if anyone slaps you on the right cheek, turn to him the other also. And if anyone would sue you and take your tunic, let him have your cloak as well. And if anyone forces you to go one mile, go with him two miles. Give to the one who begs from you, and do not refuse the one who would borrow from you.
—Matthew 5:38–42

A soft answer turns away wrath, but a harsh word stirs up anger.
—Proverbs 15:1

For if you forgive others their trespasses, your
heavenly Father will also forgive you.
—Matthew 6:14

Don't retaliate! At some point during your career, you will have students come to you and report that they are being threatened physically by other students. Take that moment to put Jesus's words into your own, and advise those students how to handle these conflicts without retaliating. Let them know that you will forward their concern to the appropriate authority, and they may be questioned by an administrator. Give them a compliment that they were correct in reporting these aggressive behaviors. Use these situations as teachable moments, and give them some strategies to hopefully avoid further conflicts with other students.

Examples of such strategies may include encouraging them to change their seat in the classroom or encouraging them to take other routes to classes in order to help deescalate situations. Discuss some appropriate verbal responses that may enable students to deescalate or resolve conflicts. *"A soft answer turns away wrath."* If the person who is being threatened tries some of these strategies, and the aggressor continues the threatening behavior, a pattern may be established and the aggressor disciplined appropriately.

Teacher, it is *your* responsibility to immediately report this issue to an administrator. Administrator, it is *your* responsibility to make every effort to resolve the conflict before it escalates. Many times, the punch thrown in retaliation is the result of intimidation that has been ongoing for a period of time.

How proactive are you when students report difficulties they are having with other students?

DAY 83

Our Disposition

Yet forty days and Nineveh shall be overthrown!
—Jonah 3:4b

God may use you, even when your disposition toward his work is negative!

God used Jonah to bring an entire city to repentance even though Jonah's disposition toward the people of Nineveh was negative. Examine the simplicity of Jonah's message, *"Yet forty days and Nineveh shall be overthrown!"* The important detail is that this was the message of God! When God is saying it, it doesn't matter the eloquence; the message gets through!

Unlike Jonah, determine to have a positive disposition toward your students, even those that are hard to love. Ask God to give you a tender heart with the right attitude so that in all that you do, you will be reflecting God's character to others.

How are you performing in your role as an ambassador for Christ?

DAY 84

Our Disposition, Part II

Do you do well to be angry?

—Jonah 4:3b

We must be mindful of our disposition toward all our students. Some are easy to love; some are a little more difficult to love. Be mindful of your attitude toward those who are a little more difficult.

Jonah had a negative disposition toward the people of Nineveh. He eventually did what God asked him to do, and when the people repented, instead of being joyful at their acceptance of the Lord, Jonah was angry. Moreover, Jonah missed the blessing of joy and made his own life miserable due to his negative disposition toward the people of Nineveh.

Take care to make sure that your disposition toward all your students is a positive one so that you can rejoice at their successes when they experience them. Realize that whether they acknowledge it or not, you were part of that small success that they experienced.

Do you have a positive disposition toward *all* your students?

DAY 85

Missing Blessings

Jonah went out of the city and sat to the east of the city and
made a booth for himself there. He sat under it in the shade,
till he should see what would become of the city. Now the
Lord God appointed a plant and made it come up over Jonah,
that it might be a shade over his head, to save him from his
discomfort. So Jonah was exceedingly glad because of the plant.
—Jonah 4:5–6

Jonah was so angry that the people of Nineveh repented he held his
own pity party outside the city. God blessed him with a plant that
gave him shade, and Jonah was glad for the plant, but he did not
change his disposition toward the people of Nineveh. Be careful
not to miss God's blessings due to your negative disposition toward
others.

Are you missing God's blessings because of a negative disposition?

DAY 86

Self-Reflection

Let us test and examine our ways and return to the Lord.
—Lamentations 3:40

Self-reflection is extremely important both professionally and, more importantly, spiritually. Spend some quiet time not just asking for favors from God but looking inward and asking God to point out all secret faults. Professionally, ask God to help you to look critically at your practice as an educator so that your effectiveness may increase.

Are you spending time daily in both spiritual and professional reflection?

DAY 87

Handling the Truth

Prove me, O Lord, and try me; test my heart and my mind.
—Psalm 26:2

What an amazing prayer! Reading David's prayer challenges us to deeper self-reflection. Is our relationship with our Savior such that we could be so bold as to ask God to prove, try, and test our hearts and minds?

A friend and colleague of mine had applied for a position that he thought that he would get. He was greatly disappointed when he learned that he did not get the position. When reflecting with another colleague who had recommended him for this position, my friend asked if some inquiries could be made as to why he wasn't selected. This colleague said, "I'll make some inquiries and will tell you what I find out, but can you handle the truth?"

When we ask God to prove, try, and test our hearts and minds, are we ready for the truth? Upon self-examination, I find myself woefully lacking; however, I am so grateful that because I have been saved, our Lord accepts me for who I am. I remember that he is not finished with me.

Examine yourself and your practice. Are you ready for the truth?

DAY 88

Keep Moving

The Lord said to Samuel, "How long will you grieve over Saul, since I have rejected him from being king over Israel? Fill your horn with oil and go. I will send you to Jesse the Bethlehemite for I have provided for myself a king among his sons."
—1 Samuel 16:1

God keeps moving. It is important to stay close and follow him, even when we don't know the full plan. Don't worry, God does! He already sees the end of the matter before we even can think about it. The Lord basically says to Samuel, get up, and get moving with me; the rejection of Saul is old news! I have plans, and you will eventually be clued in, but you must follow me! Jesus said the same thing: *"Follow Me."*

This forces us to come to that crisis of faith, "Am I willing to trust God and follow him even when I don't know what will happen?" David would have been anointed king regardless of whether Samuel did the anointing or not. Samuel made the right choice to follow God and, in doing so, was the instrument God used to communicate his plan for Israel's next king. God's plans are irrevocable. Don't miss out because you decided to stay in one place.

Are you following God with "reckless abandon"?

DAY 89

Emotions

How long will you grieve over Saul?

—1 Samuel 16:1a

God's ways are not our ways. This verse reveals an important spiritual element that we must consider. We must not always trust our emotions regarding hearing from God.

In this instance, had Samuel trusted his emotions, he would have missed being used by God to anoint David as King over Israel. In a professional sense, do not let your emotions allow you to say or do things that you will later regret.

Do you "wear your emotions on your sleeve" too much?

DAY 90

Working within Established Frameworks

Then Daniel replied with prudence and discretion
to Arioch, the captain of the king's guard.
And Daniel went in and requested the king to appoint him a time.
—Daniel 2:14, 16

Therefore render to Caesar the things that are
Caesar's, and to God the things that are God's.
—Matthew 22:21

Let every person be subject to the governing authorities.
For there is no authority except from God, and
those that exist have been instituted by God.
—Romans 13:1

Daniel exhibited prudence and discretion when speaking to Arioch, Captain of the king's guard, using the established channels of communication within this organization when requesting an audience with the king.

Professionally, when we get an idea, and we are working within an organizational framework, it is important to work within that established framework, going through the proper channels of communication. Jesus said, *"Render unto Caesar the things that are Caesar's,"* and Paul reminds us that we are subject to the governing authorities. Professionally, you will gain greater credibility when you demonstrate respect for proper protocols and work through established channels of communication.

Are you following the channels and protocols established by your school administration?

DAY 91

Our Response to Fools

And there was a man in Maon whose business was in Carmel.
The man was very rich; he had three thousand sheep and a
thousand goats. He was shearing his sheep in Carmel. Now
the name of the man was Nabal, and the name of his wife,
Abigail. The woman was discerning and beautiful, but the
man was harsh and badly behaved; he was a Calebite.
[A]nd he is such a worthless man that one cannot speak to him.
Let not my lord regard this worthless fellow, Nabal, for as his
name is, so is he. Nabal is his name, and folly is with him.
—1 Samuel 25:2–3, 17b, 25

Yes, we all have met or will meet several Nabals in our career. The
name means folly, fool, or boorish. As teachers, we sometimes encounter these types of people who are parents of the students we teach.
These types of persons tend to be selfish, want their way, and their
children, in their eyes, are the smartest, brightest, and best behaved.
They will want to blame the shortcomings of their children on you.

Notice that in this reading, Nabal's own men as well as his
wife knew that he was worthless. Be like Abigail—discerning. Do
not take to heart the guilt that these types of parents may want to
place on you due to their children's mistakes. Unfortunately, they are
teaching their children this same behavior.

Are you discerning in your responses to the "Nabals" that come
across your path?

DAY 92

Arrogance versus Confidence

Let not the foot of arrogance come upon me.

—Psalm 36:11

David had experienced much success as a warrior and as a king. God had blessed him in many ways, both financially and spiritually. Despite these successes, David realized that arrogance could become a stumbling block. Perhaps he remembered his sin with Bathsheba and the consequences that came afterward. Maybe at that time of indiscretion, he was arrogant regarding his power and success; we don't necessarily know for sure. A difference exists between being confident and arrogant.

We gain confidence when we see our students experiencing academic success as well as personal success. Arrogance is centered around our performance and does not necessarily consider the performance of our students. I know a teacher who, when engaging in any conversation regarding education, must somehow frame the conversation of his perceived success. It fascinates me that in different conversations regarding different educational topics, this person will cite the same experience.

Listen carefully to your colleagues. How are they talking about their professional accomplishments? Do you detect an air of arrogance? Examine yourself. Is there an air of arrogance when you reflect on your successes?

When you experience success and gain a great reputation as an "effective teacher," be careful and engage in honest self-examination to ensure that you are not arrogant regarding your successes in the classroom.

Examine yourself. Are you arrogant or confident?

DAY 93

Maintaining Integrity

As long as my breath is in me, And the spirit of God is in my nostrils, my lips will not speak falsehood, and my tongue will not utter deceit…till I die I will not put away my integrity from me. I hold fast my righteousness and will not let it go.
—Job 27:3–6

We all experience spiritual "dry seasons." How do we successfully navigate through a spiritual "dry season"? Job was going through such a season, and he gave us a wonderful model in the form of a vow.

I have heard it said that integrity is who you are when no one else is looking. These are times to exercise your free will and make the choice to do what you know to do from your past experiences reading God's Word and following the Holy Spirit. The decisions that you make during this dry period are made with the help of the Holy Spirit, "*He will guide you into all of the truth*" (John 15:13).

Remember, during these times, Satan will come at you just as he did to Jesus in the wilderness. Professionally, you may be feeling pressure from students, parents, and yes, administrators to "bend the rules" or to "make an exception." In fact, there may be cases where these decisions are warranted, but above all else, maintain your integrity. If the decision you are pressed to make violates your integrity with God, then do not go there. Allow the Holy Spirit to be your guide.

Are you diligent in maintaining your integrity? Is "who you are when no one is looking" consistent with "who you are when everyone is looking"?

DAY 94

Hard Decisions

But the Lord God helps me; therefore, I have not been
disgraced; therefore, I have set my face like a flint,
and I know that I shall not be put to shame.

—Isaiah 50:7

When the days drew near for him to be taken
up, he set his face to go to Jerusalem.

—Luke 9:51

Even when we are following God, when we feel ourselves and God
are "on the same page," there will be hard choices to make. Beware
of falling into the trap of Satan that the path of least resistance is
the right path. Jesus, in his humanity, had to make choices to follow
through with his mission to come and die for our sins. *"He set his
face"*; *"I have set my face like a flint"*—this is a hard face, jaw set, eyes
forward, and determined to see the process through.

We will have those choices to make both spiritually and professionally. As believers, we also have God's help, through the Holy
Spirit, to move through those difficult decisions and to make the
right choice in which God is glorified. These times in life strengthen
our faith, and we can confidently move forward allowing God to
work through us for his glory.

Reflect on times when you had to make hard choices and how
the Holy Spirit helped you.

DAY 95

Throw It Down

The LORD said to him, "What is that in
your hand?" He said, "A staff."

—Exodus 4:2

And he said, "Throw it on the ground."

—Exodus 4:3a

"And take in your hand this staff, with which you will do the signs."

—Exodus 4:17

And Moses took the staff of God in his hand.

—Exodus 4:20b

"A staff, this staff, the staff of God!"

"What is that in your hand?" God asked.

"A staff," said Moses.

"Throw it down," said God. And the rest is history!

In God's eyes, any staff would do, but he made Moses face a decision to obey. God does this with us. What prized possession do you own? Throw it down. What special talent or gift do you have? Throw it down. Whatever it is, give it to God. We must do this so that God can use it. God will not use it if we share ownership. Notice in these verses the progression. The staff that Moses held went from being just a staff to *this* staff, more specific, to the staff of God—very specific and unique. God wants to use our gifts and possessions for his glory, but first we must "throw it down!"

Have you "thrown it all down"?

DAY 96

Affirmation of Vocational Education Students

Then Moses said to the people of Israel, "See, the Lord has called by name Bezalel the son of Uri, son of Hur, of the tribe of Judah; and he has filled him with the Spirit of God, with skill, with intelligence, with knowledge, and with all craftsmanship, to devise artistic designs, to work in gold and silver and bronze, in cutting stones for setting, and in carving wood, for work in every skilled craft. And he has inspired him to teach, both him and Oholiab the son of Ahisamach of the tribe of Dan. He has filled them with skill to do every sort of work done by an engraver or by a designer or by an embroiderer in blue and purple and scarlet yarns and fine twined linen, or by a weaver—by any sort of workman or skilled designer."
—Exodus 35:30–35

Vocational and technical training are significantly important. Often, schools hold in high esteem those students who are talented in math, science, social sciences, athletics, and the arts and have less regard for those students whose gifts lie in the vocational and technical fields. God placed importance on these fields as he blessed Bezalel and Oholiab with not only the gifts of craftsmanship but also the gift of teaching others these skills. Why? Because he was preparing human hands to do God's work, the construction of his Tabernacle!

I was visiting with a student who was contemplating quitting school. He had been absent quite a bit and was anticipating withdrawing. I asked him why he wanted to withdraw as he only had a year left to graduate. He explained he always had trouble with the academic subjects—in his case, algebra—and he felt "dumb" to those teachers and classmates in those classes. In looking at his grades, however, I noticed he did very well, all As, in fact, in welding. I learned he had a part-time job at a welding shop, and he spent most nights in the shop welding. He had difficulty waking in the morning and attending school.

In our discussion, he looked at me and said, "When I put that welding hood down and start welding, my world is complete. I live for when I put that hood down and everything else disappears, and I am at work."

I believe that this young man may not have been gifted academically, but with a little affirmation and recognition of his vocational ability by his academic teachers, he may have been able to pass some of those subjects. Please understand his teachers are not to blame here. They didn't know or understand "the rest of the story" and may have been so involved with other students that this young man "slipped through the cracks" because he never was a discipline issue.

Examine the grades of your failing students and see if they are successful in other areas. If they are, affirm them, and perhaps they will respond to your invitation to give extra assistance. Be sensitive to those students who have gifts in the technical fields and encourage them to develop the gift with which God has blessed them. Remember that student studying carpentry may be an on-the-job witness one day at a construction site and another student studying cosmetology may one day be on a mission trip to a Third World country, sharing the love of Christ while doing a makeover! Remember, God chose carpentry as a vocational field for his Son as he was growing up. God works through us in many ways and contexts to share his love for all. This is his chosen method—the Great Commission!

Do you encourage and affirm the talents of those students who work with their hands to create?

DAY 97

Misuse of God's Gifts

[A]nd the Lord spoke to Moses, saying, "Take *the* staff, and
assemble the congregation, you and Aaron your brother, and tell
the rock before their eyes to yield its water. So you shall bring
water out of the rock for them and give drink to the congregation
and their cattle." And Moses took *the* staff from before the Lord,
as he commanded him. Then Moses and Aaron gathered the
assembly together before the rock, and he said to them, "Hear
now, you rebels; shall we bring water for you out of this rock?"
And Moses lifted up his hand and struck the rock with *his* staff
twice, and water came out abundantly, and the congregation
drank, and their livestock. And the Lord said to Moses and
Aaron, "Because you did not believe in me, to uphold me as
holy in the eyes of the people Israel, therefore you shall not bring
this assembly into the land that I have given them." These are
the waters of Meribah, where the people of Israel quarreled
with the Lord, and through them he showed himself holy.
—Numbers 20:7–13 (emphasis added)

No water was to be found. The people complained to Moses, and
Moses sought direction from God. All is right...yes? *No!* Moses did
not follow the directions God provided! Examine the account. God
told Moses to take *the* staff, assemble the congregation, and *tell* the
rock to give water. What did Moses do? He assembled the congregation and *struck* the rock twice with *his* staff. Moses did not follow *all*
the directions, and it cost himself and Aaron their place in the promised land! Moreover, Moses misused something that was no longer
his. Remember, Moses's staff was now the staff of God. Notice the

account. First it says "*the* staff," not Moses's staff. Once Moses misuses the staff, the account reads "*his* staff."

When we have thrown something down, like a talent we have, and God takes it, it is no longer ours. We must be careful not to misuse something that is no longer ours. This begs the question: Are we misusing a gift that we surrendered to God? As teachers, we have an unimaginable influence over the minds of our students. Use the gift of teaching God gave you for his glory!

Are you using your gift of teaching, or any other talent that you have dedicated to God properly?

DAY 98

Misrepresenting God

[A]nd the Lord spoke to Moses, saying, "Take the staff, and assemble the congregation, you and Aaron your brother, and tell the rock before their eyes to yield its water. So you shall bring water out of the rock for them and give drink to the congregation and their cattle." And Moses took the staff from before the Lord, as he commanded him. Then Moses and Aaron gathered the assembly together before the rock, and he said to them, "Hear now, you rebels; shall we bring water for you out of this rock?" And Moses lifted up his hand and struck the rock with his staff twice, and water came out abundantly, and the congregation drank, and their livestock. And the Lord said to Moses and Aaron, "Because you did not believe in me, to uphold me as holy in the eyes of the people Israel, therefore you shall not bring this assembly into the land that I have given them." These are the waters of Meribah, where the people of Israel quarreled with the Lord, and through them he showed himself holy.

—Numbers 20:7–13

Let's continue looking at the staff that Moses threw down. Remember, this staff had become the staff of God. It was no longer Moses's staff; however, Moses used the staff as God directed him up to this point. Note the text in verse 8, "Take the staff," the staff of God. Then note the text in verse 11, "With his staff." Moses took from God the staff he had thrown down!

Once we have given our talents over to God, they are *his*, and we do not get to take them back! We are obligated to use our talents for the Lord. Moses misused the staff of God. He momentarily, in a fit of anger, took what he had given to God and misused it. By this action, he misrepresented God in front of the people. This action, done in a fit of rage, cost him dearly.

Actions taken or words said in a fit of rage can be costly. We must be careful how we use the things or talents we have given to God because they are no longer ours. Remember that when we accept Christ, our lives are no longer ours.

Have you misrepresented God to others by the improper use of your talents, possessions, or by your manner of living? Ask God to show you these areas, ask for forgiveness and repent.

DAY 99

Scars

So the other disciples told him, "We have seen the Lord."
But he said to them, "Unless I see in his hands the mark of
the nails, and place my finger into the mark of the nails,
and place my hand into his side, I will never believe."
Then he said to Thomas, "Put your finger here, and see my hands;
and put out your hand and place it in my side. Do not disbelieve,
but believe." Thomas answered him, "My Lord and my God!"
—John 20:25, 27–28

Jesus, even in his glorified body, kept the scars of his crucifixion. Of course, God the Father could have removed them, but he left them for Thomas to see and touch. Oh, the love God has for us that he would leave his Son scarred for a doubting person to see and touch so that he would believe! Maybe the scars remind all the hosts of heaven that Jesus became man, died on the cross for our sins, and conquered sin and death by rising on the third day. Each time a believer enters heaven and is welcomed by Jesus, the scars on his hands are visible as he extends them in greeting. These scars serve as a reminder that no believer got there on his/her own merit. By *his* grace, we were bought with a great price! All we can say is, "Thank you, Lord Jesus!"

At the end of an in-class assignment, the teacher asked the students to exchange papers to grade. On one of the student's papers, a marginal answer was given, not a completely wrong answer, but not as the teacher announced it. The banter back and forth between the student-grader and the teacher went like this:

"What about this answer?"

The teacher responded, "Whose paper are you grading?"

The student said, "John's."

The teacher said, "Give it to him because he may need it."

John recounts how this incident left a tremendous emotional scar on him because of the awkward embarrassment he suffered that day; he will never forget it.

Scars—we all have them. At some point, we injured ourselves and the wound left a scar. We can look at that scar and relive the moment we were wounded and remember how painful it was and the inconvenience it caused. We may have had to have stitches or have had to go without the use of a finger (or limb) for a period. Nevertheless, scars remind us of events.

We also carry emotional scars. We carry scars from our past that remind us of a hurtful event. All of us carry a scar or two from a thoughtless comment made to us by someone that we held in high esteem, like a teacher. Scars serve as a reminder to us to put safety first before using sharp tools! Emotional scars help us to choose our words wisely so that we do not say words that are hurtful to others. As a teacher, take care not to be that person who gives a scar to a student who may carry it for the rest of his/her life.

Take a moment and thank Jesus again for his sacrifice for your sins and for saving you. Examine your interactions with your students. Have you or are you leaving any scars?

DAY 100

Walk the Talk

Then I proclaimed a fast there, at the river Ahava, that we might
humble ourselves before our God, to seek from him a safe journey
for ourselves, our children, and all our goods. For I was ashamed
to ask the king for a band of soldiers and horsemen to protect
us against the enemy on our way, since we had told the king,
"The hand of our God is for good on all who seek him, and the
power of his wrath is against all who forsake him." So we fasted
and implored our God for this, and he listened to our entreaty.
The hand of our God was on us, and he delivered us from
the hand of the enemy and from ambushes by the way.
—Ezra 8:21–23, 31b

Do we say we have faith but do not "walk the talk"? Have we ever seen
ourselves as "stepping out on faith" but have a safety net, just in case it
doesn't work out? In this passage, Ezra's heart is revealed. He had proclaimed earlier to the king the protection of God, and he wasn't going
to endanger the credibility of God by asking for protection on this
journey. Undoubtedly, since he had the king's blessing on this project,
he could have asked for protection and received it, but he didn't.

When reading this passage, we are confronted with a hard question. Do we question God's credibility by our actions, even though
we speak of our faith? My prayer is that I don't damage God's credibility by my actions. Ezra's credibility was also at stake here. Had he
requested protection, the people under him could have said, "I heard
him say that God would protect us, but now he is asking the king for
protection." Remember, our students watch what we do to see if our
actions are aligned with what we say.

Are your actions in agreement with your testimony?

DAY 101

Acquiring a Moral Compass

[A]s for me, I will meditate on your precepts.
—Psalm 119:78b

We hear the words often today, "moral compass," meaning a person can discern right from wrong or to make good moral decisions. This phrase is often used in discussions on leadership. This verse answers the question of how we obtain our moral compass.

First, we know that it is impossible to have a true moral compass without a saving knowledge of Jesus Christ. Notice I said "true moral compass" because some will argue that a person can have a moral compass and have no relationship or belief in God or Jesus. Yes, one can be a good moral individual, but to really have a true moral compass, one must have a relationship with Jesus.

Second, we must be constantly in God's Word, and as the psalmist says, meditate on God's precepts. Meditate—to think deeply and focus one's mind for a period on God's precepts, which are principles, commands, and doctrines intended to regulate behavior. Acquisition of a good moral compass is accomplished through our willful and consistent study of God's Word so that *his* principles saturate our thinking and our very being so that in everything we say and do, Christ is magnified.

Are you really meditating on God's Word that you read daily or are you just "checking the box" that you did your daily reading?

DAY 102

Using the Right Lens

Set your minds on things that are above,
not on things that are on earth.
—Colossians 3:2

I will never forget your precepts for by them you have given
me life. I am yours; save me for I have sought your precepts.
—Psalm 119:93–94

O how I love your law! It is my meditation all the day. Your
commandment makes me wiser than my enemies, for it is ever
with me. I have more understanding than all my teachers, for
your testimonies are my meditation. I understand more than the
aged, for I keep your precepts. I hold back my feet from every
evil way, in order to keep your word. I do not turn aside from
your rules, for you have taught me. How sweet are your words
to my taste, sweeter than honey to my mouth! Through your
precepts I get understanding; therefore I hate every false way.
—Psalm 119:97–104

Paul provides the general challenge and David provides the specifics.
Paul challenges us to set our minds on Godly things. David gives us
some Godly ideas to set our minds on! Look at what David says. We
should set our minds (meditate) on God's law, God's testimonies,
and God's precepts or rules.

Once these principles take root in our lives, our behavior is
changed (Hold back our feet from every evil way; hate every false
way), and our disposition toward the things of God is more positive,

("How sweet are your words") and Christ is magnified in every area of our being!

Oh, that we would commit ourselves to the study of God's Word and to the working out of our faith! Notice in verse 97 that the psalmist states that he is in constant meditation (setting of his mind on) the things of God. How does this work out in our daily lives as we go about our business? If we are reading and focusing on God's word, we then begin to see everything from a different lens, the lens of God. It is in this sense that we "meditate all day."

Examine your actions through the lens of God. What spiritual principles, both positive and negative, do you see working out in your life? Examine the actions of your students, and make this same assessment.

DAY 103

Handling Criticism

Do not take to heart all the things that people
say, lest you hear your servant cursing you.
—Ecclesiastes 7:21

The phrase "take to heart" is defined as a way of understanding something as having a deep significance to oneself; to consider a comment made by another to be significant to oneself. We hear the statement, "Don't take it to heart," sometimes meaning "Don't take this seriously." Interestingly, people will sometimes preface a negative comment toward you using this statement, giving them (so they think) permission to be critical.

Satan, if we let him, has a way of working in our minds to make us take something negative to heart when it is totally unnecessary. Don't be like flypaper and allow all comments, particularly negative ones, to stick. When we do this, we begin to wear those comments and develop a low sense of self-esteem. Taking all comments to heart may damage relationships as we may feel all negative comments are directed toward us. Developing this type of mindset even makes it difficult to accept compliments because we think that the person giving the compliment really doesn't mean it. Criticism will come your way. Use criticism as a point of reflection to improve practice, but do not let criticism define who you are. Beware of Satan's trap! He will use this trap to ensnare you into being ineffective.

How do you handle criticism?

DAY 104

Calloused by Sin

The harvest is past, the summer is ended, and we are not saved.
—Jeremiah 8:20

What a dismal existence that must be, to have a conscience so seared that there is enmity with anything that involves the things of God. People can become so calloused that it may be impossible for them to find salvation due to their constant, continuous, pushing away of the invitation by the Holy Spirit to come to Christ.

As Christians, we are eternally saved, but there may be sins in our lives in which the Holy Spirit has convicted us, but we have pushed him away so much that these sins have become acceptable. We need to ask God to show us these sins so that we can repent and draw closer to God.

Do you pray for your students? Pray for that student who gets on your last nerve will not reach the point in his/her life that sin no longer matters. Pray for that student to come to know Christ as his/her Savior. Make it a practice to say a quick, silent prayer for that student as he/she leaves your presence. It will help your disposition toward that student the next time a conflict occurs.

Is there sin in your life that has become acceptable to you? Turn from it and ask God's forgiveness. Do you pray for your students' salvation? Pray for their salvation and ask God to use you as his instrument to bring them to a relationship with him.

DAY 105

How It's Said

[G]uard the doors of your mouth.

—Micah 7:5b

Make this instruction a watchword for each day. The environment in which we are living and working in is exceptionally treacherous. Innocent words spoken are taken out of context to "bring down" others. Words meant for correction are taken as derogatory. Be careful not to get too familiar with your students that you say words that should not be said. The same is true in dealing with colleagues; think about how it sounds before you say it!

Are you thinking about how you say your words before you say them?

DAY 106

Don't Be a Fair-Weather Christian

Though the fig tree should not blossom, nor fruit be on the vines, the produce of the olive fail and the fields yield no food, the flock be cut off from the fold and there be no herd in the stalls, yet I will rejoice in the Lord; I will take joy in the God of my salvation. God, the Lord, is my strength; he makes my feet like the deer's; he makes me tread on my high places.

—Habakkuk 3:17–19

Habakkuk knew that awful events were in store for Israel. Knowing that these events were coming, Habakkuk considered an important question, "If everything is stripped away, if my health fails, when work issues pile up, even if I lose my job, my family, everything, what will my disposition be toward God? Am I willing to trust God himself and not in circumstances?" Like Habakkuk, consider and answer these questions before the tempest comes because when the tempest comes, you can find comfort.

In this passage is the important word, *will*, implying a decision made beforehand. *Will* also implies a conscious decision to accomplish something regardless of the condition and to see things through. "He has a will to live"; "That job was completed through his will." *Will* may also imply "hardheadedness." "That person is a strong-willed person." Hardheadedness in a good way can be pleasing to God. Resolve, like Job, to "fear God for nothing." Put your trust in God himself and not in circumstances.

We see colleagues and students bless God when things are going well and sometimes even curse God when things are not going well. Resolve that this will not be you. Don't be a "fair-weather Christian!"

Are you putting your trust in God and God alone or are you allowing your circumstances to reflect your disposition toward God?

DAY 107

Sent

I do not ask that you take them out of the world,
but that you keep them from the evil one.
As you sent me into the world, so I have sent them into the world.
—John 17:15, 18

As the Father has sent me, even so I am sending you.
—John 20:21

When the cares of the world and the job get overwhelming, it is good to remember that as Christians, we are sent. We are on a mission to win others to Christ. Remember to keep your saltiness and influence, even when surrounded by those who would tempt you to do otherwise. Jesus *sent* me; keep that thought. Remember that Jesus even prayed for me because he knew what I was going to face. He asked his heavenly father to *not* take me out of the world!

Walk into that classroom, look at those faces, and remember that Jesus sent you to them. He prayed for you so that you would not retreat into a spiritual cocoon of fear but that you would have the boldness to continue to be the influence that you were saved to be. Reminding ourselves that we are sent helps to keep the proper perspective that we are *in* the world and not *of* the world; we are sent into the world. *"As the Father has sent me, even so I am sending you."*

When the cares of the world surround you, and you get absorbed in the details of your work, do you remember that you are sent?

DAY 108

Actions Aligned with Confession

But if you call yourself a Jew and rely on the law and boast in God and know his will and approve what is excellent, because you are instructed from the law; and if you are sure that you yourself are a guide to the blind, a light to those who are in darkness, an instructor of the foolish, a teacher of children, having in the law the embodiment of knowledge and truth—you then who teach others, do you not teach yourself? While you preach against stealing, do you steal? You who say that one must not commit adultery, do you commit adultery? You who abhor idols, do you rob temples? You who boast in the law dishonor God by breaking the law. For, as it is written, "The name of God is blasphemed among the Gentiles because of you."

—Romans 2:17–24

In this passage, Paul addressed Jewish leaders regarding their failure to practice the law they proclaimed. This passage has serious application for those of us who teach. Allow me to paraphrase, "But if you call yourself...a teacher of children...you then who teach others, do you not teach yourself? You who say that one must not...do you? The name of God is blasphemed...because of you."

Beware because everyone we encounter pays truly close attention to what we do, and they measure it against what we say! In this day of social media, words we once thought were secret are now public. Careless comments made many years ago are now brought forward as people search our background. Thoughtless or flippant postings made on social media are brought forward in condemnation.

Ask this question of yourself, "Are my actions aligned to my confession of Christ?" Be careful of being the adult who says, "Do what I say and not what I do." Remember that we are role models for our students and we do not have the option to choose not to be role models.

As professing Christians, if our actions are not aligned with what we confess, people will question whether there is anything to this notion of becoming a Christian and following Christ. I pray that my actions will never inhibit someone from trusting Jesus as his/her Savior.

Are your actions aligned with your confession?

DAY 109

But Now

But now the righteousness of God has been manifested
apart from the law, although the Law and the Prophets
bear witness to it—the righteousness of God through
faith in Jesus Christ for all who believe.

—Romans 3:21–22a

Never underestimate the importance of the two words "But now."
"But now" implies that a new way of doing things or seeing things
has begun. This phrase marks a pivot point, from one way of thinking or doing to another. A new state of being has begun. The water
was hot, *but now* it is cool; I was in Texas, *but now* I am in Louisiana;
I used to be overweight, *but now* I have reached my weight goal; our
classroom rules used to be that, *but now* they have changed to this.

Never settle for the average with your students. Challenge them
to have "But now" moments in their learning and in their lives. Most
importantly, "But now" implies a new relationship has begun and is
ongoing with Jesus when we have accepted him as our Savior. The
hymn "Amazing Grace" says it best, "I once was lost, *but now* am
found, was blind *but now* I see."

Are you encouraging "but now" moments with your students?

DAY 110

Carrying the Letter

And you show that you are a letter from Christ delivered by
us, written not with ink but with the Spirit of the living God,
not on tablets of stone but on tablets of human hearts.
—2 Corinthians 3:3

Think of this paraphrase of this verse: "You are a letter from Christ
written with the Spirit of the living God on tablets of human hearts."
As Christians, *we* are letters from Christ to a lost world! Our words
and actions have the potential to carry the message of Christ to all
we have interaction.

This begs the question, what kind of letter are we delivering to
those with whom we come in contact? This letter is not and should
not necessarily be that warm, fuzzy card associated with friendship
and special occasions.

The letters of Paul give us some guidance to the type of letter we
should deliver by our words and actions. Paul provides the academic
letter that establishes the foundation of our faith to the Romans. The
book of 1 Corinthians reaffirms that our faith is in Christ alone lest
we err and follow other human teachers. Galatians displays Paul's
white-hot anger (righteous anger) at a group that was being led astray
by the Judaizers. In contrast, 1 and 2 Thessalonians offers praise
for perseverance as well as encouragement and reminders to stay the
course until Christ's return. Ephesians reminds us that we are saved
by grace.

All of Paul's letters expressed his love for Christ and his love for
those in which he interacted. May it be the same for us as we interact with students, colleagues, and parents. Sometimes our letter will

be purely academic; sometimes our letter may have to be stern; but always, our letter should offer encouragement!

Is Christ's letter being carried by you every day?

DAY 111

Aim High

So whether we are at home or away, we
make it our aim to please him.

—2 Corinthians 5:9

This statement from Paul indicates that he had a preoccupation in his mind of pleasing God. In everything he did or said, he first asked the question, "Is what I am about to do or say pleasing to God?" Was he successful in this endeavor? Of course not! Thereby comes the statement, "We make it our aim. We make it our aim." The marksman takes aim at a target, and even the best miss sometimes. Does what we do or say please God always? Of course not! We are fallen people; and in our fallen state, we cannot please God always. That is why he sent Jesus to take away our sins if we believe and place our trust in him.

Taking aim does, however, imply an act of the will. Remember, when God created us, he gave us free will to choose; therefore, we also should take aim to please God in all that we say and do.

Are you consistently "taking aim" for the target God has set?

DAY 112

Tender Heart

As it is, I rejoice, not because you were grieved, but because you were grieved into repenting. For you felt a godly grief, so that you suffered no loss through us. For godly grief produces a repentance that leads to salvation without regret, whereas worldly grief produces death.
—2 Corinthians 7:9–10

Have you ever felt so bad about a sin that you committed that you vowed never to commit it again because it made you feel so bad before a holy God? When tempted to commit it again, does a reminder of that awful feeling come to mind so that you say to yourself, "I don't want to feel this way again before God, so I won't do this." I think that this is what Paul is referring to as "godly grief." For Christians, the Holy Spirit convicts us when we sin, and through repentance, that behavior is changed. May our hearts be tender so that when convicted, we repent without regret.

How tender is your heart toward the things of God?

DAY 113

Pushing the Wrong Buttons

Fathers, do not provoke your children to anger, but bring
them up in the discipline and instruction of the Lord.
—Ephesians 6:4

James was sent to my office for talking back to the teacher and for
class disruption. Once inside my office, James said in a loud voice,
"I hate that lady! Every day, she looks for something to say to me to
get me upset."

I asked James what had happened today. James related to me
that when he arrived, Mrs. Jones made a comment regarding the
T-shirt he was wearing. James was wearing an Adidas T-shirt, the
one that has the Adidas logo on it with the leaves. Mrs. Jones accused
him of wearing a shirt out of dress code because it promoted the use
of marijuana. Mrs. Jones accused James of "liking" marijuana.

This exchange occurred as other students were entering the
classroom, and James defended himself, saying that it was not a
"druggie" shirt. The argument escalated until Mrs. Jones sent him
to my office. James related other incidents where derogatory comments were made by Mrs. Jones to him as well as to other students.
Unfortunately, I had witnessed some of this behavior by this teacher.

Ask yourself if you are/have provoked a student to anger by
making insensitive comments or "pushing the right buttons." Ask
God to guard your lips so that in every exchange, you will reflect
Christ.

DAY 114

Alertness to Learning Habits

And we urge you, brothers, admonish the idle, encourage
the fainthearted, help the weak, be patient with them all.
—1 Thessalonians 5:14

I found that the first two six weeks of the ninth grade is one of the toughest periods for students as well as for their teachers. Students are now old enough to know how to manipulate their parents into thinking that the work is too difficult, and parents are quick to come to their child's defense when their child complains about the work. Teachers spend this period trying to get to know their students as well as trying to figure out whether the learning difficulties students are saying they are having are truly present.

Students are presented with a large increase in the amount of homework in ninth grade compared to their middle school years. Suddenly, students are required to perform complex equations in algebra, to understand and use complex vocabulary in biology, to read Shakespeare in English, and to draw inferences from extended reading passages in world geography. These new expectations in high school require much more time and effort than the student has spent in the middle grades doing homework and studying.

Parents express concern because in their eyes, their child "is working harder than ever and not making good grades and crying every evening." In many cases, they state that they think their child has a learning disability and want them tested. When I ask why they think their child has a learning disability, they state, "In middle school, he/she didn't have to work as hard to get the subject. It came easier."

We begin to discuss their child's study habits. One of the common statements that I hear when discussing this issue with the parent is that the child is totally unsupervised while trying to do their homework.

We discuss supervision at home, and I offer some strategies such as completing one subject and taking a brief break before moving to the next. I also point out that the grading process is a marathon and not a wind sprint. The final grade for a course is not at the first six weeks marking period but at the end of the third marking period. I first recommend that they have a conference with the teacher and establish a working relationship with that teacher. I state that I find that when teachers are alerted to these issues that are occurring at home, they can more closely examine the student's work habits in the classroom as well as look for signs of a learning disability.

I recommend that they monitor their child's homework and study habits and then, after the second marking period, if the difficulties continue, we try other strategies and possible testing for learning disabilities. I also encourage them to have patience and to be encouraging to their child and to enforce good study habits.

Only one answer exists to this process for both teachers and parents, and that is time, tough love, and most importantly, patience.

Are you getting to know the learning habits of your students so that you can intelligently discuss their learning with their parents and offer strategies for helping them achieve success?

Pray for insight and patience with your students.

DAY 115

Use of Social Media

Nothing is covered up that will not be revealed or hidden that
will not be known. Therefore whatever you have said in the
dark shall be heard in the light, and what you have whispered
in private rooms shall be proclaimed on the housetops.
—Luke 12:2–3

These words of Jesus ring true today in this world of social media.
Our nation just witnessed the notes contained in a high school yearbook made public by our Congress during the confirmation hearings
of a Supreme Court Judge. In another instance, comments made by a
recent Heisman Trophy winner while in high school on social media
were made public, and he had to answer for them.

In our region, the local news published a picture from social
media of a teacher dressed as Mammy from the movie *Gone with the
Wind*, attending a Halloween party. That picture was called "racist,"
and that teacher was suspended from her job by the school district.

Know that when you apply for a position, your social media
accounts will be screened by your potential employer. Know also that
you already have followers of your social media by your students and
their parents. If you choose to use social media, be especially careful
regarding what you post as well as your choice of wording. Assume
that whatever you post will be public knowledge. Do not allow your
Christian witness to be compromised by what you post, like, or share.

Are there items on your social media that could compromise
your Christian witness? Examine your social media and erase anything that could compromise your Christian witness.

DAY 116

Driver's Education

The Spirit immediately drove him out into the wilderness.
—Mark 1:12

Driving. This is one of the greatest "rites of passage" in a teenager's life. To teens, driving is one of the "firsts" that allow them to be "in charge" of something; in this case, a vehicle. Being "in charge" to them means that they can now go places, visit friends, and attend activities. They now have more control of where they go and how long they stay. I can't tell you how many couples attended the homecoming dance or the prom and only stayed long enough to take the picture.

This newfound freedom that driving gives to teenagers meant parking lot issues for us as administrators. Issues such as selling parking spaces, the fight over parking spaces (he/she parked in my space), the hasty exits after school which led to fender benders—get the picture?

As a teacher, you drive your class. You give and teach the proper material and determine which methodologies to use that give your students opportunities to successfully complete your class to move to the next course or grade. The delivery of instruction is totally under your control inside the four walls of your classroom.

Let us stop a moment to linger over this verse. The Holy Spirit *drove* Jesus! In other words, in Jesus's humanity, the third person of the Trinity was in charge. Jesus, in his humanity, allowed the Holy Spirit to be in charge! If Jesus, our example of the perfect man, allowed the Holy Spirit to drive him, how much more should we allow the Holy Spirit to drive us?

Speaking of driving, I have seen the old bumper sticker that stated, "God is my copilot." As I reflected on this saying considering this verse, I realized that this bumper sticker sends the wrong message regarding our relationship with God. God being our copilot implies that we are in control of our lives and only relinquish that control to God when we see the need. That is not the rightful place of God in our lives. He is the pilot!

Give the Holy Spirit the wheel and allow every thought and action to be controlled by him. Let go to let God do what he wants to do when he wants to do it!

Are you being completely controlled by the Holy Spirit?

DAY 117

Complacency

At that time I will search Jerusalem with lamps, and I will punish the men who are complacent, those who say in their hearts, "The Lord will not do good, nor will he do ill."

—Zephaniah 1:12

So because you are lukewarm, and neither hot or cold, I will spit you out of my mouth.

—Revelation 3:16

But Jesus answered them, "My Father is working until now, and I am working."

—John 5:17

One of the traps Satan continues to set and maintain is the trap of complacency. Think about it: we strive to get to that place where routines are set, life is comfortable, we mind our own business, and have a "que sera sera" attitude regarding events that do not immediately affect us. This is exactly the disposition Satan wants us to adopt! We have become complacent, going through the motions in our work, at home, in our relationships, and in our spiritual lives. John, relaying a message from God, defines complacency in Revelation 3:16 as being lukewarm. Being complacent or lukewarm is not acceptable to God.

A common saying states, "If you are not improving, you are regressing." Take a moment and engage in self-reflection. Is there improvement in your spiritual life? Are you more like Christ today than you were yesterday? Is there improvement in your professional life? Are you current in your methodology and professional practice?

God is never complacent, and neither should we be complacent. Jesus reminds us in John 5:17 that God is always working and that he (Jesus) is also working. That is our example for every area of our lives. Remember, if we are not improving, we are regressing.

Are you making improvements in your spiritual as well as in your professional life?

DAY 118

Carry Your Corner

And when he returned to Capernaum after some days, it was reported that he was at home. And many were gathered together, so that there was no room, not even at the door. And he was preaching the word to them. And they came, bringing to him a paralytic carried by four men. And when they could not get near him because of the crowd, they removed the roof above him, and when they had made an opening, they let down the bed on which the paralytic lay. And when Jesus saw their faith, he said to the paralytic, "Son, your sins are forgiven."
—Mark 2:1–5

One of the more challenging aspects of my position as a school administrator was that of working with our homebound students, their caregivers, and their parents. I worked with students recovering from major surgeries, cancer patients, students recovering from major accidents, and even a heart transplant patient.

In the case of our heart transplant student, the family moved temporarily from a neighboring city to be closer to Texas Children's Hospital. Texas Children's told them that they needed to be close so that when they received a suitable heart for Johnny, they needed to be within one hour of the hospital so that the transplant could be successful. My point is that not only in Johnny's case, but in all the cases that I dealt with, a common thread was that these students' parents always expressed to me their desire to get the best medical care possible for their child.

These four men were of the same conviction as the parents of these students with whom I worked. Jesus had established his reputation as one who could heal various ailments, and these men wanted the best care for their friend. Carrying their paralyzed friend upstairs and digging through the roof showed their determination in getting the best care for their friend. They knew that if they could just get their friend to Jesus, he would be healed.

These men exercised their faith. Their actions, based on their convictions, supported their belief. How about us? We say "Jesus is the answer," but do our actions support our convictions? How are we doing getting people to Jesus? Regarding our students, do our speech, actions, and activities demonstrate that we are purposeful in doing everything it takes to bring them to Jesus?

Remember also that there were four men. Each carried a corner of the pallet. Each did his part in getting their friend to Jesus. How are we doing? Are we carrying our corner to get people to Jesus? Statistics say that more people come to faith in Christ, not by a single event but by a series of events that point them to the saving knowledge of Christ.

Pray that God will show you a corner to carry so that you will be part of leading someone to Christ.

DAY 119

Get to Work

For though by this time you ought to be teachers, you
need someone to teach you again the basic principles of
the oracles of God. You need milk, not solid food.
—Hebrews 5:12

He has told you, O man, what is good; and what does
the Lord require of you but to do justice, and to love
kindness, and to walk humbly with your God?
—Micah 6:8

High school freshmen are unique because they have left middle
school and are now encouraged to try new concepts with less assistance from their teacher. In a sense, they need to be weaned off constant direction and encouraged to develop some independence in
their work habits, to follow a set of written instructions as opposed to
verbal instructions, and to begin to reason and think on their own.

An example of this may be seen in a typical freshman algebra
class. Instead of the teacher and students working multiple problems
together, the teacher may work one or two examples and ask the students to take notes on the processes as well as copying the examples
given into their notes. The teacher will leave the examples as well
as the steps to complete the problem on the overhead so that the
students may refer to them as well as to their own notes during the
guided practice part of the lesson. When the guided practice part of
the lesson comes, the student has these examples as well his/her notes
to refer to as the proper procedure to complete the problems given.

Sometimes it is difficult for the teacher to know how much assistance a student really needs. Does the student really need further assistance or just encouragement or "tough love" to get the problems completed? Getting to know students' personalities is highly recommended for this reason and can prove to be such a blessing for the teacher for future classroom success.

I was observing an Algebra I class, and the teacher had done an excellent job of explaining the process of solving an equation to the students. The class was now in the "guided practice" portion of the lesson when the students were expected to complete problems on their own. They had as their reference the notes they themselves had just taken as well as the examples the teacher had provided that were left on the overhead.

"I don't know how to do these problems," said one student.

"Yes, you do," said the teacher. The teacher walked over to the student's desk and looked at the partially completed problem. "You can do this because I have shown you how, and I see that you have written down the examples that I gave you." The teacher continued by saying, "Look at the notes that you just took and look again at the example on the overhead." This student did what the teacher asked, thought a minute, continued working, and successfully completed the problems.

Spiritually speaking, we sometimes act like that freshman. We are faced with a certain situation. We know what God wants us to do; we know that there is action required on our part. But for some reason, we do not follow through and fulfill the requirements of God. We say, "I am not sure what God wants or requires from me, so I will keep on praying"; when we should be saying, "I know what God wants because he has shown me through his Word." We pretend ignorance to shirk responsibility. How do we know what God's requirements are? Because he has shown us.

Have you made the decision spiritually to "Get on with it"?

DAY 120

Proper Preparation

But the day of the Lord will come like a thief.

—2 Peter 10a

[B]e diligent to be found by Him without
spot of blemish, and at peace.

—2 Peter 14b

I watched and listened as a band director spoke with an upset young lady after a halftime performance. The young lady was upset because she didn't know her part and was embarrassed. The teacher said, "What can I do to make this experience better for you?"

The young lady looked to the ground and softly said, "Nothing." She was right because she knew she was not prepared for the performance. She wasn't prepared because as she admitted during this conversation, she had not attended rehearsals where she could have learned her part.

The teacher concluded the conversation by saying, "I'll tell you what I will do. If you come to rehearsal every day, I will make sure that you know your part, and you will be prepared for the next performance. But you must meet me halfway by coming to rehearsal."

Have you ever been nervous before an event where you are the presenter because you were not fully prepared and, deep down, knew it? Have you had that queasy feeling when the students arrive, and your lesson is not fully prepared? Have you ever "winged it"? It is a terrible feeling to know that you are not prepared for a lesson or some other event in life.

God uses these times to remind us that one day, there will be a day of reckoning and that there will be no more second chances. This day will come when we do not expect it, and Peter urges us to be prepared and to stay prepared.

As Christians, we are saved, but we do not want to be ashamed or embarrassed should Christ return and find that our actions are not reflective of our testimony regarding our faith. Strive to live each day as if Christ will return at any moment.

Are you prepared to meet Christ today? Are you prepared for your students today? Would Jesus, the Master Teacher, be pleased with your preparation, presentation, and follow up of your lesson?

DAY 121

Incremental Improvement

Not that I have already obtained this or am
already perfect, but I press on to make it my own,
because Christ Jesus has made me his own.
—Philippians 3:12

My principal and I had to have "the talk" with a first-year teacher. She had seriously poor classroom control and was not accepting constructive criticism from her department chair or colleagues. After some informal walkthroughs, I tried to offer some advice and received the "eye roll." I told my principal that I needed to speak with her and requested that he be in the room when we had this conversation.

We called her in, and I explained to her that in no uncertain terms, after completion of my formal observation, I would have to mark deficient in the areas of classroom management and knowledge of her subject. My principal reminded her that she was a probationary teacher, and she could be dismissed at any time. We encouraged her to do some self-reflection and decide if she really wanted to be a teacher, and if so, to accept the help of a mentor. She accepted the mentor's assistance and all aspects of her classroom improved.

My informal observations noted incremental improvement with each visit. She became one of our best teachers and was even asked by the district's subject specialist to present workshops on good instructional strategies to others! The mentor mentioned to me several times that this teacher was her "trophy" due to her vast improvement in her classroom management as well as her communication of her knowledge of the subject.

Press on. We are not perfect, but we keep trying because of our gratefulness for what Christ did for us. Remember that he saved us from our sins, and we accept him by faith. Because Christ made me his own, I press on to be more like him.

The words to the hymn "Higher Ground" come to mind. *"I'm pressing on the upward way, new heights I'm gaining every day, still praying as I'm onward bound, Lord lead me on to higher ground."*

If your classroom wasn't what you wanted it to be yesterday, press on to improve! If your spiritual life isn't where you wish, press on to a deeper relationship with God! Adopt this mindset: "Because Jesus saved me, I'm going to try to be the best teacher I can be!" Incremental improvement in your professional and spiritual life is the goal.

Are you "gaining new heights" each day in your spiritual and professional life?

DAY 122

Sustenance

I lay down and slept; I woke again, for the Lord sustained
me. I will not be afraid of many thousands of people
who have set themselves against me all around.
—Psalm 3:5–6

I feel far from God at times. I let my emotions gain control as I recount an event or situations that I didn't think were resolved correctly. Where was God in these times? Answer: he was right there; I was the one that had moved!

Remember that when we awaken in the morning, this is a blessing from God because he sustained us through the night. In fact, every breath we take is a gentle reminder from God that he sustains us. Resolve like David to not be afraid of circumstances because God sustains us. When you find yourself "in the moment" with an upset parent, an unruly student, or a disagreement with a colleague, think about that breath you are taking. That is God sustaining you!

Do you remember to thank God for his sustenance when you awaken every morning?

DAY 123

Ultimate Control

And when he came to the other side, to the country of the Gadarenes, two demon-possessed men met him, coming out of the tombs, so fierce that no one could pass that way. And behold, they cried out, "What have you to do with us, O Son of God? Have you come here to torment us before the time?" Now a herd of many pigs was feeding at some distance from them. And the demons begged him, saying, "If you cast us out, send us away into the herd of pigs." And he said to them, "Go." So they came out and went into the pigs, and behold, the whole herd rushed down the steep bank into the sea and drowned in the waters.

—Matthew 8:28–32

One of my colleagues was dealing with a student who refused to attend class. This young lady was walking the halls and yelling profanities at my colleague, myself, and the school police officer who we had asked to assist us in removing her from the halls. Somehow, we were able to get her into the assistant principal's office and thought that she had finished her tirade. Suddenly, she attempted to leave, but the door was closed, and she tore the blinds that were on the door as well as the blinds on the office window. She left the office and started back on her rampage in the hall. About that time, her father arrived, and he, we, and the school police officer were following her through the school again. The police officer grabbed her, and before he could subdue her, she kicked him in the groin, and he fell to the ground injured. Her father finally was able to get her into his car, and they left. She finished the school year in the district's alternative school and was under a physician's care.

I do not know what happened to her after this, but I do know that this young lady made an impression on all of us that day. The officer recovered from his injury and chose not to press charges against the young lady.

This incident reminds me of this passage. Notice that the demons knew who Jesus was, and they knew that he was in total control of their destiny, just as we had the final determination of this young lady's educational placement. Because these demons knew this, they, like this young lady, were wreaking havoc as much as they could on these two men as well as on anyone that got near them. This young lady said that she had nothing to lose, so why not continue her tirade?

Satan also has this disposition. He knows that his days are numbered and that one day, he will be defeated, but until then, he is going to do everything possible to make our lives miserable, particularly those who follow Jesus. I believe God uses these incidents to help us recall passages such as this one to remind us that one day, evil will be totally defeated.

Thank God for his assurance that evil will be defeated. Keep your perspective when you encounter such evil in your classroom, in your school, or in your life outside of school.

DAY 124

Personal Quiet Time

But he would withdraw to desolate places and pray.
—Luke 5:16

Jesus made a practice to withdraw and spend time alone with God. God the Son took time to be alone and communicate with God the Father. Linger on that statement Luke made regarding Jesus's prayer habits.

When I was a band director, the period after Thanksgiving until about the fifteenth of December was a hectic time of year. I had rehearsals to prepare for and conduct, performances for school, a faculty social, and elementary schools that expected a performance kept me quite busy. In addition to these group activities, individually, our students were preparing for their all-district auditions which were in January, right after we returned from Christmas break. In addition, for these band students, this time marked the end of the semester, and they were completing semester projects and preparing for semester exams.

At church, I was attending rehearsals and practicing my music to play in our orchestra. I would also get last-minute calls to play with other churches at this time of year.

Balancing our professional duties, our church obligations, as well as our own preparation for Christmas becomes a challenge. We see the statement "Keep Christ in Christmas," yet we get so busy that we keep Christ out of Christmas, exactly where Satan wants him!

Jesus, in his humanity, faced similar issues. Crowds of people were following him. Wherever he went, people appeared. Nevertheless, Jesus made it a priority to withdraw and pray. If God's own son, in his humanity, took time to withdraw to pray, then it is more important that we do the same. Are you making it a priority to withdraw to pray?

DAY 125

Closing Written Correspondences

But they who wait for the Lord shall renew their strength;
they shall mount up with wings like eagles; they shall
run and not be weary; they shall walk and not faint.
—Isaiah 40:31

The Lord bless you and keep you; the Lord make his face
to shine upon you and be gracious to you; the Lord lift
up his countenance upon you and give you peace.
—Numbers 6:24–26

Do you have a favorite verse that you convey to your students when you are asked to sign their yearbook? I was fortunate to be the principal of a middle school named for Dr. Clarence G. Oliver, a former superintendent who remains active in the community. Our mascot was the eagle, and he chose the mascot. Dr. Oliver and I would have lunch from time to time. I always looked forward to spending time with him because he was a wise Christian man and gave me good perspectives regarding school situations that I encountered.

Dr. Oliver was gracious to come to the school to speak to our students and to visit with our teachers. He is an icon in the community as he continues to serve on many city advisory boards and committees. One of the events that the students looked forward to was the annual yearbook signing day and having Dr. Oliver sign their yearbook. His signature always read, "'Soar with the eagles!' (Isaiah 40:31)."

I follow his example; when I close cards and letters, I use the first verse of Aaron's blessing found in Numbers 6:24–26: "The Lord bless you and keep you." This is an excellent, nonconfrontational method of giving a witness for Christ.

Have you thought of a verse that you could use as you close correspondence with others?

DAY 126

Smooth Transitions in the Classroom

So the Lord said to Moses, "Take Joshua the son of Nun,
a man in whom is the Spirit, and lay your hand on him.
Make him stand before Eleazer the priest and all the
congregation, and you shall commission him in their sight.
You shall invest him with some of your authority, that all
the congregation of the people of Israel may obey."

—Numbers 27:18–20

Joshua was God's chosen successor to be Israel's leader after Moses. In appointing Joshua, God chose to work through Moses and Eleazer so that the people would follow their new leader. First, Joshua was publicly commissioned before the people. Second, some of Moses's authority was given to Joshua to ensure a smooth transition.

In many schools, there are helping teachers, assistant coaches, assistant music teachers, and assistant principals. It matters how you treat either your assistant or your helping teacher in front of your students. Students will adopt your attitude toward that person. You can greatly enhance the helping teacher's or assistant's ability to successfully work with students as well as your own professional relationship with them by treating them with respect, trusting them to do their job, and by giving them your authority when the situation calls for it.

I recall a situation in our school when a special education teacher was assigned as a helping teacher in a regular education classroom. The lead teacher didn't want a helping teacher, so she talked down to this helping teacher in front of the students and assigned her menial tasks. The students adopted the lead teacher's attitude toward the helping teacher, and she wasn't hugely effective. We changed her assignment to another teacher who welcomed a helping teacher, and she flourished!

Be reminded that not everyone feels the call to be the lead teacher, head coach, or the principal. As the leader of instruction in your subject area, be mindful of the way you interact with other staff in front of the students. They will follow your lead; they will adopt your attitude.

Are your interactions with your colleagues such that students will respect them?

DAY 127

Spiritual Inventory

Beware lest you say in your heart, "My power and the might
of my hand have gotten me this wealth." You shall remember
the Lord your God, for it is he who gives you power to get
wealth, that he may confirm his covenant that he swore to
your fathers, as it is this day. And if you forget the Lord your
God and go after other gods and serve them and worship
them, I solemnly warn you today that you will surely perish.
—Deuteronomy 8:17–19

From time to time, we should pause and take a spiritual inventory.
Where are our priorities? Have we forgotten God? Many times, we
take this inventory when life isn't going well, and perhaps it is easier for us to take such an inventory when life isn't going our way. It
seems more important, however, to take this inventory when life is
going great!

When our professional life is going well for us, we need to be
mindful that this is a blessing from God. I have heard it said "pride
comes before the fall." Be mindful not to become arrogant and feel
that your professional accomplishments you currently enjoy are of
your own making. God blessed you with the gift of teaching.

As to your possessions, enjoy them, but take care not to let them
become your idols. And lastly, but maybe most importantly, do not
let the idol of leisure overtake you so that you are neglectful regarding the worship of God. Is life going so well for you that you have
forgotten the God who gave all that you have? Stop to take a quick
spiritual inventory.

DAY 128

Incremental Development

> But Moses said to the Lord, "Oh, my Lord, I am not eloquent, either in the past or since you have spoken to your servant, but I am slow of speech and tongue."
> —Exodus 4:10

> Give ear, O heavens, and I will speak, and let the earth hear the words of my mouth. May my teaching drop as the rain, my speech distill as the dew, like gentle rain upon the tender grass, and like showers upon the herb. For I will proclaim the name of the Lord; ascribe greatness to our God! The Rock, his work is perfect, for all his ways are justice. A God of faithfulness and without iniquity, just and upright is he.
> —Deuteronomy 32:1–4

The eloquent speech of Moses. What? Moses eloquent in speech? Yes! Note the example given. The book of Deuteronomy contains three addresses to the Israelite nation from Moses, the same Moses that confessed that he was "not eloquent…but slow of speech and tongue" when God gave him his calling at the burning bush.

As educators, we encounter students who we think will "never make it," only to see them succeed in a profession in which God called them. If a student confides that he/she is thinking of a certain profession, offer encouragement and some advice to help them get there. Leave it to God to work out the details with the student.

Be careful thinking that God will only call you to use your present abilities and talents. If God calls us to do something, he is going to develop us along the way so that we will be able to do it.

Consider Moses's progression. God gave him Aaron, who was good at speaking, to "get him by for a time." Through the next forty years or so, God developed Moses's speech so that Moses was now eloquent! Why? So that God could show himself and remind us that he alone is sufficient for all our needs.

Is God calling you to a task which you don't think you can do? Good! Allow God to work through you, and give him the glory.

DAY 129

Rationalizing Sin

But you, keep yourselves from the things devoted for
destruction, lest when you have devoted them you take any
of the devoted things and make the camp of Israel a thing
for destruction and bring trouble upon it. But all silver
and gold, and every vessel of bronze and iron are holy to
the Lord; they shall go into the treasury of the Lord.
—Joshua 6:18–19

But the people of Israel broke faith in regard to the devoted
things, for Achan the son of Carmi, son of Zabdi, son of Zerah,
of the tribe of Judah, took some of the devoted things. And
the anger of the Lord burned against the people of Israel.
—Joshua 7:1

And Achan answered Joshua, "Truly I have sinned against the Lord
God of Israel, and this is what I did: when I saw among the spoil
a beautiful cloak from Shinar, and 200 shekels of silver, and a bar
of gold weighing 50 shekels, then I coveted them and took them."
—Joshua 7:20–21a

A good friend and colleague took his high school band on a spring
trip. Prior to the trip, he met with all parents of the students who
were traveling. The purpose of the meeting was to specifically go
over the regulations regarding student conduct on the trip and consequences should their child misbehave. One of the consequences out-
lined was that a student could be sent home at the parents' expense if
the behavior was severe enough. Examples were given, such as being

out of their assigned room after curfew, inappropriate behavior with members of the opposite sex, possession of alcohol or drugs, and shoplifting or stealing.

The trip was going well. The band had played magnificently, and now there was some free time to be spent at a local mall. While at the mall, my friend received a message all teachers hope never to receive. "Mall security has one of your students, and we need to see the person in charge immediately."

My friend rushed to the security office and found that the student had been arrested for shoplifting. The security camera footage clearly showed the student purchasing a pair of $20 sunglasses, then a bit later, taking a $2 sunglass neck strap and putting it into his pocket. When asked why he did this, the student responded, "It was just a neck strap. I didn't think anyone would miss it."

That theft of $2 worth of merchandise cost many others. It cost the band director who had to get the student released into his custody as well as to deal with the paperwork and embarrassment of having to report this incident to the school administration. It cost a parent chaperone time not spent with his child because he had to sit with the student at the bus station, waiting for the bus. It cost the student's parents bus fare as well as the embarrassment over their child's behavior. That $2 theft brought a heavy price!

That is the way Satan works. He whispers, "Take it, it won't hurt anything, no one will notice." That's what he said to Achan. "It's just a beautiful cloak, 200 shekels of silver, and 1 bar of gold."

This "little" sin cost Israel thirty-six lives and a defeat in the first battle for Ai. It cost Achan his life as well as the lives of his family. Rationalizing sin can be dangerous.

Have you been tempted to rationalize sin? Ask God for forgiveness and to enable you to resist rationalizing sin in your life.

DAY 130

Second-Guessing God's Call

And Joshua said, "Ah, Sovereign Lord, why did you ever bring
this people across the Jordan to deliver us into the hands of
the Amorites to destroy us? If only we had been content to stay
on the other side of the Jordan! O Lord, what can I say, now
that Israel has been routed by its enemies? The Canaanites
and the other people of the country will hear about this and
they will surround us and wipe out our name from the earth.
What will you do for your own great name?" The Lord said to
Joshua, "Stand up! What are you doing down on your face?"
—Joshua 7:7–10 NIV

Beware of becoming content and complacent because this is where
Satan wants you! Useless! Thank goodness God didn't allow Joshua
to remain in this state. Joshua was frightened, dejected, weak, and
tired from this defeat at Ai. Sometimes, difficulties and setbacks will
occur along the path of God's will. Don't make the mistake of thinking when experiencing a setback that you are not following God's
will.

My daughter injured her ankle playing soccer in high school.
The injury required surgery and three screws in her ankle. After
going through physical therapy with a tall, beautiful former basketball player from the University of Kansas, she recovered, earned a
soccer scholarship, and played four years of college soccer. She graduated with honors with a degree in biology. Through this injury, the
tough recovery, and by God's intervention of placing a strong female
role model as her physical therapist, my daughter felt the call from
the Lord to go into physical therapy for a career.

Upon graduating from college, she had applied to several PT schools but had been waitlisted by a couple and turned down by the others. At this point, she could have been content finding a job using her biology degree. She still felt the call of God to be in the medical profession, so instead of giving up, she enrolled in courses to begin work to fulfill the prerequisite coursework needed to apply to nursing school.

On the first day of class, she received a phone call from one of the schools where she was waitlisted saying they had an opening! She took this spot, received her doctorate in physical therapy, and is now working and helping many people. In fact, in the practice where she serves, there is a waiting list of people that wish to see her because her reputation for excellent care has spread among her patients as well as physicians.

She, like Joshua, didn't decide to be content with her biology degree on the other side of the river. When God calls us to do something, the path may not always be easy. Beware of making the mistake that just because there are setbacks that it isn't God's will. Be persistent, continue to pray for God's guidance, and get up and try again!

The second time, after following God's guidance, Joshua won the battle for Ai. You will encounter students with Ai's in their lives. Will you be able to relate to them an example of an Ai in your life that God has led you through? Look for opportunities to share with a student who is struggling.

DAY 131

Role Models for Women

Now Deborah, a prophetess, the wife of Lappidoth, was judging
Israel at the time. She used to sit under the palm of Deborah
between Ramah and Bethel in the hill country of Ephraim, and
the people of Israel came up to her for judgement. She sent and
summoned Barak the son of Abinoam from Kedesh-naphtali and
said to him, "Has not the Lord, the God of Israel commanded you,
'Go, gather your men at Mount Tabor, taking 10,000 from the
people of Naphtali and the people of Zebulun. And I will draw out
Sisera, the general of Jabin's army, to meet you by the river Kishon
with his chariots and his troops, and I will give him into your
hand'?" Barak said to her, "If you will go with me, I will go, but if
you will not go with me, I will not go." And she said, "I will surely
go with you. Nevertheless, the road on which you are going will
not lead to your glory, for the Lord will sell Sisera into the hand of
a woman." Then Deborah arose and went with Barak to Kedesh.
And Barak called out Zebulun and Nephtali to Kedesh. And
10,000 men went up at his heels, and Deborah went up with him.
—Judges 4:4–10

Deborah is an interesting study because she serves as a role model
for young ladies. Deborah was a prophetess leading Israel. In today's
language, Deborah "had it all" in that she had a profession (prophetess), was married, was respected by the people because they came to
her for judgment, and was a strong leader. By her conversation with
Barak, we can see that she possessed a strong, independent, outgoing
personality, and she did her own thinking.

One of the biggest challenges working with young ladies experiencing difficulties in their relationships with others was that many times, their conflicts arose because they allowed others to do their thinking for them. After much discussion, we would find that the root of the conflict was a third party, "keeping the pot stirred"; or if the conflict involved a boy, the young ladies would allow themselves to be manipulated. In either case, the result never ended well.

Young ladies need role models of strong women who think for themselves. Deborah is an example of such a person. We don't know much about her; but from this account, we can see that she possessed a strong, independent personality, did her own thinking, and wasn't manipulated by others. Are you being or can you point to strong Christian female role models for young ladies?

Strive to be that role model for your students or be able to provide some contemporary examples of strong Christian female role models.

DAY 132

Sensitive to Change of Behaviors

There was a certain man of Ramathaim-zophim of the hill country
of Ephraim whose name was Elkanah the son of Jeroham, son
of Elihu, son of Tohu, son of Zuph, and Ephrathite. He had
two wives. The name of one was Hannah, and the name of the
other, Peninnah. And Peninnah had children, but Hannah had
no children. Now this man used to go up year by year from his
city to worship and to sacrifice to the Lord of hosts at Shiloh,
where the two sons of Eli, Hophni and Phinehas, were priests of
the Lord. On the day Elkanah sacrificed, he would give portions
to Peninnah his wife and to all her sons and daughters. But to
Hannah he gave a double portion, because he loved her, though
the Lord had closed her womb. And her rival used to provoke
her grievously to irritate her, because the Lord had closed her
womb. So it went on year by year. As often as she went up to the
house of the Lord, she used to provoke her. Therefore Hannah
wept and would not eat. And Elkanah, her husband, said to
her, "Hannah, why do you weep? And why do you not eat? And
why is your heart sad? Am I not more to you than ten sons?"

—1 Samuel 1:1–8

Mean girls are real! Many times, we encounter such persons in our
classrooms. As a principal, I dealt with several instances where a
young lady was targeted. After much questioning, discussion, and
tears, I discovered jealousy was involved in many of these situations.
Examples of jealousy included one took another's starting position
on the team; a young man had chosen one girl over the other girl;
one girl had received a higher grade on a major project, thus pushing

her GPA (Grade Point Average) higher than her rivals. The GPA issue was huge because a higher GPA influenced class rank which in turn influenced college scholarship offers.

The young lady suddenly found herself alone. No one wanted to sit with her at lunch. "Friends" shunned her in the halls. She endured snide remarks that adults couldn't hear, ugly looks from peers that went unnoticed by others, or devilishly inappropriate comments to her or made about her on social media.

These times are difficult for teens and as teachers. We need to be sensitive to these events and be there to help them cope. Observe the outward signs of depression Hannah displayed: bouts of crying, not eating, and a sad face. Be sensitive to students' change in behaviors as it may indicate there is something going on that is troubling them.

Are you sensitive to subtle changes in your students' behaviors?

DAY 133

Working with Troubled Students

After they had eaten and drunk in Shiloh, Hannah rose. Now Eli the priest was sitting on the seat beside the doorpost of the temple of the Lord. She was deeply distressed and prayed to the Lord and wept bitterly. And she vowed a vow and said, "O Lord of hosts, if you will indeed look on the affliction of your servant and remember me and not forget your servant, but will give your servant a son, then I will give him to the Lord all the days of his life, and no razor shall touch his head." As she continued praying before the Lord, Eli observed her mouth. Hannah was speaking in her heart; only her lips moved, and her voice was not heard. Therefore Eli took her to be a drunken woman. And Eli said to her, "How long will you go on being drunk? Put your wine away from you." But Hannah answered, "No, my lord, I am a woman troubled in spirit. I have drunk neither wine nor strong drink, but I have been pouring out my soul before the Lord. Do not regard your servant as a worthless woman, for all along I have been speaking out of my great anxiety and vexation." Then Eli answered, "Go in peace, and the God of Israel grant your petition that you have made to him." And she said, "Let your servant find favor in your eyes." Then the woman went away and ate, and her face was no longer sad.

—1 Samuel 1:9–18

One of our tenth-grade students was having some personality issues with a certain teacher. In this situation, a "red flag" went up in my mind. First, this student was never in my office, was normally quite pleasant to speak to, and had excellent grades in all her classes. This teacher, however, had a history of personality issues not only with students but with other colleagues and with parents. Also, this teacher was one person who could not be trusted to speak to a parent without supervision because most of the time, the problem only became worse.

The teacher would make statements to students such as "I think you may be on drugs" or "Where did you get that new backpack? Did you steal it?" These comments would be made out loud in front of the class. We dealt many times with students that this teacher targeted. It created an awkwardly difficult situation. Finally, enough documentation was collected on these behaviors that our principal was able to have a conversation with her, and she chose to retire.

Eli gives us a poor example and a good example of how to work with a troubled student. He jumped to a conclusion and made an accusation. In this case, after Eli said what he did, Hannah, to her credit, had the courage to explain to him what was troubling her. We must remember that Hannah is an adult. Many students have not yet reached the age where they will willingly explain their behavior or even explain it in a sophisticated manner. Eli listened to Hannah. After Hannah explained her issue, Eli appropriately offered a word of encouragement and Hannah seemed to feel better.

Our initial approach to troubled students is distinctly important. The tone that we use can either open communication or make the situation worse. Examine your tone of voice when speaking with a troubled student. Are you quick to listen and offer encouragement?

DAY 134

Judging Parenting

When Samuel became old, he made his sons judges over
Israel. The name of his firstborn was Joel, and the name
of his second, Abijah; they were judges in Beersheba.
Yet his sons did not walk in his ways but turned aside
after gain. They took bribes and perverted justice.
—1 Samuel 8:1–3

In our profession, we meet different types of parents. We meet parents who have rebellious children; and after several visits, we say to ourselves, "The apple didn't fall far from the tree!" Then we meet those parents who also have rebellious children and they are "doing everything right." They are disciplining their children, they are supporting your efforts with their child, they are professing Christians, and make sure that their child is involved in church activities, namely regular attendance and Bible study.

Reading this passage both saddens me and encourages me regarding how to relate to parents. I am sad for Samuel that both of his sons did not follow the godly example that he set. I am encouraged to not be quick to judge parents regarding the actions of their children and to be patient to pray for them as well as the children.

From what we can tell, Joel and Abijah were "raised in the church," knowing about God and knowing the requirements of God. We don't get any details regarding the everyday family life of Samuel and how he related to his sons. We only know that the boys didn't turn out like Samuel would have wanted.

Are you too quick to judge the parents or guardians of your challenging students? Pray that God will give them the wisdom needed to raise their children and that their children will have tender hearts toward the things of God. Ask God to give you wisdom and patience as you work with them.

DAY 135

Our Disposition, Part III

Therefore we are ambassadors for Christ, God
making his appeal through us. We implore you,
on behalf of Christ, be reconciled to God.

—2 Corinthians 5:20

We put no obstacle in anyone's way, so no fault
may be found with our ministry.

—2 Corinthians 6:3

As educators, we are under constant scrutiny by our students, their parents or guardians, our administrators, and our colleagues. It has been my experience that others take notice of our actions and demeanor before they take notice of our words. They evaluate for themselves whether we "walk the walk" before they determine if we "talk the talk." They particularly observe and evaluate for themselves our responses when negative situations occur. They watch how we troubleshoot problems and propose solutions. They evaluate our demeanor as people are saying hurtful or sometimes attacking remarks to us and evaluate our responses. They evaluate our face first and listen to our responses second.

Paul reminds us that we are Christ's ambassadors. As ambassadors for Christ, do all our actions, deeds, demeanor, and words reflect Christ? Do they implore others to be reconciled to God? Or do they place obstacles in the way for others to be reconciled to God?

Ask God for a demeanor that always invites others to be reconciled to God.

DAY 136

What Others Find When They Dig

Then this Daniel became distinguished above all the other
high officials and satraps, because an excellent spirit was in
him. And the king planned to set him over the whole kingdom.
Then the high officials and the satraps sought to find a ground
for complaint against Daniel with regard to the kingdom,
but they could find no ground for complaint or fault, because
he was faithful, and no error or fault was found in him.

—Daniel 6:3–4

It is good to remember that, like it or not, your life is an open book.
Here we find Daniel being successful in his assigned position, and
his colleagues were jealous of him. What did they do? They looked
for something in which they could make public to bring Daniel
down. But Daniel had lived his life to the point that they could find
nothing to bring against him.

What do searches around your name bring? Ask God daily to
"lead us not into temptation," and live your life so that when others
dig, they will only find good!

DAY 137

Your Students' Well-Being

But I want you to be wise as to what is good
and innocent as to what is evil.
—Romans 16:19b

Like Paul, all good teachers want the best for their students. They want their students to succeed not only academically in their class but personally in all their endeavors. Paul states this wish succinctly in the second part of verse 19.

As you look at and work with your students today, make this verse your wish for them. Pray that God will give them wisdom for good and to shun evil. Place a student's name with this short prayer. "Lord, may Johnny be wise as to what is good and innocent as to what is evil."

Have you prayed for the well-being of your students today?

DAY 138

Don't Overdo It

With many such parables he spoke the word
to them, as they were able to hear it.

—Mark 4:33

The last part of this verse, "as they were able to hear it," jumped out at me because it has wonderful application to our practice. Jesus, being the master teacher, knew how to keep the length of his lessons reasonable so his listeners truly listened and didn't tune him out! Sometimes we, as teachers, try to do too much, particularly when introducing a new topic of study.

As a new teacher, I was being formally observed by my supervisor. I had preplanned the lesson to the smallest detail and provided many different examples. Upon receiving feedback from my supervisor, he said, "Great lesson, but you overdid it." He went on to explain that the students needed less examples and more guided practice. By providing more guided practice, I could then use the other examples as needed to assist those who were having difficulty.

Jesus knew just the right example to give and just the right length of teaching to administer before he lost his listeners. Notice that his listeners always heard what he said, even though some didn't accept his teaching.

Examine your practice. Are there lessons that need to be broken down into smaller parts so that your students understand the concepts being taught? Are you providing enough guided practice so that you can diagnose learning difficulties and help your students make the necessary adjustments?

DAY 139

Loving Others

In return for my love they accuse me, but I give myself to prayer.
—Psalm 109:4

But I say to you, Love your enemies and
pray for those who persecute you.
—Matthew 5:44

David and Jesus say the same idea. Love your enemies and pray for them. Do you have that student, parent, or colleague who is at odds with you right now? First, examine your practice and see whether you inadvertently have offended them. Love them and pray for them. Your disposition toward them will immediately improve.

DAY 140

Exercising Our Authority

And as he was walking in the temple, the chief priests
and the scribes and the elders came to him, and they
said to him, "By what authority are you doing these
things, or who gave you this authority to do them?"

—Mark 11:27b–28

And Jesus came and said to them, "All authority in
heaven and on earth has been given to me."

—Matthew 28:18

Webster's Dictionary defines *authority* as "the right to give orders, make decisions, and enforce obedience." In this passage, we see the chief priests, scribes, and elders questioning Jesus, saying, "Who gave you this authority?" and Jesus not answering them. We see in the second passage of scripture Jesus saying, "All authority has been given to Me."

As teachers, we are granted a certain amount of authority and autonomy in our classrooms. Many times, we are asked by disgruntled students or parents, "Who gave you this authority?"

Students state to us, "You can't tell me what to do," questioning our authority. We must take care to use the authority given us wisely and not abuse it.

I am writing this during the COVID-19 pandemic. Our leaders and public officials have taken on much more authority during this time. We are being encouraged to listen to them for our own well-being and health. As Americans, we, like these officials in the scripture passage, tend to question authority, particularly when the requests made by them are having influences on our lifestyle.

We need to remember that all authority has been given to Jesus. When we turned over our life to him, we relinquished all authority over our lives. Every decision that we make should reflect the ultimate authority that Jesus has over us. That means that in our profession, we take care not to abuse the authority that we have been given.

Are you exercising the authority that you have been given in a way that reflects Jesus to those under your watch?

DAY 141

Sharing Our Faith

Nevertheless, many even of the authorities believed in him, but for fear of the Pharisees they did not confess it, so that they would not be put out of the synagogue; for they loved the glory that comes from man more than the glory that comes from God.

—John 12:42–43

Are there times when you are afraid to share your faith because of what others may say to you or about you? We have all heard people say, "Here comes that holy roller" or "All he/she does is try to get you to come to their church." Other times, we hear folks say that work or school is not the place to share our faith because of "separation of church and state." I find it quite interesting also that people will discuss the beliefs and traditions of different religious denominations, but as soon as you put Jesus into the context of the conversation, you are "getting too close and personal."

Satan puts those instances in our minds for us to recall so that we will not share our faith. Your testimony does not have to be the "hellfire and brimstone" type of testimony that you sometimes hear about when teenagers are rescued from drugs and all sorts of evil! Mine is simple; I came to know Christ as a second grader when I gave my heart to Jesus one night before going to sleep. I made that willful, conscious decision public the very next Sunday when I went down and made a public profession of my faith in Christ. Jesus has been with me ever since, and I always know that I can talk to him and bring my petitions before him.

Look for small opportunities to share your faith. You don't have to be "preachy." Are you using the opportunities God has given you to share your faith with others?

DAY 142

Preparation

In my Father's house are many rooms. If it were not so, would
I have told you that I go to prepare a place for you? And if
I go and prepare a place for you, I will come again and will
take you to myself, that where I am you may be also.
—John 14:2–3

Preparation. We as teachers are constantly encouraging our students
to prepare. *Prepare* defined is to either make something ready for use
or to make someone ready to do or to deal with something. Proper
preparation requires thought regarding the steps necessary to make
something ready. We prepare our lessons by thinking of and planning the steps our students need to take to learn a new concept. The
musician prepares for the concert by thoughtful, meaningful practice. The athlete prepares for the game by first getting into shape by
training the right muscles for his/her sport. Then that athlete must
carefully listen to his/her coach's prepared game plan.

We tell our students that not only is preparation important,
but *how* you prepare is of the utmost importance! My point in saying all of this is that much thought and energy go into making
something ready for use or to get someone ready to deal with something, such as a game or test. Nothing is haphazard about proper
preparation!

Jesus said he was going to prepare a place for us. The thought
that my Lord said he was going to and is still preparing a place for
me excites me! Also exciting to remember is that he said when he fin-

ished his preparations, he would come to get me! O thank you, Lord Jesus, for what you have done and what you are doing!

When we encourage our students to prepare well, remember that Jesus is doing the same for us.

DAY 143

High-Fives or Fist Bump

[A] time to embrace, and a time to refrain from embracing.
—Ecclesiastes 3:5b

A time to embrace socially.

Recently I had the privilege of being the guest clinician for a local middle school band. I had been to their rehearsals several times and had somewhat established a rapport with the students.

One day, as the students were entering the room and assembling their instruments, a young lady walked up to me and said, "I love hugs. Can I have a hug?"

I gave her a big smile and said, "I don't do hugs, but I love high-fives or fist bumps! You make the choice, high-five or fist bump?"

She smiled and raised her hand, and we did a high-five. Each day after that, it became a game of whether we were going to do a high-five or fist bump when she arrived at rehearsal.

We have all encountered students who are seeking affection. Here in the South, it is quite common to greet friends with hugs or in our Cajun culture, even a kiss on the cheek. Students may have grown accustomed to these kinds of greetings because that is what they practice in their families. When they feel comfortable with you, they may ask for a hug. These kinds of greetings are not appropriate for the school setting! Maintain your distance but remain friendly.

How do you greet your students who seek more physical affection? Are you maintaining your distance but remaining friendly?

DAY 144

Embracing Technology

A time to embrace professionally.

[A] time to embrace, and a time to refrain from embracing.
—Ecclesiastes 3:5b

School has taken on a different look given the COVID-19 pandemic. Many have said that "school is canceled," but ask any teacher, and you will know that this is not the case. This different look of school has included online learning, teachers making more personal connections with their students with technology, and many other creative ways of meeting the needs of students who may not have access to technology.

Now is the time to embrace new methods of reaching students. How are you learning to use new tools and devise new creative ways to reach your students?

DAY 145

More about Jesus

A time to embrace spiritually.

[A] time to embrace, and a time to refrain from embracing.
—Ecclesiastes 3:5b

As I write this during the COVID-19 pandemic, I am reminded that this is a wonderful opportunity to embrace God more fully. My goal and prayer are that when we come out of this and return to normal, that I will be a changed person, more committed to the things of God than ever before. With that in mind, I am making it a priority to improve my knowledge of God and his business by reading and studying the Bible; I am also making sure to make practical applications of what I am reading to my life. I am devoting more time to praying for others, for our leaders, and for my family and friends.

During this time, I am reminded of the hymn "More about Jesus." Following is the text of that hymn:

More about Jesus would I know,
More of His grace to others show.
More of His saving fulness see,
More of His love who died for me. More, more about Jesus,
More, more about Jesus.
More of His saving fulness see,
More of His love who died for me.

More about Jesus let me learn,
More of His holy will discern.

Spirit of God my teacher be,
Showing the things of Christ to me.

More about Jesus; in His Word,
Holding communion with my Lord.
Hearing His voice in every line,
Making each faithful saying mine.

More about Jesus; on His throne,
Riches in glory all His own.
More of His kingdom's sure increase.
More of His coming, Prince of Peace.

Are you spending time to learn *more* about Jesus during this season of grace that God has provided?

DAY 146

Advocation for God's Point of View

Be not overly righteous, and do not make yourself too wise. Why should you destroy yourself? Be not overly wicked, neither be a fool. Why should you die before your time? It is good that you should take hold of this, and from that withhold not your hand, for the one who fears God shall come out from both of them.

—Ecclesiastes 7:16–18

As I was reading this passage, I needed some commentary to guide my understanding because on the surface, the passage seems to say, "Don't be too goody-goody, and don't be too bad!" That does not square with what I know about God and his character.

Upon reading the commentary, I discovered that "righteousness and wickedness" in these passages were referring to being "right" or "wrong" in a legal sense or in one's cause. The question now becomes, "How do we advocate for God's point of view as we are working through issues at work with our colleagues?" The implications of this passage are vastly important as we navigate the area of maintaining positive working relationships with our colleagues.

Do you know someone who must win every argument? Do you know someone who doesn't speak up when the discussion regarding an issue suddenly turns to moving toward an ending that is unjust? This passage helps us to understand that there is a balance. The person who must win every argument will eventually alienate those around him/her. The person who never speaks up for justice or for what is morally right is also guilty.

I take from this passage that we may not win every argument, but we must always speak for God's point of view. Do not be afraid to advocate for God's point of view when engaging in discussions with colleagues.

How do you tactfully advocate for God's point of view in your discussions with colleagues?

DAY 147

Rejoicing during Difficulties

How long, O LORD? Will you forget me forever? How long will
you hide your face from me? How long must I take counsel in
my soul and have sorrow in my heart all the day? How long
shall my enemy be exalted over me? Consider and answer me,
O Lord my God; light up my eyes, lest I sleep the sleep of
death, lest my enemy say, "I have prevailed over him," lest my
foes rejoice because I am shaken. But I have trusted in your
steadfast love; my heart shall rejoice in your salvation. I will
sing to the LORD, because he has dealt bountifully with me.
—Psalm 13:1–6

Have you ever faced a situation that you wondered how long it would
take for it to be over? We all have encountered professional situations
such as working with difficult colleagues or having that difficult student (and the parent who comes with them!) in our class. We all have
had personal situations such as an illness or, in this case, being quar-
antined during this COVID-19 pandemic. We miss our students.
We miss our colleagues. We miss our church fellowship. It is okay to
ask the question of "How long?" to God.

David gives us an example of such questions and a model for
how to work through unpleasant situations. Three words are significantly important in this passage beginning in verse 5. These three
words are *but*, *shall*, and *will*. *But* implies a shifting of one's mindset from the question of "How long?" "But I have trusted" indicates
remembering a decision already made. We have trusted Christ as our
Savior. Remembering that willful, conscious decision, we now make
two more willful conscious decisions. We "shall" rejoice in the salva-

tion that Christ provided for us. Savor the simplicity of the provision that God through Christ has made for us to be his. Finally, because of our relationship with Christ, we will sing to the Lord. Paul says it especially well: *"Rejoice in the Lord always again I say rejoice!"*

Are you deciding to continue to praise God and be grateful for your salvation in Christ through difficult times?

DAY 148

How Will We Respond?

Is anything too hard for the Lord?

—Genesis 18:14a

God told Abraham that he was going to have a son. Sarah heard God tell him this, and she laughed to herself. She just knew that she and Abraham were physically too old to have children, so she thought! Our ways are not God's ways!

How do we answer this question when we are tested? How do we answer this question when confronted with difficult situations? Do we turn it over to God or do we try to pursue a solution in our own strength? Perhaps how we answer this question in every circumstance is how we can determine the strength of our faith. My prayer is this today: "O Lord, please let me always answer this question in whatever circumstance with an unequivocal *no*, nothing is too hard for the Lord!"

How do we answer the question, "Is anything too hard for the Lord?"

DAY 149

Give Ear

Many years you bore with them and warned them by your Spirit
through your prophets. Yet they would not give ear. Therefore
you gave them into the hand of the peoples of the lands.
Nevertheless, in your great mercies you did not make an end to
them or forsake them, for you are a gracious and merciful God.

—Nehemiah 9:30–31

In my early years of teaching middle school, we enjoyed noon recess where the students were able to go outside to play after they finished eating lunch. As the time for recess to end came near, some students (boys, of course!) began to make it a practice to look at their watch to count down the time remaining for the bell to ring to go inside the building. To get to the doors of the school, these students had to pass down a long-covered walkway. This walkway was a typical flat-roofed structure that had three-inch pipe holding up the roof.

One day, as these boys were preparing to race into the building, the duty teacher observed what was happening and began shouting to them, "Students, don't run down the walkway because somebody will run into a pole and get hurt." She said this same sentence repeatedly.

The boys, now en masse, yelling and counting down the time, did not "give ear" to the teacher's warnings. The bell rang, and they bolted down the walkway toward the door, and *bam*! One of them hit the pole.

I distinctly remember the incident like this. The teacher said, "Don't run because somebody is going to hit a pole!" *Bam!* "See, I told you somebody was going to hit that pole."

Luckily, the student was not seriously injured. That duty teacher did all that she could to warn those boys but to no avail.

Are we guilty of not "giving ear" when the Holy Spirit gives us a warning about sin in our lives? My prayer today is to first thank God for his patience in bearing with me and to give me sensitivity to heed any warnings that the Holy Spirit gives.

Thank God for his mercies toward you, and heed warnings that the Holy Spirit gives. Do the same for your students. Be patient, bear with them, and do not hesitate to give them the warnings they need to be safe at school.

DAY 150

Majoring on the Minutia

On its hem you shall make pomegranates of blue and purple and
scarlet yarns, around its hem, with bells of gold between them,
a golden bell and a pomegranate, around the hem of the robe.
—Exodus 28:33–34

God is very meticulous! These two verses are part of the larger context where God is giving Moses specific instructions in building the
ark of the covenant, the Tent of Meeting, and the garments for the
priests. Notice that these instructions even define the smallest details
of the priestly garments.

These instructions give us a tiny glimpse into the attributes
and character of God. God is concerned even with the most minute
details. We, as God's children, should also be meticulous about the
small items in our daily lives and in how we prepare and present lessons to our students.

When I taught beginning woodwinds, I made a very big deal
to the students about the importance of playing on a wet reed. This
small piece of wood fits onto the mouthpiece, and when air is passed
through it, it vibrates and causes the instrument to make a sound. I
would have the students put the reed in their mouths and hold it like
a lollipop while assembling their instruments. After a few class periods of reminders, this practice became important to them because I
had stressed the importance of this activity.

God leaves nothing to chance. We as teachers also need to ensure
that the instructions given to our students are clear and precise. The

importance of majoring on the minutia is vital because the students will "pick up" on your character as a teacher as well as an individual.

Are you paying attention to the small details in your life spiritually as well as to the small details professionally? Major on the minutia!

DAY 151

What Is Not Said Is Important

Now I was cupbearer to the king.
In the month of Nisan, in the twentieth year of King Artaxerxes,
when wine was before him, I took up the wine and gave it to the
king. Now I had not been sad in his presence. And the king said to
me, "Why is your face sad, seeing you are not sick? This is nothing
but sadness of the heart." Then I was very much afraid."
—Nehemiah 1:11b–2:1–2

How well do you know your students? Have you developed the type of relationship with them that you notice changes in their nonverbal behavior?

Nehemiah, as King Artaxerxes's cupbearer, developed an intimate relationship with Artaxerxes as his duties included testing and drinking all food and drink brought to the king. Artaxerxes noticed a change in Nehemiah's nonverbal behavior and asked him, "Why is your face sad, seeing that you are not sick? This is nothing but sadness of the heart."

Notice that Artaxerxes asked an open-ended question and made no assumptions in the asking of the question. He stated only his observations and facts. This serves as a good example for us should the need arise to question students.

Make it a priority to be observant of the nonverbal behaviors of your students so that you will be sensitive to changes. Should you observe such changes, before approaching the student, check with other teachers as well as the student's counselor. Sometimes they will know whether something is going on in the student's life. This information will guide you in whether to approach the student.

Should you feel a need to question the student, do it discreetly and use Artaxerxes's example of asking open-ended questions as you state facts. An example may be, "I've noticed that your face seems sad" or "I've noticed that you are putting your head down on your desk. Do you want to talk about it, or is there something I can help you with?"

Do you notice changes in your students' nonverbal behaviors, and have you developed such a relationship with them that you could ask, and they would feel comfortable responding?

DAY 152

Our "Place"

You call me Teacher and Lord, and you are right, for
so I am. If I then, your Lord and Teacher, have washed
your feet, you also ought to wash one another's feet.
—John 13:13–14

My Sunday school teacher called my attention to these two verses. He noted that the disciples called Jesus "Teacher and Lord," but Jesus, in verse 14, reversed the order and reminded them he was their "Lord and Teacher." Jesus found it necessary to gently remind his disciples that he is first Lord! This fact makes him unique, distinct, not just another great teacher, but *the* Son of God. "Lord" is an office that was given to Jesus by God the Father. In that office, Jesus forgave our sins, and all who come to him and him alone can be saved, find redemption, and look forward to living with him forever in heaven.

Perhaps Jesus had to gently remind the disciples who he was because they had become so familiar with his earthly presence that they temporarily forgot who Jesus really was. After all, he had just washed their feet!

This passage made me think about our roles as teachers. In our efforts to connect with our students, do we sometimes allow ourselves to become so familiar with our students that they forget about the office we hold as their teacher?

As a first-year teacher, I was having some discipline issues with a young man. We had a parent-teacher-student conference to find a solution to this issue. His mother, an extremely wise public-school teacher herself, said to her son: "He is the teacher, you are the student." And then she looked directly at me and said, "You are the teacher, and he is the student." She looked at her son, then turned her head back toward me and said, "He does not get to have choices. He does what you tell him to do." After that conference, that young man was wonderful! That mom taught me a great lesson: to remember the office that I hold and the responsibilities that go with that office.

Jesus stopped and gently reminded his disciples that he was first Lord and, being Lord, had all authority. Sometimes we, too, must stop to gently remind our students that we are the teacher and they are the students.

Is Jesus in his rightful place as Lord in your life? Are you maintaining your office as *teacher* in your classroom?

DAY 153

Peer Pressure

But when Cephas came to Antioch, I opposed him to his
face, because he stood condemned. For before certain men
came from James, he was eating with the Gentiles; but when
they came, he drew back and separated himself fearing the
circumcision party. And the rest of the Jews acted hypocritically
along with him, so that even Barnabus was led astray by their
hypocrisy. But when I saw that their conduct was not in step
with the truth of the gospel, I said to Cephas before them
all, "If you though a Jew, live like a Gentile and not like a
Jew, how can you force the Gentiles to live like Jews?"
—Galatians 2:11–14

Peer pressure is real! Peter succumbed to peer pressure and became
a negative influence on Barnabus. Paul had to straighten Peter out!

I enjoyed lunchroom duty because I valued the casual conversation with students as well as observing which groups sat together.
The first week of school in the cafeteria was always interesting as I
observed students making choices regarding where in the cafeteria
they were going to sit and with what friends they were going to sit.
I observed that certain groups of students formed, and in about a
week, everyone had their "place" to sit.

On occasion, I would notice a group change, and suddenly,
one person would be missing. Invariably, I discovered that the group
decided to remove themselves from that person because one person
decided that they didn't like the other person anymore. Others in
the group made their choice based on the influence of the informal
"group leader." The poor student might sit alone for a few days before

finding another group or rejoin the former group as the "leader" was no longer "mad" at him/her.

We observe examples of this behavior constantly and we encourage our students not to succumb to peer pressure, but what about us? Are we as guilty? Do we change the choices of people we associate with based on the opinions of others about them without evidence for ourselves? Are we just as guilty of succumbing to the peer pressures of getting married, buying our first house, starting a family, or even changing jobs or careers because of the influences of our friends and acquaintances? Not to imply that these are bad things, just that they need to happen in our lives with God's timing.

If it can happen to Peter, it can happen to us. We must continue to encourage students to be strong as well as continuing to examine ourselves to not succumb to peer pressure.

Examine your choices and determine that they are in step with God's timing and not due to the influences of others.

DAY 154

Our Personal Attributes

Show yourself in all respects to be a model of good works,
and in your teaching show integrity, dignity, and sound
speech that cannot be condemned, so that an opponent may
be put to shame, having nothing evil to say about us.
—Titus 2:7–8

During an interview, the potential candidate for a teaching position at our school was asked to describe some personal attributes of a great teacher. This candidate, knowing that this is a common question included in interviews, gave the typical response—knowledge of the subject, a great team player, and able to connect with students.

While these are desirable attributes, Paul provides three that take us to a much broader and deeper level spiritually as well as professionally:

Integrity—firm adherence to moral uprightness, trustworthiness, reliability, and accountability. It has been said that integrity is how one behaves when no one is looking. Will you turn in that lost wallet that you found on the jogging trail and not take the cash?

Dignity—a firm reserve or serious manner. People who treat others with respect, respond politely, and mind their manners in difficult situations have dignity. As teachers, we must maintain our dignity with our students. We must be careful to maintain that distance between ourselves and our students.

Sound speech—not given to coarse jesting or sarcasm but speaks wholesome words, offers encouragement, and always speaks the truth.

This raises the question, how would our colleagues and students describe us? Would they or could they use the terms of integrity, dignity, and sound speech to describe us? Remember, people will make judgments about us by our actions and then our speech.

Do you have the reputation of having integrity, dignity, and sound speech?

DAY 155

Reflect on Student Success

I have no greater joy than to hear that my
children are walking in the truth.

—3 John 1:4

As a former band director, one of the joys of my life is on occasion to get to sit down and play in the church orchestra or in an ensemble with a former student. These folks have chosen to follow Christ and serve him with a talent that I had a part in developing. I feel that these occasions are times when God allows me to see the results of the seed that I have sown. God grants us these blessings of seeing or hearing of former students serving Christ and experiencing success in their chosen occupation to affirm our calling and to encourage us to continue to sow good seed. When you hear or see the successes of your former students, remember that you were a part of the positive influence on that person's life.

Have you taken a moment to reflect on the successes and Christian influences that your former students are now having on others? Pray for them and for their continued influence for Christ.

DAY 156

No Regrets

After making purification for sins, he sat down
at the right hand of the Majesty on high.
—Hebrews 1:3b

There comes a point in time during the educational process that the teacher has done all that he/she can do to prepare the students for an exam. Advanced Placement (AP) testing at high school serves as a good example. The teacher prepares the students, the students hopefully study, and then they take the test. As a result of their performance on the test, they either receive college credit for the course or they do not receive college credit for the course. No "in-between" exists. I remember many times our AP teachers saying, "I've done all I can do. Now it's up to them."

Jesus did all he could do! He obeyed God the Father, came to earth, lived a perfect life, and paid for our sins by his death on the cross. He said, "It is finished." After finishing his work, he sat down at the right hand of God. Sitting down implies that he had done all that he could do for us. We can now either believe and accept his offer of salvation or reject him. This proposition, like the AP exam, is an either/or proposition; no "in-between" exists.

This passage begs us to examine ourselves on multiple levels. First, have we made the decision to accept Christ as our Savior? Second, if we have accepted Christ, are we obeying his commission to do all we can do to lead others to him? Third, are we doing all that we can do in our profession to prepare our students? I used to challenge my students to leave no "woulda, shoulda, or couldas" on the table, meaning, "I woulda done that," "I shoulda done that," or "I coulda done that!"

Are you leaving any "woulda, shoulda, couldas" on the table in your spiritual and professional life?

DAY 157

Rebuke

About this we have much to say, and it is hard to
explain, since you have become dull of hearing.
—Hebrews 5:11

And he said to them, "Then are you also without understanding?"
—Mark 7:18a

Are you so dull?
—Mark 7:18a NIV

It gives me great comfort to read that the greatest teachers who ever
lived sometimes had to rebuke their students because they "weren't
getting it!" Paul and Jesus had to pause in the middle of their lesson
and say, "You have become dull of hearing."

"Then are you also without understanding?" was also said by
Jesus during the lesson. The NIV translates Jesus's words as "Are you
so dull?"

I once heard a pastor say, "People tell me that my sermons are
over their head, that what I say is too complex."

My answer to them is, *"Raise your head!"*

Examine Paul and Jesus's methodology in handling this issue.
They paused the lesson, gave their rebuke, and then moved back to
their lesson. Before moving further into the lesson, they gave a quick
review of the material. In both cases, they didn't go on and on in
their rebuke; they didn't put down their students. They made a quick
comment regaining their listeners' attention.

Sometimes we as teachers must stop to give a gentle rebuke when we see our students "checking out." Be mindful that before *you* noticed them "checking out," *they* were already "checked out!" At that point, follow Paul and Jesus's example of giving a quick reteach; it will prove to quite beneficial for the students.

A gentle rebuke given in the appropriate manner is needed when our students begin to "check out." Sometimes slight humor or a witty remark gives a "commercial break," and the class can return to the lesson. When you must rebuke your students, are you using the proper tone so that you do not exasperate them?

DAY 158

What Your Superiors Will Say about You

> Now there was a day when the sons of God came to present
> themselves before the LORD, and Satan also came among
> them. The LORD said to Satan, "From where have you come?"
> Satan answered the LORD and said, "From going to and fro
> on the earth, and from walking up and down on it." And
> the LORD said to Satan, "Have you considered my servant
> Job, that there is none like him on the earth, a blameless and
> upright man, who fears God and turns away from evil?"
> —Job 1:6–8

It was spring, the time of the school year when the master schedule
was being developed for the next school year. This particular year,
our district required that we offer a new course called "Principles of
Engineering." This course required a teacher with specialized training offered by the creators of this course. It also required the teacher
to have a heavy math and physics background. These requirements
made the pool of people who could be considered to teach it unusu-
ally small. We discussed possible candidates on our staff, and this
conversation centered around their academic qualifications, their
performance in their current teaching assignment, their willingness
to attend the training required to teach the course, and of course,
their personal attributes such as their integrity and how well they
worked with students as well as with their colleagues.

   During this conversation, one of my colleagues said, "Have you
considered Jamie? She is a great person, works well with the kids, gets
along with everyone well, and remember, she is alternatively certified

to teach because her degree is in engineering. She could be the perfect person to teach this course."

As God and Satan discussed Job's attributes, the same will be true for your superiors who at some point will discuss you. What will they say? Keep in mind that your classroom performance and your general disposition toward your students and colleagues are always being observed and evaluated.

Is your performance and disposition such that when your superiors discuss you, the discussion will be positive?

DAY 159

Punctuation Is Important

Then Satan answered the LORD and said,
"Does Job fear God for no reason?"

—Job 1:9

We learn in English class that proper punctuation symbols are necessary to communicate our written thoughts effectively. We use a question mark when writing a question. We use an exclamation point to express surprise, excitement, or a strong emotion. We use a period to indicate an end to a sentence. The question mark of Satan should be the exclamation point of our faith.

Satan asked God a remarkably important question. "Does Job fear God for no reason?" This question should cause us to pause and examine ourselves and our relationship to God. Do we fear God because of the blessings he has given us? If we lost everything, would we still fear God or would we blame him? We know that Job continued to fear God even when all was taken from him.

Let us now return to the punctuation of this verse. Literally, Job turned the question mark of Satan into the exclamation point of his faith by maintaining his integrity and proper disposition toward God. We, like Job, must also turn the question mark of doubt that Satan puts in our lives into the exclamation point of faith in God in our spiritual journey. Fear God for no reason!

Can you testify that you fear God for no reason?

DAY 160

Sanded and Shaped

For we are his workmanship, created in Christ Jesus for good works, which God prepared beforehand, that we should walk in them.

—Ephesians 2:10

At the high school where I served, we had a fantastic industrial arts department. I remember listening to the woodworking teacher discussing with the students their choices regarding what they were going to make. They would begin their project with bare pieces of wood and end with nice furniture. Many times, the students sold what they made and were happy to make a handsome profit.

I visited the class from time to time and watched their progress. As the semester progressed, I noticed the students taking greater care of their project and taking greater pride in their craftsmanship. When they had finished their project, they would stand back and admire it. I remember how proud they were of their workmanship. Over the course of the semester, they had carefully molded and crafted pieces of wood into a fine finished product.

If we have been born again, we are Christ's workmanship, and we are created to do good works. The good works come because we have been saved by grace. Sure, there are going to be some rough experiences as he sands and shapes us, but we must be willing to be sanded and shaped! As the great hymn "Have Thine Own Way" says, "Thou art the potter, I am the clay. Mold me and make me after thy will while I am waiting yielded and still."

Are you being sanded and shaped in the way Jesus wants so that you can do the work that he has called you to do?

DAY 161

Dealing with Arrogance

We know that "all of us possess knowledge." This "knowledge" puffs up, but love builds up. If anyone imagines that he knows something, he does not yet know as he ought to know.
—1 Corinthians 8:1b–2

In this passage, Paul is specifically addressing the issue of food offered to idols, but there are some interesting aspects of this passage that may assist us as we deal with arrogant students. The passage puts quotation marks around two quotes; "all of us possess knowledge" and the word *knowledge*. Upon examining commentary regarding the reason for these quotation marks, I discovered that Paul was quoting Corinthian sayings and implying they didn't have all the answers; even though in their arrogance, they thought they did. Paul was addressing a problem of arrogance among the Corinthians, and as teachers, we occasionally must address this issue with some of our students (and their parents) from time to time.

Working with intelligent students sometimes presents a unique challenge because they may become arrogant and feel that they are smarter than you as well as smarter than their peers. Working with younger students who are exceptionally bright presents a unique challenge because not only may they be arrogant, but sometimes, their parents are as well and have told their child how smart and wonderful he/she is.

Paul makes two observations regarding this type of behavior. First, he acknowledges that this "knowledge" puffs up; in other words, people become arrogant. Second, he states that, "If anyone imagines that he knows something, he does not yet know as he ought to know." In other words, you may not know what you think you know in the right way, and there is *always* more to learn.

The key to working with these students is to acknowledge their arrogance and challenge them to move deeper into their learning by saying something like, "I know that you already know this, but what about this?" It may take some mental gymnastics on your part to accomplish but remember to love them and challenge them. "Love builds up," as Paul says.

Are you tactfully dealing with your students who are arrogant and challenging them to take their "knowledge" to a deeper level?

DAY 162

Follow the Policy

Then Jesus was led up by the Spirit into the wilderness to be tempted by the devil. And after fasting forty days and forty nights, he was hungry. And the tempter came and said to him, "If you are the Son of God, command these stones to become loaves of bread." But he answered, "It is written, 'Man shall not live by bread alone, but by every word that comes from the mouth of God.'" Then the devil took him to the holy city and set him on the pinnacle of the temple and said to him, "If you are the Son of God, throw yourself down, for it is written, 'He will command his angels concerning you,' and 'On their hands they will bear you up, lest you strike your foot against a stone.'" Jesus said to him, "Again it is written, 'You shall not put the Lord your God to the test.'" Again, the devil took him to a very high mountain and showed him all the kingdoms of the world and their glory. And he said to him, "All these I will give you, if you will fall down and worship me." Then Jesus said to him, "Be gone, Satan! For it is written, 'You shall worship the Lord your God and him only shall you serve.'" Then the devil left him, and behold, angels came and were ministering to him.

—Matthew 4:1–11

I received a phone message from an irate parent regarding a low grade her child had earned. This parent told me in no uncertain terms that I needed to change that grade to a higher grade. Instead of just telling her no, I cited Texas Law to her. Texas law states: "Pursuant to a TCTA-initiated law, an examination or course grade issued by a teacher is final and may not be changed unless it is erroneous, arbitrary or inconsistent with a school board-approved district grading policy" (Texas Education Code 28.0214 Finality of Grade).

I explained to this parent that I had investigated this grading issue, and the grade assigned was not erroneous, arbitrary, nor inconsistent with our district's grading policy. Referring to the policy, I explained that what she was asking me to do was illegal, and I could not do this. We concluded the conversation by agreeing to disagree regarding getting the grade changed.

Many times, teachers came to me seeking advice on how to speak with an irate parent regarding a low grade. I would immediately go to our district's grading handbook, cite the policy, and encourage the teacher to do the same with the parent. The conversation always ended better when a policy was cited instead of just saying no because it moved the conversation to the third person. Instead of a discussion of "I want you to do this, and you won't do it," the discussion was moved to "I'm following the policy, and you are asking me to go against the policy."

Satan came to Jesus three times in the wilderness and tempted him. Three times, Jesus cited scripture as he resisted Satan's temptations. Jesus "followed the policy!" Satan even tried to use scripture, but Jesus knew scripture so well (he inspired it) he successfully refuted Satan.

Regarding your district's grading policies, do you know your district's policies so that you will be able to cite them when confronted by that irate parent? How well do you understand your district's grading policies so that you may effectively apply them when you are questioned regarding a grade that you assigned? How well do you know and "follow the policies" that are given in God's Word?

DAY 163

Quick, Slow, Slow

Know this my beloved brothers; let every person be quick
to hear, slow to speak, slow to anger; for the anger of
man does not produce the righteousness of God.

—James 1:19–20

I was in a conference with a parent and her child's team of teachers. Her child was failing all the core subjects. As we went around the table addressing each subject, I noticed the different body language each teacher exhibited when addressed by the parent. Some teachers listened and addressed each concern the parent expressed. Other teachers gave short answers and "couldn't be bothered." Still others immediately became defensive regarding their teaching practice when the question the parent had did not even address their teaching practice.

James provides the perfect formula for working through issues that will arise. My pastor put this formula into a succinct phrase in which we can remind ourselves when faced with issues or conflicts, "Quick, slow, slow." Repeating those three words can help us as we work through issues.

"*Quick to hear.*" First, be a good listener! Write the concerns down, repeat them back to the speaker so that your mind is clear as to what the concerns are. Repeating and writing allow the person to perceive that you are really listening. Many times, the situation will begin to deescalate because the person on the other side feels that he/she is being heard and not being "put off."

"*Slow to speak.*" Let your responses be measured and directly address each individual concern the person has. Try to give some positive solutions that may help to resolve the issue.

"*Slow to anger.*" Do not allow your emotions to get the best of you, even if you feel verbally attacked. This type of anger does not give an accurate reflection of who we are as Christ's followers. We are Christ's ambassadors and should always reflect *his* point of view!

Are you a good listener? Do your responses always reflect your profession as one of Christ's followers?

DAY 164

Making Application

But be doers of the word, and not hearers only, deceiving yourselves. For if anyone is a hearer of the word and not a doer, he is like a man who looks intently at his natural face in a mirror. For he looks at himself and goes away and at once forgets what he was like. But the one who looks into the perfect law, the law of liberty, and perseveres, being no hearer who forgets but a doer who acts, he will be blessed in his doing.

—James 1:22–25

I remember straight up failing my first exam in a low-level history course when I was in college. I told myself that "it was just history," and I could remember names and dates. Remembering my previous experiences in these types of classes, the multiple-choice question section would not be difficult because with only three answer choices, I would be able to figure out the correct answer choice. Boy, was I ever wrong! When I received that test, the wording of the questions was in no way the types of questions that I had experienced before. After that test, I had to change my study habits, and I spent the rest of that semester digging myself out of the "hole" I had created for myself because this class only had four tests which included the midterm and final exams.

I had totally deceived myself into thinking that this class was not going to be difficult. I did all the right things: I attended every class, took detailed notes, and read the assigned readings (somewhat); I was a hearer and not a doer. I realized that I didn't remember what I had read and I did not know the material at the depth of knowledge needed to be successful.

That experience has helped me professionally as I have had conversations with many parents who were having difficulty understanding why their child was not passing a course such as Algebra I. I would explain to them that these courses were not the same courses that we took in high school. For example, Algebra I is no longer a course where a student completes the odd-numbered exercises and checks the answers in the back of the book. Now the questions on the tests are such that the student must make application to concepts learned and not just memorize processes to complete the problems.

James is telling us the same idea. We must do God's Word so that it takes root in our lives and not just listen to or read God's Word. To just listen or read God's Word and not make application to our lives causes us to deceive ourselves and to think, *I've got this*, when we really do not.

Spiritually, are we sometimes guilty of "checking the boxes," having read our Bible but not applying what we read into our daily routines? Professionally, are you challenging your students to do some "mental gymnastics" with the material so that they put it into long-term memory and can make applications to it in different situations?

DAY 165

"Soak Time"

But be doers of the word, and not hearers only, deceiving yourselves. For if anyone is a hearer of the word and not a doer, he is like a man who looks intently at his natural face in a mirror. For he looks at himself and goes away and at once forgets what he was like. But the one who looks into the perfect law, the law of liberty, and perseveres, being no hearer who forgets but a doer who acts, he will be blessed in his doing.

—James 1:22–25

Let's pause for a moment and linger for a bit on the last two words of verse 22 and then verses 23 and 24 of this passage. Spiritually, are we sometimes guilty of remembering only the first part of verse 22? Given my own experience, I think it is entirely possible. I find that I need to slow down and allow the Holy Spirit to help me apply what I am reading into my daily routine of life. I need to allow for some "soak time."

Our math department chair experienced much success teaching, given the results of her students on standardized tests. When asked her "secret," she replied, "It's not that hard if you don't move too fast and give them (the students) plenty of "soak time." Watching her teach, she introduced new concepts by linking them to concepts the students knew. She moved decidedly slowly, her words carefully measured, pausing frequently to make sure the students understood.

During these pauses, she made sure to read nonverbal cues as well as verbal responses. She broke down concepts into small, doable chunks and included much guided practice. Her homework assignments were small but poignantly directed at what had been taught in class that day. The next day, she would check the homework by asking students to demonstrate what they had done. She didn't ask for volunteers. She made sure that all students were held accountable for the work.

As a student in her class, you knew that at any moment, you may be asked to demonstrate your knowledge regardless of whether you raised your hand to volunteer! She never moved to another topic until she was sure the students understood and could put the concept into practice in different scenarios.

Reflecting on my own devotional practice after watching this teacher made me realize that many times I have "checked the box" spiritually. For example, I had a goal of reading the Bible through in one year. To accomplish this, I had to read about three chapters per day. I reached the goal, but I didn't remember all that I had read! Sometimes I would discover that I was reading but not remembering what I had read. Have you ever had this experience of reading and then realizing that you were only moving through the words and not remembering what you were reading?

Do we sometimes "move too fast" in our study of God's Word and not give ourselves enough "soak time"? Are you including enough "soak time" for your students in your class routine?

DAY 166

Personal Accountability

For if you live according to the flesh you will die, but if by the
Spirit you put to death the deeds of the body, you will live.
—Romans 8:13

We tell our children and our students, "Make good choices." We tell
them that "you can determine the type of life you lead by whom you
associate with, by the decisions you make, and by the way you feed
your mind." Are we ourselves guilty of not following what we tell our
students to do?

This verse contains a hugely large "but if." Examine it closely.
Paul tells us that, as Christians, we have the Holy Spirit to lead and
guide us; but we have a responsibility to put away sinful habits and
desires. Do we sometimes abdicate our own responsibility for sin? Do
we explain it away and lower our standards? Quite possibly, we need
to not only continue to hold our students and children accountable
for their actions but more importantly to hold ourselves accountable
before God for our actions.

How well do we hold ourselves accountable for our actions?
Have we adopted the world's standard in accepting sin in our lives?

DAY 167

Dress Code

But put on the Lord Jesus Christ, and make no
provision for the flesh, to gratify its desires.
—Romans 13:14

One of the most difficult tasks that I had as a principal was enforcing our school's dress code. As a male, enforcing the dress code was difficult, particularly in addressing standards of dress with our young ladies. In this day of the "Me Too Movement," male teachers and administrators are reluctant to address female students for fear of being accused of "looking at them in an inappropriate manner." Personally, I am vastly appreciative of our female administrators and teachers who are proactive in addressing dress code issues as well as modeling appropriate dress at school.

I was walking down the hall in our high school when I saw one of our young ladies dressed inappropriately. Not wanting to embarrass her, I began walking faster to catch up with her when one of our female coaches came out of her classroom. She saw me, saw the young lady, and immediately went up to her and diplomatically said to the young lady, "Sweetie, that just isn't a good look for you today. Let's go to the office so that you can call someone to bring you another top that covers your stomach better." Immediately, the young lady reached and rolled down the top and covered her stomach!

Interestingly, many of our dress code issues are solved in a few minutes because those students know the dress code but decide to violate it. Many times, they already have a coverup or another piece of clothing in their backpack ready to use if approached. The point is that they made a conscious decision when they were getting dressed to wear that inappropriate top or blouse to school.

Paul, in this one sentence, reminds us that when we wake in the morning to get dressed for the day, we, as Christians, have two conscious decisions to make. We are to remember to "put on the Lord Jesus Christ" and "make no provision for the flesh." In other words, put Christ first; and don't entertain worldly thoughts and desires. Putting on Christ and making no provision for the flesh are two conscious decisions that we make each day.

How well do we remember to "put on the Lord Jesus Christ" and "make no provision for the flesh" as we prepare for our day?

DAY 168

Maintaining Perspective

So we do not lose heart. Though our outer self is wasting away, our inner self is being renewed day by day. For this light momentary affliction is preparing for us an eternal weight of glory beyond all comparison, as we look not to the things that are seen but to the things that are unseen. For the things that are seen are transient, but the things that are unseen are eternal.

—2 Corinthians 4:16–18

Have you ever had "one of those days"? We face problems every day dealing with difficult students, colleagues, and sometimes parents! I remember one day during the Christmas season, my colleague and I were dealing with multiple issues of discipline as well as irate parent phone calls. It had become "one of those days!" I remember my colleague saying to me, "The hits just keep on coming."

At about that time, our principal came out of her office and said, "It seems quiet today, I think I'll run down to Starbucks and get a cup of coffee. Can I bring something back for you?"

We both declined. After she walked out of the building, we frustratingly looked at each other and said at the same time, "What school are you working at, lady?" We now laugh about this incident every time we recount it.

Perspective is hugely important! Paul tells us that we need to keep our minds on Christ and keep our hope on the future. When all seems to be going badly, we need to remind ourselves that this issue, or issues, are only temporary, that we are *his* and *he* is ours and that this too will pass. It may pass like a kidney stone, but it *will* pass! When I became a new principal, one of my colleagues told me to not sweat the small stuff and to remember that it is *all* small stuff! When compared to the eternal life that we will have with Jesus, the temporary issues we deal with really are all small stuff.

How well are you keeping your perspective when issues seem to be coming at you from all sides?

DAY 169

Affections

You are not restricted by us, but you are
restricted in your own affections.
—2 Corinthians 6:12

You shall have no other gods before me.
—Exodus 20:3

Affections. *Websters Dictionary* defines them as "a gentle feeling of fondness or liking." We see examples of affection in our schools by the behavior of our colleagues and our students and experience affection for different people and objects ourselves. In high school, we see the "cute couple" looking for one another between classes to have that brief conversation and quick hug or kiss before moving to the next class. I used to say to such congregations, "Walk and talk."

We as teachers know that we must not show affection for one student over another but acknowledge that it is difficult not to have "favorites" in our hearts for those who are willing learners. We all have affections for our favorite food, drink, social settings, stuff, even money!

That takes us to the question, are we allowing our affections for fleeting pleasures to come between us and God? "You shall have no other gods before me." We may need to spend some time in self-reflection and allow the Holy Spirit to show us areas where our affections are coming between us and God and hindering our spiritual walk with him.

Professionally, do we allow our affections for certain learners to be revealed by our interactions with them in the classroom? Personally, what affections hinder our walk with God?

DAY 170

Blaming Others for Our Shortcomings

> You are not restricted by us, but you are
> restricted in your own affections.
> —2 Corinthians 6:12

Yesterday we examined the last half of this verse; and today, we will examine the first half of this verse. Putting this verse into the context of the Corinthian letters, we know Paul was dealing with issues and personalities within the Corinthian church, and when some of these people were exposed, they blamed Paul. I heard a teacher tell a group of students one time, "Don't blame me for your shortcomings. I'm just telling you where they are and how to fix them."

One of our freshmen was failing Algebra I. Her mother was concerned, and we had a parent-teacher conference. During this conference, it was agreed that the student would attend tutorials with the teacher before school twice a week for a three-week period, and then we would reevaluate her progress. Three weeks later, the student was still failing. The mother blamed the teacher; she stated she had rearranged her work schedule to take her daughter to school early to attend the tutorials, but the tutorials were not effective as her daughter was still failing Algebra I.

The teacher, exasperated with both the parent and child, said to me, "Here I am trying to help, and I can't get her to even come to my tutorials like we agreed. Why am I the bad guy here?"

The truth was that the parent was dropping off her daughter at the right time, but the daughter chose to socialize with her friends instead of attending the tutorials. This student was restricting her success in Algebra I because her affection for socializing with friends was more important to her. The parent, not knowing that her daughter was not attending the tutorials, placed the blame on the teacher for her child's failure.

This exact issue was the same that Paul faced. He called out the Corinthians' bad behavior, and they made him out to be the "bad guy." He was quick to point out he wasn't the problem; the problem was in their affection for items that were not in line with God's expectations.

This verse challenges us to engage in some self-reflection. Professionally, understand that there will be times that we will be given the credit for the failings of others. Know and accept that. Personally, do we sometimes blame others when our shortcomings are exposed?

DAY 171

All Things New

And he who was seated on the throne said,
"Behold, I am making all things new."
—Revelation 21:5a

And I am sure of this, that he who began a good work in
you will bring it to completion at the day of Jesus Christ.
—Philippians 1:6

The area where I now live was devastated by two hurricanes less than six weeks apart. When we returned to our home, we found eighty-two trees that had been blown down. By God's grace, none of them fell on our house; however, the cleanup process will take months. We have many friends and acquaintances who did have major damage to their homes and are not yet able to live in them. The entire area still looks like a war zone even after two months of debris cleanup and new construction. This area will never look like it did before these hurricanes.

At our home, among the many stumps left from the downed trees, as well as the bare limbs of trees that were not downed, new growth appeared in a matter of days. I was amazed at how quickly this new growth emerged and was reminded that God breaks down and he also heals. So it is with our lives. Sometimes we must be broken to be made new! And the new will not look like the old.

Watching our recovery reminds me that sometimes the process of "making all things new" may be a lengthy, painful, and arduous process. However, we can look at nature and be reminded that God is consistent and faithful and "He who began a good work in you will bring it to completion at the day of Jesus Christ." We, as Christians, must remember that God is not finished with us.

Thank God for his continued consistency and faithfulness, even when everything around you seems to be crashing. Offer an encouraging word to that student or colleague who may be going through a crisis in his/her life.

DAY 172

Spiritual Tension

He also told them a parable: "No one tears a piece from a new garment and puts it on an old garment. If he does, he will tear the new, and the piece from the new will not match the old. And no one puts new wine into old wineskins. If he does, the new wine will burst the skins and it will be spilled, and the skins will be destroyed. But new wine must be put into fresh wineskins. And no one after drinking old wine desires new, for he says, 'The old is good.'"
—Luke 5:36–39

In marching band, one of the biggest issues we faced were tears. Tears occur when part of the ensemble does not play at the same speed or tempo with the rest of the ensemble. Suddenly, you hear that the ensemble is not together, and one of two events can happen. One, that group that is playing out of tempo with the ensemble gets back in time, and the problem resolves itself. Two, the problem or tear continues to get larger and the entire ensemble falls apart. The point is that tears cause tension within the ensemble, and the entire ensemble suffers because something small develops into something big. In rehearsal, we know that we cannot ignore the small tears. They must be fixed so that there will be no tension in the ensemble.

Jesus came to earth and ushered in the new covenant of grace. In doing so, he abolished the old covenant of laws and sacrifices. The Pharisees, however, favored the past and wanted to continue their old ways of doing religion, thus creating tension between their way and Christ's way. Jesus was saying that you cannot mix the old with the new!

This passage takes us to an important time of reflection spiritually. Am I retaining my old way of doing things, my old sins, and affections, while trying to be the Christian who I profess to be? Perhaps some of the tension we experience spiritually is the result of trying to "put a piece of new material on an old garment" or "putting new wine into an old wineskin." We dismiss sin in our lives by not dealing with it, and it may or may not become a big issue. Whether or not sin becomes a big issue is beside the point. If we are to walk with our Lord, we must put all sin away and not dismiss it as a small issue. Remember, we have "put on Christ" and are making "no provision for the flesh."

In what areas of your life are tensions hindering your walk with God?

DAY 173

Good Documentation

Inasmuch as many have undertaken to compile a narrative of the things that have been accomplished among us, just as those who from the beginning were eyewitnesses and ministers of the word have delivered them to us, it seemed good to me also, having followed all things closely for some time past, to write an orderly account for you, most excellent Theophilus, that you may have certainty concerning the things you have been taught.

—Luke 1:1–4

One of the most often used statements that we hear in education is, "Document, document, document." While serving as the Student Support Administrator for our school, I became extremely aware of the importance of the accuracy of the minutes of Special Education and Section 504 meetings. The minutes of these meetings captured the essence of conversations had during the meeting as well as to how a student's Individual Education Plan (IEP) or 504 Accommodation Plan was to be implemented.

Many times, we would find it necessary to refer to the minutes of the meeting when the parent or the teacher had issues regarding how an IEP or 504 Accommodation Plan was being implemented.

Personally, I kept a log of phone conversations I had with parents. Many times, I found it necessary to go through my notebook, gathering dates, times, and the essence of multiple conversations I had with a parent regarding his/her child. Being able to produce precise, accurate, and descriptive documentation gave me credibility.

This same process is exactly what Luke did. One of the remarks made by commentators about Luke's prologue stated that this single sentence ranks among the finest Greek writing of the first century and demonstrates Luke's skill and credentials as a writer. Luke "followed things closely for some time" and provided an "orderly account." This proves to be important because Luke's account provides facts and details about Jesus's life here on earth that the other gospels do not provide. More importantly, Luke's gospel gives us assurance of Jesus's Messiahship, his authority over nature, demons, death, and his purpose to deliver all of us from our sins and be reconciled to God the Father through our belief in him.

Accuracy and precise documentation provide credibility to the event as well as to the person reporting the event. Do you make it a habit to maintain a log and notate how a lesson went and to document conversations with students and with parents?

DAY 174

Our Credibility

After he had finished all his sayings in the hearing of the people, he entered Capernaum. Now a centurion had a servant who was sick and at the point of death, who was highly valued by him. When the centurion heard about Jesus, he sent to him elders of the Jews, asking him to come and heal his servant. And when they came to Jesus, they pleaded with him earnestly, saying, "He is worthy to have you do this for him, for he loves our nation, and he is the one who built us our synagogue." And Jesus went with them. When he was not far from the house, the centurion sent friends, saying to him, "Lord, do not trouble yourself, for I am not worthy to have you come under my roof. Therefore I did not presume to come to you. But say the word, and let my servant be healed. For I too am a man set under authority, with soldiers under me: and I say to one, 'Go,' and he goes; and to another, 'Come,' and he comes; and to my servant, 'Do this...'" When Jesus heard these things, he marveled at him, and turning to the crowd that followed him, said, "I tell you, not even in Israel have I found such faith." And when those who had been sent returned to the house, they found the servant well.
—Luke 7:1–10

This passage is quite remarkable because it reveals that Jesus healed a centurion's servant, and the centurion never had a face-to-face conversation with Jesus. Just to be fair, in the Matthew account of this event, Matthew has the centurion himself asking Jesus to heal his servant. For today's thought, let's focus on the Luke account of the centurion sending others on his behalf. In this account, Jesus responded to the centurion's request based on information given by others on his behalf. This man had earned his credibility and respect of these people, even though he was a Gentile representing an oppressive government.

Luke provides some important information about this man. First, because Luke identifies him as a centurion, an official of Rome, we can deduce that he is a Gentile. Even though he is a Gentile, he is held in high esteem by the Jews under his authority. We know that he is held in high esteem because these Jewish officials were willing to speak to Jesus on his behalf. They told Jesus that "He loves our nation," "He built our synagogue" and "He is worthy to have you do this for him." We also can tell from this text that this centurion was a humble man, sending his friends to tell Jesus that he was not worthy to have Jesus come under his roof and that he didn't presume to come to Jesus. All this impressed Jesus, so we can also deduce that this man was a believer.

Two different sets of people were willing to honor the requests of this man and to speak to Jesus on his behalf. Our credibility is earned by our actions and not necessarily by what we say. Our love for Christ is demonstrated by how we treat others, particularly those under our authority.

How good is your credibility with those who are under your authority? Is your reputation such that others would be willing to speak on your behalf?

DAY 175

A Servant's Heart

"Will any one of you who has a servant plowing or keeping
sheep say to him when he has come in from the field, 'Come at
once and recline at table'? Will he not rather say to him, 'Prepare
supper for me, and dress properly, and serve me while I eat and
drink, and afterward you will eat and drink'? Does he thank
the servant because he did what was commanded? So you also,
when you have done all that you were commanded, say, 'We are
unworthy servants; we have only done what was our duty.'"
—Luke 17:7–10

I heard an interesting exchange between a teacher and a student. The
student was complaining to the teacher that he didn't offer praise for
anything that the student had done. The teacher responded, "Why
should I praise you for something that you are supposed to do?"

Do we sometimes forget that as teachers we are servants? As
Christians, do we possess a servant's heart? Countless times, I have
found myself witnessing others condemning those who failed to
show gratitude for something done for them when what was done
was just part of their job duties. For some reason, it was felt a debt of
gratitude was owed.

Sometimes, we as Christians, expect accolades for our Christian
service. As Christians, we are servants of the living God! Before we
look for a "pat on the back" from others for our Christian service, we
need to humbly remind ourselves that we are unworthy saved sinners
doing what we are called to do. God owes us nothing. We owe him
everything. Remember that we are saved to serve.

Jesus reminds us at the end of this parable to keep a servant's heart. Let's ask God to remind us to keep a servant's heart in everything that we do.

DAY 176

Opportunities to Share Christ

The poor man died and was carried by the angels to Abraham's side. The rich man also died and was buried, and in Hades, being in torment, he lifted up his eyes and saw Abraham far off and Lazarus was at his side. And he called out, "Father Abraham, have mercy on me, and send Lazarus to dip the end of his finger in water and cool my tongue, for I am in anguish in this flame." But Abraham said, "Child, remember that you in your lifetime received your good things and Lazarus in like manner bad things; but now he is comforted here, and you are in anguish. And besides all this, between us and you a great chasm has been fixed, in order that those who would pass from here to you may not be able, and none may cross from there to us."
—Luke 16:22–26

And he said to them, "I saw Satan fall like lightning from heaven."
—Luke 10:18

One day during my lunch duty, I happened to come upon two students engaged in a conversation regarding whether hell was a real place. One student asked me whether I believed hell was a real place. I said, "Short answer, yes. But if you want, I can explain my logic as to why I believe hell is a real place."

Their curiosity was piqued, and they allowed me to relate the *Cliff Notes* version of the passage regarding the rich man and Lazarus. They were both familiar with the passage.

After relating the story, I said, "You see, I believe that Jesus was and is who he said he is, the Son of God. That means that he was with God before creation and is with God now since his resurrection. Can you imagine the events Jesus witnessed before becoming a man and the things he has witnessed since his return to be with God until he returns to Earth? He saw hell created. He said that he saw Satan fall from heaven like lightning.

"The characteristics of hell Jesus relates in this passage are places and events he has seen firsthand. So when he speaks of hell being a hot place of torment, and that there is a great chasm between heaven and hell, I believe him. That is why I believe hell is a real place. See, Jesus tells us just enough about this place called hell that I know that I don't want to go there, and that is one reason I have accepted him as my Lord and Savior."

They listened, and then the bell rang, and they left the cafeteria for class. I do not know whether my witness convinced either of them, but I do know that this was an opportunity to share Christ.

Are you ready to share Christ in some way when you are asked your opinion regarding a subject such as your belief in hell, heaven, creation, or even abortion?

DAY 177

Try It! Don't!

And the Lord God commanded the man saying, "You
may surely eat of every tree of the garden, but of the
tree of knowledge of good and evil you shall not eat, for
in the day that you eat of it you shall surely die."
—Genesis 2:16–17

And the woman said to the serpent, "We may eat of the
fruit of the trees in the garden, But God said, 'You shall
not eat of the fruit of the tree that is in the midst of the
garden, neither shall you touch it, lest you die.'" But the
serpent said to the woman, "You will not surely die."
—Genesis 3:2–4

Lunch duty was always interesting. Lunch duty had only three rules:
(1) sit where you wish; (2) clean up after yourself and place your tray
and leftovers in the proper receptacle; and (3) remain seated and visit
with your friends until the bell rings.

It was always fun on the first day of school because when we
gave these three rules to the freshmen students, they were elated
because they were able to choose their own places to sit. I enjoyed
watching them "find their place" over the next week. After the first
week of school, groups of friends were formed as "their places" in the
cafeteria were established.

We always, however, had to address one particular issue. A few
students would attempt to sneak out of the cafeteria to walk the halls
before the bell rang. My fellow duty teacher, exasperated with this

behavior, said to me one day, "They have the whole cafeteria and their pick of friends to visit, yet these few want to try to leave."

Eve did the exact same thing! God gave Adam and Eve the entire garden with only one prohibition, that of eating of the tree of knowledge and the tree of good and evil. We exhibit this same behavior. For example, when we are young, we are told, "Don't touch that stove! Don't open that cabinet!" As teens, we are told, "Don't go over to so and so's house when their parents aren't home! Don't go to that store! Don't leave the cafeteria!"

When someone says, "Don't," there is a little part of us that says, "Try it, it won't hurt anything!" We should not be surprised that as teachers, when we issue a prohibition, there will always be a few who want to try. Personally and spiritually, we need to manage those invitations of Satan to "try it."

How well do we manage Satan's invitation to "try it" when we are told "Don't"?

DAY 178

Waiting for the Ride Home

And when the feast was ended, as they were returning, the
boy Jesus stayed behind in Jerusalem. His parents did not
know it, but supposing him to be in the group they went a
day's journey, but then they began to search for him among
their relatives and acquaintances, and when they did not find
him, they returned to Jerusalem, searching for him. After
three days they found him in the temple, sitting among the
teachers, listening to them and asking them questions.

—Luke 2:43–46

After reading this passage through the lens of a middle school principal, I observed the following: (1) Luke does not say whether Jesus
asked permission of Mary and Joseph to stay behind in Jerusalem; (2)
apparently, Jesus didn't inform his earthly parents where he was; and
(3) Mary and Joseph didn't confirm with one another where Jesus
was. They "supposed" he was with the group. In other words, they
didn't communicate!

As a middle school principal, one of my least favorite activities
was evening events held on campus, such as basketball games and
school dances. At these events, parents would drop off their children
and leave. Even though we were diligent and specific in communicating the time frame for these events, there were always students
who did not get picked up until long after the other students had
departed. I remember many awkward moments waiting there with a
child, trying to start a pleasant conversation. The child was embarrassed and would be looking away toward the entrance to the parking lot to see those familiar headlights of their ride finally arriving.

When that parent finally arrived, he/she sometimes would thank me and offer explanations, such as, "I thought his/her father was coming to get her, 'I got held up at work' or 'We thought he/she was coming home with a friend's parents.'"

God the Father had entrusted the care of God the Son to human parents; and in this instance, they blew it. As a parent, it gives me great comfort to see Mary and Joseph in this situation and reminds me to give parents some slack when they fail to retrieve their children from an event in a timely manner.

What is your disposition toward children as you wait with them for their parents to arrive? What is your disposition toward their parents? Should you have a conversation with them when they arrive?

DAY 179

Divine Appointments

And Adam knew his wife again, and she bore a son and
called his name Seth, for she said, "God has appointed for me
another offspring instead of Abel, for Cain killed him."
—Genesis 4:25

The son of Enos, the son of Seth, the son of Adam, the son of God.
—Luke 3:38

It is interesting to note that Jesus's human genealogy goes through
Seth. Remember, Cain killed Abel, and later, Seth was born. Satan
attempted to use Cain to spoil the plan of God for the salvation of
the world. But God took care of that attempt! Thank goodness that
God's plans are irrevocable! Eve said, "God has appointed," possibly the first divine appointment recorded in the Bible. Luke then
records Jesus the Anointed One's genealogy back through Seth, the
appointed one!

As we go through our sometimes-mundane days, remember
that God continues to make divine appointments. We must be sensitive and diligent to look for and to seek them. Events that are called
coincidence may in fact be divine appointments. Thank God for his
faithfulness to carry out his plans, and remember to look for God's
work even in the mundane, everyday events.

Are you sensitive to and looking for God's divine appointments
in the routine of everyday life and work?

DAY 180

Handling Transitions

David commanded to gather together the resident aliens who were in the land of Israel, and he set stonecutters to prepare dressed stones for building the house of God. David also provided great quantities of iron for nails for the doors of the gates and for clamps, as well as bronze in quantities beyond weighing, and cedar timbers without number, for the Sidonians and Tyrians brought great quantities of cedar to David. For David said, "Solomon my son is young and inexperienced, and the house that is to be built for the LORD must be exceedingly magnificent, of fame and glory throughout all lands. I will therefore make preparation for it." So David provided materials in great quantity before his death." Then he called for Solomon his son and charged him to build a house for the LORD, the God of Israel. David said to Solomon, "My son, I had it in my heart to build a house to the name of the LORD my God. But the word of the LORD came to me, saying, 'You have shed much blood and have waged great wars. You shall not build a house to my name, because you have shed so much blood before me on the earth. Behold, a son shall be born to you who shall be a man of rest. I will give him rest from all his surrounding enemies. For his name shall be Solomon, and I will give peace and quiet to Israel in his days. He shall build a house for my name. He shall be my son, and I will be his father, and I will establish his royal throne in Israel forever.' Now, my son, the LORD be with you, so that you may succeed in building the house of the LORD your God, as he has spoken concerning you. Only, may the LORD grant you discretion and understanding, that when he gives you charge over Israel you may keep the law of the LORD your God. Then you will prosper if you are careful to observe the statutes and the rules that the LORD commanded Moses for Israel. Be strong and courageous. Fear not; do not be dismayed. With great pains I have provided for the house of the LORD 100,000 talents of gold, a million talents of silver, and bronze and iron beyond weighing, for there is so much of it; timber and stone, too, I have provided. To these you must add. You have an abundance of workmen: stonecutters, masons, carpenters, and all kinds of craftsmen without number, skilled in working gold, silver, bronze, and iron. Arise and work! The LORD be with you!" David also commanded all the leaders of Israel to help Solomon his son, saying, "Is not the LORD your God with you? And has he not given you peace on every side? For he has delivered the inhabitants of "the land into my hand, and the land is subdued before the LORD and his people. Now set your mind and heart to seek the LORD your God. Arise and build the sanctuary of the LORD God, so that the ark of the covenant of the LORD and the holy vessels of God may be brought into a house built for the name of the LORD."

—1 Chronicles 22:2–19

David received some news from God that he didn't necessarily like. He was told by God that he would not be the person who would build the temple. That task was to be assigned to Solomon, David's son. David's response to this news provides us with some majorly important insights into David's character and provides us with an example of how we should behave professionally when we receive information that we do not necessarily like.

First, David accepted the news; he didn't pout. He didn't make the lives of those around him more difficult. Second, if not more importantly, David not only secured the materials necessary so that Solomon could successfully complete the project, but he also prepared the people of Israel for this transition by commanding them to assist Solomon. David did everything in his power to prepare both materials and personnel to ensure Solomon's success.

Whether we like it or not, another person will always be there to follow us into the professional role that we now occupy. How well do we secure materials, inform subordinates or inform our students so that there is a seamless transition for the person that follows us? It becomes vitally important that we do all we can to set up the person following us for success.

Transitions are inevitable. How we prepare for them reveals much about our character and reflects on our Christian witness.

Professionally, are you willing to accept "bad news," maintain a Christ-like attitude toward those around you, and continue in your assigned role to the best of your ability? How well do you prepare the path for the person who follows you in your role?

DAY 181

Indifference Is Dangerous

Once when Jacob was cooking stew, Esau came in from the field, and he was exhausted. And Esau said to Jacob, "Let me eat some of that red stew, for I am exhausted!" (Therefore his name was called Edom.) Jacob said, "Sell me your birthright now." Esau said, "I am about to die; of what use is a birthright to me?" Jacob said, "Swear to me now." So he swore to him and sold his birthright to Jacob. Then Jacob gave Esau bread and lentil stew, and he ate and drank and rose and went his way. Thus Esau despised his birthright.

—Genesis 25:29–34

Commentary regarding this passage stated that Esau was indifferent toward his firstborn status. This statement caused me to ponder how dangerous an attitude of indifference can be. I define indifference as having no interest or sympathy, care, or apathy toward someone or something.

One afternoon, I passed by a classroom that looked to be out of control as there were students out of their seats, and some were even sitting on their teacher's desk! I entered the room and asked a student why this was going on. His reply was, "She doesn't care if we do this." Sure enough, the teacher was in the classroom. I had not seen her because of the many students who were up and milling around.

Another time, I overheard a conversation between two teachers discussing their supervisor. They didn't respect this person. One teacher stated, "She always chooses the path of least resistance."

Esau was indifferent to his place as the firstborn son and reflected his indifference by selling his birthright to Jacob for some stew. Because of this attitude of indifference, Esau made a decision based on expediency and took himself out of God's plan. This one decision changed the entire course of history for Esau and his descendants! Hebrews 12:16 describes Esau as "unholy." The attitude of indifference can be significantly dangerous!

Have we compromised our Christian witness by reflecting an attitude of indifference when given an opportunity to take a stand for Christ? In the same way that those students could tell the indifference of their teacher toward their behavior or those teachers' observations of their supervisor's decision-making, others can sense our disposition by observing our responses to issues that we face.

Esau's indifferent disposition caused him to miss God's plan. Many miss becoming Christians because of their indifference when they encounter Christ. They choose not to make a choice. Not making a choice to accept Jesus is really a choice to reject him.

Like Esau, we all occupy a "place" and others are observing and listening to what we say and, more importantly, don't say.

Ask God to help guard against the attitude of indifference and for wisdom in making decisions. Ask for help to not make decisions based on expediency.

DAY 182

Listening to the Right People

Rehoboam went to Shechem, for all Israel had come to Shechem to make him king. And as soon as Jeroboam the son of Nebat heard of it (for he was in Egypt, where he had fled from King Solomon), then Jeroboam returned from Egypt. And they sent and called him. And Jeroboam and all Israel came and said to Rehoboam, "Your father made our yoke heavy. Now therefore lighten the hard service of your father and his heavy yoke on us, and we will serve you." He said to them, "Come to me again in three days." So the people went away. Then King Rehoboam took counsel with the old men, who had stood before Solomon his father while he was yet alive, saying, "How do you advise me to answer this people?" And they said to him, "If you will be good to this people and please them and speak good words to them, then they will be your servants forever." But he abandoned the counsel that the old men gave him, and took counsel with the young men who had grown up with him and stood before him. And he said to them, "What do you advise that we answer this people who have said to me, 'Lighten the yoke that your father put on us'?" And the young men who had grown up with him said to him, "Thus shall you speak to the people who said to you, 'Your father made our yoke heavy, but you lighten it for us'; thus shall you say to them, 'My little finger is thicker than my father's thighs. And now, whereas my father laid on you a heavy yoke, I will add to your yoke. My father disciplined you with whips, but I will discipline you with scorpions.'" So Jeroboam and all the people came to Rehoboam the third day, as the king said, "Come to me again the third day." And the king answered them harshly; and forsaking the counsel of the old men, King Rehoboam spoke to them according to the counsel of the young men, saying, "My father made your yoke heavy, but I will add to it. My father disciplined you with whips, but I will discipline you with scorpions." So the king did not listen to the people, for it was a turn of affairs brought about by God that the LORD might fulfill his word, which he spoke by Ahijah the Shilonite to Jeroboam the son of Nebat."

—2 Chronicles 10:1–15

I had a wise principal tell me that when faced with important decisions, it is best not to make a snap decision. His advice, "Don't be shy about telling them that you need some time and will get back to them in a day or so." He continued, "You then have some time to let it (the issue) percolate down and maybe discuss it with some folks so that you can make a good decision."

Listening to the right people to receive good advice is powerfully important. Not listening to the right people was the mistake that Solomon's son Rehoboam made. He chose the wrong set of advisers, and consequently, the kingdom was divided.

As leaders, the types of people we choose to surround ourselves with is very important so that when needed, we can get competent, trustworthy advice. Professionally, are you surrounding yourself with godly colleagues who will offer solid advice when asked? Socially and spiritually, are you surrounding yourself with godly friends so that you have accountability as well as advice that is in line with God's perspective?

Ask God for wisdom to surround yourself with wise, godly people who will give you sound advice so that the decisions you make are aligned with God's plan.

DAY 183

Our Vulnerability

And Jehoshaphat stood in the assembly of Judah and Jerusalem, in the house of the LORD, before the new court, and said, "O LORD, God of our fathers, are you not God in heaven? You rule over all the kingdoms of the nations. In your hand are power and might, so that none is able to withstand you. Did you not, our God, drive out the inhabitants of this land before your people Israel, and give it forever to the descendants of Abraham your friend? And they have lived in it and have built for you in it a sanctuary for your name, saying, 'If disaster comes upon us, the sword, judgment, or pestilence, or famine, we will stand before this house and before you—for your name is in this house—and cry out to you in our affliction, and you will hear and save.' And now behold, the men of Ammon and Moab and Mount Seir, whom you would not let Israel invade when they came from the land of Egypt, and whom they avoided and did not destroy—behold, they reward us by coming to drive us out of your possession, which you have given us to inherit. O our God, will you not execute judgment on them? For we are powerless against this great horde that is coming against us. We do not know what to do, but our eyes are on you."

—2 Chronicles 20:5–12

Times occur when we as teachers and leaders need to publicly admit we don't have all the answers and admit our vulnerability. In this passage, we see a leader in total desperation, publicly admitting his vulnerability, calling out to God. In some fashion, we have all been in Jehoshaphat's shoes and can identify with his raw, transparent admission of his lack of wisdom. Professionally, we face dilemmas with students, their parents, and with our colleagues. Personally, we may be dealing with tragedy such as serious sickness, the death of a loved one, or an unexpected financial hardship.

This king gives a powerful example of how to pray when times of hardship come. Examine Jehoshaphat's prayer. He first acknowledges God's sovereignty. He then recalls the blessings that God has granted the nation. He acknowledges and accepts God's timing because he acknowledges that God did not allow Israel to defeat these people at an earlier time, yet he asks God to now execute judgement on them and admits that they are powerless to defend themselves. Then there comes the significant final statement, *"We do not know what to do, but our eyes are on you."*

In tough situations, we know that we can call on Jesus and he will answer! With what dilemma are you currently dealing? Use Jehoshaphat's example by admitting your vulnerability, calling out to God, and most importantly, vowing to keep your eyes on Jesus!

DAY 184

Our Influence

And Jehoiada made a covenant between himself and all the
people and the king that they should be the Lord's people.
—2 Chronicles 23:16

Joash was seven years old when he began to reign, and he
reigned forty years in Jerusalem. Joash did what was right in
the eyes of the Lord all the days of Jehoiada the priest. Now
after the death of Jehoiada, the princes of Juda came and
paid homage to the king. Then the king listened to them.
And they abandoned the house of the Lord, the God of their
fathers, and served the Asherim and the idols. And wrath came
upon Judah and Jerusalem for this guilt of theirs. Yet he sent
prophets among them to bring them back to the Lord. These
testified against them but they would not pay attention.
—2 Chronicles 24:1a–2, 17–18

Beloved, do not believe every spirit, but test the
spirits to see whether they are from God.
—1 John 4:1a

Examine closely verse 2. This verse indicates that Jehoiada, the priest
was a positive mentor and influence on Joash; but when Jehoiada
died, Joash listened to the wrong people and did not follow God's
plan. We tell students all the time, "You are hanging around and
listening to the wrong people!" It breaks our hearts when they don't
listen and end up in deeper trouble.

As a teacher and a leader, I find two takeaways from this passage. First, I am reminded of the responsibility that God has given me to be a positive, godly influence on others. I pray that like Jehoiada, I will be a positive influence on others. Second, I am warned that no matter how many years I have been walking with Jesus, I must be careful about who I listen to and whose advice I follow. I am reminded to "not believe every spirit but test the spirits to see whether they are from God."

Are you being a positive, godly influence on others? Even if right now you enjoy a close relationship with Christ, do you "test the spirits" as you listen to others?

DAY 185

Rebellion or Repentance

And the Lord sent Nathan to David.
Nathan said to David, "You are the man!"
David said to Nathan, "I have sinned against the Lord."
—2 Samuel 12:1a, 7a, 13a

Then the Spirit of God clothed Zechariah the son of Jehoiada the priest, and he stood above the people, and said to them, "Thus says God, 'Why do you break the commandments of the Lord, so that you cannot prosper? Because you have forsaken the Lord, he has forsaken you.'" But they conspired against him, and by command of the king they stoned him with stones in the court of the house of the Lord. Thus Joash the king did not remember the kindness that Jehoiada, Zechariah's father, had shown him, but killed his son. And when he was dying, he said, "May the Lord see and avenge!"
—2 Chronicles 24:20–22

How do we react when confronted with sin in our lives? How we react when confronted with sin gives us an indicator about our relationship with God. Christian accountability partners are ever so helpful. Having someone in our lives who will tell us straight up when we have sinned is quite refreshing and good for our soul. When we hear God's message via our pastors, we should find it important to make appropriate application to our lives.

In these passages, we see two totally contrasting reactions when David was confronted by Nathan and Joash was confronted by Zechariah. David repented, and Joash rebelled. I am reminded that God sends people our way to let us know when we have sinned to keep us close to him because he is always pursuing a relationship with us.

Do you react with an attitude of rebellion or repentance when confronted with sin?

DAY 186

How We Answer Is Important

And when your children say to you, "What
do you mean by this service?"
—Exodus 12:26

And when in time to come your son asks
you, "What does this mean?"
—Exodus 13:14

When your children ask in time to come,
"What do these stones mean to you?"
—Joshua 4:6b

When your son asks you in time to come, "What is the
meaning of the testimonies and the statutes and the rules
that the LORD our God has commanded you?"
—Deuteronomy 6:20

These four examples are included from different times and places because in them, God reveals to us a tremendously important characteristic of children. Children are naturally inquisitive. God gave all of us this gift of inquisitiveness so that we can explore, seek, and question. Through our engagement in these activities, we come to know him and then get to know him better.

Accepting this characteristic of students reminds me as a teacher that my response to their questions is extremely important. How I answer their questions can either pique their curiosity more or stifle it. Am I validating them as people of worth by how I respond to their questions? Am I being patient and kind using my responses to get them more interested in my subject or are my responses short and "huffy"? Am I viewing their questions as opportunities to further arouse their interest and appreciation of my subject? I hope and pray that my responses to students' questions will lead them to a deeper knowledge and appreciation of my subject.

Ask God for wisdom in giving answers to your students' questions that will lead them to greater understanding and deeper appreciation of your subject.

DAY 187

A Wake-Up Call

(The flax and barley were struck down, for the barley was in
the ear and the flax was in bud. But the wheat and emmer
were not struck down, for they are late in coming up.)
—Exodus 9:31–32

For if you refuse to let my people go, behold, tomorrow I
will bring locusts into your country, and they shall cover
the face of the land, so that no one can see the land. And
they shall eat what is left to you after the hail, and they
shall eat every tree of yours that grows in the field.
—Exodus 10:4–5

When God sends a wake-up call, do we listen or ignore it? Wake-up
calls from God may come in various forms. Professionally, a wake-up
call may come when a parent, colleague, or supervisor questions a
classroom routine or teaching practice we have adopted. Remember,
teaching practices may work for some and not for others. There defi-
nitely is not a "one size fits all" approach. Personally, we may commit
a sin, and the consequences are minor; but we realize that the consequences for this sin could have been much greater.

The parentheses in this first passage are there for a reason. They
are there to remind us that even in the middle of this calamity, God's
grace was evident. God didn't destroy all the crops. God is over
everything, even the timing of the crops for harvest. Not everything
to eat was ruined.

God gave Pharoah another chance, but Pharaoh hardened his
heart, did not heed God's warning, did not accept the goodness and

grace of God, and the remaining crop was wiped out by the locusts. I pray that when God sends a wake-up call, I will listen.

Are there areas of your professional and personal life when God has sent you a wake-up call?

DAY 188

Incremental Progress

I will not drive them out from before you in one year, lest
the land become desolate and the wild beasts multiply
against you. Little by little I will drive them out before
you, until you have increased and possess the land.
—Exodus 23:29–30

Incremental progress is sometimes a good thing! Currently, we are accustomed to having (and wanting) everything instantly. This passage makes me stop to realize that sometimes God gives us only parts because he knows we are not yet ready to handle the whole.

I am now living in Louisiana where we are recovering from two major hurricanes as well as a severe winter weather event. Progress in recovery is quite slow because of the unavailability of labor and materials. I have noted that many people in this area have adopted the disposition, "Baby steps, but we are making progress!"

Professionally, do we break our lesson content down and give our students small enough "chunks" so that they are not overwhelmed with the material that they must learn? Do we take the time to encourage the students who are struggling in our classes to celebrate and remind them of the incremental progress that they are making?

In my spiritual life, I find that I must from time to time stop to thank God for incremental progress. Are you grateful for small steps of progress both professionally and spiritually? Stop to acknowledge the professional and spiritual progress that you have made and give thanks and praise to God.

DAY 189

Limping Along

And Elijah came near to all the people and said, "How
long will you go limping between two different opinions?
If the LORD is God, follow him; but if Baal, then follow
him." And the people did not answer him a word.

—1 Kings 18:21

We sometimes tell our students, "Make a decision because right now
you are just treading water." Let's stop to linger a moment on the
word *limping*. The King James Version translates as "Halt ye." The
Christian Standard Bible and New International Version translates
as "wavering." Finally, the New King James Version translates as
"falter."

Spiritually, do we sometimes find ourselves limping, wavering, or faltering? Could it be that as we examine ourselves, we have
inadvertently allowed ourselves to slip into a state where we are not
depending upon Christ for everything? That is exactly where Satan
wants us to be! A born-again Christian, reconciled to Jesus through
his death, but not living the Christian life through his resurrected
life! When we find ourselves limping, wavering, or faltering, we are
not productive in advancing God's kingdom. God tells us, "Snap out
of it and make the decision to follow me."

Spiritually, do you find yourself limping, wavering, or faltering? Ask God to give you an undivided heart and trust Christ for
everything.

DAY 190

Following Through

You shall be careful to do what has passed your lips,
for you have voluntarily vowed to the LORD your God
what you have promised with your mouth.
—Deuteronomy 23:23

One of our teachers was having difficulties with classroom management. Upon observing the class for several weeks, I noticed that the teacher had no follow-through as to classroom routines, discipline procedures, and consequences; and the teacher was inconsistent in the enforcement of assignment deadlines. I heard students remark that she never does what she says she will do. She had not established any credibility with the students by not carrying out and enforcing the procedures and processes that she had established at the beginning of the school year.

Do your students know that you will follow through with what you say that you are going to do? When you make an assignment and specify a due date, do you hold that date, if possible? Are you known as a person of your word?

DAY 191

Worthy of Imitation

Remember your leaders, those who spoke to you the word of God. Consider the outcome of their way of life, and imitate their faith.
—Hebrews 13:7

The author of Hebrews challenges us to remember our leaders and to think about the outcome of how they live and to imitate their faith. This passage reminds me that as a teacher, my students are observing (considering) every word that I speak and noticing every action I take; they are cognizant of how I live my life. I pray that my words, mannerisms, and actions all reflect Jesus so that my students and colleagues want to imitate my faith.

Are you the type of godly leader the author of Hebrews speaks?

DAY 192

Knowing about versus Really Knowing

Now Samuel did not yet know the LORD, and the word of the LORD had not yet been revealed to him. And the LORD called Samuel again the third time. And he arose and went to Eli and said, "Here I am, for you called me." Then Eli perceived that the LORD was calling the boy. Therefore Eli said to Samuel, "Go, lie down, and if he calls you, you shall say, 'Speak, LORD, for your servant hears.'" So Samuel went and lay down in his place. And the LORD came and stood, calling as at other times, "Samuel! Samuel!" And Samuel said, "Speak, for your servant hears."

—1 Samuel 3:7–10

This passage reminds me that a big difference lies between a person who *knows about* someone else and a person that *knows* someone else. For example, I know about the US President, but I do not know him personally. I don't have a personal relationship with our president. Beginning in verse 7, we see that Samuel knew about the LORD, but he didn't know the LORD! Samuel knew many facts about the LORD, having been taught and served in the temple from the time Hannah gave him to Eli. Samuel, however, at this point, did not yet have a personal relationship with the LORD.

Many around us know the facts about Christ but do not know Christ! It wasn't until Samuel said to the LORD, "Speak for your servant hears" that the relationship between Samuel and the LORD changed from Samuel knowing about the LORD to Samuel knowing the LORD. Samuel followed Eli's advice and made a willful decision to submit himself to the LORD.

I pray that as I interact with others that I will be sensitive to the difference of whether they know about Christ or that they know Christ as their Savior. When the subject of religion or personal beliefs enters a conversation, are we sensitive and discerning as to where others are regarding their personal relationship with Christ? Be ready to give a personal witness as to your relationship with Christ as your Savior.

DAY 193

Approval by Our Silence

Though they know God's decree that those who practice
such things deserve to die, they not only do them
but give approval to those who practice them.
—Romans 1:32

As I was reading this passage, I was reminded of a Virginia physical education teacher who was temporarily suspended from his position after speaking out against a proposed policy requiring educators to address students by the pronouns that align with their gender identity.

In his address to the school board, the teacher said, "I'm a teacher, but I serve God first, and I will not affirm that a biological boy can be a girl and vice versa because it's against my religion. It's lying to my child, it's abuse to a child, and it's sinning against our God."

I was pleased to hear that the county circuit court judge said that the teacher was exercising his free speech and ordered the school to immediately reinstate him. The ruling remains in effect until a full trial can be held.

In this day of "woke culture," it is sad to see that more and more boards of education as well as big businesses are making requirements of employees that are contrary to the teachings of the Bible. By making these requirements, they implicitly are voicing approval to those who choose to engage in such practices. This caused me to ask this question of myself: "Is my silence when I witness these events interpreted as my approval?" I would hope not. I pray that God will give me the strength to do as this teacher did and voice my disap-proval should ungodly requirements be made by my superiors.

Are you ready to speak a word against ungodly requirements should they be imposed by your superiors?

DAY 194

"Woke"

Be on guard, keep awake. For you do not know when the time will come. It is like a man going on a journey, when he leaves home and puts his servants in charge, each with his work, and commends the doorkeeper to stay awake. Therefore stay awake—for you do not know when the master of the house will come, in the evening, or at midnight, or when the rooster crows, or in the morning—lest he come suddenly and find you asleep. And what I say to you I say to all: Stay awake.
—Mark 13:33–37

So then let us not sleep, as others do, but
let us keep awake and be sober.
—1 Thessalonians 5:6

While visiting a high school, I heard a student declare that he was "woke" to a new concept learned in class. Hearing his comment caused me to realize that a new term had entered our vocabulary.

Isn't it interesting how the word *woke* has entered our vocabulary? People now use this word meaning that they have reached clarity or a new understanding on a subject. We hear this word being used by those that wish to rewrite history or to take facts out of context to support their ideology.

Jesus challenged us to be "woke." He told us that he is returning one day, and no one knows when. He challenges us to "stay awake" and be watchful. Paul reminds us to do the same. This causes me to pause and ask myself, "Is what I am engaged in, in every moment of my life, pleasing to Jesus should he return?"

Are you "woke" to the fact that Jesus is returning? Are you ready?

LIST OF VERSES

Matthew 5:13–16
James 2:17
James 3:1
Proverbs 4:26
Psalm 111:10
Proverbs 9:10
Proverbs 1:7
Proverbs 4:5
Proverbs 4:7
James 3:13–18
Deuteronomy 6:7–9
Luke 12:8,12
James 1:5
Acts 24:16
Ecclesiastes 8:12
Psalm 37:13
1 Kings 17:13b
Proverbs 13:11
Matthew 6:24b
Philippians 4:8
Proverbs 29:20
2 Timothy 4:16–17
James 2:1
Ecclesiastes 9:10
Proverbs 16:3
Colossians 3:23
Colossians 4:6
Proverbs 13:3
Proverbs 4:24
Matthew 12:34b
Luke 12:15
Proverbs 1:23, 33

Proverbs 10:17
Mark 9:42
Proverbs 2:1–5
2 Chronicles 7:14
Proverbs 10:9
Proverbs 17:27–28
Proverbs 29:20
Proverbs 17:27
Proverbs 22:1
1 Samuel 16:18
Proverbs 22:6
Proverbs 29:15
Proverbs 29:17
Proverbs 27:17
Ecclesiastes 7:8
2 Peter 1:5–10
Amos 8:11
Micah 4:5
Joshua 24:15
Daniel 1:8a
Matthew 6:24
Matthew 6:33–34
Daniel 3:18
Philippians 4:6
Micah 7:6
Ephesians 5:16b
Ephesians 6:1
Romans 12:18
1 Corinthians 4:3b–5
Malachi 2:16b
Proverbs 4:23 (NIV)°
Galatians 6:1b
Ephesians 5:15–16
Philippians 2:5
Colossians 3:22
Philippians 2:5–8

Romans 13:14
Philippians 3:17
2 Timothy 3:10
Acts 22:3
Acts 5:34
Acts 5:35–39
1 Timothy 1:7
1 Timothy 2:1–2
1 Thessalonians 5:17
1 Timothy 2:9
1 Timothy 4:7
1 Timothy 4:12, 16
1 Timothy 5:1
1 Timothy 5:22
1 Timothy 5:24
2 Timothy 1:7
2 Timothy 3:1
John 16:13
2 Timothy 1:13
2 Timothy 3:2–5
Philemon 1:6–7
Hebrews 2:1
Hebrews 3:13
Matthew 15:16
Hebrews 5:11–12
Hebrews 5:13–14
1 Timothy 6:6
Philippians 4:11b
Hebrews 13:5
Matthew 12:34b, 36–37
Matthew 15:11, 18–19
Psalm 141:3
Matthew 13:13b–15
John 18:12–14
Matthew 26:57
Acts 4:6

John 18:15
Acts 4:8–13
1 Samuel 3:17
1 Samuel 16:7
1 Samuel 15:3,9,13–23
Genesis 39:6b–20
1 Peter 22b, 23
John 15:4
Judges 6:3–6, 11–12
1 Peter 3:1–4
James 2:18
2 Chronicles 7:14
John 14:26
2 Chronicles 7:14
1 John 1–9
2 Peter 1:12,10,5–8
Matthew 5:16
John 21:15–17
Luke 22:61
2 Peter 1:12–13, 15
2 Peter 1:16–18
Acts 4:13b
2 Peter 1:19–21
Acts 2:16–21
Joel 2:28–32
2 Peter 3:9–10
Luke 22:61–62
Matthew 2:4–5
Matthew 3:12
Matthew 13:28–30
1 John 4:1
Joshua 24:15
James 4:7
Matthew 13:7, 22
Deuteronomy 6:5–9
Proverbs 3:3

1 Corinthians 13:13
1 Peter 4:8
Deuteronomy 12:28:30
Matthew 5:38–42
Proverbs 15:1
Matthew 6:14
Jonah 3:4b
Jonah 4:3b
Jonah 4:5–6
Lamentations 3:40
Psalm 26:2
1 Samuel 16:1
Daniel 2:14, 16
Matthew 22:21
Romans 13:1
1 Samuel 25:2–3, 17b, 25
Psalm 36:11
Job 27:3–6
John 15:13
Exodus 4:2, 3a, 17, 20b
Exodus 35:30–35
Numbers 20:7–13
John 20:25, 27–28
Ezra 8:21–23; 31b
Psalm 119:73b
Colossians 3:2
Psalm 119:93,94,97–104
Ecclesiastes 7:21
Jeremiah 8:20
Micah 7:5
Habakkuk 3:17–19
John 17:15,18
John 20:21
Romans 2:17–24
Romans 3:21, 22a
2 Corinthians 3:3

2 Corinthians 5:9
2 Corinthians 7:9–10
Ephesians 6:4
1 Thessalonians 5:14
Luke 12:2–3
Mark 1:12
Zephaniah 1:12
Revelation 3:16
John 5:17
Mark 2:1–5
Hebrews 5:12
Micah 6:8
2 Peter 10a
2 Peter 14b
Philippians 3:12
Psalm 3:5–6
Matthew 8:28–32
Luke 5:16
Isaiah 40:31
Numbers 6:24–26
Numbers 27:18–20
Deuteronomy 8:17–19
Exodus 4:10
Deuteronomy 32:1–4
Joshua 6:18–19
Joshua 7:1
Joshua 7:20–21a
Joshua 7:7–10 (NIV)
Judges 4:4–10
1 Samuel 1:1–8
1 Samuel 1:9–18
1 Samuel 8:1–3
2 Corinthians 5:20
2 Corinthians 6:3
Daniel 6:3–4
Romans 16:19b

ABOUT THE AUTHOR

Alton Royer, Ph.D, spent thirty-eight years serving in public schools in Louisiana, Oklahoma, and Texas. He taught middle and high school bands. His roles in administration included being the middle school assistant principal, middle school principal, high school assistant principal, high school assistant principal for instruction, and student support administrator.

In retirement, he remains active as a clinician and adjudicator for middle and high school bands and as well as consulting in curriculum areas at the university level. He and his wife, Pam, have two grown children and two grandchildren. Teaching continues to be an ongoing topic as their daughter is married to a college professor, and their son is a music educator. Alton and Pam serve by playing in their church orchestra and are members of the local community band.

THE
MARIPOSA CIRCLE

MARIAN MCMAHON STANLEY

Concord River Press

Concord River Press

ISBN Trade Paperback: 979-8-218-68613-0

First Edition: June 2025

Printed in the United States of America

Read more from
Marian McMahon Stanley

The Immaculate

Buried Troubles

To My Sister Jane Compagnone

What is hidden will be revealed. Nothing will remain unavenged.
— All Souls Requiem

1

THE UNDERGROUND RAILROAD
JENNA – PRESENT DAY CAMBRIDGEPORT

The rosy early morning light was flattering to the old Cambridgeport neighborhood. Perhaps like the effect of pink-hued light bulbs, the ones that ladies of a certain age might use in hopes of softening the appearance of little wrinkles and imperfections. The tall trees on the street were stately in the dim light, the cracked sidewalks and rusted chain link fences airbrushed to an earlier version of themselves.

Memorial Drive would soon start to hum with traffic, but for now only a few random vehicles and city sparrows broke the silence.

An aging black Corolla with a collection of bumper stickers—*My Other Car is a Broom* and *Don't Shop, Adopt Rescues*—made its way up the street, and slowed to a stop in front of a small yellow house in the center of the block. The driver flashed the Corolla's headlights several times before coming to rest.

Inside the house, Jenna Conway checked out the dining room window before heading back to the kitchen where her guests, two teenaged girls, were finishing bowls of Cheerios and bananas at a cluttered table. "Becky's here. Gotta go before traffic," she called.

Both girls, each roughly fifteen, got to their feet. The soft, pale one straightened her off-the-shoulder lace shirt. It revealed both the outline of a black bra and a small wolf's head profile tattoo on her shoulder. She picked up a pink knapsack with a collection of Beanie Boo google-eyed plush toys clipped to its zipper. "Okay, thanks, Jenna," Harper answered.

"Yeah," said Nadia. Darker and thinner, dressed in plain jeans and a black T-shirt over a large long-sleeved white shirt. She leaned on the table as she got up and reached for the unadorned navy duffel bag at her feet. "Yeah, thanks."

"No problem." Jenna adjusted her glasses and hustled to the

1

kitchen sideboard. "We have some other business. Just a minute." She pulled her phone from her jean pocket. "Let me text Becky and tell her we'll be about ten minutes."

She stopped mid-text to look up at the taller, pale girl. "Harper, I smelled smoke in the downstairs bathroom this morning." The girl looked off to the side and set her mouth.

"Yeah, I'm *nervous,* Jenna, for shit's sake."

"I get it. I smoked for years. Would nicotine gum help?" Jenna pulled open a drawer and extracted a pack of gum—tossing it to the girl. "Becky won't let you smoke in the car. She's asthmatic."

Harper took a deep breath. "Okay. Okay. I got it. Thanks."

"What's that?" Nadia pointed to a T-shirt with a Sister Connection logo under Jenna's blue flannel shirt. "What's that about?"

"Where I work," Jenna said over her shoulder on her way across the kitchen. "We match up girls who might need a friend with women who maybe could be that friend." She poured hot coffee into a large *Strong Coffee, Strong Women* travel mug. "You know, just to have an older friend, like a big sister, to do things with, hang with, talk to. You know."

"That sounds nice. We didn't have that where I was."

"Well, they probably did, but the connection just didn't get made."

"Guess not." Nadia inhaled deeply and let out a long breath.

"Maybe someday you will or maybe you'll be somebody else's big sister or friend like that." Jenna held up the travel mug. "For Becky. I ran out of milk, so she'll have to drink it black. But . . ." she reached for the sugar bowl and heaped three large spoonfuls into the coffee. "I know she needs her sugar fix along with her caffeine fix, so maybe this'll do."

"Are you doing this thing, you know, this thing with us, as part of your job?"

Jenna reached for the raisin toast that had popped up in the toaster and paused to look at Nadia. "No, no—this is different, Nadia. Sister Connection, where I work, is a regular nonprofit. We're a separate bunch of volunteers in this work. We connect girls in situations like yours with people who can help get them to better places."

"Girls in situations like ours." Nadia used a sing-song voice and air quotes. The cuffs of her large shirt dropped to show light scars near her wrists. "Girls who are getting pimped out. You can say it, Jenna."

"Well, yeah, honey." Jenna gave the girl a long look. "Yeah, like you. You deserve better. It's not your fault."

"Right."

"It's not."

"Are you a Mariposa?"

Jenna looked at Nadia again for a moment before responding. "Yeah. We try to be pretty low-key, though. Just better and safer that way, right?"

Nadia nodded.

"So, I don't know where you heard that name, Nadia, but can you forget you heard it?"

Nadia cocked her head and raised her eyebrows. "Okay."

Jenna buttered the raisin toast, and wrapped it in a napkin. "Best I can do today for a breakfast sandwich. Okay, right." She clapped her hands twice. "Let's get a move on here." She went into the back hall and pulled down a metal box with a Bruins sticker from the top shelf. She lifted out two burner phones. "You can take these." The girls looked at each other with pleasant surprise.

"You gave yours in, right?" she asked the girls. "The way you're supposed to?"

Nadia, the thinner girl nodded. "Yeah, yeah."

The other girl hesitated.

"Christ, Harper." Jenna held her hand out. "Give it to me."

Reluctantly, in slow motion, the girl reached into the small silver purse clipped to her waistband and took out a purple cell phone with flowered stickers on its case. Jenna grabbed the phone and put it on the counter hard her eyes not leaving the girl's.

"How the hell did that happen? You were supposed to turn your phone in." Jenna put her hand on her forehead. "Did you give them some other phone or just get a new one?"

The girl didn't answer.

"You did, didn't you? Holy shit, I hope you didn't screw us,

Harper." Jenna shook her head and looked to the ceiling for a moment before facing Harper again. "You know this could be dangerous. You know that, right?"

The girl lowered her head, rebuked, but looked sidelong at the purple phone on the kitchen sideboard. Nadia stared at Harper, her dark eyes fierce, reading the other girl's face, her mouth tightening. Harper shifted her feet.

"Stupid. What are you are thinking? What are you THINK-ING?" Nadia shouted. "You called that asshole, didn't you? What's the matter with you, Harper?"

She advanced on the other girl.

"Okay, Nadia, okay." Jenna raised one hand. "Enough. I'll take care of this. Now we really have to hurry. She's right, Harper. Shit. She's right."

Harper put her chin up defiantly, her lower lip trembling, her eyes starting to water. Nadia retreated to the other end of the back hall, staring at Harper with disgust.

"Did you tell him where we are, Harper?" Jenna asked.

Harper shook her head and murmured "No, no."

"She told him," Nadia sprat.

"I did not!" Harper shouted in a fury. "Did not."

She did, thought Jenna. *Shit.* She closed her eyes briefly and let out a long breath.

"We've got to get you out of here pronto."

"Dumber than dumb," Nadia muttered.

Harper whirled to face the other girl. "You just shut up. Just shut up. You're no better than me."

"No, I'm just smarter, that's all."

"Oh yeah, you're so smart." Harper leaned forward and hissed, "At least I don't cut myself."

Nadia lunged at Harper, but Jenna inserted herself between the two girls and faced Nadia.

"Oh, Nadia," she said, looking at the girl's long sleeves. "We have to deal with that, honey."

The girl shrugged and closed her eyes. "I'm okay. No big deal."

"It's not okay and it is a big deal and you need help with it. But

right now, you're both getting out of here."

She leaned down as Harper tried to hide her face. "This is your chance, Harper. He may be nice to you and buy you things, sweetheart, but in the end, you're just a commodity to him." She touched the girl's tattooed shoulder. "He brands you like he would cattle. Don't mess this up for yourself." Then Jenna looked over at Nadia. "Or, for everybody else. Got it?"

Harper nodded. Jenna took the girl's face in her hands. "Hard, I know. We'll get through this. We have to stick together."

She glanced through the hall to the dining room window and saw Becky looking at her watch. Jenna clapped her hands together again. "Okay, Okay. Let's go. Let's go."

Hustling the girls out the front door to the waiting car, Jenna gave each a quick hug. For a moment, she could feel their heartbeats against her, quick and light, like small animals. "Stay safe," she whispered.

She leaned into the open passenger side window, and handed Becky her coffee and raisin toast. "Sorry, had a few things to sort out."

"Always are," responded Becky, a cheerful redhead, with a grin. "Not a problem. We'll make up the time."

"Wait a sec." Jenna took off her blue flannel shirt and threw it in the back seat. "Harper, put this on and cover up that damned tat." Then she turned back to Becky. "You better get going fast. I think we have trouble. Could get ugly."

"Got it." Becky's coffee spilled over the console as she rammed the car into gear and shouted, "Takeoff—seat belts, seat belts. Hang on, sisters."

Jenna blew the old Corolla a kiss as it sped up the street with its bumper stickers and its young passengers—God willing, headed for a better future.

* * * *

Pulling her cell phone out of her pocket as she watched Becky's car round the corner toward Memorial Drive, Jenna called the Mariposa contact line. She got an automated message in Frederica Strauss's calm and measured voice. "Leave a message. Back as soon

as I can. Stay safe."

Dammit.

Jenna took the stairs two at a time to her front door as she left her message. "Jenna Conway in Cambridge. Both my girls have just left with Becky. They're fine, but one girl somehow still had her personal cell and called her pimp. I'm pretty sure she told him where she was. I'm leaving the house for a few days in case there's trouble. Call me as soon as you can."

Jenna hoped Frederica called back soon with some guidance. She was usually prompt in responding, in spite of everything she had going on in her high-powered life. As a Mariposa volunteer, Jenna hadn't been in this kind of exposed situation before. She wasn't sure what to do. She needed Frederica's advice.

2

FREDERICA STRAUSS – BRISTOL LOUNGE FOUR SEASONS HOTEL, BOSTON

"Thanks, Frederica. You probably saved me a fair amount of money today."

The older woman picked up her handbag and, holding it in her lap, leaned back in her chair. "Now, I'm thinking maybe I shouldn't have had a second glass of wine at the dinner party. There was that tech startup guy and a lady who's made money investing in commodities. Before I knew it, with all the chatter at the table, I got excited." She laughed. "Yeah, I got excited and thought, well, maybe I should be putting my money there too."

"Understandable." Frederica Strauss gathered printouts of her client's asset management figures from the table and put them back in her linen portfolio. The activity of the service staff and the conversations in the Four Seasons Bristol Lounge was becoming more muted now that the business breakfast crowd was starting to thin out.

"At my age, what was I thinking, wanting to invest in tech startups and commodities?" The woman brushed a wayward gray blonde bang from her forehead. "You get interested, you know, wanting to be involved in the exciting new things. You don't want to be left out."

"Of course, we all get excited. But some things are much riskier than others, especially the really exciting things."

The woman laughed. "That's why they're really exciting."

Frederica smiled. "True. True. You're better off investing a modest amount in a tech index fund. Then, you can feel you're part of all the excitement without exposing yourself too much. And commodities are too risky, Rachel. Leave that to the big players. Smaller players often get wiped out fast. You've got a good, moderately conservative steady return portfolio. Stick with it for the most part."

"You're right. You're right. As always, Frederica." She sighed.

"Okay—I'm off."

"What's up today?"

"Library—the board's looking at the library branches. They're so busy. We need more of them."

"Absolutely. Well, have a good day, Rachel. I think we have a regular review scheduled in a few weeks."

"Right. See you then, Frederica, and thanks again." She walked away, stopping to chat at another table on her way out.

* * * *

Frederica walked out of the Four Seasons into the bright early spring sunshine. She was satisfied she'd met her client's need to have at least a small window onto the exciting world of tech without exposing herself unnecessarily at this stage of her life. And, thank heavens, she'd saved her from commodities. Good grief.

Frederica's growing portfolio of clients like this one had gained her a partnership in her investment firm last year. Word of mouth, especially among wealthy older widowed or divorced women, had brought her into an enviable position. Things were good and she was beginning to feel comfortable with the increasing visibility success was bringing her.

While she was walking from her office this morning, she'd been startled to see a Business Roundtable banner with her image on it outside the Parker House. The banner advertised the Mover and Shaker award she was about to receive from the Roundtable at its annual dinner next month.

There she was on the banner. Auburn hair pulled back in a stylish roll, her favorite dark green dress setting off signature chunky gold jewelry.

Crossing the Common, she'd called her admin to ask when and how the Roundtable had gotten the picture of her. Her admin proudly reported she'd taken the initiative of sending the image along ("I thought it was the best one") since there had been a deadline to produce the banner and Frederica had been in back-to-back meetings that week. She hadn't wanted to bother Frederica. She was sorry that she'd forgotten to mention it. Was there a problem? She thought the picture looked great and the Business Roundtable had

put the banners up all over the city. Frederica remained quiet and then said they could discuss it when she got back to the office.

Frederica had thought accepting the honor of this award would be helpful to her firm's image, but she hadn't expected quite so much fanfare. She blamed herself for not anticipating publicity. Over the years, she'd maintained a low profile in the city. High visibility came with complications, and she had been succeeding without it. She'd have to think about how to manage this new and unwelcome role.

But, for now, she'd better concentrate on the day ahead. She walked across Boylston Street to the Public Garden. She'd find a bench near the lagoon and check on her cell to see what she had in front of her for the day.

After that, she'd walk over to the Sister Connection offices. A board task force had discussed a merger with another nonprofit also working with vulnerable young people. The executive director at Sister Connection was eager to discuss the recommendations.

The walk down the Commonwealth Avenue Mall to the Massachusetts Avenue offices of the nonprofit would give her the time she needed to plan that complicated conversation. The other nonprofit served both girls and boys. There was a concern in the task force that a merger would dilute Sister Connection's singular focus on girls, so often underserved.

Frederica was glad to find an empty bench near the foot bridge over the lagoon. The paths in the Garden were busy this morning—runners, tourists, and people headed to appointments in Copley Square or shopping on Newbury Street, dog walkers, nannies with sweet toddlers in strollers. An active procession on a sunny day in the city.

Frederica scrolled through the office texts and voicemail list first—nothing looked like it needed urgent attention. A couple of numbers she didn't recognize were left for later. Separately, she reminded herself, she also needed to check on any calls to the dedicated Mariposa line. She was late on that. She'd do that on the walk to the Sister Connection offices. Right now, everything looked under control.

3

JENNA CONWAY – CAMBRIDGE

The house was quiet after the girls had gone. Time to get a move on. Chug a quick cup of coffee, pack up, lock up, and get out of here. Jenna walked to the kitchen, poured herself a cup of coffee and reached for milk in the fridge. Oh right. No milk.

Something else in her coffee. In the dining room she reached under the credenza for her bottle of Jameson Irish. She could use a good slug in her coffee after this complicated start to the day.

Jenna was not entirely surprised when she'd lifted the bottle out to find half the whiskey gone. It confirmed that it wasn't only smoke she'd smelled in the downstairs bathroom. She poured a generous measure of Jameson into her coffee and took out her phone to send Becky a quick text.

FYI. Nadia's a cutter. Harper's a smoker and a drinker. They hate each other. Harper called her pimp before I got her phone away. I think she told him where she was. I'm leaving for a while. Have a wonderful day. Love and kisses. Jenna.

Gulping the last of the coffee, Jenna sprinted upstairs to her bedroom and took a large blue duffel bag from the closet. She threw clothing, shoes, and toiletries for three or four days into the bag, though God knew where she was going to stay or how long. Maybe on the couch at her cousin's in Somerville, at least for now.

On the way through the living room, she tucked her chargers and laptop into the duffel. Pausing at the front door, she went back into the dining room and slipped the bottle of Jameson into the bag.

Minutes later, Jenna was fast-walking down her block when she ran into her older neighbor George Hennessey and his overweight apricot poodle Princess coming around the corner.

"Sorry, George, I'm racing to get somewhere."

"No problem. They give you a quote on your car repair?"

Jenna didn't stop but responded. "Not yet—thanks for your help

getting it to the shop. What would I do without you?"

"You'd be in deep shit, sweetheart, but I'm glad to help out when I can."

She laughed and raised her hand in agreement as she kept her pace. She had long blocks to go and the duffel bag was feeling heavier by the minute. She thought about calling an Uber, but decided she could cover the distance herself faster.

She looked down to check her phone. No response on her message to the Mariposa contact line. Shit. Frederica Strauss was usually very responsive. Of all days for her not to pick up.

Jenna rationalized the danger by telling herself that maybe Harper's pimp had other things going on instead of chasing after two of his underage trafficked girls and that she was overreacting. His operation was based on Route 91, a busy thoroughfare running from New York City to Vermont that invited drug trafficking and prostitution despite law enforcement's best efforts. Maybe he had enough to think about besides her two guests.

On the other hand, Mariposa had been doing some damage to his growing business. Hard not to believe there would be a response at some point. Mariposa needed a game plan.

* * * *

Overall, Jenna was gratified with her Mariposa volunteer work. All she did, as part of a network of women volunteers who helped girls escape a life of trafficking, was give the girls a safe place to stay for the first night or two before moving them on into the system and a structured process with state services. Maybe a small contribution, but it was something. It made a difference, she told herself.

Jenna liked to make a difference. Sometimes it was life-changing, as it was for her when she was a confused and lost seventh grader living in a triple decker with her grandmother in Gloucester. The staff at the Y and the teachers at the O'Maley Middle School and the High School had changed the trajectory of Jenna's life. She knew that a helping hand to a young person in trouble could work, and believed in the work with all her heart.

Now, though, she thought she might have walked herself out on a bridge too far. She was frightened. Harper had called her pimp and

Jenna was afraid for the first time. She'd been warned of the danger during her Mariposa training, but the reality of it was another thing.

Jenna had read somewhere about the different placement of eyes on predators and prey. The eyes of predators like wolves or large cats sit squarely in the front of the skull, looking straight ahead. The eyes of the prey are toward the side of the skull—ensuring a better peripheral vision to catch sight of approaching predators.

Her own blue eyes were kind of wide-set. If they were moved just a little more to the side, perhaps she would look like a cow or a sheep with their wide-spaced eyes. Always watching for those straight-ahead eyed predators. Like Harper's pimp.

Jenna ran her fingers through her dark curls and told herself to get a grip. Another block or two to the T station.

Her cell pinged. "Frederica?" she asked.

"No, it's me, George."

Jenna's heart sank. "Hi, George. No time to talk right now."

"Someone broke into your house."

Jenna stopped.

"What do you mean 'broke in'?"

"What do you think I mean? *Broke in.* The door's open and the lock's broken. Must have been right after you left. I took a chance and looked in before I walked down the street. Didn't look like there was anybody there, but I didn't want to take any chances, you know?'

"Yeah."

"Everything's been thrown around in there. Probably some damage. Looked like someone was pretty mad. You should call the cops."

Jenna thought quickly. Cops. Questions. Complications. She needed to talk to Frederica first. Where the heck was she?

"I will. I will. I'll call from work. I'm almost there," she lied.

"Do you have like an ex with a grudge or something? Somebody looked pretty damned mad."

"No, No."

"Whoever it is might come back. You should stay somewhere else for a while. Is that why you're running down River Street with

that big bag?"

"Yeah, I'll be gone for a few days anyway. I really have to go now."

"Okay, Jenna. I don't know what's going on. I'm worried about you, but I won't push it. You get to a safe place. I'll secure the door. Then, once the cops are done here, I'll straighten things out for you and fix the door. Give them my cell number."

"Thanks, George. You're so good."

"That's what old retired guys do. You can make me a meatloaf and that red velvet cake when you're back."

4

FREDERICA STRAUSS – BOSTON PUBLIC GARDEN

Frederica would ordinarily have scrolled past the email from the Chamber of Commerce reminder about their upcoming CEO Breakfast except for the speaker's name on the subject line.

Except for the speaker's name on the subject line.

The chamber was welcoming a new CEO to town, Alex Massey of the New You national chain of women's fitness clubs.

Alex Massey.

Frederica didn't know how long she stayed on the bench, staring at the sun on the water in the lagoon, the ducks on the little island in the middle, quacking softly. It could have been a minute. It could have been an hour. She could hear the cars along Boylston and Beacon Streets, the footsteps and voices of people passing by, but all seemed muffled and far away.

She ran her fingers slowly along the wooden bench, avoiding splinters and inspecting a name scratched inexpertly in one area. "Kyle." She wondered what had prompted someone to carve their name. Maybe "I'm here, world. I matter."

Frederica returned to the two unknown numbers on her voicemail list. One was a request to speak at an MBA program event. The other was a message from a frighteningly familiar voice from the past. Alex Massey's voice. Frederica looked up at the blue sky while she listened. A light wind blew flurries of wispy white clouds toward the river. Frederica felt a gentle trembling begin in her body, and her breath slowed and deepened.

As she listened to the voicemail, in her mind's eye she saw the buildings, the brownstones around her quaking, the ground opening silently to swallow Frederica Strauss, respected investment advisor with her carefully constructed life and closing over it all as if it had never existed. Like the event horizon on a black hole, the point of no return for falling matter, Frederica Strauss and her invented rich life was

swept into a point of no return.

"Long time, Vickie. Such a big shot now—new name and all. Very classy. Frederica Strauss. I'm a big shot now too, you know." A deep inhaled breath, shaking with anger, *"No thanks to you, bitch."* A pause. "So, I'm riding into the damned city here and what do I see . . . what do I see?" The voice tightened. "What do I see all over the place but pictures of Vickie Czinski, that skinny, ungrateful bitch."

He started to laugh. She remembered that laugh when he was in a mood—when he was in an ugly, dangerous mood. *"All cleaned up and classy—getting a big award—a Mover and a Shaker. That's a funny one, isn't it? I could have given you one of those."

Another silence. *"You might be a mover and a shaker here, honey, but you're still the old Vickie Czinski to me."* She could hear him taking a deep breath as he slowed down. "We have some unfinished business, Vickie. Did you think I'd forget that you and the pack of losers screwed me after all I did for you?" He paused. **"After all I did for you,"** and then more loudly, "I **made** you. I **made** you, Vickie. I **made** you." She could almost see him jabbing the air with his thick fingers.

He drew quiet on the line for a few beats. His voice was low now, close to the phone. "Oh no, I never forget. You're done, Ms. Mover and Shaker. You are so done. In every way, you are so done." After a few moments of silence, when she could hear him breathing, he closed the call.

Frederica sat very still, holding her phone open. The sounds around her stayed muffled for some minutes, until the high-pitched laughter of a duck-feeding toddler near the lagoon broke through and brought her back.

Shutting off her phone, Frederica reached into her bag for a bottle of water. She drank in large gulps before capping the bottle with unsteady fingers and putting it carefully into her bag. Then, with effort and holding to the back of the bench, she rose unsteadily to her feet.

"You all right, ma'am?" A runner stopped and reached for Frederica's arm.

"Yes, yes—just a got up too fast. A little dizzy. Nothing really, thanks."

Unconvinced, the man released her arm but waited.

"Please, I'm fine. Thank you so much for stopping. Very kind of you."

"You should have that checked. Not a good sign."

"Absolutely. I will. Yes, you're right."

He looked at her doubtfully.

"I will. I will. Please." She held her hand up, palm out.

The man shook his head again and threw his hands up. "Okay, okay." He resumed his run slowly, looking back at Frederica several times.

She continued to hold the back of the bench, breathing steadily through her mouth. When she felt she'd regained her equilibrium, she started to walk slowly—dream-like—toward the exit from the Garden to the Commonwealth Avenue Mall.

She needed a plan. For now, she'd carry on, follow her original schedule and walk to Sister Connection offices. The walk would give her time to come up with a rough short-term strategy. She thought she had structured a solid long-term strategy before. New name, new city, new persona. But—it can happen—everything could blow up.

She felt the fresh, slightly damp spring breeze on her face. She'd dealt with ugliness before. She could deal with it again. She might have a new public persona, but she was still at heart the tough and smart Vickie Czinski from the Slopes. Still Vickie.

5

BUILDING A STRATEGY

As she walked the path among trees on the Commonwealth Avenue Mall, Frederica continued to feel a light tremble in her body and, as much as she tried to moderate her breathing, she was still breathing in short, shallow bursts.

She could sense her mind operating on another frequency—a higher frequency. Almost a light whirring and buzzing in her brain as she walked. A gamma state—alert and focused.

She had to think smart now. Was this situation salvageable? Maybe she could finesse it –make a deal with Massey. He didn't need his past brought up either. Frederica caught herself up short. Ridiculous. Alex Massey didn't forget betrayals and he didn't do deals with people who crossed him. If he could, he destroyed people who crossed him.

Okay, maybe she could be realistic, just accept the fact that it might be too late to save life here as she knew it. Pity. It suited her. She loved it all. Working with her clients on investment decisions that stabilized their lives. Building out her mission to help vulnerable young girls with the Sister Connection and, separately, her personal mission with the Mariposa Circle – focused on a population of trafficked girls.

And then there was all the rest. The old house in Charlestown—such a wreck when she'd bought it, keeping close ties with her young Sister Connection mentee Antoinette Mackey—now a sophomore at Howard, and deepening her relationship with the very interesting Boston Police Department Detective Abe Leone she'd met at a homeless shelter fundraising dinner.

Thinking about Abe stopped Frederica. Maybe it was a good thing she hadn't become even more deeply involved with him, though that possibility tugged at her heartstrings. He might have been the one.

She wanted him to be the one. Now she guessed she'd never know. She'd been foolish to permit herself to set down roots in Boston when she knew that at any time someone from her past could come and rip it all up. Thinking about how content and maybe careless she'd become, she got angry at herself.

Her steps were getting steadier, the sun felt warm on her face. Still a light vibration to her body, though moderating. Frederica started to reconsider the situation. She couldn't be sure if her new life was salvageable but, just maybe, with the right strategy it might be.

Right now, she needed to buy time. She needed time to figure this all out. She could create some plausible excuse to go away for a while, close up shop temporarily, disappear, make some space. Maybe Massey wouldn't make a move if she weren't here in the city. At least her going might delay any move and, meantime, she would have a better chance of being physically safe.

Out of nowhere, in the midst of this worried strategizing, Frederica started to chuckle. She couldn't help herself. Unbelievable. Those damned Mover and Shaker banners with her picture all over the city. Could there be worse timing?

Somehow, laughing at the ridiculousness of that circumstance calmed her down. She'd met so many challenges. This one was gigantic, but perhaps not entirely beyond her. No. Not entirely beyond her skills to solve if she were smart and brave.

And maybe ruthless.

Ruthlessness was the only way to deal with someone like Alex Massey and there was too much at stake now to do anything else. Her survival or his.

* * * *

Once Frederica had reached that decision, her nerves calmed and now, she could concentrate on the immediate tasks at hand. A quick stop by Sister Connection offices to give the executive director, as kindly as she could, the bottom line on the proposed merger – that the board was unlikely to support it. Better to do that in person. She was unable to discuss it further today. A family emergency, but another member of the task force would follow up.

Then, she'd take a cab back to her offices on State Street. Find one of the partners and have a quiet conversation about her family emergency—an old aunt in the Midwest, her godmother, all alone in her last days. Frederica had to be out for a while. She couldn't say exactly how long she would be gone, but she'd make sure nothing fell between the cracks. Would someone at the firm be kind enough to attend the Mover and Shaker Dinner and accept her award on behalf of the firm?

She'd alert her admin of her family emergency, quickly sort through her projects and prepare a list of assignments to be handled by various staff. She would be taking no calls or communications while she was out. Oh, and would her admin please call the Business Roundtable to say that she regretted, with this family situation, she would not be able to attend the Movers and Shakers Dinner. She was sure that someone senior at the firm would be pleased to attend in her stead.

Antoinette Mackey, the young woman she mentored through the Sister Connection, would still need some support when she came home from Howard at the end of the term. Antoinette had landed a plum summer intern job in community development in the mayor's office. It would be helpful for her to have an experienced mentor to call on, so she could make the most of that assignment. Maybe Frederica would ask someone to pitch in and be available for Antoinette over the next few weeks. She knew the perfect person for that assignment. Maybe she could make that happen.

And Abe. What to do about Abe? For now, the old aunt story would have to do for Abe too. She had to stay consistent, avoid getting too ornate. Not great, and he probably would not be fully convinced of her story about a dying aunt in the Midwest, but she would finesse it as best she could.

Frederica recognized with sudden clarity that she may not be able to navigate the Abe thing. She may have to lose Abe. A wave of sadness washed over her.

Frederica remembered standing at Halibut Point—the rocky point at the end of Cape Ann, north of Boston—on a recent weekend

trip with Abe. It had been a chilly early spring day. She still remembered the warmth of Abe next to her as they stood close together on the rocks with the waves crashing below.

Abe had watched the cormorants on the rocks, spreading their wings to dry, though the sun was weak. "Did you know the name cormorant means *sea raven* in Latin?"

"No. I didn't know that."

"Of course, they aren't really ravens. Back then, almost all large black birds were referred to as ravens."

Frederica had smiled and tucked her arm under his. "I love that you know these things."

"That's good. Useless information but interesting," He sighed. "Where's Agamenticus? You can usually see it from here."

They both looked out to the sea then, searching through a light fog for Mount Agamenticus in Maine on the horizon, before finally giving up to drive to Farnham's Famous Clams in Essex for two orders of clams, fries, and coffee.

They'd sat at a wooden picnic table looking over the expanse of green, undulating grass of the Essex marshes reaching to the back of Crane beach. The pages of Abe's tattered and well-used birdwatching guide, bookmarked to the shore birds section, fluttered in the breeze in the middle of the worn table.

"You ever climb Mount Katahdin?" he asked.

"No, where's that?"

"Up in Maine in Baxter State Park. You go to Millinocket, outside Presque Isle. It's north, almost at the New Brunswick border. Beautiful old mountain," he continued. "You'd love the view from the top—endless pine trees. Gorgeous. And the Knife Edge walk near the top would be a piece of cake for you."

"I'd like that."

"Nice B and Bs up there. Presque Isle has some pretty good restaurants too."

"Sounds like fun."

"Well, let's do that."

"Okay. It's a deal."

And she'd thought it was a deal. She thought they were a deal.

Now, a dream not likely to be. She couldn't see the Abe thing ever rolling out in a good way, given the bombshell that had just been dropped in her life. It would be hard even for a long-term relationship to handle, never mind one that was just a few months old.

Frederica stopped herself again. She had no time to linger on these thoughts, and she couldn't handle that now anyway. She had too many other, immediate, practical things to figure out in a short time. Her mind was buzzing, working on multiple tracks—multiple calculus programs running through her head. She couldn't linger on Abe today.

Besides, it hurt.

By the time she got to Mass Ave, Frederica had a workable rough plan. To be refined, of course, but workable for now.

With a jolt, she realized she hadn't picked up any messages left on the dedicated Mariposa line that morning. She was so late checking in. It was important to make sure nothing went off the rails with the Mariposa activities. A lot could go wrong if not caught right away.

6

JENNA CONWAY – HOMELESS IN BOSTON

The large bag on Jenna's shoulders couldn't be more awkward—bouncing and banging as she fast-walked toward Central Square, away from who-knows-what danger. She adjusted the straps and forged on with ragged breaths, trying to concentrate on what had happened – a threatening break-in at her small house—and what could be next.

The T ride to the Mass Ave stop was next. Then, the safety of the Sister Connection offices. She'd use the stairs when she got to the lobby. No elevator. She couldn't handle the thought of talking to anyone yet. She had to get her head together. Think it through when she got to the office. Time to stay calm. Why was Frederica not returning her calls?

She'd try the number again before work. She needed some support here. There would never be a quiet moment at the office for a call like this and there was no privacy on the T. Better do it now. She stopped at the First Baptist Church just before Central Square, pulled out her cell and leaned against the stone wall, breathing heavily and starting to hiccup. She had to pause to get her now shaking hands under control before she punched speed dial.

Shit. Voicemail. That maddeningly calm, measured voice saying "Can't talk now. Leave a message. We'll get back soon. Stay safe."

Jenna closed her eyes, willing herself not to cry. She left a breathless message, interrupted by wet hiccups. "This is Jenna Conway in Cambridge again. My house was been broken into and ransacked. I'm on my way to work now and will try today to find a place to stay until I get some guidance from you. I didn't report the break-in to the police yet. Was this the right thing to do? Please get back to me."

She'd done all that she could do. She closed the phone and headed for the subway.

The railing down to the subway felt cool and the air smelled a little dank. The crowd was moving in its thick, early morning daze. It felt good to be with so many people. Anonymous, but some kind of community, like a bee hive. She liked bee hives. All that busyness, with purpose and well-defined roles. A coherent universe. Here at the Central Square MBTA station, fellow humans moving together, bumping into each other, sitting together wordlessly, just . . . together. Jenna found it comforting.

A busker stood just inside the turnstile – a long-haired violinist in a blue dress playing a Corelli piece. Jenna thought she would weep as the music washed over her. She wasn't all that spiritual a person but this had to be some kind of sign. She fished in her pocket for a dollar and dropped it gratefully into the open violin case.

Jenna didn't usually get a seat on the crowded subway car, but she did today. She sank heavily into the seat, arranged her bag under her legs and gave the man across the aisle who'd been watching her a tentative smile. He gave her a long look in return before moving his eyes down to the neck of the Jameson bottle protruding from the blue duffel bag. He then glanced at her again before turning to his iPhone.

Swell. Well, better here than in the office. She tucked the neck of the whiskey bottle into a sneaker and buried both at the bottom of the duffel bag, to the amusement of the teenaged boy beside her.

She sat back in her seat.

Breathe. Just breathe, she told herself. Jenna felt her heart pounding and her body quivering. She was surprised the people around her didn't notice the shaking, like a tiny personal earthquake. With some determined breathing discipline—feet flat on the floor, eyes closed—she managed to bring herself to a fragile equilibrium by the time she got to the Mass Ave T stop.

The exit stairway was jammed with commuters and the large duffel bag didn't make the climb any easier. She craved another strong cup of coffee. Probably a bad idea when she was already so hopelessly wired, but she needed what she needed right now.

At the Dunkin Donuts on Mass Ave, Jenna maneuvered her way

up to the counter through throngs of students from the Berklee College of Music, many with instrument cases. She felt a small flash of triumph on an unsettling day when she emerged from the crowd a few minutes later holding a large coffee with two shots of espresso.

"Need help with that?" The street person who stationed himself every morning at the entrance of the Dunkin Donuts staggered to his feet from a grungy Red Sox blanket he'd arranged on the sidewalk. He reached for her bag.

"No, no." She moved quickly aside to protect her bag and her coffee. Then, she hesitated, placed her coffee down to reach in her pocket for the change from her purchase.

Jenna dropped the change into the empty Dunkin cup on his blanket saying, "You know, I keep telling you that this is a lousy place for you to collect. Nobody has any money in this crowd. I mean, look around. Nobody's fighting with you over this spot."

"Yeah. See, these are my kind of people." He sat heavily on the blanket again. "I'm okay, sweetheart." He raised his eyes and a grimy hand with broken nails in benediction. "God bless. I'm good. Take care of yourself."

"Thanks, you too." Jenna was surprised to find her eyes filling as she turned away.

Coffee in hand, she reached her building and rushed through the small lobby, her head down to avoid conversation. She entered a dimly lit stairwell at the side of the lobby and had just started up when she saw a figure further up on the stairs.

7

STAIRCASE CONVERSATION AND FOLLOWUP

"Wait up, Freddie."

Cell pressed to her ear, Frederica paused in her climb up the four flights to Sister Connection offices and turned to see Jenna Conway behind her, struggling with a large bag.

Frederica closed her phone, paused for a moment, gathering strength. Her mind was clouded with her own personal dangers, but she needed to respond and deal in the moment. And she did.

She rushed down the stairs. "Just listening to your call, Jenna. God, I'm so sorry—it was crazy today—of all mornings." She picked up Jenna's duffel bag. "Let me take this for you. I didn't have a chance to pick up messages until now. It must have been awful for you." She reached for Jenna in an awkward stairwell hug.

"Yeah." Jenna's voice wavered. "It was awful. Thank God the girls were gone and I had just taken off. Could have been much worse." She closed her eyes briefly, imagining "the much worse". "What should we do, Freddie?"

Frederica hoisted the duffel bag straps to her shoulder. Complication after complication. Get a grip.

"I need to think." She headed back up the stairs before responding. "Okay. Let's see. First, call Becky and Social Services up on the North Shore to make sure the girls are okay. We'll need their help to get a protection plan for the girls."

"You want me to handle that?" Jenna was working hard to keep up with Frederica.

"Yes, please. Then, I'm going to call Abe."

"Abe? Won't that get complicated?"

"Abe is a good cop. He knows from complicated and BPD has a good relationship with the Cambridge force. They'll call you, check the house out, make a full report, and then keep an eye on it when

25

you're away."

"Where am I going to be away?"

"You can be at my house. I have to go out of town for a while. You can stay at my place while we sort this out."

"What do you mean sort out?"

"Their pimp is that guy who runs his girls along Route 91, right?"

"Yeah. He's based in Springfield."

"As a start, he'll probably get a visit from the local or state police. He's already on their screen. It's impossible to tie him or his people directly to your house ransack but it should put him on notice. For now."

They'd reached the fourth-floor offices of Sister Connection. Frederica gestured toward the corner offices further down the hall and gave Jenna the duffel bag. "I have to do a quick stop down there. I'll be by on my way out. In just a few minutes."

Before turning to go, she gave Jenna a quick shoulder squeeze. "I know it's tough but we'll deal with it. We'll make a plan."

* * * *

Jenna walked slowly over worn carpeting down the corridor to her cubicle. The Sister Connection offices, located above Daddy's Junky Music Store, while well kept, bore all the markings of a frugally run nonprofit. Still, there was color. Lots of color. Artwork and banners by the girls and the Sisters and photos of various group activities covered the walls. Large, dusty windows looked out on a vibrant Mass Ave filled with students milling on the sidewalks and jaywalking in the traffic.

Jenna threw the duffel bag under her desk, and placed her large coffee on one of the few clear spots on her cluttered desk. She leaned back in her chair and closed her eyes. *Breathe.*

Having Frederica in the mix relieved some – though certainly not all—of her anxiety and went a long way toward giving Jenna some confidence that this scary situation could be managed. But not entirely. It was still pretty damned unnerving.

The phone rang. *Oh God, I can't stand it. I'm going to cry. Let it go to voicemail while I get my act together.*

But she couldn't let it go to voicemail. She had clients, sometimes in delicate situations. No slacking off, even if her own world seemed suddenly weird and dangerous. She opened her eyes, ran her fingers through her hair and picked up her phone.

"Hi Jenna. It's George Hennessey." Her old neighbor.

Oh, no. I hope it's not another break in.

"Hi George."

"Do you want me to pick up your mail and bring it to you every few days at work?"

"No, no, that's okay."

"It's no trouble. You're just across the river and I do my errands in town anyway."

"Okay," she surrendered. "Yes, okay, that would be helpful. Thank you, George."

"I could bring you some of my Irish bread sometimes too."

"No, No, that's okay."

"It's my mother's recipe. She used to say that with a hot cup of tea and good butter, it can solve the problems of the world."

Jenna didn't respond, even though she knew he was trying to be kind.

"And, if you don't mind my saying so, you seem pretty shaky. It can't hurt."

Jenna rubbed her forehead and looked up at the ceiling.

"Yes, that would be lovely. Thank you, George. I have to go now."

"Right. You take care of yourself, Jenna."

"Yes, yes. Goodbye, George."

Jenna closed the call and continued rubbing her forehead. She could feel a migraine coming on.

8

A PLACE TO STAY

Frederica stopped by Jenna's cubicle a short time later. She took several folders off the single black plastic chair in front of Jenna's desk and put them on a crowded credenza before she sat down.

She smiled at Jenna and scanned the pictures on the cubicle walls. A large one recorded an expedition with the Sister Connection group, kayaking on the Essex River. Frederica and her mentee Antoinette Mackey stood beside their kayak, grinning at the camera.

"That was a good day." Frederica brushed some strands of hair from her brow and straightened in her chair. "I talked to Abe."

"He's okay with our having helped the girls?"

"He's not entirely comfortable, but he's okay. He's a reasonable guy."

"Good." Jenna nodded. "What will happen about the break in?"

"Cambridge Police are going to do a check on the house. Anybody there to let them in?"

"I think the lock has been broken and they can get right in. But I have a neighbor with a key if they need it. He's going to clean up for me."

"Okay. Just don't let him do anything before the police give it a good going over."

"Okay. I'll call them and I'll call George to let him know. Thanks."

"You get in touch with Becky and Social Services?"

"Yeah. They're on it, working with the Gloucester and Lynn Police."

"Good." Frederica reached into her jacket pocket and took out a set of keys, which she put on Jenna's desk. "Charlestown. 140 Winthrop Street. Make yourself at home. There's some construction going on in the house, but it shouldn't bother you too much.

Nice guys. And it's not a bad idea to have them around while you're there. I'll have a little extra security there too."

Jenna looked at Freddie.

"Won't hurt. Anyway, I've got to go now."

"Okay. Thanks, Freddie."

"Not a problem. Have to stick together here." She stood, leaned over and, resting her hands on Jenna's shoulders, she faced her. "That's how we survive."

* * * *

After Frederica left, Jenna took a long and thoughtful look at the group picture from the Essex kayak excursion. Frederica in the front row, with that mass of reddish-brown hair, a broad white-toothed smile, and those direct close-set green eyes. A wave of irrational relief swept over Jenna. Maybe Frederica was not a predator but she was nobody's prey.

9

MORE THAN SHE HAD BARGAINED FOR

Maybe Jenna had been reckless to sign on to support the Mariposa Circle. She certainly had a full career at Sister Connection, helping match young girls in challenging situations with women mentors and working to ensure that the relationship had the best chance of succeeding.

But this – the Mariposa work—this was important work too. And urgent. These girls were often in desperate straits.

It was odd the way it started. She'd been hiding out at the Au Bon Pain on Mass Ave, working on her laptop. She had a report due the next day and was unable to get anything done in the office with all the interruptions. So she'd decamped to Au Bon Pain, bought a large coffee and croissant, and settled down at a small side table to work.

A little later, deep in thought, she was startled by a bump to her table. Opposite her stood a tall, fit woman in workout clothes. She was of indeterminate age, anywhere between 35 and 45, with a long blonde braid. The woman pulled a chair out and moved to sit opposite Jenna. The tables were small, perhaps two and a half feet wide. Jenna's cup of coffee, laptop, and papers took up almost the entire surface. She was thinking it was pretty intrusive of this woman and wondering if she should tell her there was no room for her. Or maybe if she should move her own stuff and sit at one of the other unoccupied tables. It would have been rude but Jenna had to get this project done.

"Hi, Jenna."

Startled, Jenna asked, "Do I know you?"

"Not yet, but I'm told you'd be the right person to join an initiative some of us are involved in."

"I'm not looking for a job."

"Not a job. Something bigger."

Oh joy, Jenna thought. *A hard-core political activist or some kind of religious extremist.*

"Not interested. I'm already run ragged between my job and too many volunteer commitments. " Jenna pointedly started to look at her papers and to type on her laptop, ignoring the woman. "Excuse me. I'm on deadline here."

The woman sat quietly before saying, "I'm Alyssa Thomas."

Jenna nodded without responding.

"We work to rescue local young girls being prostituted."

At that, Jenna stopped working. Supporting young girls was Jenna's life's work. That's how she'd ended up at Sister Connection. She had closed her laptop then. Annoyed but curious, she leaned forward on her elbows and looked at the woman. "Talk."

And Alyssa did. She told Jenna about a group that was founded by women who had been trafficked in their youth and had escaped to build new lives. They called themselves the Mariposas ("after the butterfly") and the group was called the Mariposa Circle.

"So, this is like a nonprofit?"

"It's not a registered nonprofit now. It could be in the future but right now we work informally with social workers in the state system."

"Who funds this?"

"Some of the original Mariposas did very well."

"What happens to these girls after they're rescued?"

"With a lot of help, most of them are able to reinvent themselves. Some don't make it. Maybe too troubled, too far gone or addicted—and they go back to their old lives. But, the rest, with a ton of counseling and support, they make it. They get jobs, they go to school. Maybe even talk about getting married, starting a family someday. Making a real life." Alyssa Thomas inhaled deeply before continuing. "It's not an easy road and they can never get back what's been taken from them. They'll always be shadowed by that pain and confusion, but they absolutely can build another, better life."

And so, after more conversations in coming days, Jenna's work with the Mariposa Circle began. It had been two years now. The work was often emotionally hard, but with her Sister Connection career during the day and the Mariposa activities, Jenna felt she was

making a real difference in these girls' lives. Single, in her late twenties, a little more than a decade older than the girls, she could understand them. Even if sometimes, perhaps because she'd been an only child, an old soul raised by her grandmother and a little matronly even as a child, she knew the girls thought she was older. That was just fine with Jenna.

Yes, she was gratified by her work. But now, on this morning, she could feel a fluttering of fear in her chest, like a small trapped bird. She felt . . . what? Vulnerable. Yes, that was the word. She felt exposed and vulnerable. Had she been naive and foolhardy to sign up for something so close to the edge of danger – so close to the edge of sex trafficking operations? What was she thinking?

10

JENNA TO CHARLESTOWN

The headache she'd had for most of the day had gone but not wandered far when Jenna left work early that afternoon.

She'd been off-kilter all afternoon, lost in a fog of anxiety. She stayed in the office for lunch, eating something stale and tasteless from the vending machine, and then checking the people around her constantly on her way to the T station when she left the office for the day.

She'd dropped her Charlie Card transport pass when she entered the turnstile in the station and felt on the verge of weeping as she scrambled to find it on the ground. An older woman nearby looked at her with concern, perhaps ready to ask if she could help. Jenna averted her eyes.

Jenna knew she looked wrecked. A poor soul on the cusp of falling apart, or maybe already falling apart, she couldn't bear a stranger's intrusive kindness right now.

* * * *

She caught the Orange Line, a straight shot to Charlestown and the Bunker Hill Community College stop. From there, a walkable distance to Freddie's Winthrop Street address. Still, despite years of hiking, Jenna was not sure that she was equal to walking the distance and climbing the steep incline on Winthrop Street, especially with her damned duffel bag.

She picked up a small spinach and feta pizza and a diet coke at the Domino's in the Bunker Hill Mall, and tucked both into the netting on the side of her bag. Then, she surrendered and caught a cab at Thompson Square.

The cab climbed up a steep hill and then drove a few blocks to the right. The Monument—a tall and impressive plain granite obelisk commemorating an important battle of the Revolution—loomed ahead.

The green around the monument was quiet on this late afternoon. A couple of park rangers and a few tourists stood at the base of the obelisk. Groups of children and dogs played on the green, Frisbees flying. A small white dog caught a ball thrown by a tall, muscular bald man in a blue sweatshirt, and then ran back to receive effusive praise and pats. Looking at the scene, Jenna could almost feel the tension leaving her body. So peaceful and normal.

Freddie's house was midway down Winthrop Street from the Monument, a handsome old house painted sage green with a cream trim. A few people sat on benches in the small, park across the street. In front of the house, a short steep set of stairs, bracketed by blue ceramic planters filled with shrub roses and lavender, led to a heavy maroon door. At the side of the house, she could see a fence around a patio and another entrance with long French doors. This was certainly better than her original plan of sleeping on her cousin's couch in Somerville.

* * * *

Jenna climbed the stairs to the house and had almost reached the top when the front door opened and a crew of workmen came through.

"Sorry, she's not home," the first man out the door said.

"Hold on, Conor. Freddie has a guest coming to stay a while," corrected a burly man coming to the entrance. He walked down a few steps and extended a work-hardened hand to Jenna. "Matty. Matty Cronin."

"Thanks. Jenna Conway," she responded as she took his hand.

A couple of other workmen passed them, nodding to her in greeting and saying their goodbyes to Matty Cronin, who Jenna gathered was the foreman or crew chief.

"See you in the morning, Matty," the first man called back, smiling at Jenna rather than Matty.

"Be on time and be awake, for Christ's sake, Conor," Matty responded.

The other man didn't turn around but laughed and raised his hand in acknowledgment.

Matty turned to Jenna. "Okay, now, Jenna Conway. Let's get

you settled."

He had a kind, angular face, unruly black hair, and startlingly bushy eyebrows—like small woodland creatures, thought Jenna, smiling. Something about him made her feel safe.

He picked up her bag and commented that his son's hockey equipment bag felt lighter. "You have a body in here or what?" he asked.

"Oh, you know, I had to pack everything so fast, I had no time to think. I have my laptop, some books and probably have four or five pairs of shoes in there, but just one top."

"You got trouble?"

Jenna hesitated and shrugged. "Yeah, I guess I do."

"Nice of her to offer you a place while she's gone."

"Yeah, I was really surprised. Kind of a life saver." *Maybe in fact*, thought Jenna.

"She's a class act in my book. I guess she's in the big leagues in town, but you'd never know it. Down to earth, you know? Doesn't think she's better than anyone else and would do anything to help you."

"That's the truth."

"Well, you're in good hands with Freddie. Johnny and Alyssa just got here today too—so you shouldn't have any problems."

"I don't think I know them."

"Oh, I thought you might. Close friends of Freddie's from a long time ago, I guess. Anyway, they just came to stay for a while." He turned to face Jenna. "Johnny seems like a really nice guy to me, but not too many people would want to mess with him. Or with Alyssa, for that matter. You know what I mean?"

"I'm not sure I do. "

"Well, never mind."

This information about the other guests in Freddie's house was probably supposed to make her feel more secure, and it did. But, not for the first time, she wondered what she had gotten herself into. What she did wonder about for the first time was Freddie's life "from a long time ago" with friends "that no one wanted to mess with".

Matty started up the stairs. "You're in the guest room toward the back. It's nice. You look out on the park."

Before heading up the stairs, Jenna peeked into the front parlor. A beautifully appointed room in greens, gold, and ivory with a lush oriental carpet, floor to ceiling bookcases and long windows. But she was more taken, stunned really, by the large oil painting over the carved marble fireplace. An enormous butterfly—orange and black. The image wasn't graceful, delicate or pretty. This being was a triumphant and glorious spirit, a triumphant crescendo dominating the room.

"This way, Jenna."

"I'm coming," Jenna responded, deep in thought.

* * * *

On the way up the stairs, Jenna asked, "Do you know how long Freddie's gone for? She didn't say."

"Beats me. She said she wasn't sure herself but she'd be in touch, and she prepaid me for the work we're doing. Like I said, a class act."

They reached the upstairs hall when a storm of white fur and four little racing feet came charging up the stairs. "Sorry", a deep voice downstairs called. "Got away. He's too fast for me."

"Not a problem, Johnny. He'll be looking for Freddie."

The "he" was an energetic West Highland Terrier who was charging into what Jenna assumed was the master bedroom. "Not here, Archie. Sorry." The dog immediately barged past him and started to check the other rooms.

The last room he checked was the guest room Jenna would be sleeping in. Matty put the duffel bag on the bed and then crouched down to pet the dog. "Not here, buddy, but—look, a new friend."

He lifted the dog up to face Jenna. She stretched her hand out for Archie to sniff and then stroked him. The dog leaned his head into her hand.

"I think you've made a friend, Jenna Conway. You're not allergic or anything, are you?" Jenna shook her head. "You like dogs?"

"Oh yes."

"Good."

Matty put the dog down. "You know, the one who's been asking the most about what's going on with Freddie is Abe."

"Really?"

"Yeah. They're kind of a thing, you know. Or becoming a thing. Made for each other."

"I figured, but I don't really know much about it, other than they go out."

"Yeah, pretty regular now. He's been around here a lot. Anyway, I guess she called him too this afternoon to tell him she was going out of town for a while. Abe's being chill about it, but I'm pretty sure he doesn't buy the dying old aunt out in the Midwest malarkey. He's got good cop instincts. Not too much gets by Abe Leone. So, now he's poking around a little." Matty walked to two large windows and pulled up the shades. "Nice view, huh."

It was. "Yeah, it is," Jenna said.

"So," he continued, "I don't know what's going on, but I hope it doesn't screw up what could be a good thing for both of them. Great people—so smart, so good, the both of them." He shook his head. "Okay, gotta go. I'm talking too much. I see you've got your dinner." He pointed to the pizza and diet Coke in the netting on the side of the duffel bag.

"I'm all set. To tell you the truth, I'm exhausted. It's been quite a day."

"I figured."

"Thanks. I'm going to just eat right here and collapse."

"Good plan. You want me to leave his nibs?" he asked looking at Archie.

"Oh yes, he's probably good company."

"That he is, though he can get noisy. We call him the Speaker of the House. Anyway, 'night—see you tomorrow."

"'Night, Matty. Thanks very much"

"My pleasure, Jenna."

Jenna shared her pizza with Archie and took a small bowl from the bedside table to fill with water for him. That night, he seemed content to sleep at the end of the bed with her.

She went into a deep, uneasy sleep, interrupted once in the middle of the night by a strange dream about a large butterfly hovering outside the window.

11

PROTECTION

Jenna woke up the next morning later than usual, feeling unsettled and anxious. She took a moment to enjoy the view of the small green park and to stroke Archie, who greeted her enthusiastically. Nevertheless, the troubling events of the day before were still top of her mind.

She would be late for work unless she got going soon. She could hear the construction crew already starting their day, replacing the old horsehair plaster on the third floor. She took a quick shower and dressed, with the dog close behind her every step. Clumsy in her anxiety and distraction, Jenna was afraid she would trip over him. Her nerves were frayed. She could only hope she could get through the work day and that the situation would resolve in some way.

Jenna opened the door to the hall to the comforting smell of fresh perking coffee. Why did that smell always make her feel that she could handle whatever the day threw at her? Well, maybe not everything, but enough. She started down the stairs. Behind her, an impatient Archie barreled down the stairs, barking as he went.

Matty Cronin leaned over the railing on the third floor, wearing a mask and dropping heavy cloths against the plaster dust around him. "Hey, Jenna. Watch for Conor on the stairs."

She turned to see Conor with two large buckets and a mask hanging from his neck. "Sorry, no way not to be clumsy with this stuff."

Jenna hadn't intended to but she noticed his hazel eyes. Just for a moment. "Thanks, Conor." He smiled and seemed pleased she'd remembered his name.

Jenna walked into a spacious kitchen at the back of the house. Centered in the kitchen was a heavy round maple table and captain's chairs, a cozy grouping that seemed incongruent with the kitchen's high-end appliances, sleek fittings, and granite counters, but somehow it worked.

"Coffee?"

She turned and saw a Dorchester Building Supply T-shirt stretched across the muscles of a big man's broad back as he washed coffee cups and placed them in a wooden draining rack. He turned and came toward her, extending his hand. "You must be Freddie's friend Jenna Conway."

"And you must be Freddie's friend Johnny." She realized that this was the man she had seen throwing the ball to Archie up at the Monument green when she arrived in the taxi last night.

"Right. Johnny Thomas. Pleased to meet you." He turned to the coffee pot. "Almost done here."

"I'm so late. I can't wait—but thanks. And, I'm sorry, I didn't have a chance to take the dog out."

"Don't worry, I'm at his service. And the coffee's just about done." The coffee pot stopped its perking. "Just in time." He reached for the drying rack and picked up a Bruins travel mug. "You can take it with you." The cup was lost in his large hands. "You like the Bruins?"

"I guess."

"You guess? Well, I'll let you use it anyway. It'll give you a little street cred walking through the 'Town. "

"Thanks." Jenna smiled as she took the cup and started to leave.

"Alyssa's waiting outside. She'll be with you on your way to work. I'll be with you on your way home."

Jenna felt a wave of relief. "Really? That's very nice of you."

"Glad to do it. Frederica's orders."

Jenna cocked her head. "Are you Mariposas?"

"Oh yeah. The originals, honey. The originals."

"You were friends from a long time ago?"

"Oh yes, long time ago in another world. We're a good team. I like working with her." He was quiet for a moment. "We won't go into that now. You'll be late for work, and Alyssa will be mad at me for keeping you."

He glanced toward the hall. "Oh God, I'm in trouble. Here she comes. I'd know those footsteps anywhere."

A tall, fit woman with a long stride and a thick blonde braid

came around the corner. She grinned, "Yes, I will be mad, Johnnio. Let's get this girl on the road or there'll be no seats on the T." She put her hand out to Jenna. "It's me again. Alyssa. Alyssa Thomas. The one who originally recruited you about a year ago when you were trying to get some work done at Au Bon Pain on Mass Ave, and I as a real pain in the ass. Wouldn't stop bothering you."

They both laughed. Jenna extended her hand. "Hello, Alyssa. Good to see you again."

"Same here. Let's get a move on now." Alyssa turned to go.

"Okay, ready." Jenna held up the coffee cup to Johnny. "Thanks again. Go Bruins."

On their way out of the kitchen, Johnny called to her, "Jenna." She turned back. "Freddie, Alyssa and I can handle this. Freddie knows how to take care of business and so do we."

He picked up a Sox cap from the counter, slipped it over his balding, close-cropped blonde hair and picked up a leash on a hook near the door. He snapped the leash on Archie and opened the door. "Come on, dude. Let's go water the monument."

12

BUTTERFLY ON THE BOSTON WATERFRONT

The butterfly sat lightly on the man's half-opened mouth, orange and black wings with their stained-glass pattern spread wide, tiny claws perched on the man's full bottom lip. The polka dots along the side of the butterfly's wings continued over its head where two antennae quivered in the morning breeze from the harbor. The proboscis balanced delicately over the man's mouth, as if to suck nectar from a flower.

BPD Detective Abe Leone squatted on his long legs by the man's body and studied the paper butterfly. "Looks real."

"Yeah." Sergeant Janelle Mahoney stood next to him, surveying the body. "Kinky."

"I'd say so." Leone's eyes moved down to the man's blood-soaked torso before coming back to the man's face. "We know who he is yet?" He scanned the man's clothing and expensive shoes. "Looks like a serious suit."

"I guess. Alex Massey, CEO of the New You chain of women's gyms." Sergeant Mahoney checked her notes. "Just finished giving the CEO Breakfast Forum talk in the hotel. About social responsibility." She paused to glance at Mr. Massey's body before continuing. "He was moving the operation's headquarters to Boston after buying out the Harbor Sports gym chain here."

"No kidding. I used to lift there." Abe Leone smiled. "In my youth."

"Yeah. That must have been impressive."

"Shut up."

Janelle Mahoney cocked her head at Detective Leone. "Kick in the pants, right? Gives a talk about social responsibility in his debut performance for the chamber, walks into the hotel garage to pick up his Beemer," she looked over at the car, "and gets done. Then, someone sticks a pretty butterfly on his mouth." A thoughtful, puzzled

look covered her honey-colored face. "Hell of a way to come to a new city and start your day," she said softly.

Leone rubbed his bald head. "Got a nice kiss too."

Mahoney cocked her head and looked at him. "Excuse me?"

"Head butt." Leone said. He used a pen to lift the man's sandy hair to reveal a deep bruise on the forehead. "Looks like that took him down, and on the way, he took a bunch of plugs to the stomach."

He stood. "And, unless we have a mugger who forgets to take a wallet full of money and cards and runs around sticking little paper butterflies on the vic's mouth after stabbing him . . ." He paused, looking at the wounds. "After *viciously* stabbing him. Brutal." They were both quiet for a moment before he said, "Anyway, I guess we have to say that this is not a random act."

Leone circled the victim again. "We'll wait for the examiner. I think Reardon's on call," he said. "This looks angry. Not just business or a hit." He turned to Janelle Mahoney. "What do you make of the butterfly?"

"Personal. Real personal." She squatted to take a closer look at the small butterfly.

"It does look real, as if it just landed there and might fly away."

The victim looked surprised, his brown eyes still open and staring ahead. One would have thought he was more surprised by the magical winged creature alighting on his lips than by the rest. The rest being a brutal head butt followed by several quick, savage stabs to the midsection at a toney waterfront hotel parking garage on an ordinary weekday morning.

Sergeant Janelle Mahoney took another long look at the paper butterfly. About three inches wide, wings brilliant orange and black, a thin, delicate black body. "I've seen those in One Thousand Villages in Harvard Square. Maybe Mexican or Latin American. "

She looked lost in the butterfly for a moment before standing and turning to Leone. "Something feminine here."

"Stabbings like this aren't female." He gestured to the torso. "See how powerful these cuts are? And that head butt? Looks pretty masculine to me."

Sergeant Mahoney took some time before replying. "Maybe, but

I'd still say something female here." She looked up to face Abe. "Angry female."

"Why do you say that?"

"No guy is going to leave a beautiful memento like that."

"Why not?"

Mahoney paused and ran her hand down the side of her face. "Yeah. I suppose a guy might. And those cuts are angry. Deep. So, maybe. Or maybe a mix."

"What's that mean?"

"I don't know."

"Well. Whatever. Let's not circulate the butterfly part of this yet. Whoever did this wants that part publicized. Let's not give him that satisfaction yet."

"Okay. We'd better caution the garage crew and the security guard that found him."

"Right. Can you do that?"

"Yep."

* * * *

At the sound of someone approaching in, Abe turned to see Reardon the medical examiner.

"Decorative," Reardon commented.

"Well, decorative, but otherwise standard issue. Stab wounds to the stomach and abdomen are pretty nasty, though."

"We'll see," Reardon responded.

Abe Leone gave a heavy sigh. "Yep." And sighed again.

Reardon stopped at the sound and looked at the detective. "Jesus, Leone. You sound like my mother with that sigh. My father used to say she sighed for all of Ireland."

Abe gave a small smile. "It's my own mother. She sighed like that all the time."

Reardon pulled gloves out of the pocket of his crime scene suit. "I thought you were Italian. What? Italian mothers sigh like that too?"

"Probably. My own mother's a Conneely from the west of Ireland, Connemara. Father's Italian-Jewish." Abe moved to give Reardon more room near the victim. "You can be both, you know."

"No shit." Reardon leaned over the victim.

He stared at the body for some time before saying, "Now, give me some room. I can't work with you bunch crowding me." He dismissed them with a wave of his hand. "Go search the crime scene or something."

Sergeant Mahoney looked at Abe with raised eyebrows and a small grin. Abe nodded at her. "Have them start in the stairwell."

"Yes, sir."

Abe stepped back a few feet from the body to give Reardon ample room. He pulled out a small spiral pad and started to make some notes.

Reardon was quiet as he worked, except for the soft mutterings under his breath. The department knew that the medical examiner had these whispered conversations with victims as he went along. Abe figured this was the real reason Reardon didn't want everyone hanging over him. Chatting with the victim didn't play well with the rank and file.

After some time, Reardon stood. "Well, there is the bug . . ." he began, pointing at the butterfly.

"A butterfly is an insect," Abe said without looking up from making notes on his small black pad. "All insects are bugs. Not all bugs are insects

Reardon stared at Abe until Abe raised his eyes.

"Whatever." Reardon inhaled deeply before continuing. "Including the *insect* . . ." He paused. "Well, have to do a full autopsy, but I'd say that, aside from the *insect*, this is not a standard issue case at all."

Abe walked closer to the body. "In what way?"

"In the way that one broad, large knife did damage to the abdomen and the stomach—really violent, powerful blows. But . . ." he gestured to the man's chest, "the one that did him in finally was a thin stiletto—very precise, right to the heart. I would say he was given that after he collapsed from the blow to the forehead and the thrusts to the stomach and abdomen."

"I didn't even see that."

"Well, you wouldn't," Reardon responded generously. "Too

much blood from the other wounds."

He pulled off his gloves and stood, facing Abe directly. "It's different from the others." He inhaled deeply again. "I'd say that the head blow and the stomach and abdomen were done by a very angry guy. An in-a-rage, powerful guy. These are savage thrusts."

The medical examiner rolled his gloves, put them in the pockets of his crime scene suit and straightened his glasses. "The *piece de resistance,* the one to the heart—whole different story. Calculated, careful." He paused. "But fierce. Fierce."

Abe furrowed his brow. "That complicates things."

Reardon continued as if Abe had not spoken. "Like two different murders. The big, broad knife cuts him down. That's all violent, masculine, a strong man." He tuned to face Abe. "The careful penetration to the heart is different. That and the butterfly. That part of the murder is not a man. Just a guess, but I'd say that's a woman. A woman taking revenge, I'd say."

He shrugged. "Of course, you can't always guess at the gender of the murderer by the style—could go either way—but that's my guess."

As he spoke, Reardon moved his blue crime scene boot further away from the pool of Alex Massey's congealing CEO blood, which didn't look any different from anyone else's.

13

LEAVING THE SCENE

The big man slipped behind the wheel, and efficiently maneuvered the car out of a tight space near the South Station bus terminal. The morning traffic was thick along the waterfront, the congestion advancing sluggishly in a semi-organized flow through a knot of intersections and turnoffs.

Once out into traffic, he spoke without looking at the woman beside him. "Bottle of water beside you. Breathe."

The woman in the passenger seat was breathing deeply, eyes closed. "Slow it down," he said. "Breathe in Calm. Breathe out Relax."

He repeated the breathing mantra a number of times, even as he worked his way through congested morning traffic. "Breathe in Calm. Breathe out Relax."

The woman, eyes still closed, gradually moderated her breathing. The man turned onto Congress Street by the Federal Reserve Bank, passed over the Fort Point Channel bridge, drove by the giant milk bottle beside the Children's Museum, and headed to South Boston.

"It's done. Massey's done." She closed her eyes. "I'm still wired. I can't stop my heart."

"Yeah." He looked out the window for a few moments. "Of course you're wired. This is a big deal. It'll last a while, but you'll be okay."

"How can you stay so calm? Never understood that."

"I'll have a drink later." He turned to check the side view mirror before merging into traffic. "I've had experiences that you haven't. I'm different." They were both quiet for a few moments.

"Besides, you know me. I go to another place. I'm there, but not there. Felt pretty intense for that moment though," he continued.

"I could tell." She studied her hands. "I could go to another place too. Been there before, and it's not a good place."

"No, no. It's not. Well, now, you won't have to go to that place ever again if you work on it and watch yourself. It's all over."

"Yeah," she responded.

He turned to face her. "I know why you did it, but I wish you hadn't done the butterfly thing. It's like an announcement."

"Yes, it is an announcement. You know that I had to do that."

"Right."

"Where're we headed now?"

"We're going to take a slow walk around Castle Island. Then, I'm going to drive to that place I got in Eastie. You're going to take a long nap. I'll stay on the couch. Then, I'll get takeout at Mario's and we'll both have a glass of wine.

* * * *

In a few minutes, they pulled into an open parking place at Castle Island. He put his hand on her shoulder as she reached for the door handle. "Check for splatters when we get out." She nodded.

Afterward, they headed across the causeway. The morning air was fresh, the walkway pleasantly busy with joggers and young mothers with strollers. Senior citizens sat on park benches to enjoy ocean breezes, the views of freighters on the harbor, and planes taking off from Logan.

They walked slowly. He kept his hands in his pockets and rolled his head in small neck exercises.

She looked out over the water. "I thought I would feel—what?— complete when this was over. When we'd finally done him. But I'm not feeling it."

"Been carrying it for a long time. It's a lot to take in. Give it time."

"Yeah, so many years." She hesitated for a moment, thoughtful. "SOB looked so smooth. Did you see that suit and that haircut? Son of a bitch."

"Not so smooth anymore."

"No, he's not."

He smiled at her. "But the bastard's done. One more to go. Need to get the other one."

"Did you send the message to him?"

He waited until the sound of the plane taking off overhead from Logan subsided. "Yeah. I think he'll rise to the bait. He's got a good survival instinct. These guys always do."

They had reached the old Fort Independence at the end of Castle Island and at the mouth of Boston Harbor. The man looked up at the gray granite fort built by the British and captured by the colonists during the Revolution. "You know, there's a legend about a guy walled up in those walls," he said. "A soldier who killed someone in a duel. Killed someone who was really popular, I guess. Anyway, guess what happened?"

"I give up."

"The murdered man's friends got this soldier drunk, put him in a wine cask, and walled him up inside the walls." He shrugged. "I don't think it's true, but somebody wrote a story about it."

The woman stopped on the walkway, staring at him with red-rimmed eyes. She shook her head. "I can't believe you. Just the kind of thing I don't want to hear about right now," she snapped. Her eyes tearing, she gazed out at the gray walls of the fort. "That's so awful."

And then, she started to laugh. "What goes on in your mind? I can't believe you," she said again.

"Just a little local color." He threw his head back and laughed along with her while stepping aside for two walkers coming up behind them.

"They'll wonder what our problem is," she said, wiping her eyes

"Well, we did have a problem." He straightened his jacket. "But now it's okay." He put his arm around her shoulder as she sobbed and laughed. "We're taking care of it."

14

A THIN THREAD AND A SUBSTANTIAL ONE
TREMONT STREET HEADQUARTERS, BPD

"Hey, Mahoney. Got lucky." Abe Leone strode over to Sergeant Janelle Mahoney's desk at the Tremont station and pulled out his phone. "You know, I asked to see all the images from the hotel garage."

He pulled up an image of two blurred smudges and held them before her. "Got two partials – not great, but something to work with. One was on the vic's name badge from the CEO breakfast, maybe when he'd been pushed in the chest." Abe demonstrated with a hand on his chest. "So, a partial on the name badge and the rest on the fabric, where they couldn't pick up the image."

He pointed to the second image. "It's a very small impression on his New You corporate lapel pin. Same thing. The impression could have been when Massey was shoved."

Janelle put on her reading glasses and squinted at the smudges for a few moments before leaning back in her chair and giving Abe a dubious look. "I'm sorry, Abe. They look like blotches to me—no definition at all." She raised her hands in apology.

Disappointed, Abe looked at the image again. "You sound as bad as the captain."

"I guess that doesn't put me in good company."

Abe sighed. "No, it doesn't, Mahoney. No, it doesn't. You're being just as negative as he is. Open your mind up to possibilities. We get them cleaned up—somebody must be able to do that even with prints this bad—then we run them through the system." Abe put his hands on his hips and exhaled another long breath. "Everyone around here is so damned negative."

"Come on, Abe." Janelle defended herself. "We're not on some detective show where technology magically solves the case. I haven't seen that happen in real life—at least not around here."

"Come on, Mahoney. Think bigger. Software's improving all the time. They can bring details up. And, you know, if they put the prints through the system, it may give us something. May be enough. The process takes a while, but it may be enough."

"Who's *they*?"

"If not our tech team—maybe somebody across the street at the College of Computer Science at NU. Maybe MIT. Maybe the FBI. Don't just give up. Christ, our first break and I'm not getting any response. Why am I the only one who's excited here?"

Mahoney held her hands up. "Okay. Okay. Sorry. God knows we could use a break."

"Good attitude adjustment. Glad you're open to new learning, Mahoney."

Mahoney gave Abe an encouraging smile. "Want me to take it from here?"

"Yeah. Yeah." He punched her number into his cell. "Just sent you the images. Take them down to tech support and see what they can recommend, who we can go to if they can't help." Abe nodded to himself. "A thin thread, but we'll take it."

* * * *

More threads in the case emerged later in the day, just in time to save Abe Leone's sinking morale. Janelle called Abe on his cell as he was leaving another meeting with his captain, a meeting in which the captain emphasized how much pressure he personally was under from the city and his bosses in the department to get some results on the Alex Massey Harbor Hotel murder. "Let's see some action, Leone. Give me some concrete results. I'm dying here."

The captain was unimpressed with the smudges that Abe insisted on calling fingerprints. "Okay, check them out, Abe—but I'm not seeing much there."

Abe had started back down the hall when his cell phone buzzed. "Yeah?" he answered wearily. "Hope you've got some good news, Janelle."

"Massey had an interesting history."

"Is it relevant? Got some background to follow up on?"

"Yeah."

"I'll be right there."

Janelle was still flipping through her notes when he sat in the chair opposite her and leaned forward. "Give it to me."

"Okay. Here we go. Originally from Pittsburgh. I called the PPD and spoke to a Detective Compagnone. He sent me the file. Very interesting."

"Hurry up."

Janelle narrowed her eyes, gave Leone a look, and muttered "Great work, Sergeant Mahoney. Thank you," before continuing.

"Our guy was Skip Massey, born Alex Massey. Ran a gym in Bloomfield with some kind of community, after-school programs." Janelle paused, reading through her notes again. "He had a setback when it all burned down. They couldn't prove arson, so he got the insurance money—but it was always viewed with some suspicion. The word is they didn't think that he did it—maybe somebody was trying to teach him a lesson. One source said he borrowed money from the wrong people."

"Run with a bad crowd in general?"

"There was always talk about some of the activities in the gym."

"Like what kind of activities?"

"He had a nice collection of young women in the gym community programs. Very young women. Some of them lived in the house next to the gym."

"I see."

"Anyway, he moved on after the fire and bought another small gym, made a number of other acquisitions and built it all up to the New You national chain. And, as I said, he just acquired Harbor Sports and was moving the headquarters to Boston. And," she added, "no talk about this national chain of gyms having any funny business with young girls or anything."

"Well, well, well." Abe let out his trademark heavy sigh. "You just never know, do you?"

"I saved the best for last."

"Yeah?"

Officer Mahoney smiled, leaned back, and waited before responding, savoring her best news—tasting it, rolling it around in her

mouth before sharing it.

"Christ. Get on with it, Mahoney."

"Right." She gave him a slow smile before carefully enunciating the words in the next sentence. "Another butterfly murder in Pittsburgh eight years ago."

"You're kidding."

"Nope."

"Who flies direct to Pittsburgh?"

"JetBlue does. But the department will never give us the budget to fly down."

"Yes, they will. They're really feeling the heat on this one."

"There's a 7:30 JetBlue in the morning from Terminal B. I'll see if we can get in to see Detective Compagnone. He was the lead in the case."

"You're so good."

"Yes, I am that good." She smiled as she picked up the phone to make travel plans for Pittsburgh. "Remember that when my review comes up."

15

A NEW MENTOR FOR ANTOINETTE

Frederica found an old friend to mentor Antoinette Mackey while she was on an internship at City Hall and Frederica went away. Dorinda LaPierre was only going to be in Boston from Philadelphia for a few weeks on a short-term assignment, but she was glad to help out. Could Jenna help with introductions and logistics?

"Delighted," responded Jenna in her text. Sometimes things just turned out right. They appeared to do just that when Frederica's new Sister Connection volunteer arrived at Jenna's office a couple of days later.

Dorinda LaPierre was a warm, gracious, kind IT professional and black. Perfect. It would be helpful for Antoinette to have a mentor who was a professional of color. After an accelerated vetting process, Jenna set up an introductory meeting.

Normally, these introductory meetings happened at the Sister Connection office conference room over sandwiches and coffee from Au Bon Pain, or during a small excursion, perhaps to the Rose Kennedy Greenway for ice cream and the carousel. But, this time, Frederica insisted on making reservations at Maison Robert--a toney restaurant in the old City Hall section of Boston known for executive dining. "Let's make it special for Antoinette. She's growing up and she's starting out in the world." Frederica had said. "It's on me."

Dorinda LaPierre, no stranger to power lunches, was still pleasantly surprised. On the other hand, Antoinette Mackey was beside herself. Jenna and Dorinda were seated before Antoinette arrived from the mayor's office.

Petite, lively and expressive, Antoinette raised her eyebrows in delight as she stopped to take in the brick walls, the brass fixtures and white linen tablecloths, the quiet conversations between well-dressed diners.

"Oh, Jenna," she whispered as she lowered herself into her chair. "When I told people where I was coming for lunch, they were *so* impressed."

"I'm impressed too." Dorinda smiled. "Hi, Antoinette, I'm Dorrie."

"I'm so glad to meet you, Dorrie. You're wonderful to pitch in to help support me with this internship. It's really important to me." Antoinette held her hands up, palms out and closed her eyes. "I mean *really* important. Community development is what I want to do with my life. This is the best opportunity."

"I can see that." Dorrie grinned. "I'll do my best to help you where I can. This is a good experience for me too. I'm looking forward to it."

The waiter came for their orders. "Give us a few minutes," Jenna asked him before turning to Antoinette and Dorrie. "Okay, ladies. Let's attend to this fabulous menu and then we can chat away. What time do you have to be back, Antoinette?"

"In about forty-five minutes. Will that be a problem?

"No, no. But let's get down to business here."

The time flew after they had placed their orders. Over lunch, Antoinette talked about her time at Howard, her goals in community development, and what her new summer assignment entailed. Dorinda gave a brief outline of her IT consultancy for small businesses. "We can talk more about that later, but you might find the small business aspect helpful as you think about community development."

As the lunch drew to a close for Antoinette, Jenna said. "And now, a little surprise from Frederica."

She pulled two tickets from her jacket pocket for the upcoming Alvin Ailey dance performance at the Wang Theatre. "Oh, my goodness." Antoinette clapped her hands, her eyes misting "We go to that every year. I thought we'd miss this year. She is just the best."

"Always has been," Dorinda said. "A star in every way."

* * * *

At the Sisters Connection fund-raising dinner a week later, Dorinda LaPierre generously filled a table with her colleagues and

customers. Antoinette and Jenna were also introduced to two new Boston friends of Dorinda's—a big handsome guy named Dan, also new to town, who was running a program for vets near the Charlestown Navy Yard, and Dan's sister Sheila, a hospice nurse.

What a great addition to the Sisters Connection organization Dorinda turned out to be, thought Jenna. *I wonder if she could be persuaded to continue to be involved in the Philly branch.*

Jenna noticed a clear spark between Dorinda and Dan. Watching them dance at the fundraiser together, she saw Dorinda--elegant, tall and slim--put her head on Dan's shoulder. Dan, large, muscular and gentle, put his head on hers as they swayed to the music. Jenna's eyes moistened from the trust and sweetness—and the what? The obvious history.

She wondered about that history for a moment and meant to ask Dorinda if Dan came from Philadelphia too. But things got busy and she forgot.

16

STEELER CITY
PITTSBURGH POLICE – WESTERN AVE STATION

Abe and Janelle's flight into Pittsburgh was blessedly uneventful. "Not bad," Janelle commented, surveying the modern, efficient and organized Pittsburgh airport.

"Gives Logan a run for its money," Abe said, referring to Boston's busy Logan airport, always under construction to keep up with heavy air traffic in a tight geographic area.

"Oh, yeah. You can feel almost human here."

Within an hour and a half, they were sitting in the offices of Detective Salvatore "Toto" Compagnone of the Pittsburgh Police Department on Western Avenue. Broad and husky with a genial, bushy-browed Italian face, he shook their hands and gestured to the two comfortable chairs in front of this cluttered desk. "Coffee? We have time for a quick cup. It's pretty good and all ready. I make my own in here." Compagnone waved his arm toward a window sill where a French press coffee maker sat next to a bag of Dunkin Donuts.

"I could use a good strong coffee right now," Abe replied and Janelle agreed.

"Good, Good." Compagnone walked to the window sill and filled two Steeler mugs full of the hot coffee. "Want a doughnut? Already had mine. I'm kind of addicted to the glazed ones."

The visitors declined, and Compagnone indicated the sugar and milk on the side of the desk.

"Welcome to the Burgh, Patriots Nation. You're in Steelers territory now."

"Oh yeah, we got that." Both Leone and Mahoney had remarked earlier on the proliferation of Steeler signs and flags all through the city. "We respect the territory. Great team and a great city," Abe responded, raising his coffee mug in a toast.

Receiving appropriate homage, Compagnone smiled and retrieved a file from the side of his desk. "Like I told you on the phone, Sergeant Mahoney," he looked at Janelle, "the Roger Coombs murder—our own butterfly murder—has been pretty stone-cold case until now. We didn't close the case, but among ourselves, we chalked the murder up to a drug deal gone bad or, more likely, stiffing the wrong people out of money. We never figured out the butterfly, but in the end we decided it was just a personal quirk. We never had another butterfly murder." He looked at Abe. "Until now."

Compagnone placed his hands on top of the file. "A truckload of candidates in those days for who the bad guys and wrong people might be. We got to any number of dead ends and then our resources were just too tight to keep on the case. We have too many other needs in a big city. You know the score."

Abe and Janelle both nodded. "Oh yeah," Abe agreed.

"But it looks like we can take another look now with similar butterfly murder in Boston. For the background of the case here, I've got somebody who can tell the story better than I can." Compagnone leaned back in his chair. "Not a member of the department but thinks he is and – I hate to say it," the detective smiled, "but he can be useful. Name is Henry Murdoch. He was a journalist at the *Pittsburgh Post-Gazette* who got interested in this case and then became kind of a helpful pain in in the ass. Nebby—that's the word for nosy here—nebby as all hell, but a great guy. Retired now, he still can't let go of the Coombs murder case—he's obsessed with it."

"How come?"

Compagnone patted the file folder again. "You'll see. The case just stuck with him. Mostly, it was the butterfly part that got to him. Kind of weird. But, also, the story of the vic's downfall. Here's Roger Coombs, your basic standup guy in his everyday life, at least according to people in Oakmont. Then, suddenly, it's like he was living two lives—community leader in his hometown, a drowning-in-debt drug addict when he crossed the city limits."

Compagnone looked out the window and then back at them with a smile. "Anyway, Murdoch's a persistent old bastard. Wouldn't leave the case alone, always bugging us. I can't tell you how happy

we were when he retired. We all went to his retirement party down at the River City Inn, thinking that was the end of him always getting in our faces about this or that."

Compagnone snorted and gave a chuckle. "Then we find out, the SOB's writing a book about the Coombs case." He shook his head. "Can't catch a break around here."

He reached for his jacket on the back of his chair. "And now, it looks like the old bastard was right to stay with it. Anyway, take a few more sips of my excellent coffee and finish up. We're going to meet Murdoch in half an hour at one of his favorite haunts. He'll bring his read on the case—he already knows everything in here." Compagnone tapped the thick file folder. "He'll remember more detail. And, honestly, he tells the story better."

"Great." Abe hesitated, looking at his watch. "His favorite haunts? It's a little early in the day for us."

"Oh, I wouldn't worry about that."

17

BACKSTORY AT THE TEA ROOM

The Sarah Barnes Tea Shop was tucked into an ornate turn-of-the-century brick building on East Ohio in the Deutschtown neighborhood.

"Nice to know there are still gentlemen around," Janelle Mahoney murmured as Detective Compagnone held the door for her.

"I do that too," Abe objected.

"Yeah, Leone, you do." She entered the tea shop. "And you don't even give off that shit about how if I'm a feminist, I shouldn't expect any of those . . ." She searched for a word. "Niceties."

"There's the old bastard." Compagnone waved at an older man with the face of a medieval saint, heavy glasses, and carefully combed sparse gray hair on his freckled scalp.

"I mean I just like it when a man does that," Janelle continued over her shoulder as they approached Murdoch's table. "Makes me feel special."

Abe rolled his eyes.

Henry Murdoch was waiting for them at a back table underneath a large sign against the brick wall that read "Keep Calm and Drink Tea." Murdoch stood as they drew closer. "See what I mean?" Janelle whispered.

"Welcome to our fair city. Your football team may have been arrogant bastards in their day, especially your ex-number twelve, but welcome to Steeler City, Boston."

Leone ostentatiously pulled out a chair for Janelle Mahoney. She lowered herself into it gracefully with a satisfied smirk on her face.

"Well, Mr. Murdoch, you guys had a long run yourselves. It was time to give someone else a chance." Abe said and extended his hand to shake Murdoch. "And somebody else will have a turn soon."

Murdoch snorted in reply and Compagnone muttered, "We'll see."

A china teapot smelling of fragrant jasmine tea sat in front of Murdoch, an old-fashioned tea cup and saucer to the side atop a thick, tattered file folder. As the group settled at the table, the tea shop proprietor approached the table.

"Let me introduce my friend Sarah Barnes, retired teacher, school principal, and tea connoisseur," Murdoch announced. They stood to be introduced to Sarah, an older black woman with bright, knowing eyes. She greeted each of them with a wide smile.

"Henry told me he was expecting guests from Boston. What brings you to Pittsburgh?"

"Researching an old case," Abe replied. "With the expert." He gestured toward Murdoch.

"Well, you've got the right gentleman. Solid gold." She cast her incandescent smile in Henry Murdoch's direction. "Solid gold."

Murdoch shifted in his seat, happily uncomfortable to be so recognized.

"So, what can I get for you today? Many choices." Sarah waved at the long list of teas on a side white board. Leone looked flummoxed.

"Well, I've just had a cup of *excellent* coffee." Janelle glanced at Detective Compagnone who nodded in acknowledgment of her taste. "But that," she pointed at Murdoch's teapot, "smells so good, I'd like some of that."

"Jasmine for the pretty lady," Sarah said approvingly. "An appropriate choice for you. Fitting." Janelle almost preened with Sarah's approval.

"And no caffeine. Not to worry," she added.

"Henry here," Sarah looked at Murdoch, "is not really a jasmine tea type but he's always wandering out of his lane—as they say."

"You got that right," muttered Compagnone with a side glance at Murdoch.

"And Toto," she looked at Detective Compagnone, "a ginger tea for your digestion." Compagnone nodded with a small smile and patted his stomach.

Sarah turned to Abe, who was still looking at the long tea list, a bewildered expression on his face.

"Want me to choose for you?"

"Sure."

"Let's see." She gave Abe an appraising look.

"My special masala chai tea for you," she said finally, "because you're interesting."

"Well, well," Janelle grinned at Leone who beamed with pleasure.

"He's interesting, she's exotic, and I have bad digestion," complained Detective Compagnone. "I get it."

"And a plate of my own lemon shortbread—on the house for Boston's finest." Sarah gave them one last bright smile before she left.

18

THE FALL OF ROGER COOMBS

"So, Murdoch, what've you got?" Compagnone glanced at the old man's thick folder. "The short version, not the long version with side notes."

"The strange story of Roger Coombs, upstanding businessman and civic leader," Murdoch intoned as he removed his tea cup from atop the thick file and pulled the tattered folder closer." A man who started to lead another, secret life when fate threw him some curve balls. Wife sick with cancer, business reversals, getting paunchy." Here, Murdoch patted his own middle. "One thing led to another. He couldn't handle it. Borrowed too much money from the wrong people—the same ones your friend Skip Massey did, started consuming too many illegal substances, and picked up a sweet girlfriend younger than his kids. Hell, he probably had a watch older than she was."

"Sounds like a prince." Abe gave a heavy sigh.

"Real stand-up guy," muttered Janelle.

"Well, now," Murdoch said in response, "Some people are made for hard times. Other people break easy. He was one of those. By all accounts, he was a good guy for years before he hit a rough spot. Great father, devoted to his family."

A waitress brought their order and a plate of warm lemon shortbread.

Murdoch searched through his file folder and pulled out a photo, caught between two pages. He laid it on the table in front of them. "Roger Coombs before the fall."

A smiling, ordinary-looking guy with a brown crewcut. An athletic-looking teenaged son and a scrubbed pretty daughter stood between Roger Coombs and his wife. The woman's blonde hair was long enough to cascade over her shoulders onto a light blue sweater. A gold cross with what looked like a small diamond rested in the V of the sweater. Beautiful family.

"I suppose he belonged to the Rotary Club."

"Of course, he did," responded Murdoch. "Rotary, Lions. CCD teacher, Pop Warner coach. You name it. All-American guy."

"Funny, isn't it?" mused Compagnone. "I mean funny how it can all go to hell so fast."

"Oh yeah," Murdoch continued. "One minute it's the American dream. Then, the wife gets a serious cancer, the business has problems, the medical bills pile up. It wasn't supposed to be that way. He couldn't hold it together."

He took a sip of jasmine tea from Sarah's delicate tea cup. "That's when he got involved with Skip Massey—your guy Alex Massey before he changed his name. Another friend brought Coombs to the gym—and not for the hot yoga, at least the kind they teach in most classes. You now the score with the young girls at that gym?"

Abe nodded grimly.

"Just for the record, it wasn't Massey who introduced Coombs to his pusher during this time. Coombs found that guy on his own – bottom of the barrel pusher, by the way. A real creep. Anyway, Massey didn't do drugs." Murdoch leaned back in his chair. "But apparently Massey did get some kind of a finder's fee for getting Coombs—who by this time was in big financial trouble – connected with the loan shark operation."

"You know, I can't tell you how many times I've seen this movie," interjected Compagnone. "You're over your head. You start taking a little something for the stress, then a little more and the next thing you know, you've got an expensive habit. If you have a business, it's tanking, mostly because you can't focus anymore. You need to borrow some money, but the only people who will give you a loan now are the wrong people."

"His family know what was going on?" Abe asked.

"God, no. His wife was too sick to know much of anything. She was on comfort drugs. The kids came home every time they could. They knew their father was under serious pressure because of his business problems. Then one week he told them things were going to be okay—he was able to get an infusion of cash to hold it together."

"That must have been when the money came in from the loan shark," Abe said.

Janelle shook her head. "What a story."

"Coombs never knew what hit him," Compagnone commented.

"No, he didn't," Murdoch said. "So overwhelmed, so naive. He went down fast." Murdoch hesitated. "And, you know, when you're that desperate, you do things."

"Like what things?" Abe asked.

"One of the saddest parts," Murdoch responded. "I told you he picked up this young girl—looks like she might have been at the beginning of a pro career." He paused. "Her mother was a pro—not that it's a given the daughter would end up staying in the business too, but the kid didn't have a great start in life." Murdoch shook his head. "Anyway, Coombs is crazy about this young girl. But his pusher's on him about money, threatening to hurt his wife, who's now dying, his daughter who's in nursing school and his son who's up at Penn State. One night, Coombs—desperate—brings his young girlfriend to his pusher and offers to share her as partial payment. The pusher likes the girl. Nice. He knocks down a little of the debt that Coombs owes him. So it becomes a regular thing after that."

"This is all from what I heard on the street. I told Detective Compagnone." Murdoch cocked his head at the detective. "But no one wants to go on record. Just talk in the neighborhood. And talk dries up when police start asking questions. Nobody knows nothin'."

"I'm familiar," Abe commented.

Murdoch took a sip of his tea before continuing. "Anyway, the pusher gradually feeds the girl some stuff—looks like horse with some fentanyl. She's getting hooked. One night he gets rough with her and feeds her too much. They find her next morning up on Polish Hill in the alley beside the church."

"Poor baby," whispered Janelle Mahoney.

"Yeah. Right after that, Coombs's wife died. He went into some kind of shock. His wife and his girlfriend gone—and he was straight-out responsible for the girlfriend. All downhill fast from there. He was using like crazy, not paying anyone back, not making his kids' tuition payments—which used to be sacrosanct. Then, it

came to a real bad end in Saint Peter's Cemetery. It was pretty ugly, even for the characters he got involved with—the loan sharks and the pusher. The theory was that someone decided to make an example of him."

"Got to do that if you're going to have any kind of business," Compagnone commented.

Murdoch looked at him with raised eyebrows. The detective just shrugged.

"What happened to his family?" Janelle asked.

Compagnone gave her a kind look. "Nice that you should care, Sergeant Mahoney."

"The kids?" Murdoch asked. "Well, the daughter moved out west somewhere, finished nursing school in Phoenix. Never came back to Pittsburgh, as far as I know, and doesn't keep in touch with anyone. Wanted to put the whole thing behind her, I guess. Can't blame her. Couldn't trace her after a couple of jobs in the Phoenix area."

Murdoch sipped his tea. "The son signed up for multiple tours in Afghanistan, I hear. And then some assignments in the Middle East. Still there now, I think. One way to deal with it."

19

WHAT'S THE DEAL WITH THE BUTTERFLY?

In the quiet of the tea shop, the four considered the case. Abe broke the silence. "If everyone assumed, with good reason, which Coombs was done by a pusher or loan shark, even if it wasn't proven—what's the deal with you sticking to the case for so long?"

"The butterfly."

"Yeah. The butterfly in the victim's mouth. What's with the butterfly?"

"A little strange. Too hinky. Just kind of caught me."

"Yeah, there's that, but so what?"

Murdoch pulled out another photo—a high school ID photo—from his folder and lay it in front of Abe.

"Who's that? The girlfriend?"

"Yep. Agnieszka Urbanowski."

"So young," Janelle whispered.

Murdoch nodded. "Tragic."

No one spoke until Murdoch took another sip of his tea and said, "Just couldn't get it out of my head. Roger Coombs was a naive, immature man who couldn't handle life. He was like a lamb to the slaughter himself when he got involved with these guys, and he brought this pretty little lamb to the slaughterhouse with him."

"Beautiful too," commented Janelle. "Looks like a young Mrs. Coombs."

"You're not the first one to make that observation," Murdoch responded softly. He paused before continuing. "Sort of a lost soul herself. She had an older brother—good, hard-working guy who really tried to look out for her, to take care of her, but he was just a kid himself. Anyway, she was a foster child, but not in one of the better foster situations. Lived up on the Slopes somewhere with a family that always struck me as sketchy themselves. The older son was a

66

troublemaker. She should never have been placed there."

He helped himself to a second piece of Sarah Barnes's short-bread. "I heard she spent more time down at a gym program on Liberty Avenue than with her foster family. She lived in the house next door to the gym after a while." Murdoch looked up at them. "And you already have a handle on what was going on there."

Mahoney and Leone looked across the table in a wordless conversation.

"Didn't she have a social worker?" Janelle asked.

"Sergeant Mahoney was sociology major before she switched to criminal justice," Abe said. "Gives her a different perspective."

"Well, that's a good balance, I'd say. Fact is that she did have a social worker but not a good one or maybe just overworked. I think they all are." He screwed his mouth up and inhaled deeply. "Not a pretty picture. Not a pretty picture."

Murdoch licked some crumbs off his fingers and started to search in his file folder again. "But I wanted to show you why I was intrigued with the butterfly in Coombs's mouth at Saint Peter's that night. With the help of one of Detective Compagnone's guys, I found a picture that got lost in the system, for some reason."

"Happens." Compagnone grimaced. "Misfiled. If Murdoch hadn't been such a pain in the ass, we might not have located it."

"You're welcome, Detective." Murdoch murmured as he shuffled more pages. "What the heck did I do with that?" he complained to himself.

"Ah, here it is." He laid another image on the table. A fuzzy, slightly crumpled and cracked crime scene photo of a sweet and pretty young girl with a halo of blonde curls. Aggie Urbanowski lying on the hard concrete surface of an alley beside the church on Polish Hill.

Janelle closed her eyes for a moment. "Damn."

Murdoch pointed to one detail in the photo. The sleeve of the girl's jersey was pulled down and on her shoulder was a bright little orange and black butterfly.

Abe looked across the table at Detective Compagnone.

"Yeah," Compagnone said," this by itself would argue that we

needed to take another look at the Coombs case, what with his relationship to this young girl in Massey's gym. We knew that Coombs was a heavy user and the girl OD'd. We also knew that Massey was bullshit about losing the girl." Detective Compagnone paused. "She seemed like a sweet kid."

After a moment, he continued. "Anyway, the captain agreed and we were ready to talk to Massey again when we got the news from Boston. And it's another butterfly murder, this time Massey himself. That makes everything more interesting, doesn't it?"

"I'd say so." Abe Leone leaned back in his chair and looked at the group.

20

DISTURBING THOUGHTS COMING HOME

Later that night, on the return flight to Boston, Abe felt a touch on his arm.

"Abe, you want coffee?"

He jerked himself out of his musings and turned in his seat to face Janelle and the JetBlue flight attendant. "Sorry. Yes, yes, coffee would be great. Black, no sugar. Thanks."

The attendant handed Abe's coffee to Janelle to pass along to him in the window seat. Janelle's tray was already down, and she placed his coffee next to hers. She glanced at the multiple newspapers on Abe's tray that he'd picked up at the airport, saying "Only time I have to read." But the Post-Gazette, the Washington Post and the New York Times lay largely unopened.

Abe had been thinking about butterflies. Butterflies placed on the mouths of two murder victims. The butterfly tattoo on Aggie Urbanowski's shoulder. The oil painting of a glorious butterfly he'd seen in Frederica's living room when he'd walked her home one night.

But mostly he thought about the shadow of a small butterfly tattoo on Frederica Strauss's shoulder. The kind of shadow that a laser tattoo removal treatment left. He had meant to ask her about it, but the moment passed. He didn't exactly forget about the tattoo. Then, it hadn't been top of mind either. Everyone was young once and maybe got some reckless ink.

How much did he know about Frederica Strauss? Frederica knew all about his family. His sister Karen in Lexington with her husband Saul and their kids. His late mother Maureen and his father Abe Leone Senior, who'd been living with Karen after Maureen died. Abe was hoping to bring Frederica to a family party in the fall at Karen's house, to celebrate his dad's birthday.

Frederica, on the other hand, had sketched her background in

69

broad strokes. Growing up in Mount Lebanon, outside Pittsburgh, her dad a scientist at Bayer, her mom a volunteer at the Carnegie Museum, a close family of three sisters and a dog named Archie, who was spoiled and allowed to sit on the couch.

No, Frederica did not go home to Pittsburgh anymore. Her dad had been transferred to Bayer headquarters in Germany. After that, the family home was sold, and her mom and dad didn't come back very often either.

Why hadn't he asked if she ever flew to Germany to see her parents? Or just asked to see a family picture?

He thought Frederica's sister Dorrie lived somewhere in the Mid-Atlantic and maybe Lissy lived closer, maybe even New England? He couldn't remember, but he did know that they were close and communicated a few times a week, even if just with a quick text. He remembered now too that they'd had another, beautiful younger sister who had died early of some rare disease.

What was the name of the youngest? Abe let that question sit in the back of his mind for a few minutes as he stared out the plane window, watching soft clouds as the plane continued its flight through them. When the youngest sister's name finally came to him, Abe felt his body jerk with a startle response.

Aggie. Her name was Aggie.

Abe heaved a long sigh, rubbed his bald head and closed his eyes as he leaned back in his seat. Who was Frederica Strauss? And where was she?

* * * *

That night, walking through his condo front door and dropping his jacket on a chair in the hallway, Abe immediately went to his bookshelves and looked for the Audubon Society Field Guide to North American Butterflies.

He opened the book to a section on the Monarch butterfly and read as he walked to the kitchen for a bottle of Sam Adams. Still reading, he used the cap remover beside the fridge to flip off the beer bottle cap and walked back to the living room.

In his big green reading chair, with his feet up, he continued to read about the butterfly's innate navigation system, its compound

multifaceted eyes for seeing everything, and its anaerobic endurance during migration, much like the long-distance runner. And he read about the toxicity of the butterfly—a poison called cardiac cytosides, which it absorbs from the milkweed plant as a larva. The gorgeous colors of the Monarch butterfly are designed to ward off predators.

Because the beautiful and graceful Monarch is deadly poison to predators.

He began to understand why humans have always been fascinated by the butterfly as a symbol of rebirth. Brilliance from a lowly caterpillar. For the ancient Greeks, the butterfly held the soul of a deceased person. What soul was the butterfly in the painting over Freddie's fireplace carrying? Murdoch's photo of Aggie Urbanowski came to Abe's mind.

Abe slept restlessly. He dreamt of an orange cloud, a battalion of butterflies flying alongside his window on the JetBlue flight. He dreamed of the enormous butterfly in Frederica's painting following the plane, circling the plane, its butterfly face with its twelve thousand flicker and fusion fragmented eyes staring at him through the window.

He woke up sweating. Time to do some unraveling here. He speed-dialed Janelle. "Need some deep dive research," he announced without saying hello.

21

BROKEN BIRDS
PITTSBURGH – EARLY 2000s

They'd each been broken birds in one way or another. Perhaps the parents were still around but not functioning, or functioning in a bad way. Or the parents could be long gone, maybe alive, maybe dead, lost to the street or gone to find their dreams elsewhere. So, it was foster homes or an older married sister or other relatives.

Maybe, for some girls, an uncle or a brother-in-law or a foster father occasionally visited her room in the middle of the night. Maybe her sister or aunt or foster mother knew about those visits. Maybe not. Nobody talked about it. It just was. Each girl knew too that if night-time visits ever did get talked about, it would be her fault. For such girls it was always her fault.

Vickie Czinski's mother was alive and present—sort of. A quivering ghost of a woman scrambling for the next fix, dazed, incoherent half the time. Men visited her mother, going back to the bedroom with her and closing the door. As Vickie got older—but not all that old, as she remembered – the men would notice her too. The length of her legs and that thick red-brown hair pulled back into a long ponytail. When her mother was out of the room, they'd give her that look and that smile. Or buy her a gift—once even a cellphone—but there was always a price to be paid. Maybe her mother knew. Maybe not.

The gym on Liberty Avenue had been a sanctuary for a while. A city-sponsored after-school program for girls. Volley ball and basketball, dance classes, some gymnastics—and a room where they could do their homework. In their own homes, there was never a place to do homework.

The young guy who ran the gym and the program, Skip Massey, had after-school snacks for them. He'd run down to the Giant Eagle supermarket and pick up fruit or cheeses. An even bigger deal was

that he'd line up tutors for them in math and reading. Something special because, in the girls' minds, somebody thought they were worth getting tutors for. Somebody assumed they had brains. For the first time in her life, Vickie thought she might graduate from high school. She thought she might even have a shot at something beyond that—another life.

* * * *

Dorinda LaPierre was the one who suggested Vickie start staying overnight at the Liberty Avenue gym. Dorrie leaned against the wall near Vickie's locker at school that day and examined her face. Behind them, the noise of the students changing classes in the hallways was thunderous.

"You look wiped," Dorrie said.

"What?"

Dorrie put her free hand beside her mouth and shouted. "I said you look wiped."

Vickie shrugged, "Yeah."

"You were falling asleep in algebra," Dorrie said, shouting again

Vickie shut the locker, and nodded, leaning against the door. Dorrie moved to stand closer. "What's up?"

"Sleeping in Judy's sister's car."

"What the hell?"

"Can't stay at my house."

"Why? Why can't you stay at your house?"

"My mom's boyfriends."

"Whoa." Dorrie pulled back. "They bother you?"

"One does."

Dorrie nodded. "So, the best you can do is Judy's sister's car?"

"Judy's mom said a week on their couch was enough. I had to find another place. I told her I would, but then Judy's older sister caught me outside and said I could stay in her car for a few nights till I figured things out. So, it's best I can do." Vickie shrugged. "She brought out a pillow and an extra blanket, but it's really uncomfortable. At least it's not terrible cold out."

"Ladies. Ladies, ladies." The assistant principal walked briskly down the hall. "Where are you supposed to be now? Not chatting in

the corridor. Get going." He waved his hand up the hallway.

"Yes, sir." Dorrie turned to Vickie as she was leaving. "See you at the gym."

"Too tired."

"No, come. I have a fix for you."

"Let's go, Miss La Pierre," the assistant principal clapped his hands.

"Coming. Coming."

* * * *

Late that day, after volleyball, Dorrie caught up with Vickie as she gathered her knapsack and jacket.

"Listen, here's the deal. I had a talk with Skip—you know, the guy that runs the place here. He has some beds – those old iron ones, but they're okay—made up in the back room. He looks the other way when I have to sleep here. You know, when it's bad at home."

"Why? What's going on?"

"You know, my mom. Ever since she took that fall coming off the bus, she's just not right in the head some days." Dorrie paused. "She can get pretty mean, especially to me. It's like she hates me. I don't know why. She screams at me to get out." Dorrie's eyes watered.

Vickie put her arm around her friend.

"She getting treated?"

"Yeah, not working so far. My brother Darrell's the only one who can handle her. She'll do whatever he says." She inhaled deeply. "But he's a piece of work too. Handles her disability checks and takes care of business that way. But he has some friends with 'other interests', if you know what I mean."

"Not really, but I get that it's not great."

"No, not great."

"Come on, Vickie, we'll go get your shit from Judy's sister's car. You can stay with me here, and we'll watch out for each other."

* * * *

Lissy Kelly joined Dorrie and Vickie two weeks later.

"My stepmother hates me. Always at me. I laugh too loud. I'm too fat. My jeans are too tight. I don't pick up after myself in the

bathroom. I hang out with the wrong people. Jesus. I could go on and on."

She ran her hand up her arm and looked to the side. "You know, one day she told me I was trash, just like my mom was." Her eyes teared. "I mean my mom's dead. She doesn't have to talk about her that way."

Dorrie inhaled deeply. "No way."

"Oh yeah. That's when I thought I'd better get out before I killed her. I'm way bigger and stronger than she is. I could have killed her right there in the kitchen."

"Where's your father?"

"Oh, him. "Lissy rolled her eyes. "He can't handle her—he just stays out of the way—takes extra shifts, goes in the other room, says he doesn't want to get in the middle." She looked up. "I'd like to say he'd miss me if I go, but he's not that kind of dad."

* * * *

Aggie Urbanowski was the last one. She and her brother, Tommy, were fostered in two different families. Tommy's family was a better fit than hers.

Lissy told Vickie and Dorrie that Aggie stayed late at the gym at night to avoid the family's older son, whose eyes followed her everywhere in the house.

"I can believe that," Dorrie said. "She's so sweet and pretty. Parents don't do anything?"

"Nothing. They tell her to ignore him. She put a lock on her bedroom door, but it's only a matter of time. She's afraid to tell her brother. He'd probably go after the guy and she doesn't want trouble."

"Come stay with us, Aggie" Dorrie said to her the next day. "Skip's good. He might even talk to the family to make it okay. All they care about is they get their money from the state. Ain't your model foster family."

"My brother Tommy's fosters are so nice. Wish I could have been with them."

"Yeah, but that's not how it ended up. Better you be with us."

* * * *

It was hard for the girls not to be a little in love with Skip Massey—big, athletic, bossy, so good to them. And ambitious. Real ambitious. Skip had a kind of drive and energy they were not used to seeing in their worlds. He wanted to expand the gym—add space for more spinning classes, maybe even a hot yoga studio. He'd already hired another fitness instructor and was interviewing a yoga instructor. They had opened the classes to men. The gym had been a women's fitness center, but Skip said that including men would build the business.

About this time, the owner of the large blue Victorian next door confided in Skip that he was ready to move to Florida with his wife, and that the house would be coming on the market soon. Skip's plans and dreams enlarged.

"Big step," he told Vickie. "I'd be really stretched but, you know, I can see buying it and moving my offices, the four of you and this program over there. The city will be okay with it." Skip paused. "Though it's just as well not to mention that you'd be sleeping there. Anyway," he continued, "then I can expand this place for more class space. We'd keep the volley ball and the basketball courts here. You guys can come from next door to use them."

"It's a beautiful place. Real pretty." Vickie hadn't really listened to anything after the part about moving all of them to the house next store.

"It is, isn't it?" He gazed out a nearby window at the house. "A little rundown, but we can fix it up. I can just see it."

He glowed when he talked about renovating the house, refinishing the old woodwork, rebuilding the porch and the turret. "We'll get it all redd up, Vickie."

"Will there really be room for us to sleep there?"

"Oh yeah, nice bedrooms." Then, in a conspiratorial whisper, "with gas fireplaces." He put his hand on her shoulder. "After I get my approvals from the city. They don't need to know about your sweet bedrooms with fireplaces yet."

"Nice." It felt like some kind of dream to Vickie.

"Yeah." Skip took a deep breath. "I'm going to have a short-term cash flow problem, but I'll figure that out." He turned to

Vickie. "You know what that means, right? Cash flow?"

"Sure. We covered it in Business Accounting last semester." Vickie couldn't believe those words were coming out of her mouth, and neither could Skip.

He grinned. "You're my star, Czinski. I'm making you into a frigging star."

22

GONE FOR NETS

Lissy was the first one. A big, bouncy, wide-faced blonde—her laugh a little too loud, a little too raunchy, always a little too much skin showing.

One day, Skip asked Lissy to join him on an errand across town with his friend Frank, going to pick up new nets for the gym. Vickie could still remember Lissy as she left the study room, delighted to be going on an errand with Skip and his friend. "Toodles!" Lissy had called, popping back through the doorway to blow kisses at the other girls on her way out. "See yinz later!"

But Lissy was subdued when she got back. Her face was closed and she didn't talk in anything other than monosyllables. Just grabbed her books and left.

The girls looked at each other without speaking after the door had closed behind her. Vickie looked for the new nets, but never found any.

"What happened, Lis?" Dorrie asked her later as she lay red-eyed, curled on her bed.

"No fucking nets," she mumbled. Inhaling deeply, she sat up, wiping her eyes. "We pull up behind a warehouse on Smallman Street in the Strip. I'm thinking we're going to pick up nets there, but the place looks closed and there's no one around. Then, Skip hops out of the car. He leans in the side door and says, 'I'm going for coffee down the street. Do me a favor, Lissy. I promised Frank you'd show him a good time. I'll make it up to you."

Lissy hit the pillow with her fists. "Like I had a choice."

"Shit. *Show him a good time.*" Dorrie clenched her teeth. "Did he hurt you?"

"No. No. He wasn't a total animal—but you know, I'm like fifteen."

"What did you do?" Vicki asked.

"What do you mean, *what did I do?*" Dorrie challenged. "Shit. What kind of question is that?"

Vicki shrugged and asked again, "What did you do, Lis?"

"I . . . I just froze. I looked at the ceiling, but mostly I closed my eyes." Her lip quivered and she started to sob.

"Yeah," Dorrie rubbed Lissy's back. "Yeah."

Dorrie lay on the narrow bed next to Lissy. "I'll stay with you tonight."

The next day, Skip took Lissy clothes shopping at The Gap in the Ross Park Mall and got her a new phone before taking her out to dinner. "Thanks, Lissy. I really owed this guy and he thinks you're hot."

* * * *

Over the course of a few weeks, the Liberty Avenue girls learned they were now in a different game.

"I think that's how Skip expects us to pay our way," Vickie said one night in her bedroom. She reached behind her bed and took out four nip bottles of Smirnoff Ice from a small cooler.

"What the heck? Where'd you get those?" Dorrie asked.

"Traded them for math homework. Patrick's dad bought drinks for some family event they were having. He didn't miss these."

Dorrie opened her Smirnoff. "Well. *Paying our way.* That's for shit."

"Yeah, it is, but I figure he thinks we owe him. For everything he's done to help us out. Now, he's got new expenses with buying the house next door."

"Well, Jesus. I didn't sign up for that part of the deal."

"None of us did. I'm thinking that now he thinks of us as assets because he needs cash."

"Dressing all this up with fancy terms like *assets*." Dorrie responded in a sing-song voice. "Doesn't make it any less of a shitshow. Disgusting. Where did you get that – your accounting class? Jesus."

"I thought it sounded better than pros." Vicki stretched her neck from side to side before speaking again. "He took care of us and now we need to pay him back. That's what he thinks."

"He can twist this any way he wants – it's for shit."

Vickie leaned forward. "Yeah, I know. But I've thought about it. What choice do we have?"

"We can just get the hell out of here."

"You want to go back to your stepmother's house, Dorrie? I'm not going back to the hellhole I was in."

"Maybe they won't be such bad guys," sweet Aggie said in a soft voice as she took a sip from her Smirnoff.

"What the hell, Aggie?" Dorrie snapped.

"I mean, if they don't hit you or anything."

"Did anyone used to hit you, Aggie?" Vickie asked.

Aggie didn't answer.

"Oh, yeah. I don't think Skip would let them hit," Lissy said uncertainly "or be druggy."

"Jesus. I can't believe this." Dorrie threw up her arms.

Vickie straightened up. "I guess what I'm saying is that we all were in really bad situations. That's why he thinks he can do this and he can. Nobody cares about us."

"My brother cares about me. Tommy cares about me," Aggie protested.

"Yeah, you're lucky, Aggie." Vicki gave Aggie a long look. "But he's still underage. I'm talking about adults that can help us, can get us in a better situation. I don't see that right now." She looked down at her hands, tracing the lines in her palms. "I mean, Skip cares about us in his weird way, but he will use us to pay for whatever he wants to accomplish. And he thinks that's okay for him and for us. In his mind, he'll do better, pay his expenses, and he'll take better care of us too."

"Twisted," from Dorrie.

"Yeah, twisted," agreed Vickie, "but there'll be no changing him. That's just the way it is right now."

The room was quiet for a while before Vickie, her jaw set, looked around at the other girls. "Well, that's the way it is, but—for me—I'm never going back to where I was and I don't want to roll the dice on fostering. I just want to graduate so that I can make my own life. Maybe even get a scholarship somewhere."

"You're so smart, Vickie. So smart," Aggie whispered.

Vickie smiled at Aggie. "Thanks, honey." She drew her breath in. "And nobody else is going to help us. If I have to do these things for now, I will—if it's safe and just for now. I can handle it."

"Fuck, Vickie, you sound so old and cold." Dorrie ran her hands through her hair.

"Maybe not old, but maybe cold, Dorrie," Vickie said. "I just want a chance at a good life. I'm in the wrong life here. We're all in the wrong life. There are better lives out there. We have to somehow get to them. Maybe I'm missing something, but I don't see any other way for me to do that right now. That's just for me."

Vickie looked out the side window at the alley next to the gym. "For now. Just for now. Then out and never looking back."

The room went quiet. "That's just for me," she repeated. "You do what you want. I can see the way things are going with Skip. He's not totally bad, but he's bad enough and he's not what we thought." Vickie looked out the side window at the alley beside the gym. "If he can manage the people we're with – no rough stuff, no drugs—I think I can handle it for now," she repeated. "For now. Then out."

* * * *

There were more Franks and, over time, there were no more charades about going on errands for nets or anything else. Skip came to the door and crooked his finger at one or sometimes two of them. They'd leave the study room or the gym, and if it was during a game, someone would replace them. It became routine. Sometimes there were dinners or parties or they went to the mountains with several Franks. The men didn't bother even to take off their wedding rings and they showed the girls pictures of their kids.

Skip bought all the girls mobile phones with a speed dial to him. "Just in case." He took them on a shopping trip to the Ross Park Mall and gave them each a generous allowance.

"Nothing slutty," he said. "Show some class." He looked at the girls. "Dorrie's got the best look. That's what we're aiming for. Let her see what you're trying on. I'm not buying anything unless she clears it."

Dorrie looked surprised and not pleased.

Skip turned to Dorrie and spread his arms. "Just cooperate and help me out here, Dorrie. I'll be back in a couple of hours. Meet you here."

Dorrie rolled her eyes and nodded. "Okay, okay."

Skip turned to leave but called over his shoulder "And you, Lissy, no cutoff tops, no holes in the jeans. I've been shopping with you and I'm telling you again—I'm not paying for that shit."

He continued on his way and smiled pleasantly at two startled middle-aged women shoppers. "Morning, ladies."

* * * *

No or minimal makeup. A little lipstick and mascara. That was it. He corrected their grammar and slang and was quick to come down hard on bad language. And absolutely no smoking.

Gradually, they didn't look or talk like Liberty Avenue girls anymore. They looked and talked and had manners like wholesome girls from nice homes in Mount Lebanon or Squirrel Hill. He was proud of them, he said. None of them ever remembered anyone being proud of them before in their lives.

It didn't take long for the kids at the high school to figure out the game at this after-school gym program. Sly comments—or not so sly comments. Someone said something ugly to Aggie Urbanowski. His friends laughed. There was a little grabbing and touching in the crowded corridors between classes.

When the grabbing and touching started, Skip began to visit the school occasionally, chatting with coaches and guidance counselors he knew. He might sit on the wall outside during breaks. Just making small talk.

Skip was big, and there was something very still and very dangerous behind his wide, toothy smile directed at certain boys. Everyone else saw it too, and the comments, the little laughs, the touching stopped.

Next trip to the mountains with the girls, Vickie was not surprised to see one of the guidance counselors from the school join them.

23

THE DIET DR PEPPER RAID
AND AN OBSERVATION

One afternoon, as Vickie and Lissy walked down the corridor toward the gym, Lissy pointed at Skip's office.

"He has a little fridge in there where he keeps his secret stash of pop—Diet Dr Peppers." She made a face. "As if."

"As if what?"

"As if anybody would want to steal that stuff—tastes like Drano."

"How would you know, Lissy? You never drink it."

"I took one, of course."

Vickie laughed. "Of course you did. No wonder he keeps it in there. He catch you?"

"Yeah." Lissy smiled. "I kind of wanted him to. I wanted to see what he would do." She poked Vickie. "He's good-looking, don't you think? Big, nice build."

"Well, he does run a gym. He can't run around with a big paunch."

Lissy rolled her eyes. "You know what I mean—the way his hair falls over those big brown eyes." She sighed.

"Oh, stop it." Vickie opened the door to the volley ball court.

"What, you haven't noticed?"

Vickie shrugged. "Whatever. Does he have a girlfriend?"

"I don't think so. I've been watching. No sign."

"Maybe he has a boyfriend."

"Thought about that too. No sign of that either. You know what?" She held Vickie back to look directly at her.

"What?"

"I'm thinking he doesn't like girls or boys."

"You don't know anything about that."

"Well, I can kind of tell. You get a vibe, you know, one way or

83

the other. I get nothing from him. No vibe of any kind—nothing. Like there's nothing there."

"Good. At least he's not pawing at you."

"Right."

Vickie started to walk away, but turned to ask. "What did he say when you snitched his Diet Dr Pepper?"

"Told me to get the hell out of his office. He'd ban me from the gym for a week if he caught me in there again."

"Guess he didn't feel under the spell of your charms, Lissy," Vickie laughed.

Lissy straightened up and threw her long blonde hair back. "That's what I mean. Nothing there. No vibe." She pursed her lips. "I was lookin' good too."

They walked onto the court. "No vibe," Lissy continued. "Kind of creepy—nothing there."

"He's better than most. I'll take that. I don't need no goddamned vibe."

* * * *

Someone said Skip had a complicated childhood. That's why he went into this line of work with the after-school program. There were whispers that Skip was used by an uncle when he was a kid. Used by an uncle and sometimes the uncle's friends. That story only made Skip Massey more attractive to his charges. One of their own.

Dorrie asked him about his childhood when they were sitting around the study room late one day. "How'd you grow up, Skip?"

"Oh, I was bumped around a little," he said after a long moment. "Maybe bumped around a lot. Rough times." He looked down at his hands before he looked at the group again. "But I made it through. You will too."

24

LET'S GET SOME INK

The tattoos were Lissy's idea. She brought it up at study hall. "Why don't we get some ink together?"

"Looks cheap," Dorrie commented without looking up from her homework. "Skip would go bananas."

"Doesn't look cheap. Everybody gets them now," Lissy objected. "Nothing Goth, like a skull. Maybe like a rose." She hesitated. "No, not a rose, too many roses around. Maybe a butterfly?"

"Well, that might be cool. A little butterfly. I'd love that." Aggie pulled the sleeve of her sweatshirt down and pointed to the top of her shoulder. "Right here would be perfect."

Dorrie leaned back and stuck a pencil in her tight black curls. "You guys are something." She laughed. "Well, okay. Don't leave me out. Vickie?"

"Sure. Why not?"

That week, Lissy borrowed a book of tattoo designs from a classmate whose cousin was a tattoo artist. After much back and forth, they settled on Aggie's choice—a small orange butterfly. No flowers or design with it. Just a small realistic butterfly with delicate black markings, looking as if it might take off from the shoulder at any moment. They might be caterpillars now, but they were going to be butterflies.

* * * *

"So, I think we're all set on our tats, if none of you have chickened out," Lissy announced as she came into the study room a few days later. "Everybody still in?"

"I'm in. I'm in." Aggie called out.

Vickie raised her hand and Lissy followed. "Dorrie?"

"Who's going to pay for it?" Dorrie folded her arms across her chest. "And don't tell me you're going to do him for tats. I don't want to start anything like that."

"Don't be a jerk, Dorrie." Lissy sighed. "My friend Joey's arranging. He's going to pay his cousin who does tats—with a big discount, of course. Then, Vickie's going to coach Joey for the math exam. Right, Vickie?"

Vickie shrugged. "Yeah. Joey's not stupid, just kind of lazy. He'll be okay."

"And I'm going to help him with workouts and a little power-lifting," Lissy added.

"What kind of workouts?" Dorrie asked.

Lissy looked offended. "Jesus, not that kind of workout. Besides, Dorrie, Joey doesn't like girls that way."

"Oh."

"So, when are we going to get it done?" Aggie asked. "I can hardly wait."

"Can everybody do Wednesday night? Joey's cousin can hold the shop open for us. If Skip has a job for one or two of us, we can do a couple of separate appointments. But let's shoot for Wednesday."

"Don't we have to have an adult with us or a birth certificate or something?" Vickie asked.

"Joey's cousin said not to worry about that."

"Well, I don't know about that, but . . ." Dorrie slowly raised her hand. With a reluctant "Okay."

"Good Karma Tattoos, here we come!" Lissy squealed.

"Should we ask Skip?" Aggie asked in a quiet voice.

"No," Vickie and Dorrie chorused together.

"He'll get mad when he finally sees them," said Vickie." But it will be a while because we should keep them covered for maybe ten days."

"And besides," Lissy added, "we're not getting anything really out there. Just a little butterfly."

"A sweet little butterfly." Aggie smiled and rubbed her arms.

* * * *

"Does it hurt much?" Aggie asked as they walked toward the Good Karma Tattoo Studio near the Strip on Wednesday night.

"Not much, I don't think." Vickie laughed. "You're only worrying about that now?"

"Well, I'm nervous about somebody shooting dye into my skin," Dorrie complained. "And I don't even know if the sweet little butterfly is going to show up on me."

"Don't worry, Dorrie. It's safe. Look how many people have them," Lissy said. "And Joey said his cousin is going to make the little butterfly more of a reddish orange, since the red shows up better on darker skin."

"Okay," said Dorrie, somewhat mollified. "But I'm going last and if I get real nervous, I'm just walking out."

"Oh shit, Dorrie. Don't be like that."

"You have to be with us, Dorrie," Aggie pleaded and pulled Dorrie's arm.

"Okay, okay. Let go of me, Aggie. I'll do it." She took Aggie in a hug.

"Let's go," Lissy shouted as she entered the small shop. "I'm going first. Let's do this."

And so she was and so they did.

Years later, Vickie had seen their butterfly in the Butterfly Garden at the Museum of Science in Boston. She was surprised and disappointed to learn the butterfly's life cycle was so short. Just two to six weeks. After all that hard struggle of emerging from a cocoon, she had wanted that butterfly to live in glorious splendor for months and months, sipping on milkweed, gliding back north from Mexican forests. Victory in flight.

25

WE'RE NOT THE ONLY ONES

Dorrie leaned against the headboard of Vickie's bed one night. "You know, we're not the only ones getting used like this. There are lots of girls getting used like us."

"Like what?" Lissy asked.

"Jesus, Lis. Like getting pimped out."

"I hate when you say it like that." Across the room, Aggie teared up.

"Oh, come on, Ag. What other word is there for it? Should we say something like Skip did when this all started, when he wanted Lissy to do a favor for him and be good to his friend?"

Aggie bit her lip. "Okay. Okay."

"We're not pen pals with these guys. They pay money to Skip for using us. He's selling our bodies."

"Leave her alone, Dorrie," Lissy snapped. "She said okay. Shit."

Vickie had been sitting quietly on the floor, arranging some notecards for a presentation she had to make in a class the next day. "Well, this won't be forever – once we graduate—if we can just hang on." She looked up. "But Dorrie's right. We're not the only ones." She frowned as she changed the order of two of the cards. "And we have it better than a lot of them do."

"I wish we could help some other girls when we get out," Lissy said. "We probably could do that because we know what it's like."

"Yeah," Dorrie mused. "They always pick the girls in shitty situations, like us. That's why they get caught in this game, just like we did. Nobody to help them in the right way." She stopped for a moment before she added in a low, soft voice, "What are we talking about? We can't even help ourselves. We can't even get ourselves out of trouble."

Vickie stood, wrapped the index cards with an elastic and put them on the small bedside table. "Not today, Dorrie." She looked at Dorrie. "Not today. But we will get ourselves out of trouble – we

will for sure. We will get ourselves out of trouble. And then maybe sometime we can help someone else get out of trouble."

* * * *

Sometimes late at night, the girls talked quietly together about the future and what their plans might be after they got out of this life. They vowed to stay in touch and to reach back to help other girls in these kinds of situations.

"Maybe some of those girls won't want to leave the life," Aggie mused. "Maybe sometimes a girl might like her guy, like Skip, because he's nice to her, takes care of her, you know."

"He's not just her *guy,* Aggie." Dorrie jumped in. "Call it what it is. He's a pimp." She looked up at the ceiling before continuing. "And he's not taking care of her from the goodness of his heart. She's a money-maker for him. Jesus."

"I know, I know, Dorrie." Aggie held her hand up. "But maybe too they think they won't be able to make their way, don't even know where to start. Like maybe they don't think they have a choice either, like us?

"Right", said Lissy. Maybe it's like the only real home they have, and he's the only one who cares for them."

The room was quiet as that observation sank in. "Yeah, there is that," Vickie commented with a sad smile.

Finally, Lissy said, "Yeah, anyway, there's that. We know about that. And," she added, "maybe he feeds them stuff and maybe, you know, they're afraid of the guy."

"Are you afraid of Skip?" Vickie asked.

"Yeah, a little," Lissy said. "He hasn't ever done anything—much—but I think he could do damage. He looks pretty scary to me when he's mad." She paused. "Yeah, I think he could go over the edge."

"I think you're right. We haven't seen much of that. But I think you're right."

"He's a mix too – it's like he loves you, even if he's using you. And then it really hurts when he pulls back."

"Oh yeah, he's good at that." Vickie gave a sad smile. "A real talent."

"He can pull back all he wants from me", Dorrie stretched her arms. "I just don't want any hitting. And I think he could do that."

"Yeah." Vickie and Lissy agreed.

Aggie's eyes widened. "Really?""

Dorrie threw her head back and laughed. "Yeah, Aggie. Really." She reached over and started to tickle her. "What planet are you on, girl?"

"His mind works different," Lissy said.

"You know," Dorrie said, releasing Aggie. "He has a different software in his brain—a different program running than most people."

"You're just showing off now, Dorrie." Lissy interrupted.

"What the hell is that supposed to mean?"

"Ever since they sent you for that computer course, you just throw around these words – like software program. Who's talking about a software program?"

"*We* are, Lissy," Dorrie shot back. "It's how our brains work too. It's how we're programmed."

Lissy held up her hand in surrender, though she clearly still didn't get the connection.

"He's programmed differently. Like," Dorrie paused to choose her words, "he can love you in his twisted way but totally damage you, screw up your life. And . . ." Dorrie's hand slapped the bedcover, "*and* he thinks you should be grateful to him. Fuck."

* * * *

"You know, it's great to talk about helping other girls," Lissy said a few days later as she folded her clothes in the gym laundry. "But we wouldn't know what the hell we were doing."

"We'll figure it out, "Vickie said. "We'll learn and be the people we wish had reached out to us, looked out for us."

"Like become social workers or something? They didn't do a whole lot for us."

"Well, maybe we didn't have the right ones," Vickie responded. "Anyway, maybe what we do is help them make connections with the right people. Talk to them if they will let us."

"Pimps can get pretty mad." Dorrie caught the conversation as

she entered the laundry. "At them and at us. Not nice people. Interfering with the business can get pretty dangerous. Skip can be tough but he's a cakewalk compared to some of those other guys."

"I guess." Vickie agreed. "And if we helped them escape, they have to have a place to go." She nodded to herself. "Yeah, we'd have to learn how to do this – like learn the systems, study, so that we know what chances the girls might have."

"Are we all going to be social workers?" Lissy frowned. "I kind of want to be a personal trainer."

"Well, that's kind of a social worker, Lis." Vickie smiled. "No, we'd do other things for a living, but we'd have this as a mission. Yeah, as a mission. To do what we can. But they have to be linked into the system. It won't be easy."

"Right, and we can't adopt them all." Dorrie yawned. "We have to help them get somewhere better. We didn't take a chance on the foster system ourselves."

"Maybe we should have. Aggie's brother's got some really nice fosters."

"Well, yeah, but we're close to out – so that ship already sailed," Vicki shrugged.

"You know, it really won't be easy helping other girls. We could a get into deep trouble, not knowing what we're doing." Dorrie pursed her lips. "These are some bad dudes, and some girls might be too messed up, too far gone – guy gets her hooked or whatever. A girl might tell us to get lost. She'd say she's okay."

"Yeah, but there might be a few others," Vickie persisted. "Maybe not too far in, girls that don't want to be in that world. We know what this world is like from the inside and we haven't had it at all as bad as some girls. We can help move them into the system."

She nodded to herself. "Just learn and try. We can do that. Deal?" Vickie put her hand down on a stack of gym towels. "Deal?" Dorrie added her hand first, then Lissy and Aggie. "Deal," they said in unison.

Aggie put her clothes in a washer and raised her hand. "We need a name. Let's find a name for us."

"The Crusaders," Lissy offered. Dorrie snorted and gave a

thumbs down.

"The Guardian Angels," Aggie volunteered. Dorrie put her hands over her face. "That is *so* bad, Aggie."

"Too holy, Aggie." Vickie smiled.

"Maybe the Avenging Angels." Dorrie chuckled.

"Don't ruin it, Dorrie." Lissy threw a gym towel.

Ignoring them, Aggie looked at the ceiling, thinking. "How about Butterfly Girls – like our tattoos?" She turned her shoulder to the group.

"Too cutesy," Lissy laughed. "Like you."

Aggie hissed "Stop it!" and snapped a towel at her.

"Wait." Vickie held her hand up." Aggie's idea is not bad. How about Mariposa? The word for butterfly."

"Nice." Dorrie smirked. "The Mariposa Gang."

"No, no. The Mariposa Circle." Vickie nodded to herself,

"That's so pretty." Aggie clapped her hands.

"I like it, "Lissy agreed

"Yup." Dorrie sat up again. "*Classy,* like Skip would say."

26

BUSTED

The girls had covered up their arms and butterfly tattoos for the ten days recommended by the tattoo artist at the Good Karma Tattoo Studio. This was convenient, since none of them had wanted to face Skip with their new tats.

Just after the ten days were up, they were scheduled to host a group of girls from the Upper St. Clair YWCA for a pickup volley ball game. A few other girls from the various exercise programs joined the core group of Vickie, Lissy, Dorrie, and Aggie, to round out the team and necessary subs.

Skip had met the Upper St. Clair gym manager, Marcie, at a city event for community programs. He liked her style and decided the Upper St. Clair girls would be a good influence on his team at the Liberty Avenue Gym.

Dorrie and Lissy also thought Skip had kind of a thing for Marcie, a tall and lithe, ponytailed brunette who'd just graduated from Duquesne. Though they were pretty convinced Skip was asexual, he seemed enchanted with Marcie's style.

"Watch her. She's smooth, you know, classy," he'd said. Lissy elbowed Vickie. The girls all agreed that Skip was way too hung up on *class*. "You could do a lot worse than Marcie for a role model of what you could look like and act like." Skip had added.

In spite of themselves, the girls liked Marcie when they were introduced to her and her team. "Okay, she is pretty classy," Lissy said.

"I'll bet her family really does go to Martha's Vineyard, and doesn't just wear the Black Dog sweatshirt," said Dorrie as Skip took his Upper St. Clair guests for a tour of the gym. Skip had recently taken to wearing the Black Dog sweatshirts to the gym, though the girls were quite sure he had never visited the island.

"Speaking of sweatshirts," Vickie said, "we're going to have to

93

ditch these now to play. Our tats are going to show. Get ready. Just act normal."

"It's not that I'm afraid . . ." Lissy started.

"You bet your ass you are," Dorrie retorted.

"I'm just nervous."

"It was your goddamn idea. So brave about getting butterfly tats and now afraid to show them." She laughed.

"Maybe we should just keep them covered up," Lissy volunteered.

"That's stupid, Lissy," Dorrie shot back. "All of us with gauze bandages on our shoulders? Like he wouldn't notice that. And we'd look ridiculous playing in our sweatshirts."

"I feel really afraid," Aggie whispered. "Not just nervous. You know how he is. He'll say we should have asked permission."

"As if he'd ever say yes," Lissy snapped.

"He'll say that it looks cheap, just like I said at the beginning," commented Dorrie, slipping her sweatshirt off and admiring her little red/orange butterfly. "But I have to say it's growing on me."

"Skip might be upset but I don't think he'll make a really big fuss in front of company – maybe a little fuss, but not a really big fuss." Vickie said, checking her own shoulder. "It healed pretty nice, I think."

"Yeah, but he'll be really mad after they leave," Aggie looked glum. "That'll be worse, because we embarrassed him."

"We'll see," Vickie said. "Not much he can do about it. I don't think he wants to pay for laser removal treatment. And not much we can do about it now either. Let's go, ladies."

With Vickie leading, and her teammates tentatively following, the girls took to the court and play commenced. It was a good, fast and well-matched game, so that the girls almost forgot about Skip and their orange butterfly tattoos. It also took some time for Skip to notice the tats.

Then, suddenly, out of the blue, the girls heard a loud "What the hell?" from Skip's sideline and the atmosphere in the gym changed. "What is this shit?"

"Oh fuck." Lissy hissed while she spiked the ball over the net.

"What?" Distracted by Skip and Lissy's reaction, the Upper St.

Clair player missed the ball. "No fair," the girl shouted. "What's going on?"

Grimacing, Lissy whispered "Sorry."

Marcie called a timeout. Arms spread and head cocked, she strode across the court to Skip, who stood stone-cold with his arms crossed. "What the heck's going on, Skip?"

"Vickie, get over here," he called. Vickie slow-walked over. Skip reached for Vickie's arm and, holding it, rubbed his fingers on the butterfly tattoo. "Is this thing real?"

"Yep." Vickie looked directly at Skip. "Yep. It's for real."

"Something wrong, Skip?" Marcie asked as she reached him. "What's going on?"

"Nothing. Nothing. I'll deal with it."

"Deal with what?" Marcie looked at Vickie's arm, which Skip was still holding. Red marks were beginning to show where his fingers pressed Vickie's skin.

Marcie gently put her hand on Skip's, took it off Vickie's arm, and stared at him. "What do you think you're doing?" He shook his head, blew out an angry breath and crossed his arms again.

Dorrie and Aggie came to stand behind Vickie. Lissy walked across the court.

Skip looked at their arms. "Shit. All of you? What were you *thinking*?"

"He's mad about our tats," Dorrie blurted, turning her shoulder to Marcie and pointing to the little butterfly.

"Just a little butterfly", Aggie bit her lip nervously.

"Hey, very cool," Marcie said. "Let me see." She moved Dorrie's arm so that she could get a better look. "Nice work. A really fine job. Almost looks real. Where'd you get it done?"

"Good Karma down near the Strip."

"Oh yeah, they're good." Marcie turned to Skip. "What's the problem, Skip?"

He still had his arms crossed over his chest. "Don't like tats. Looks cheap." Skip looked at her. "You know I'm trying to have them show a little class."

Marcie stared at him. "Right. When did you get so old and

crotchety, Massey?"

Marcie pulled the sleeve of her sweatshirt down to reveal a delicate rose tattoo.

"Get with the program."

Nearby, Dorrie covered her mouth to hide a laugh and elbowed Vickie.

"You think I don't have enough class, Skip?" Marcie continued.

Skip reddened. "I don't think that, Marcie. You know I don't think that."

Marcie walked closer to Skip and whispered, "Then just leave those girls with their classy, pretty butterfly tattoos alone. And," she looked at Vickie's arm, "keep your hands off the girls. Hear me?"

Reddening, Skip nodded and shifted his feet.

Marcie started to walk away but turned back to say, "And would you please uncross your arms?" Skip dropped his hands to his side, shook his head and raised his hands in defeat, a small smile on his face.

Marcie clapped her hands. "Okay, timeout's over, everybody. Let's play."

* * * *

"Is she the best or what?" Lissy said in her room that night, dropping on her bed.

"Skip's right – she's a great model. Just not the one he expected." Dorrie laughed.

When one of the gym cats had a litter the next week, the girls named a sleek gray kitten Marcie before they gave it away to one of their classmates.

Skip and Marcie engaged in a few more activities together with their respective gym teams. Skip apparently never lost his admiration for her – in spite of her rose tattoo and her dissing him in front of his Liberty Avenue team.

But Vickie could see how disappointed he was when, at one of their last games, Marcie mentioned she was headed to law school in New York. Vickie registered the shock on Skip's face, though she was quite sure Marcie did not. Marcie couldn't have realized the impact on Skip of her moving out of his orbit – going to New York

City—and leaving him behind on Liberty Avenue.

Later, as Vickie learned of Skip's successes, long after the days of the Liberty Avenue gym, she always thought he was still trying to impress young Marcie – so long gone from his world.

27

A NEW HOME AND AN OPPORTUNITY

Vickie had a different math tutor from the other girls. A tougher one. She was in three AP classes. "No slacking off," Skip would order. "Keep those grades up. You're gold, Czinski. My star. Don't fail me."

Vickie had long ago stopped dropping into her mother's dirty and unkempt apartment with all its random visitors and her mother in another world. She'd made out a change of address at school for Skip's blue Victorian next to the gym and forged her mother's signature on it. No one asked any questions or noticed that the address was that of the house next to the gym.

She wasn't sure her mother even noticed she was missing or remembered she had a daughter—she was so lost to the world. One day, Vickie walked by her mother's apartment building and there was someone else's name on the mailbox. No one knew where she had gone.

Since Vickie used the blue Victorian as her mailing address, that's where the letter came advising her of the scholarship to the University of Pittsburgh. It was a full academic scholarship, but no funding for living expenses or books.

The on-campus jobs Pitt suggested to help defray expenses could in no way cover the costs of books, room, and board. Vicki was advised to apply for a student loan but she knew that, essentially having no parents and living in an unorthodox arrangement at the gym, her application could never withstand the scrutiny of the process. She'd have to commute to Pitt and continue living at the blue house with her expenses picked up by Skip and her earnings from her clientele.

Still, Vickie knew the scholarship was an enormous accomplishment. To celebrate, Skip took her to a special restaurant called Le Mont, way up near the funicular carrying people up and down the

steep incline on Mount Washington and overlooking the Pittsburgh skyline.

Vickie and Skip dined on filet mignon and a special chocolate lava cake for dessert. They sat at a corner window table, with views of the city where the three great rivers meet—the Ohio, the Allegheny, and the Monongahela. Vickie had never seen this view before—the Three Rivers Stadium, the Pittsburgh Plate Glass building, and the whole skyline. So beautiful, it almost made her dizzy – could it be real? Was this the city she'd been living in?

Skip gave her a new laptop for her studies and the week off. He told her she was his pride and joy. For that night, Vickie felt no one had ever loved her like Skip Massey.

28

THE WORLD OPENS

Vickie met a boy the first day of registration at Pitt, chemistry major named Josh. He had dark curly hair and glasses and made her laugh in a way she couldn't ever remember doing before.

He brought Vickie to the Cathedral of Learning at Pitt, with its ornate nationality rooms. He couldn't believe she had never been there before. "Didn't your parents ever bring you here?

"Oh no, they were always traveling overseas and I went to boarding school in Vermont."

"Wow, that must have been interesting." Vickie thought Josh sounded a little envious. She must seem so exotic to him. What a joke.

"It was okay. I'll tell you all about it sometime. Have we been to the Chinese room yet? Let's see that before we go."

They walked through Schenley Park and talked forever. Vickie continued to make a lot up about herself and her life, but that was okay. It rolled off her tongue easily—she'd looked up small private schools in Vermont for details and just made up her parents' lives overseas in broad, nonspecific brushes. It was like writing a movie script. She'd figure out how to deal with it later.

Josh loved to take Vickie places she'd never been. She was transported by the day they spent at the Phipps Conservatory and Botanical Gardens. Looking over a sea of orange and red chrysanthemums in an autumn display, she told Josh "I'm in heaven".

To Vickie, during these times the very air seemed to throb with the possibility of a different life.

Later that same week, she had to make her apologies for not being available for dinner at Hemingway Café and a preseason Panthers exhibition basketball game. She knew Josh was disappointed, but when she told him she had an engagement with old friends of

her parents, he understood.

In truth, the engagement she had was a date with a lawyer from McKeesport that Skip had set up for her. *Don't be late. Dress nice. He's a class act.* In fact, the class-act lawyer had something more exotic that he wanted her to wear when they'd driven to a no-name motel out of the city, but that's another story.

Vickie was careful not to accept dinner or drinks dates with clients, arranging instead to go directly to hotel rooms where she usually entered the back way. She took no assignments anywhere near the university or Mount Lebanon. She couldn't risk being seen.

Josh lived in the dorms for the full college experience, although his family was in Mount Lebanon outside Pittsburgh. Vickie told Josh her parents had arranged for her to board in a private home and the lady did not want Vickie to bring guests back to the house. She always managed to catch the bus from Pitt alone, so the Josh didn't have a chance to see the house where she was supposed to be boarding. Again, she'd figure that part out later.

Josh seemed to accept the explanation in general, though he never fully understood why her parents did not want Vickie to live in the dorm. He guessed they just thought about things differently.

* * * *

Being with Josh was different—tentative and sweet, something she'd never experienced. Afterward, he would bury his face in her hair, murmuring her name. He'd trace the veins in her arms and neck with his fingers and then kiss them lightly before reaching her mouth. No one had ever revered Vickie like that. She remembered a word from poetry class—consecrated. She felt consecrated.

"I'm not your first," he said.

"No, but you're my best."

"Tell me."

"No."

* * * *

That month in Vickie's Psych 101 class, the instructor touched on the defensive mechanism of compartmentalization—keeping

parts of our lives and the emotions around them separate—for survival. Boy, she'd thought, I could have written the book on that. Now, she had a name for how she'd gotten through her life so far.

* * * *

When they could find a good space together, Josh and Vickie usually studied in one of the reading rooms at the Hillman Library. Afterward they'd go to the Fuel and Fuddle Bar near campus to unwind.

At the Fuel and Fuddle, they agreed they would try for the Beer Cult. Once they drank—over time—each of the 100 craft beers the bar stocked, they would become official Beer Cult members and would get their names on a special list of Beer Cult members on the wall. Vickie and Josh wanted to have their names up there together at the same time.

After a while, Josh invited her home for dinner with his family in Mount Lebanon. Josh's family lived in one of those solid Tudor-style brick homes that Vickie had only seen in magazines. A row of asters and late blooming shrub roses bordered the brick walkway as they approached the heavy maroon front door with a wide overhanging portico. Large blue ceramic planters were filled with more shrub roses. Through a large window, with the golden light from the living room, she could see Josh's parents laying out appetizers.

"Wait," she said, putting her hand on Josh's arms. "I want to imprint this." She inhaled deeply and leaned her head on his shoulder for a few moments.

Smiling, Josh opened the front door and ushered Vickie into this paradise. Thick oriental carpets lay on the wooden floor, the upholstered furniture comfortable and rich, like the carpets, in various shades of green, gold and ivory. Josh called out. His parents came down the hall. When they reached Josh and Vickie, they hugged them both in welcome. Soft music played in the background. "We've heard all about you. We're so glad you're here." For Vickie this was a dream image she never forgot.

They had a dog. She'd always wanted a dog. Skip allowed cats at the gym to keep the mice under control, but he'd refused a dog. The girls had promised to walk and feed a dog faithfully, if they could get one for the gym, but Skip was unmovable. "Yeah, you say that now.

Too much trouble. Anyway, a dog would probably bother the clients. All that barking, jumping, and slobbering."

Josh's dog was a West Highland Terrier named Archie. Blocky, white and spirited. The family let Archie sit on the sofa and Josh fed him cheese from the plate when his mother wasn't looking. His mother said the vet had told her that Archie was not supposed to eat people food.

Such nice people. Just like on television, thought Vickie. She was glad Skip had spent so much time teaching her and other girls table manners. Glad too she'd been listening carefully to some of the other students from places like where Josh came from. Glad she'd been trying to mimic how they talked and expressed themselves.

Josh's dad—gray at the temples, wearing rimless glasses and dressed in a white button-down shirt and a navy cardigan—was a scientist at Bayer. Josh's tiny bird of a mother—a lively and witty blonde in black leggings with ballet slippers and a colorful, swingy top—spent her time volunteering at the Carnegie Art Museum.

Over a Moroccan chicken dish ("Maybe you've had this in your travels. Did your parents ever visit Morocco?") Vickie danced through questions about her parents and prayed that Josh's mother and father didn't go too much deeper. They didn't, the conversation flowed smoothly, and she could tell they found her charming.

"They really like you", Josh gushed afterward. "Pretty *and* smart, they said."

29

THE END OF THAT DREAM

One night shortly afterward, Skip came into Vickie's small bedroom behind the gym. He stood in the doorway, and leaned against the door frame with his Diet Dr Pepper in one hand. Vickie was sitting on her bed, pillows behind her, one of the gym cats beside her. Immersed in a Fundamentals of Finance textbook, it took her some time to realize that Skip was at the door. When she looked up, she saw him taking in the scene and studying her.

"Have your fun, honey. But don't get serious. You're too young." He took a sip of his Dr Pepper and smiled. "And, well, you still have to earn your keep here. I've made a big investment in you. You're my lead girl. My flagship for a first-class operation. Don't give it all away to some little boy, sweetheart. I can't let you do that."

Vickie didn't respond. Skip smiled again before leaving and walking back down the hall. They never discussed the subject directly again.

The next time Vickie went to the Fuel and Fuddle with Josh, Skip was sitting at the bar. He gave her that wide smile as he ambled over to their table. When he pulled out a seat, Vickie could feel some part of her dying.

"Hi, Vickie, fancy seeing you here." He turned to Josh after he sat down. "This your friend Josh? Good to meet you, Josh. I'm Skip." He reached over the table to shake hands with Josh, who looked bewildered.

There was a rerun of a Steelers game on the bar TV. "You a Steelers fan, Josh?" Skip asked. "Hey, but who isn't?" He settled into his chair. "You know, I'm thinking they'd better trade down in the first round drafts this year to get more picks in the later rounds, right?"

Josh looked confused and stunned but recovered enough to respond weakly, "Oh yeah, we're all Steelers fans, I guess, but I like the Penguins myself."

"Okay, hockey's a good game too. If they could just keep their injuries down this season, they should do okay."

And so it went, with Skip talking in an aggressive torrent of sports commentary, getting himself a beer and pushing one toward Josh. "Here you go. A different one—called the Fancy Girl. Help you get into the Beer Cult. You want a Fancy Girl, Vickie?"

Vickie shook her head slowly without looking at Skip.

"Okay, too bad." He looked over the extensive list of beers on the wall. "Boy, a lot of choices there." He shook his head and repeated, "Yep, choices, choices, choices."

Josh had stopped talking. He stared stonily down at his empty glass and did not pick up the fresh Fancy Girl beer. Vickie looked across the table at him once. He wouldn't meet her eyes. She saw him now as he was—a really nice guy from the suburbs who was far out—so very far out of his depth. She would never be part of this solid, funny, wonderful guy's bright future. Who was she kidding? Right now, she was an on-call girl. Maybe not forever, but right now that's what she was.

Finally, having made his point, Skip stopped and looked at both Josh and Vickie for a long time. "Well, gotta go. Just thought I'd stop by to say hello." He stood, leaned down to give Vickie a proprietary kiss on the lips. She could feel Josh's physical shock across the table.

"See you later, Fancy Girl." Then, Skip left and all was quiet.

"Who the hell was that?" Josh stammered.

"A guy I know." Vickie murmured.

"Seems like more than that to me. Weird." He frowned. "A little scary, if you want the truth."

"I guess." She shrugged, at a loss for words. She willed herself not to cry, but she could feel her body trembling.

They were both quiet. Vickie traced the condensation on the side of her glass and didn't look at Josh.

"Can't handle this," Josh said finally.

Vickie watched him leave.

After some minutes, she picked up her jacket and went up to the bar where, with shaking hands, she erased both names from the Beer Cult candidate list.

Josh didn't ghost her. He invited her for coffee at Pamela's Diner. She listened in polite silence as he explained that since they were both young—only freshmen—it probably was a good idea for them not to get too serious. Besides, he had a heavy course load and he really needed to buckle down on his studies right now. He didn't have a lot of time for a social life and she probably felt the same, since she seemed to have other interests.

Vickie did not respond to the "other interests" part. Neither of them directly touched on Skip's showing up at the Fuel and Fuddle and all that it suggested. But what was there to say about that event except to follow it to other questions and lies? She couldn't handle that.

She just nodded. "I get it. We'll let it go." Josh left shortly after.

His whole careful script sounded to Vickie like something his mom had coached him on, while they sat in the captain chairs at the round maple kitchen table with in their Mount Lebanon home.

Even as her heart was broken at a dream destroyed, that was the part she envied to her very soul. Josh's mom sitting with him at the maple table helping him do things right. He had a mom who could help him do things like that. Only very occasionally did Vickie feel the profound, aching wound of not having a mother in any real sense of the word. This was one of those times.

Every once in a while, she would see Josh in the food court or walking across campus with friends. But he didn't call. Not the next day or the next or ever again.

Skip bought her a Canada Goose coat. "Going to be a cold winter, sweetheart."

Vickie didn't study as much at the Hillman Library at Pitt after that. She started to come directly home to the blue Victorian after classes.

30

BURGERS AND ICE CREAM –
DANGER ON THE HORIZON

One night, some weeks later, Vickie was in the study room at the gym with Aggie when Dorrie stuck her head around the corner of the door.

"Your brother's here, Aggie."

Aggie looked up, clearly relieved to leave her geometry workbook. "Thank God. I've *had* it. I hate this stuff." She pushed a curtain of white-blond hair from her eyes. "I don't know why Skip makes us do this shit."

"It's for your own good, Aggie," Vickie murmured behind her own book. "You need it to graduate from high school."

"I'm never going to use it," Aggie wailed, throwing her arms out. "I'm not going to get some big college scholarship like you. Besides, I want to be a hair stylist."

"Well, maybe it will help you cut someone's bangs straight," Vickie commented, again without looking up from her book.

"Can it, Aggie." Lissy put her hand on her hip. "If you don't go out with your brother, I will. He's a big, good-looking guy."

"Oh, Lissy, listen to you. You leave him alone." Aggie laughed as she got up, shooting Lissy a warning look.

"And he takes you out to eat too," Dorrie said.

"Just to CC's for a burger." Aggie picked up her jacket. "And afterward for ice cream."

"Sounds special to me." Dorrie sighed. "Burgers and ice cream with a regular guy, not drinks with some old dude." She brushed something off her jeans. "Hope I can get some of that someday."

She leaned against the door frame and looked up at the ceiling dreamily. "I'd get me one of those CC burgers with all the fixings and then I'd go get one of those Banana Split Blizzards. Oh yeah."

"Shut up, Dorrie. I gotta go." Aggie moved Dorrie out of the

way with a half shove, half hug.

"Bring me back one? One of those Blizzards?" Dorrie called after her.

"Maybe. You know Tommy can't go treating everybody, Dorrie." Then, Aggie turned. "Okay—what kind again?"

"Yes!" Dorrie squealed. "Banana split, honey, banana split."

"She's lucky," Dorrie said to Vickie after Aggie left. "He comes every week." Dorrie dropped into a chair next to Vickie, crossed her long, elegant brown legs and peeked at Vickie's cost accounting book. She grimaced. "Ugh."

"Her brother work?" Vickie asked. "He's foster too, right?"

"Yeah, he got some good ones. I wish Aggie could have been with them instead of where she ended up."

"Me too. She's better off here. That guy in that last house was a creep."

"Plenty of creeps here, Vickie girl."

"Yeah, but at least they pay and there's something in it for us."

Dorrie didn't speak for a moment and then said softly. "Speak for yourself, girl."

"Where's her brother work?" Vickie asked, ignoring Dorrie's comment.

"Car wash. Takes Aggie out once a week. Little presents for her birthday and for his fosters on the holidays. The rest, he pretty much saves for when he's eighteen and can get an apartment for him and Aggie."

Lissy sighed across the room. "He's a prince."

"Yeah, that he is." Dorrie agreed.

"No parents?" Vickie asked.

"Mom got on the pills and went pro to keep herself supplied. Father's forever gone—a long-haul trucker, I think. Got another family for himself in West Virginia." She threw her head back, the beads in her long black braids slapping the back of the chair. "We're a sad bunch, ain't we? Nobody wants us except for our asses."

"Not true, Dorrie. We've got a chance here."

Dorrie snorted. "How did we get so lucky?"

Vickie broke the silence that followed. "What's with that dry

cleaner guy and Aggie. He's always picking her up. I thought Skip said no exclusives."

"I don't know. I think maybe he pays extra." She laughed. "Maybe he gives Skip a deal on getting all those fancy suits cleaned at one of his shops. He owns a chain of shops, you know."

"No, I didn't know that," Vickie smirked. "That sounds like Skip—taking his suits to a client's business." She twisted her mouth slightly. "But a bad idea to let the guy have an exclusive. Does she like him?"

"Naw. He was okay at the beginning but now he's kind of creepy. Likes her too much. Doesn't want her having other dates. She's getting a little nervous with how into her he is. He's even talking crazy about leaving his wife and family. *And . . .*" Dorrie put her face closer to Vickie's, "his wife has a bad cancer—what do you think about that? Isn't that for shit?"

"Pretty bad. Jesus."

"Besides, he's like . . . really old. He's got kids in college. She's a few years younger than they are." She winced. "Ick."

"Yeah, ick," murmured Vickie, still looking at her textbook, but no longer studying.

Then, Dorrie smiled. "He's got one smokin' good-looking son, though. Aggie showed me a picture. Aggie said he was a football player up at Penn State. That's who Aggie should be dating."

"Another world, Dorrie," Vickie said softly. "Another world. Not ours."

"You're telling me." Dorrie sighed. "I looked him up on the internet when I was supposed to be doing my English essay." She grinned. "Whoa—yeah, way better than his old dad. Forget the dad. I'm falling for the son."

They both laughed. "Anyway, maybe the dad has one of those midlife crisis things they talk about. Maybe he'll get over it."

"Or maybe not." Vickie closed her textbook. "Shit. What's she going to do?"

"I don't know. I think she should tell Skip. She's afraid to tell her brother, Tommy—he might go after the guy. He doesn't really know everything. He'd go crazy."

Dorrie was quiet briefly, looking into the distance and chewing her lower lip. "I don't know. Skip won't stand for this foolishness. And . . ." Dorrie shifted in her seat. "And, I really don't think this guy is good for her in lots of ways. A couple of times lately, she looks kind of slammed when she gets home. She called and asked me to let her in the side door so Skip didn't see her."

Vickie looked at Dorrie. "What do you mean *slammed?*"

"Like maybe he gave her something. Like maybe she was on something." She looked down at her hands. "And I think he might be taking her to meet with one of his friends."

"Oh Christ. That's all we need. We need to tell Skip."

Dorrie put her hand on Vickie's shoulder. "Now I'm thinking we should wait up on that. He'll kill the guy. God, he might kill Aggie."

"Don't talk like that, Dorrie."

"Well, anyway, he might throw Aggie out. He said he doesn't want any junkies in his girls—brings down the image." She rolled her expressive brown eyes before continuing, "Said he's not running a rehab here. No second chances—once and we're out. Aggie doesn't have anywhere else to go. I'm worried for her."

"Then we need to talk to her."

Dorrie looked out the window near the study desk. "I want out of here so bad."

"Look, you got enough credits for your diploma. And with the computer courses you're taking, you've got a good chance at a future. Just a little longer. You'll have a real life." Vickie put her hand on Dorrie's knee. "We all need to get ourselves real lives."

"You really think he'll let us go? I think he expects us to stick around."

"He doesn't need to *let us go*." Vickie paused. "Lissy and Aggie are almost out too. Then, we can all go together."

Dorrie gave Vickie an inquiring look. Vickie returned the look with a soft one of her own. "And, besides," she said, squeezing Dorrie's knee, "We've got each other. We're family."

31

FROM WHEN WE'RE CATERPILLARS TIL WE'RE BUTTERFLIES

Aggie shook off her black jean jacket. Looking around CC's restaurant, she slipped the right strap of her pink tank top down and turned sideways toward her brother, Tommy, to reveal the top of her right shoulder.

A small, sweet monarch butterfly tattoo sat on her shoulder, about two inches tall and three inches in wing span—all anchored by a slender black body.

Tommy smiled. "Pretty. How come you got that?"

"Because we're caterpillars now, but we're going to be butterflies, Tommy." Aggie slipped her strap back up and put her arm back into her jacket.

"Who's *we*?"

"The other girls at the gym and me."

"Got it, Aggie. You're going to be butterflies." he chortled.

"Don't laugh at me, you jerk. We even have a name."

"And what's that?"

"You can't tell anybody. It's a secret."

"Oh, like a secret society," he said and leaned across the table toward her with a broad grin.

"Yeah, a secret society. Only us. To stick together. Like family."

Tommy pulled back and sat against the back of the booth. "You and me, we stick together. We're family. They're not family."

Aggie waved her hand and said softly, "This is different, Tommy. We look out for each other in a different way."

"Better than I look out for you?"

She put her hand on his and looked at her brother for a long time. "Nobody looks out for me the way you do, Tommy."

Tommy relaxed and smiled at her. "Damned right, little sister. Damned right, Butterfly Girl."

"Stop it. Do you want to know the name?"

"All right. I give up. What's the stupid name?"

Aggie looked around the diner to see if anyone was listening before she leaned forward and whispered, "The Mariposas."

"The Mariposas?" Tommy screwed up his face. "What the fuck does that mean? It sounds like some gang."

"Shh. Not so loud," Aggie said in an urgent whisper, followed. "Watch your language, shithead."

Tommy laughed and fell back against the plastic booth. "Okay. I'll be good. What's it mean?"

Aggie took another sip of her orange juice. "Vickie looked it up. It's Spanish."

Tom raised his brows. "Fancy. What's it mean?"

"Right. It's two words. *Mari* is for Mary, the Blessed Mother." Her brother nodded approvingly. "And *posa* is like posing or perching on a flower. Isn't that pretty?"

He nodded again, enjoying his sister's company.

She paused to bite into a French fry. "And you know what else?"

"No, what else, beans for brains?"

"They travel thousands of miles from up North to special places in Mexico."

"Going on a little butterfly vacation?"

"Stop it," Aggie snapped.

"Whoa." Tom put his hand up. "Don't get too cranky here."

Mollified, Aggie continued. "They go to lay their eggs and then the new butterflies fly all the way back North." Aggie touched his arm. "What I wanted to say is that they fly so far, *so far*. They have such a *long* journey." She nodded to herself. "Vickie says we have a long journey too. Butterflies."

"You going somewhere?" asked Tommy. "Don't get me worried, Aggie."

"Listen. What Vickie meant was the trip from when we're caterpillars till we're butterflies."

Her brother grinned. "Well, just let me know when you start growing those little antennas." He put his hands on either side of his head, index fingers extended. "And wings," he added as he lowered

his hands. "We'll have to cut holes in your jacket."

They both laughed.

"You laugh now, Tomaz Janek Urbanowski. You'll see."

"Just hang on, Aggie. I'll graduate and be eighteen in May. The car wash says that with my experience I can supervise the afternoon shift." He nodded to himself. "Goin' places." He squirted his beef patty liberally with ketchup before biting into it.

"That's disgusting. You bury everything with that slop."

"Shut up, little sister. My burger. You don't have to eat it." He made a face at her.

"Anyway, as I was saying before I was so rudely interrupted," he continued, "then, I'll get a little experience and I can go somewhere else." He licked ketchup off his fingers. "Supervising looks good on the resume, you know. Even at a car wash." He chuckled.

"Oh, you're going to go far, Tommy." Aggie responded. She rubbed her forehead and smiled at him.

"And," Tommy took another bite of his burger, "by then I'll have enough money and I'll be of age. We can rent us a place of our own and get you out of that goddamned *gym*." He leaned forward, his face pained. "I can't stand you there, Aggie."

"I don't have a choice right now, Tommy. *We* don't have a choice. I have to live. I have to graduate from high school. Just a little longer."

Her brother covered his eyes.

"Don't cry, Tommy. Don't."

Tommy lowered his hand and inhaled deeply.

"I can't stand it, but maybe just a few more months." He pointed his finger at her. "You have to keep your grades up so that we can both graduate, Aggie. We have to have a future, you and me. We have to make a future for us out of this big mess."

"That would be wonderful. We will, Tom, we will." Aggie sighed, touching her forehead again. "God, this headache just won't go away."

Tom put down his burger and stared closely at Aggie. "Look at me."

Slowly and reluctantly Aggie looked up into her brother's eyes.

"Where were you last night? What did you take?"

Aggie let out a long breath and leaned back in the booth. "Always the big brother, Tommy."

She reached for his hand. He snatched it away. "Don't *Tommy, Tommy* me, Aggie. Is it that dry cleaner jerk?"

"No, no. I didn't see him last night. Just coming down with something."

"Shit. Be careful, Aggie. We're almost there." Tommy leaned forward. "Listen to me. You have to be careful." His eyes filled. "You and me. We got plans, Aggie."

"I know, I know. Hey, I promised Dorrie I'd bring her back a Blizzard. Don't let me forget."

"I suppose I'm buying." He smiled a proud smile.

"Yes, you are, Big Bro." Aggie pointed at his ketchup-covered burger, laughed. "Eat that mess."

32

COLLATERAL DAMAGE

Lissy let Aggie in the side door again one night later that week while Skip was downstairs watching a Netflix DVD. Some-one had banged on the side door until the inside hall light went on. Then, that someone hopped back in his car and sped away.

Lissy half-carried and slow-walked Aggie up the back stairs into Vickie's room. Vickie looked up and, without speaking, helped Lissy bring Aggie to Vickie's bed.

Aggie rolled over once when she hit the bed. "Thanks, Lissy. So tired."

"Christ," Lissy said, looking at a dazed and disheveled Aggie. Dark blood dried on her nose, her blouse open, her black lace bra askew and her breasts bruised, deep bite marks on the nipples.

"Go get Dorrie," Vickie told Lissy. "Skip will kill her if he sees her like this. She's not right. Totally out of it. Shit." She surveyed Aggie on the bed. "We should wash her."

"No, no," said Lissy. Leave her that way. It's evidence for the police."

"Are you crazy? There will be no police. God. Too many ques-tions, about this, about Aggie. Skip would kill us and he'll kill us for bringing her in." Then Vickie muttered under her breath. "Be-sides, police responding to a complaint about another beat-up whore. As if," she muttered under her breath.

Lissy gasped, her eyes filling with tears. "Stop it, Vickie."

"I'm sorry." Vickie rubbed her forehead. "Go get Dorrie."

When Lissy left, Vickie got a washcloth and filled a small clean plastic wastebasket with soapy water. She sat next to Aggie on the bed and started to gently wash her injuries.

Aggie woke and turned her head to Vickie and giggled softly. "Hi, Vickie. Can I sleep here? Maybe the Big Guy won't find me." She buried her face in the pillow. "Oh, God, he'll be so pissed." She

giggled again.

"What'd that asshole give you?" Vickie asked.

Aggie's head lolled on the pillow. "What? What?" Then her eyes closed again. "Dunno. Stuff. Talk in the morning," Aggie murmured without opening her eyes. "Can't think now."

Vickie dried her and buttoned up her clothes. Then, she wrapped her arms around Aggie and lay back with her.

"Looks like it was a rough night, Aggie."

"Yeah." Aggie's mouth twisted. "He has a friend. Rough. Mean." She gave a sob and then turned her head on the pillow away from Vickie and closed her eyes—gone again.

Dorrie came back with Lissy, who stopped at the door and took in the scene. Her mouth tightened. "I'm telling Skip right now. Better he be mad and we all get in trouble than her be dead." She paused. "And he'll kill that dry cleaner shithead."

"In the morning," Vickie heard Aggie whisper as she turned and moved her head next to Vickie. "Night. Talk in the morning."

But there was there was no next morning.

* * * *

Vickie could hear Skip coming down the hall, his feet heavy on the floor. "Fuck, fuck, fuck."

He straight-armed the door to the bedroom and walked directly over to the bed. Dorrie and Lissy stood tentatively in the hall, inching their way into the room, terrified.

"Who let her in?"

"I did," Vickie said.

"The hell you did." Skip swirled to look at Dorrie and Lissy, who both stepped back several feet.

"Never mind," he snapped. "She was supposed to be with that Coombs guy—right?"

Vickie nodded.

"I'll kill him."

Skip turned to the door where Lissy and Dorrie stood watching. "Get out of here," he shouted, starting toward them. They held each other's arms as they backed into the hallway. "And keep your mouths shut," he yelled after them.

Pushing Vickie aside, Skip lifted Aggie by the shoulders and started to shake her. Aggie's blonde hair flew around her head in a wild golden storm. Her head flopped back and forth as if it might snap off her body.

"Stop it, stop it, Skip." Vickie rushed him and pulled frantically on his arm.

"Shut up, Vickie. Shut up." He pushed her to the floor with one arm, gave her a powerful kick to the ribs and returned to shaking Aggie.

Vickie rolled over in pain but lifted herself up enough to reach for Skip's leg and pull at it. He kicked her off again. She'd rolled away when suddenly everything became very still, quiet. Skip had stopped shaking Aggie.

"Jesus Christ." He dropped Aggie on the bed like a rag doll. "Jesus Christ. She's gone."

Skip rubbed his face with his hand and sat on the edge of the bed. Vickie crawled to the bed and reached for Aggie. "Aggie. Aggie. Are you okay?"

He pushed Vickie to the floor and began to kick her again. "Aggie's not fucking okay. Aggie's dead. Got it?" Vickie folded her arms over her stomach and ribs, as Skip kicked her again and again in a rhythmic pattern "You got it? She's dead. You got it?"

Vickie crawled under the bed and squeezed herself against the wall in a fetal position. Her efforts to protect herself enraged Skip further. He started to lift and shake the bed, reach for her. "She's goddamned dead. Fuck. Fuck. Fuck."

He stopped after a couple of minutes, and she could hear him drop heavily on a side chair. She crept out enough to see him with his face buried in his hands. Hearing her, he raised his face and said tiredly. "Come on out, Vickie. Get me a blanket for her."

Vickie's body ached all over, but she crawled out from under the bed, stood and made her way to the end of the bed where she picked up a baby blue fleece blanket. She had no tears.

"Where're you taking her?"

"Never mind. Never mind," Skip growled, his jaw set, the area round his mouth white.

"Why the hell didn't you tell me he was doing her like this?"

"Didn't know," Vickie murmured.

"The hell you didn't." She flinched and backed up as he rose and came toward her again. The first blow knocked her against the wall, but she didn't fall. The second blow hit the left side of her head and eye area like a clap of thunder. She knew the bruises would show. So did Skip.

He shook his head and averted his eyes from the look of her bruised face. "Hurry up."

She had tears on her face now, her nose running. He took a tissue from a side table and threw it at her.

"Clean yourself up." She didn't pick it up.

"Clean yourself up," he roared, stepping toward her.

Vickie picked the tissue up and wiped her nose with shaking hands. She touched her face where his blows had struck her, and handed him the blanket.

She breathed in ragged short breaths as she watched Skip's rough, angry movements wrapping Aggie in the blue blanket. Like a butcher wrapping a roast—rough and efficient.

"Thought she was different," he muttered. "But she turned out to be a piece of trash like her mother. I can't run a rehab house here."

"She's not a piece of trash. She's a good person. You're the one that gave her to that guy."

He came toward Vickie in a slow, menacing stride. She stood unsteadily, her whole body aching, and braced for the blow that didn't come. He waved his hand dismissively and turned back to Aggie's bed.

"Can I come?" Vickie asked in a hoarse voice.

"No, you can't come." He finished wrapping Aggie's body up in the blue fleece, and stopped to stare at her face looking out from the blanket, her light blonde hair fanning out like the sun from her sweet, round face. He lightly fingered a necklace on Aggie's throat – a thin gold chain with a multicolored butterfly on it. "Her brother gave her this, right? Not the shithead?"

"Right," Vickie murmured.

"Then we'll leave it on her. If the other one gave it to her, I'd

shove it down his throat after I beat his head in." Vickie thought she might have heard Skip's voice crack with a sob. "Shit. A sweet kid. One of my best."

Eyes red, he turned to Vickie. "No, you can't come with me. If you'd called me last night, I wouldn't have to carry her out like this. You must have known, Vickie. You must have known."

He stood for a moment by the bed before he walked over to her. "You knew. You knew. You all knew." Vickie closed her eyes and didn't move. Then, inhaling deeply, Skip stopped, walked back to the bed and picked Aggie up.

"Where's the family she's supposed to be living with?"

Vickie searched her mind. "I think Flynn on Wiggins Street— up on the Hill," she whispered.

"Pack up all her shit and bring it up there after you clean yourself up." Skip didn't look at her when he added, "Straighten yourself out. And put on sunglasses. Maybe wear a scarf."

He stroked the side of his face with his hand, thinking, "Tell them to put it all back into whatever room she was supposed to be staying in," he continued." I'll be by there in a couple of hours to pay them and tell them what to say."

Aggie had no suitcases, so Vickie used trash bags to hold her things. She only broke down when she packed up Aggie's stuffed animal collection.

* * * *

Later that night, Skip dropped Vickie off at the emergency room at West Penn Hospital. He didn't go inside with her. Imaging at the hospital showed that Vickie had two broken ribs, which they could do little about except to do a wrap. Her back was heavily bruised, but nothing broken. They gave her painkillers and a prescription for more. Looking at the bruises on her back, the left eye swollen shut, and the split lip, the nurse arranged for a social worker to stop by before Vickie left, to interview her and discuss domestic abuse.

Vickie stuck to her falling-down-the-stairs story with the social worker. Afterward, she tossed the literature they gave her in the trash barrel outside the emergency room exit. Skip drove over from the back of the parking lot and picked Vickie up at the exit. She

knew he was embarrassed to face the emergency room staff and didn't want any possible abuse conversation complications.

"You okay?" he growled and pulled away while she was fastening her seat belt.

"Just fine." She looked to the side, out the window.

"Good—take the week off. They give you a script for painkillers?"

She nodded. His eyes still fixed ahead, Skip held out his hand, took the script, and slipped it into his jacket pocket. "You don't need to start taking those. You can take some Tylenol."

* * * *

Over the years, this night would return to Vickie. There was really no way to process the life she was in then. She just had to move through it in those days. But later, long after she'd left Liberty Avenue, this cruel night would come back to her in the early morning hours. A regular uninvited, unwanted visitor that would sit with her until the sun rose.

33

THE BLONDE MADONNA ON POLISH HILL

The next morning, the Pittsburgh Police Department responded to a report of a body on Polish Hill. Rolled in a blue fleece blanket, the body was found in the alley between the Immaculate Heart of Mary in Heaven Church and Rosary Hall, not far from the image and prayer plaque of Our Lady of Czestochowa, the Black Madonna.

"Another one." The responding officer looked at the blonde Madonna who'd been Aggie Urbanowski, her hair spilling on the asphalt like white gold, that soft, sweet Aggie smile still on her face.

"Tough. They forget to breathe with that stuff," his partner commented. "Good looking kid—I'm getting fucking tired of this. Any ID yet?"

The first officer shook his head. A passing EMT pulled down the shoulder of Aggie's jersey. "I noticed this. Might help."

The small butterfly could have just alighted on Aggie's shoulder. A slight breeze coming down the alley could almost have fluttered its orange wings. A little butterfly keeping Aggie Urbanowski company as she passed to the other side.

* * * *

The obituary notice for Agnieszka Natalia Urbanowski reported her *sudden death* at a young age, often a code for overdose and/or suicide. Her brother, Tomaz, was listed as her survivor. To their surprise and eternal gratitude, so were Vickie, Dorrie, and Lissy. Tommy refused to put her mother's or father's name on the survivor list—they had disappeared from Aggie's life long, long ago. He also left off Aggie's foster parents, who had essentially sold her to Skip Massey. Everyone but her brother, Tommy, and the Mariposa girls had betrayed Aggie Urbanowski.

A sparsely attended funeral Mass in Polish was held at the Im-

maculate Heart of Mary in Heaven Church. Skip did not attend. Neither did Aggie's nominal foster parents.

Tommy sat between his own foster parents, the mother close to his side, the father's arm around his shoulder. The owner of the car wash where Tommy worked sat beside Tommy's foster father. A small, made family that the Mariposa girls, sitting behind them in the second row, could only look at longingly.

* * * *

One of the police officers who'd responded to the report of a body in the alley slipped into a seat in the rear of the church just before the funeral service began. He noted the sunglasses and scarf on one of the victim's friends, heavy pancake makeup only partially covering telltale bruising. He was too familiar with these bruises in his work. Never ends. There's a story there, he thought, possibly connected with the deceased?

The deceased had already been written off as an overdose and no one was going to open a case because one of her friends had been roughed up. Maybe not even related. You never know, but not enough to open a case again.

He'd come to the service because he had a rare break in his schedule and, yes, because there was always the off chance there might be something or someone worth following up on at the service. But he was one of the guys who found this poor young kid, wrapped in a blue blanket, left in the middle of the night outside a church. He couldn't take a moment to mark each one of all the tragedies that he witnessed in his profession, but every once in a while, if he could, he thought it was right to stop and give some respect.

* * * *

The only other attendees at Aggie's funeral were several elderly Polish ladies scattered around the church, their lips moving quietly as they whispered the mysteries of the rosary.

After Mass, the soloist sang the recessional hymn *Witaj Królowo Nieba* "O Queen of Heaven, We Greet You" as Aggie's coffin was carried out by the funeral staff, with Tommy and the Mariposa girls following. The funeral cars took Tommy, his foster parents, his boss,

and the girls to Saint Stanislaus Cemetery where the priest said a brief prayer before Aggie's coffin was lowered into a grave in a side area of less expensive grave sites.

In lieu of flowers, donations were requested to an account at the Pittsburgh National Bank to help pay for funeral expenses. There was a large check from the dry cleaner guy in Oakmont. Tommy instructed the bank to return it. Tommy's boss at the car wash paid for the pink headstone, which included a delicate engraving of a butterfly and a sweet photograph of Aggie.

Afterward, the world moved on without Aggie Urbanowski. Sort of.

34

VENGEANCE

Two weeks later, a car burned in Saint Peter's Cemetery above the area known as the Slopes. When the crew from the Arlington Fire Department arrived, the first firefighter to the car called out. "Christ. There's someone in there."

It was difficult identifying the body. Eventually, through dental records, the police were able to name the victim as Roger Coombs of Oakmont, owner of a chain of dry-cleaning establishments in the Greater Pittsburgh area. He was an outstanding family man and civic leader, Christian Doctrine teacher, and youth ministry volunteer. No history, no bad business deals, no threat that the family knew of.

The medical examiner determined that Coombs had been shot in the head. Both his legs and a number of fingers had been broken, apparently beforehand. In his mouth was stuffed a small black wire frame roughly in the shape of a butterfly, with tiny black antennae.

"God knows," Detective Sal Compagnone, the lead detective on the case, said. "These things can get pretty weird, but I don't know what the hell *that* means."

And, despite the best efforts of Detective Compagnone and the Pittsburgh Police Department, they never did find out for sure. But they had their suspicions. The area around Saint Peter's and the Arlington neighborhood was known for drug dealing. Perhaps a drug deal gone wrong. They also knew that Mr. Coombs had some serious money troubles, what with his wife's medical bills and his chain of businesses struggling with new competition.

The word on the street was that he'd borrowed money from the wrong people. Again, nothing conclusive, and no one knew what to make of the butterfly. The crime scene photo of the young girl found on Polish Hill – the image showing the butterfly tattoo on her shoulder—was somehow misfiled and was never connected to the butterfly murder in Saint Peter's Cemetery.

For this reason and for the demands of other cases at the time, investigators decided that the butterfly was just a quirk. The Coombs case was still officially open, but in the department the working assumption was that Mr. Coombs had fallen victim to either loan sharks or drug dealers. In time, the police department had to move on. No one worked on the cold case. The department had more than enough pressing current cases to work on.

35

"GROW OR DIE" AND OPPORTUNITY ARRIVES IN A BLACK RANGE ROVER

A fog of sadness enveloped the girls in the following Aggie's funeral. Their rooms were quiet, though the gym was not. Skip had finally put together enough money between his own cash and a loan to finance the building-out of areas for new spinning classes and a hot yoga room. The renovations of the blue Victorian next door had also continued in earnest.

On the first floor of the house, he'd put the gym administrative offices, a meditation room and a parlor where they could welcome guests. Upstairs, his own suite and rooms for the girls were ready and occupied.

Skip described the girls' activities to the outside world as being part of a work study program, going to school and working in the gym. No one in the high school administration ever pursued the rumors that the girls were living next door to the gym or inquired what kind of work the girls were doing or indeed what they were studying that was relevant to the gym.

Skip was very busy. All the activity and supervision around the renovations of the gym and the blue Victorian absorbed his energy and, most importantly, his rage after Aggie. He softened toward the girls and let them choose the wallpaper and decorations for their rooms in the house. He bought them tickets to the Springsteen concert at the Civic Center downtown. The Center's roof was opened to the stars, the music was incredible and the girls were transported. Even with all that happened later, they never forgot that night—the stars, the music and each other.

One day, he called Vickie into his new office suite in the blue Victorian—a charming area with a fireplace, comfortable seating arrangement and bay windows looking out on the street. In the sunny bay area sat a tiger's eye maple antique desk with a laptop on it.

126

Skip was standing with his hands in his pockets, looking out the bay windows onto Liberty Avenue, as Vickie came into the room. He turned as he heard her and smiled, shaking his head. Looking around the room, he made a sweeping gesture with one arm. "Do you believe we made this happen?" He closed his fist and punched it down through the air. "We made this happen, Vickie."

Closing his eyes briefly, Skip looked out the bay windows again and inhaled deeply before turning to her. "This operation is going to be yours to run, Vickie."

Vickie frowned. "What's that mean?"

"We both know you're worth more now that you're a *college girl*," he said, the last in a sing-song voice with his brows raised. "You graduate from Pitt next year with your finance degree and you're gold to the operation. You and me, we're going to build this business."

Vickie didn't tell him that she was graduating this month, that she'd accelerated her classes. Better he not know. She wanted to graduate and just get out.

"Honey, I have a big investment in you." He looked at her fondly and said in the loving voice that could terrify her. "You're not a whore, Vickie, you're an escort. I don't know where you got it. You mother's a mess and God knows where your father is, but you're different from the others. You've got class. That's what this operation needs—*class*."

He dropped into the upholstered chair behind the antique desk with a smile. "And we're growing here. I'll need help in the business. You graduate—only the best for you here, a few guys with money – cream of the crop. But mostly, you're going to help me run this shop." He waved his arm around the office. "You can have this office, manage the business, bring on some new girls and train them. I'm going to be busy expanding in the North Hills." He nodded to himself in satisfaction and ran his fingers slowly over the tiger's eye maple desk. "You know what they say: *Grow or die*."

* * * *

Later that week, Vickie passed by Skip's office when he had a visitor. She heard a snippet of conversation though the door was

closed. She decided to linger.

"I'm keeping up with all the payments, aren't I?"

"You are, Mr. Massey, but we have some circumstances right now. You know what happens in business sometimes."

Vickie frowned. She pressed her body further against the wall and remained still.

"What kind of circumstances?"

"Another client didn't come through the way he should have, and we've had a couple of other—reversals. As they say."

"Well, that's not my fault, is it? I'm holding up my end of what we agreed to. Those business reversals aren't my problem."

Vickie listened to a deadly silence in the room before the other man said in a low, slow voice. "Oh, yes, Mr. Massey, those business reversals would be your problem."

"I don't have the money to increase my payments that much. It's just not there."

"It would be there if something happened to the gym and this place. An unfortunate fire. You've got good insurance, I assume."

"No, no. I've spent years building this all up."

"You could pay us and have a good amount left to start over with. I know you've been interested in expanding in the North Hills. There's a nice little place over there that could be for sale soon. Called New You."

"I don't want another place—this is what I want," Skip objected, but followed with "I didn't know that place was for sale."

"Neither does the owner, but he could be persuaded."

"Wait a minute, I don't want any part of that kind of stuff."

"Well, then, Mr. Massey. I suggest you just find money for the extra payments."

Skip didn't answer immediately. "I'll try," he murmured.

"No, Mr. Massey. Don't *try*. *Do*. You've got till the end of the month. Here's my card. Call me if you want to go the insurance and the New You route that I suggested."

Vickie could hear the man rising from his chair and the door of Skip's mini-fridge opening. "Just take one of these, if you don't mind." She heard the cap of the Diet Dr Pepper fall on the floor.

"Oops. I'll see my way out, Mr. Massey."

The man left Skip's office and passed Vickie in the hall. A fit man in a sports jacket over a black cashmere sweater. She guessed he must be the owner of the Range Rover she saw parked outside. He smiled and looked Vickie up and down appreciatively. "Another gorgeous work-study student, I see. Massey sure knows how to pick 'em." Then, he was gone.

Vickie retreated to a small alcove near the office. She heard Skip in a rage. "Son of a bitch! Son of a bitch!" She heard a shelf of books and gym trophies crash to the floor. He slammed out of the room. After she saw him stomp down the hall, hitting the walls with his fist, she crept into his office. There on the floor alongside the books and the trophies, was the cap of the Dr Pepper that the man had taken. The door of the small refrigerator was still open to reveal the neatly arranged bottles inside.

And at the front of the desk lay the visitor's business card. Just a phone number under the title *Prestige Investment Advisors, Alternative Financing.* Vickie took the business card over to the small copy machine in Skip's office, copied it and left the office.

36

PROTECT THE BRAND AND PLANS DEVELOP

One night later that week, Skip called the girls to a meeting in his office. He gestured each one to a chair in front of his desk as they came in.

Once they were comfortable, Skip came around and sat on the edge of his desk. He had started wearing a white open-neck shirt, slacks, and loafers with no socks to work—no more sweats unless he was spending the day in the gym. When he was at the gym now, he still wore Black Dog sweatshirts from Martha's Vineyard. Again, although Skip had never been to Martha's Vineyard, he looked like he had, which was the whole point.

He didn't want to be called Skip anymore. He wanted to be called Alex. Alex sounded more professional, he said. A name was an important part of the brand.

The only one who really understood the full transition Skip was making was Vickie. She knew the heights of his ambitions.

"I just wanted to take a little time to go over some things—to make sure we all understand what my expectations are here", he said this night.

Is this what a corporate staff meeting looks like? thought Vickie. It was straight out of her management class at Pitt.

The talk was about staying clean. Aggie Urbanowski had made a mistake, a bad mistake, and she paid for it. The fact was that they all paid for it because everybody cared about Aggie and missed her. And the gym paid for it—the *brand* paid for it—because of how Aggie died. But he was warning them on this because he cared for them. He really had their best interests at heart. He was the only one who really looked out for them. They were his responsibility. They should just remember that.

He had big plans for the operation – a *first-class* operation, he emphasized – and they would all be the better for it too.

The talk was only about twenty minutes long. Skip had an appointment for a haircut. He asked if there were any questions, but the girls were silent. He had never given them a talk like this before, at least in this way. As they were leaving the office, Skip called out, "Just remember the one who loves you. The only one who really loves you."

* * * *

Back in Vickie's room, they sat on her bed and the floor with a bottle of wine Lissy had retrieved from the back of her closet. Vickie plugged in the electric tea kettle and pulled out a box of spice tea.

Lissy broke the silence. "The *brand* paid for it," she said bitterly. "Fuck all."

"Yeah, he *cares* about us. More like he cares what he can make off us." Dorrie traced the raised pattern on the bedspread with her long index finger and sculpted nail. "He thinks we love him."

"Of course he does." Lissy took a sip of wine from one of Vickie's willow-patterned blue and white mugs. "We don't love him. We're afraid of him. Look at what he did to Vickie—his favorite." She lifted her chin toward Vickie, who was pouring water from the electric kettle into her tea cup. "Beating her up so bad on the night Aggie died. As if it was Vickie's fault."

Lissy covered her eyes as she spoke. "I can't stand the fact that he beat Vickie up and I really can't ever forgive him for Aggie. He blamed us and her, but he's the one that pimped her out to that creep." A sob broke Lissy's voice. "And then that creep *shared* her. He *shared* her."

A long silence ensued.

"Well, what are we going to do about it?" Vickie asked, swirling a tea bag around in her mug. "We know the score."

"What's he going to do when we all age out?" Dorrie asked leaning over to pour herself a mug of wine. "I'm not sticking around here." She turned to look at Vickie. "When do you graduate? What are you going to do?"

Vickie dropped her tea bag into a wastebasket. "I accelerated my classes. Got all my credits, finished all my requirements. Picking up my diploma next week."

Dorrie jumped up, squealed and threw her arms around Vickie, spilling wine on the floor. "You're shittin' me—goddamn." She pulled Vickie close and then held her out again in her arms. "Goddamn, goddamn."

Lissy was crying. "Jesus. You did it. Oh my God. You did it, Vickie." She walked over and put her head on Vickie's shoulder.

Vickie's own eyes were moist, but she waved it all away with a smile. "Don't tell Skip. I haven't figured things out yet."

"Are you going?"

"Skip wants me in the business. He wants me to run this shop while he expands to the North Hills." She stopped and looked directly at Dorrie and then Lissy. "He's bringing a couple of new girls in. They look so young. He wants me to train them."

"We were so young," said Lissy.

"He wants you to help them turn pro." Dorrie's voice was flat. "Christ." She got up from her seat on the bed and stood in front of Vickie. "You know what they call that job in our line of work, Vickie? That would make you the *bottom bitch*. The one running the shop, teaching the newbies—the head girl."

There was a silence.

"I hate him," Lissy said quietly, looking down at the mug.

"We all hate him." Dorrie responded.

Vickie looked out the window. "I'm nobody's bottom bitch." She picked a few dead leaves off the geranium she kept on the windowsill. "We can stop it. We can go."

"Where would we go?"

"Plenty of places to go."

"With no money."

"We all know how to work. Dorrie, with all your IT classes, you'll be set. Lissy, you could get a job at a real gym tomorrow and be certified as a personal trainer in no time."

"Doesn't seem real," Dorrie said. "After all this time."

"Besides . . ." Vickie stopped and looked out the window again. "Besides, Skip has money. He keeps cash so he doesn't have to declare it or explain where it comes from. It's our money. We earned it. I know where it is and I know the combination."

The room went quiet. Then, Dorrie and Lissy looked at each other with raised brows. "Shit," Dorrie whispered.

"And I have another idea," Vickie said with a small smile.

* * * *

And so it began. A liminal time – a moment-in-time space between old lives and, if all went well, new lives. Anxious and hopeful days for the girls, still working hard to keep up an outwardly normal routine and demeanor.

If things had been moving at an ordinary pace in the gym and the house and if he had not been distracted with renovations, Skip might have noticed the quiet, focused energy. To the girls, the very air seemed to vibrate with it. But Skip was busy with workmen, with arrangements. So he missed the clues, even when the girls found new homes for the several cats in the gym that they took care of as pets. Skip was usually sharp. He never missed a clue.

Until he did.

37

DR PEPPER MAN AND THE PLAN

It wasn't a hard phone call to make. "I'm Skip Massey's business manager. I wonder if we could talk privately about the business suggestion you had for him when you visited recently."

"You the doll in the corridor outside the office that day? Business manager?" He laughed for a long time. "Multi-talented girl."

"So?" Vickie said evenly.

"Pick you up at the Black Coffee House on the South Side."

"You're not picking me up anywhere. I'll meet you outside the area—Squirrel Hill. Coffee Tree Roasters is good."

"Damned bossy for staff." He paused. "Skip know you're calling me?"

"No, but I'm looking out for his best interests."

"Smart girl."

Vickie and the man she called Dr Pepper Man, for the drink he took from Skip's fridge, might have been friends. Or maybe a small business owner and a staff member sitting together in Coffee Tree Roasters the next afternoon. Except perhaps for Dr Pepper Man's habit of continually surveying the room. *Scanning for what?* Vickie wondered. *Clients? Delinquent borrowers? Physical threats?*

In any case, he was pleased with the maple scone he'd ordered with his black coffee. "I usually don't like these – they tend to be dry, you know? But this is a good one. You don't have anything. Let me get you one."

"No. No. I'm good."

"I insist. I'm not going to be here eating while you don't have anything in front of you but a little – what is that you're drinking anyway?"

"It's a latte – coffee with steamed milk."

"Oh right. Looks good. But I think it's kind of a girly kind of coffee, right?" Without waiting for an answer, he got up to get Vickie a maple scone.

A short time later, he returned with a plastic knife and a paper plate. "I guess I got the last one. We'll split this one."

"No, really, I'm okay."

"Cooperate, Vickie. I will enjoy mine more if you have some."

"Okay. Thank you."

"You're welcome."

"I don't even know your name."

He smiled. "You don't need to know my name, sweetheart."

"I think of you as Dr Pepper Man because you took one from Skip's fridge that day."

He laughed. "Oh, that's a good one. You know, that was just to aggravate him. I tossed it when I got outside."

"Do you want me to keep calling you Dr Pepper Man?"

"God, that's awful. But you can keep calling me that. I told - you don't need to know my name. I'll just make one up anyway."

They snacked in silence. When he finished his scone, he wiped his mouth with a napkin and leaned back. "So, it's simple. I just need you to give me a night the gym will be totally empty and that heavy door in the back will be propped open. Can you do that?"

Vickie nodded. "For a consideration."

"But of course." He leaned forward, his forearms on the table. "What are you going to do with that gym gone? Follow Massey? I'll set him up in the North Hills after this place goes and he gets the insurance payout. He'll have a good operation there."

"No, we have some other plans. We'll leave that night."

He gave Vickie an appreciative look. "Good idea. I think our Mr. Massey probably has some unrealistic expectations about your sticking around, but he'll get over it. Maybe. He's kind of a strange dude, don't you think?"

Vickie didn't answer.

And so the date was set. A night Skip wouldn't be at the gym. A night the gym would have been deserted except for the girls, who would leave that night. The bolted metal door at the back would be propped open when they left. "I have professionals working for me to take care of the rest, sweetheart."

Before they left, Vickie also negotiated an additional generous pay-out for each of the girls. "Think of it as a thank you and as a severance program," she told him.

"Love that. Your own little severance program." He laughed as he got up from the table. "You got it, sweetheart." He looked at Vickie. "Wish you worked for me. You ever consider that? We'd be a great team."

"Not my thing," she replied evenly.

"Naw, you're made for bigger things, Vickie. You got a lousy start in life, but you're going to make it big." He gave her a thoughtful smile and headed for the door.

* * * *

Vickie only saw Dr Pepper Man once more in those days

Out of the corner of her eye one day, as she was walking down Liberty Avenue, she saw the black Range Rover slow to a crawl and then stop on the opposite side of the street. Or maybe she sensed the presence of the vehicle, as you might a predator slowly moving into position.

She turned to see him leaning out of the driver's side window. He smiled broadly at her until the car behind him gave a light beep, urging him to move on. At that, he lost the smile and leaned out of the car window to stare at the other driver. Just a stare, but an uncomfortable, stare—exuding menace. The driver of the other car quickly held up his hands in surrender.

He nodded at the driver and turned back to Vickie, resuming his genial smile—could she say a *loving* smile? Yes, a loving smile, like a new lover. She was annoyed to find herself responding just a little. How could she? In his line of work, he was a brutal animal, she was sure.

He put his finger to his lips, which were sensual and full, his diamond pinky ring catching the sun. She could see, not hear, those lips softly, shushing her.

They stayed like that—Vicki very still, the man staring at her. After what seemed like minutes, though it was probably no more than fifteen seconds, he smiled again and rejoined the traffic stream.

Vickie never forgot that image. Years later, she could see Dr Pepper Man leaning out of the Range Rover, finger to his lips, the pinky ring sparkling in the sun. *Just our little secret.*

38

THE DEED IS DONE

The Pittsburgh fire captain adjusted his helmet and squinted against the wind and the smoke. "Gym's a total loss. Shame. Nice facility. I hear they did some good work here. And that one," he pointed to the handsome blue Victorian next to Liberty Street Gym, "maybe we can save it, but I doubt it. Shame. Beautiful renovation."

"Is there any idea how it started yet?" the young reporter asked. She held the news mic with one hand while holding her long hair back against the wind with the other.

"Naw. Too early. Right now, we're thinking it could have started with a short in the gym's electrical system and then spread to the house. So much construction going on, that could be a good guess right now, but fire investigators will issue a statement later. We really can't make an assessment yet." He turned to leave and looked up at the sky. "Burned fast with this wind."

"Was anyone hurt?"

"No, thank God. I guess there had been some people living in the house, but no sign of them. I don't know if they were permanent residents. We'll check." He scanned the area again. "Looks like just property damage, but a big, big loss."

"Yes, must be really tough. Thank you, Captain."

As she turned from the fire captain, the reporter caught a glimpse of a man she'd been told was the gym's owner, Skip Massey. Standing stock still in front of the crowd, his face was a mask of heartbreak and fury. The reporter worked her way through the spectators with her cameraman working hard to follow, calling to her, "Kimmy, don't. Wait up."

"Mr. Massey," she called. "Could I ask you a few questions, Mr. Massey?"

The man made no response.

137

"I know how hard this must be for you, Mr. Massey. You lived in the house next door, didn't you?" She leaned forward to try and catch his eye.

Massey didn't turn his face. No acknowledgment. Only a dangerous flicker of an eyelid.

"Mr. Massey?"

A shift to the shoulders.

Skip Massey swung around and loomed wordlessly before her for several frightening seconds before turning back to the fire.

She'd involuntarily stepped back several paces when he faced her and there was a slight quaver to her voice when she began speaking into her mic again.

"Clearly, a distressing time for the gym and homeowner here. One can only imagine. Channel 4 reporting from Liberty Avenue, Bloomfield."

The reporter unsteadily walked back to the news truck with her cameraman. "Christ. I thought he was going to smack me. Guy gives me the shivers. Who the fuck is he?"

The photographer placed his camera carefully on the seat of the van. "Tried to tell you."

"Yeah, you did. I was kind of wired. Wanted to get the story, you know?" She raised her brows. "But, Jesus, he is one scary dude."

"Oh yeah. If this wasn't an accident, I wouldn't want to be the guy that started it." He glanced back at the fire. "Unless the dude that started it is even scarier than this guy."

39

BUTTERFLIES TAKE WING

Quick hugs in the dark and the Mariposa girls went their separate ways. Each carried in their small knapsacks a packet of cash from the safe in the gym, in addition to a generous severance from Dr Pepper Man.

"Unbreakable" they whispered together—the secret code they had chosen when they communicated on the web. The unbreakable bond of the Mariposa Circle. Bound together forever, they took flight separately, leaving Liberty Avenue—just like the other beautiful butterflies that, against all odds, fly to the other place where they should be.

Dorrie went to Philly, where an old family friend had a small business and could use some IT help. Lissy went to Buffalo, where Aggie's brother, Tommy, had landed in a construction company and had a spare room in his apartment.

Vickie decided to go to Boston with her finance degree, and already had an interview lined up at a boutique investment house. She'd also admitted to Dorrie that she liked the movie *Good Will Hunting*. As good a reason as any to choose Boston, she and Dorrie decided. With the legal paperwork now completed, she was going to have a new name too—Frederica Strauss. It sounded kind of classy to Vickie.

40

A STRATEGIC RETREAT FROM BOSTON

After receiving Alex Massey's threatening message, Frederica made plans to leave from Boston for now, to buy time and figure things out.

When she left, she used only cash. No credit or debit cards. She'd also left her cell phone and laptop in her State Street desk drawer, with messages saying she was unavailable, out of town on a family emergency. She bought a burner phone and used no apps. Only Alyssa had the burner phone number.

Lissy and Johnny were holding the fort in Charlestown with their guest Jenna Conway – resident until her own issue with an angry trafficker went away and she could return to her little yellow house in Cambridgeport.

Maybe it was all overkill, Frederica considered, but she trusted her instincts. She knew Skip, his focus and determination. If he could find her, he would. She was his equal in this match, but she needed to be prepared.

After some thought, she took the Downeaster train along the coast to Portland, and then the bus to Presque Isle, a small working-class city in Aroostook County—potato country, near the Canadian border. And close to Abe's "beautiful old mountain" Katahdin.

A sentimental decision to go there, Frederica acknowledged. A way to keep some kind of mental connection with Abe in spite of all.

Of course, there'd also be little chance of anyone from her Boston world coming to Presque Isle. Boston visitors tended to be more coastal—Portland or maybe to Kennebunkport, Boothbay, Bar Harbor or Camden, all with charming harbors filled with expensive sailboats. Or perhaps to Moosehead or the Rangeley Lakes to the west. They would not be coming to struggling Presque Isle unless they were on their way to Millinocket and Katahdin. And then, they'd

probably go straight to Millinocket, at the base of the mountain without stopping in Presque Isle. Perfect.

It didn't take Frederica long to find a sublet in a multi-family on one of the steep uphill side streets off Main. For a little extra cash, her new landlord, a Mi'kmaq Indian who was driving his pickup over the border to a job in a zinc mine, lent her the keys to his car for the duration of her stay. The car was an ancient Honda Civic, which featured New Brunswick plates and a *Protect Native People's Rights* bumper sticker, and she was grateful for it.

Apparently, as part of the deal, she was also responsible for a gang of mooching, quarrelsome feral cats who lived in the building's overgrown backyard.

Her first call from Presque Isle when she got settled was to Alyssa.

"Hey, Vic. How's it going?

"Good. Nice place. The apartment's small but comfy. I don't need much. Working plumbing, good microwave. I didn't really need the big screen TV but it's here. And a porch full of feral cats looking for their next meal. Perfect hideaway."

"What are you doing with yourself?"

"Well, I just got here, but I plan on long walks, so that I can think all this through. Probably climb the mountain. The library is right down the street, but I won't take out a card or use the computers – no need to leave too many traces. I'll stop in to catch up with the newspapers, follow the markets. I'll have to restrain myself from sending messages to the staff about client investments. I'll hold off unless something really big happens in the market."

They both laughed without humor.

"Sounds restful – will it be?"

"Not really. It's not a vacation – more of a strategic retreat. I'll be antsy as I work through the other stuff, but it will keep me busy. How's it going there?"

"All quiet on the Western Front," Alyssa reported.

"No unexpected visitors?"

"Nope, no sign of Skip and I haven't seen him mentioned in the

papers. Could be something happening, but I don't see any movement. You want us to track him, follow him?"

"No, no. Let's not look for trouble. He might even recognize you."

"Never. I'm an Amazon now, not a fat fifteen-year-old."

Vickie chuckled. "Stop it. Well, anyway, better to just hang back for now. How about our guest Jenna Conway?"

"She's good—I'm walking her to work, Johnny's picking her up. She's settling in. The dog likes to sleep with her at night."

"Of course he does, the faithless pooch."

"And Matty Cronin's carpenter Conor O'Leary has eyes for Jenna."

"Romance on Winthrop Street. That wasn't supposed to be part of the deal."

"No accounting for these things."

"Dorrie in town?" Vicki asked.

"Yeah. She sends her love. She had a nice lunch with your Sister Connection mentee Antoinette Mackey already, and has scheduled regular get-togethers."

"I really appreciate her parachuting in to support Antoinette. She'll be great at it, and it's not a bad idea for Antoinette to get to know her. Dorrie gives a whole other layer and perspective."

"True."

"Where's Dorrie staying?"

"I don't know. She avoided my questions about that. Just said 'I'm good'. So that I let it be."

"That's not like her."

"I know, but I'm not pushing. I think she has a guy she won't tell me about."

"Hmm. Strange. She'd usually be talking your ear off about something like that. But, yeah, probably better to let it go."

"That's what I figured."

"Well, on a lighter note, I got my hair cut short." Frederica chuckled.

"You didn't. I loved your hair."

"It's still there, just less of it. And besides that, hair grows."

"Is this part of the whole incognito thing? Heading up to almost New Brunswick, using a burner phone, only cash, now cutting your hair off. Who do you thing is going to go after you—the feds?"

"Skip. When he's focused on something, he's probably better than they are."

"Yeah. I get that."

"Just until I figure things out."

"So, you going to color your hair? You could bleach it. You'd be a cute blonde."

"Naw. Too much work."

"You been thinking about how to handle the Skip thing?"

"Yeah, I have."

"He's dangerous, Vickie. He could blow up your life or, I hate to say it, he could do worse."

"I know."

"So?"

"Well, I think I need to blow up his life, even if I have to blow up my own while I'm at it. Or kill him. I think those are my only choices."

"Seriously? You'd think about doing him?"

"No, no, Jesus, Lissy, don't get carried away. I need some time to think how to do all this the right way. I think I'm almost there."

"Easier to put a bullet in him."

"Stop it, Lissy. Don't fool around like that."

"Who's fooling around?"

"Enough." Frederica sighed. "Gotta go now—have to do a grocery run. No food in the fridge. I borrowed a car here—it's pretty old but runs fine. It has a *Protect Native People's Rights* sticker on the bumper."

"Good. Stand up for the right things. But listen, Vickie, don't take too much time and overthink this. He's a threat."

"Stop talking like that. I'll have a good plan and it will work. Have any of my plans not worked yet?"

"No—but I'm so done with the Skips of this world. So done." Lissy stopped. "Wait, what's that noise?"

"Bells. A church down the street."

"That happen all the time?"

"No. I guess just midday. I think it could be the Angelus. I don't know."

"Boy, you're in a different place. Wild."

Frederica laughed softly. "It's all wild, yeah. But, so is everything right now. I gotta go, Lissy. Thanks for everything. Love you."

"Love you too, Vic."

41

BREAKING NEWS –
MURDER ON THE WATERFRONT

The next day was rainy. Frederica had planned to spend it in the Turner Library followed by, assuming the rain let up, a long walk and a phone call appointment. Then, if all went well, an early dinner at the Riverside Inn.

The dinner would be a solo celebration, marking the beginning of her strategy to counter Skip Massey's catastrophic reappearance in her life. She'd considered the strategy from multiple angles. This one was hardball and risky, but Frederica thought it had the best odds for success.

She was walking down the hill toward the library, using a red umbrella with two broken spines that she'd found in her rental's hall closet, when her phone vibrated.

"Hi. It's Lissy."

"Of course it is. You're the only one with this number. Everything okay?"

"Something happened."

"Tell me."

"Somebody got Skip."

"Got him how?"

"Killed him."

"Jesus. Hang on. Let me get out of the rain."

Frederica jogged to the sheltering portico of the library. "Okay. Talk."

"Offed him in the parking garage of the Boston Harbor Hotel right after he made some big speech to a bunch of CEOs." Alyssa gave a bitter laugh. "All about social responsibility. A real pillar of the community, our Skip."

"How?"

"Stabbed. I guess it was ugly."

145

Frederica felt a wave of . . . what? Relief? Fear? Horror? Sadness? Grief? Craziness?

"You'll see it in the Globe—front page."

"Of course."

"It was godawful and he wasn't just some regular guy, you know. He was kind of a big shot." Alyssa paused. "You got to be a big shot too, Vickie. Maybe Liberty Avenue was kind of a—what's the word?—training ground for big shots."

Frederica gave a little snort. "Yeah, and look at us now. He's in the morgue and I'm hiding out up near the Canadian border. We did real good, we did."

"You did, Vickie. Just bad luck. But you'll be okay now."

"Maybe. Do they know who did it?"

There was a long pause at the Boston end of the phone call. And then, a distant, matter- of-fact response. "Not yet, but somebody did us all a big favor."

Frederica did not reply.

Alyssa continued. "Maybe he crossed someone. He may have gotten over his head money-wise again. You know how ambitious he was, even back in the day—always wanting to be somebody."

"Oh yeah, I remember."

Alyssa broke the long silence that followed. "Guess who the BPD lead on the case is?"

"You're kidding."

"Yep. Your friend Abe."

"Lissy? You all didn't?"

"Oh Jesus. I gotta go. I'll be in touch, Vic. Let me know when you decide to come back. Coast looks clear. Love you." And Alyssa closed the call.

42

NOT AN EASY STORY, ABE
PLOUGH AND STARS PUB IN CAMBRIDGE

Janelle Mahoney approached Abe's desk, a notebook under her arm. "You ready for this, Abe?"

"Not really, but let's do it."

Abe knew he was right to ask Janelle to research Frederica's background after the details that had emerged on the Pittsburgh trip. A murdered girl with the same butterfly tattoo as Freddie and the same name as Freddie's younger sister. Still, he was anxious about what he might learn.

"Want to talk here or go somewhere else?"

Abe looked around the busy station. "Let's go for a ride—maybe across the river. Get out for a while. I can't breathe in here."

They left the station, got into Abe's car in the parking lot and started up Tremont Street to Mass Ave. Within fifteen minutes, they crossed the Mass Ave Bridge, traveled up the Avenue toward Harvard Square and pulled in across from the Plough and Stars Pub.

Janelle raised her eyebrows. "Bit early."

"Not today."

The Plough was quiet, just prepping for lunch and they were the first customers.

Abe shooed the waitress away with the menus when she approached. "I'll have the gumbo special with a Speckled Hen and so will the lady."

Janelle waved her hand. "No, no. I'll have coffee and a glass of water. No Speckled Hen."

"And the gumbo?"

Janelle smiled. "Oh yes, I'll have the gumbo."

Abe surveyed the long room of the Plough as the waitress walked away. Neither he nor Janelle spoke until the waitress delivered Abe his beer and Janelle her coffee and water.

147

Then, Abe inhaled deeply, dropped back in his chair and blew out a long breath before facing Janelle.

"What've you got?"

Janelle reached over and put her hand on Abe's. "Take a sip first."

He took a long draught of the beer. "Okay, I'm ready."

"Right." She opened her notebook, placed her palms on the table and began to read.

"I started in Pittsburgh—since it looks like that's where all this is connected. I looked through various databases for the name Strauss, and didn't find anything until I got to a legal database that showed a legal name change. Vickie Czinski became Frederica Strauss."

"How come?"

"Well, the story's a little complicated but I guess I'd have to say it was to escape her past and become a new person. It's not hard if you don't have a criminal record."

"True."

"Nice new name."

"Yeah, it is."

"This is going to be rough, Abe."

He nodded without looking at her. "Go."

Janelle looked at him for a moment and then returned to her notes again.

"Born in Pittsburgh. Mother a nurse's aide who developed a drug habit and then picked up clients to keep herself supplied. Pretty much out of it when Vickie was growing up. Men in and out of the house. Dad was a construction worker and part-time bouncer at a local bar. Marriage was always rocky. He walked out after a few years. Last trace, out in Wyoming working in an oil field. Never divorced, but he had no presence in Vickie's life. Mother OD'd up in Buffalo a few years ago."

"What happened to Vickie?"

Janelle hesitated before picking up her report. The lunchtime customers in the Plough arrived steadily and the noise level rose with them. Abe and Janelle leaned closer together at the table to hear better, their heads almost touching.

"Apparently during freshman year in high school, she joined a community program at a gym down on Liberty Avenue—the same gym Aggie Urbanowski was involved in. Vickie ended up living there and eventually in a house next to the gym."

Abe winced and looked aside at his steaming gumbo, which had arrived and remained untouched.

"Massey's gym."

"Yeah. At the time Skip Massey."

He didn't look at her. "Residential program?"

"Wasn't supposed to be, but three or four of the girls resided there—including Aggie and Vickie."

"Did anybody approve that? School, family?"

"They were the kinds of kids that weren't exactly on anybody's screen."

"Expendable?"

"I don't know if I'd say that but they were pretty much on their own. The counselor at the school that had originally recommended them for this community program at the gym moved down to Wilkes-Barre with her family at some point. If she had still been around, things might have been different, but after she left, the school was understaffed. There doesn't seem to have been any handoff and the girls just fell out of the system."

"How often does that happen?" Abe asked rhetorically.

"Probably more than we can imagine. Want to take a break?"

"No. Keep going." He responded brusquely, eyes reddened.

"Okay." Janelle turned a page in the notebook. "The address for the house next to the gym was listed as Vickie Czinski's home address. Nobody picked that up."

"Nobody cared."

Janelle moved her finger down the page. "She managed to get a good education. Not only managed but did pretty well. Graduated in three years and took a couple of courses at Pitt her last year through some special program."

Abe smiled. "Way better student than I was."

"Got me beat by a mile too," Janelle chuckled. "Anyway. Played on the basketball team." She stopped and then said gently,

"Actually captain of the basketball team at one point until her . . . work . . . got in the way of night games and she had to quit."

Abe dropped back in his chair. "Jesus."

"Want me to go on?"

"Yeah, yeah," he murmured. He looked to the side while Janelle continued.

"President of the Finance club." Janelle looked up at Abe. "Real star in the making. Too bad her mom was too spaced out to notice and her dad was long gone. She had some strong teachers who were probably more role models to her than they ever knew. School and Massey's gym were the only real anchors in her life."

"Sounds that way."

"Got a scholarship to Pitt."

"Of course she did," Abe said with a wry smile. "Of course, she did."

"Yeah, but unfortunately, only an academic scholarship. Not enough money for the dorms or an apartment, so she had to stay on at the gym."

"Her life would have been so different in a dorm. Her life would have been so different period."

"Yeah. And apparently, she was Massey's best money-maker."

Abe closed his eyes.

"Sorry." Janelle shook her head. "Anyway, he probably wouldn't have let her go."

"Go on."

"She had a boyfriend at Pitt."

"Yeah?"

"Josh. Josh Brown." Janelle searched her notes. "Ah, here we are. There was a picture of them together as freshmen in one of the yearbooks—don't have the photo with me. Cute kids together. Anyway, I looked him up at the alumni office. Still lives in the area with his wife and kids. Didn't work out but he said he never forgot Vicki."

Janelle paused for a moment before continuing.

"Anyway, just for background, Josh grew up in Mount Lebanon, his dad worked at Bayer and his mom volunteered at the art museum, and . . ."

"And he had a dog named Archie," Abe said.

"How did you know? I wasn't going to bother with that. Josh mentioned a lot of details that I didn't think were important."

"Just a guess."

She looked at him curiously before speaking. "Anyway, guess it didn't end so well."

"How come?"

"Josh said some older guy came up to them at a bar and seemed to be Vickie's boyfriend or handler or something . . . and was obviously trying to scare Josh off. Vickie wouldn't explain. Anyway, it worked. Josh thought it was too weird and just cut it off right afterward."

"That bastard Massey."

"Oh yes. Want me to finish?"

"Okay."

"She majored in finance, minored in sociology and psychology. Graduated magna cum laude."

Abe looked up at Janelle for the first time, with a small proud smile. "Amazing woman."

"Amen, Abe. Amen."

Janelle looked down at her notebook again. "Shortly after that, the gym burned down in what the Pittsburgh Fire Department thought was suspicious circumstances, but nothing came of that."

Abe pursed his lips. "Convenient."

"Yes, but we don't know anything about that, Abe."

"Right. Keep going."

"We're almost at the end anyway." She found her place in the notebook. "Changed her name to Frederica Strauss and didn't have any problem getting a good job in finance in Boston." Janelle closed the notebook. "And the rest is history."

Abe slowly massaged his forehead. "History is still being written. Let's get back to the station."

Before Janelle could respond, the waitress approached their table and looked at the untouched bowls of gumbo. "Didn't appeal to you after all?"

"Just not hungry, I guess. Could you wrap them up? We'll bring them back to the station. Be gone in two minutes."

The waitress carried the bowls of gumbo away.

Janelle reached for her jacket.

"Janelle?"

"Yeah?"

"Thanks. Appreciate it. Nice job."

"Glad to do it. This can't be easy for you, Abe."

"Something else?"

"Okay."

"I don't know if it's realistic, but try and find out the names of the other girls that lived in that house with Vickie and Aggie."

She gave him a questioning look while she jotted that down in her notebook too. "Glad to. You think you need that?"

"I'm guessing there's a Dorrie and a Lissy."

43

VIOLENCE

With the passage of time and the comfort she felt in her surroundings, Jenna had almost forgotten about the angry pimp who'd broken into her house, driving her from her home.

It was as though she had lived in Frederica's sophisticated home for years. As though her own little yellow house in Cambridgeport had never been ransacked. Alyssa encouraged Jenna to stay longer at Freddie's—"until the smoke clears." Jenna wished she knew what that meant or what that would look like—the time when the smoke cleared.

In many ways, she felt she had started a new life in a new place, all the while trailing complicated detritus of her old life.

According to Alyssa, two or three other girls before her own two recent guests in Cambridgeport had been rescued from the stable of that particular angry pimp. She also knew that this man was furious and that he wanted to send a message. He'd find a way to do that.

Still, weeks had passed without incident. Jenna had grown accustomed to camping out in Frederica's guest bedroom, with Frederica's dog Archie—the Speaker of the House, the Cronin Construction crew, and Johnny and Alyssa as company. Conor O'Leary frequently stayed after work with Jenna for Regina's pizza and beer from the North End or Thai takeout from the Sweet Rice restaurant down the street. His visits extended longer each time, gradually including a Netflix he and Jenn watched while stretched out on the sofa in Frederica's comfortable den.

In Cambridgeport, George Hennessey was taking care of Jenna's house and bringing her mail into the Sister Connection offices every week. Lately, he included a round of fresh Irish bread ("my mother's recipe") with the mail packet. "I like to spoil you, Jenna. I never had a daughter. Humor me."

Johnny and Alyssa—either separately or together—continued to accompany her to and from work. She'd been objecting for some time, without effect, that she didn't need to be walked to work. The emergency had apparently passed. This pimp was on to other things and she could manage on her own. They both listened without response and maintained their schedules as her escorts.

It was a beautiful day when it happened. Alyssa was watchful as usual, walking a little in front of Jenna as she crossed Massachusetts Avenue. Johnny had joined them that day and walked some distance behind.

Jenna heard someone calling her name. She stopped and turned to see George Hennessey on the sidewalk, his two hands holding up a plastic bag of what looked like an Irish bread and an elastic-wrapped stack of mail.

In that confusing moment, a dark van pulled between Alyssa and Jenna on the street. As Jenna was trying to understand what was happening, a man in a dark hoodie, black jeans, and red sneakers leapt from the van, grabbed her and started to pull her into the van. Her head hit the door of the van—hard—and she went limp. Everything blurred and—half in, half out of the vehicle—she couldn't make out the source of all the loud noises around her.

She thought she saw George Hennessey fling himself at the van, holding the door open as the van pulled away. Why was he doing that? They were moving at increasing speed down Mass Ave, dragging George as he tried to keep up on his aging legs. He could get hurt. She tried to call out to him but no sound came.

She heard another set of feet pounding along the side of the van and then a terrible roar as she saw—in a slow-motion blur—Johnny pull the man in the dark hoodie, still holding Jenna, from the van. The man let go of Jenna and she fell to the street.

George Hennessey fell away from the van and the driver quickly sped away, leaving his partner on the street to fend for himself. The man in the hoodie got to his feet. A knife flashed in the man's hands. Her shout "Johnny, watch out!" came out in a whisper.

Johnny kicked the man's legs out from under him and picked him up in a headlock as the man waved the knife close to Johnny's

face. Suddenly, Jenna heard a shout of "fucking slimeball!" followed by a terrible and efficient crack. The man in the hoodie fell to the pavement like a rag doll. Johnny gave the man's body a gratuitous kick just as the blue lights and siren of Boston Police cruisers came down the avenue.

"Jesus, Mary and Joseph." George Hennessey appeared and knelt at Jenna's side, "Are you okay, Jenna?"

She nodded weakly.

"That guy in the hoodie—that was the guy I saw at your house."

Of course it was.

The BPD and the EMTs from the Boylston Street Station were all over the place. George stayed by her side until Alyssa and an EMT rushed over. Then George hurried to collect Jenna's National Grid and Comcast bills and her other mail that lay scattered all over Mass Ave.

BPD officers surrounded Johnny. She heard one of them comment to the other. "Jesus. This guy a SEAL or MOSSAD or something? Look at that clean neck break. He knew what he was doing."

Officers collected names and information from witnesses, who were excited and eager to talk. One witness wanted Johnny's autograph, but Johnny was accompanying officers to the Tremont Street station.

"Christ," said one cop. "I think everyone who saw it wants to give him a medal."

Traffic stopped for the crime scene and the medical examiner did his job. Jenna was taken to Boston Medical Center for evaluation.

The victim was quickly identified as indeed a "fucking slimeball" known to police in Springfield, a western Massachusetts city. Naturally, police wanted to know more about Jenna and why said slimeball had wanted to pick her off Mass Ave in broad daylight.

Jenna wished Freddie had been available to explain their Mariposa work to the police, but she did the best she could. Being able to identify the state social workers they coordinated with mollified the police officers for the moment. She restrained herself from mentioning Abe's name. He had his hands full already.

She sensed they could absorb her part of the story, though it all had to be dissected and checked. But then there was Johnny and that very professional neck snap. That part needed a lot more attention.

* * * *

Later that night, the homeless man who usually stationed himself on a grubby Red Sox blanket outside Dunkin Donuts on Mass Ave noticed a plastic bag lying between two parked cars. He ambled over to pick it up.

"Well, Mother of God, would you look at that?" he murmured. He peered into the bag and broke off a piece of George Hennessey's fresh Irish bread, dabbing it with butter from the small cup in the bag.

Several minutes later, he sat beside his Dunkin cup—still out for donations—beside him as he feasted on the heel piece and a large Americano.

He gave passers-by a wide, missing-a-few-teeth smile. "Doesn't get any better. God loves me."

"I guess he does, man," said one passer-by as he dropped a dollar into the paper cup.

44

A HERO IN CUSTODY REVEALED

Abe held the door for Janelle and entered the Tremont Street interview room behind her.

"Hi, Johnny."

Johnny nodded without expression. He was seated at a table with another man. His public defender rose and shook hands with Abe and Janelle.

"Had to beat my way through the reporters outside, Johnny. You're a hero. The mayor may give you the keys to the city."

Johnny gave a tight smile.

"But you killed a guy. Right?"

Johnny shrugged.

"So, Johnny, doesn't matter if he was a scumbag lowlife. You killed a guy. We have to deal with that."

Johnny did not respond.

"Tell me about it."

Silence.

"Okay, if you won't tell me, I'll tell you about it."

Abe walked through the incident on Mass Ave and ended with, "And then you snapped his neck. Very professional. Where'd you learn to do that?"

"No need to respond to that, Mr. Thomas," the public defender said.

Johnny looked at Abe. No emotion in his clear blue eyes beyond a flicker of sympathy for Frederica's friend Abe. There was depth in those eyes, but emotions were locked up tight.

Abe sighed. "We have to hold you; you know that, Johnny."

He saw a slight twitch in Johnny's left eye and then a small nod.

* * * *

A few hours later, Abe closed a call on his cell and looked thoughtfully into space for a few moments before speaking. "Got an

157

interesting complication."

"Yeah?" Janelle looked up from her desk.

"Just got a call from Murdoch. You know, that retired reporter in Pittsburgh? The one who's been tracking the Roger Coombs murder?"

"Yeah?" A hint of impatience this time.

"He was watching the news—kind of a news junkie—and I guess Johnny made the national news. It was a pretty dramatic scene."

"Yeah?" She started to move her index finger to get Abe to move the story along.

"He recognized Johnny."

"No kidding." Janelle turned her chair to face him and leaned forward, hands on knees.

"Tomaz Janek Urbanowski."

"Urbanowski?" She frowned, looked down and thought for a moment before lifting her face to Abe again. "Agnes Urbanowski." She widened her eyes. "Oh, my God. The brother. Aggie's brother, Tommy."

"Jesus." Abe said. "Let's find out where Johnny was the morning Massey was killed."

45

RETURN FROM THE NORTH WOODS AND REVELATIONS

With all of these events, Abe's mind was elsewhere the next day as he crossed Ruggles at Tremont to get to Peet's and his tall latte. No lunch today. Too busy. Just coffee, and he couldn't handle another cup of burned coffee from the workroom pot.

Abe's thoughts were not so far away, however, that he wasn't annoyed when a Honda Civic beater with New Brunswick plates stopped in front of him in the crosswalk.

He knocked on the side window. "Lady . . . "

"Abie! Want a ride?" The voice sound familiar, but for just a moment the short-haired driver did not. Then, she did.

"What the hell. Your hair."

"Like it?"

"Doesn't seem like you."

Frederica gave a small smile. "Well, that depends on what me you're talking about, doesn't it?"

"Right," Abe responded testily. "Pull over to the side. You're holding up traffic, whoever you are."

Frederica gave him an apologetic shrug and pulled over. He leaned in the window and looked at her hair. "It's different but not bad."

"That's me. Different but not bad." Frederica shrugged. "Let's go for a ride and we can talk."

"Just like that? You disappear and then just show up? I don't even know who the hell you are."

"Yes, you do. I'm sorry I just took off. I'll explain."

"I hope so. I should probably just pull you in now. Besides, I'm busy. I can't just take off." He screwed up his mouth. "Unlike some people."

"Stop it. I'm sorry. I'm sorry. Do you have an hour or so? I'll explain everything."

"You could have confided in me. Trusted me."

"Maybe I should have."

Silence.

Abe took out his cell and punched a speed dial. "Something's come up, Janelle. I'll be out for a while."

He listened on the phone for a minute or two before looking at Frederica and responding to Janelle. "Yeah, I know. Bad time. I'll be back soon." He listened. "This is the craziest case, like a house of mirrors." He listened again. "Yeah, yeah. You're right. I'll be back later this afternoon and I hope I'll have more."

Abe closed the call with Janelle still making commentary, and put his cell phone away. He walked around the car to get into the passenger seat. "Tell me what the hell is going on," he said as he clipped his seat belt.

"I will. I will. I need to eat."

"Okay. Let's go."

"Good." Frederica pulled out and crossed Tremont Street heading for Mass Ave. She looked around her at the bustle of the city and the traffic. "I've missed this, Abe."

"Well, why'd you leave?"

"It's complicated."

"I hope to understand it better when you start explaining," he responded testily.

"I know. I will."

As she pulled up to a red light at Mass Ave, Frederica reached behind her to pull a baguette and a block of cheese out of a cooler bag. Tearing off two pieces of bread and expertly breaking two chunks of cheddar from the cheese block, she placed them on the console and started to eat and talk.

"Have some," she offered as the light changed and she started up again.

"Talk," Abe pleaded.

"Okay, but we're going to start at the beginning," she said between bites.

"That's always a good place to start." Abe reached behind the seat and pulled out two cold cartons of water. "Go."

Frederica talked all the way across the Mass Avenue bridge over the Charles and down Memorial Drive along the river. Without looking at Abe, she talked without interruption as she drove. Talked straight out, matter-of-factly between bites of crusty bread and cheddar cheese and told Abe the story about her life in Pittsburgh. Vickie Czinski and the Liberty Avenue gym and Skip Massey. And Agnes. On the subject of the fire at the gym, she left out some key details.

Abe sat in the passenger seat, baguette and cheese untouched, staring transfixed at Frederica.

"This is hard for me to process, Freddie." He looked out the front window. "Even if, you know, we figured out a lot of this already."

"I thought you would. Christ, even I can't process it all." Frederica gave a dark laugh before she looked at Abe's stricken face.

"I'm sorry."

Abe nodded, continuing to look ahead. "I'm sorry too. It's a terrible story. I was just," he turned to her, "you know, so worried."

"I get it." Frederica took a left on Mount Auburn Street and pulled into the gates of Mount Auburn Cemetery.

46

NO PICNICS ALLOWED

"Our destination?" Abe asked, looking around at the grounds.

"I always loved this place. I'll show you my favorite spot. Used to bring my Sister Connection mentee Antoinette here for picnics all the time."

"I thought you weren't supposed to bring food in here."

"You're not."

"Of course. By the way, tell me how is Antoinette doing? You know, the other person you walked out on?"

"Stop it."

"Sorry. Kidding – sort of."

She made a turn around the corner of Fountain Avenue. "She's doing okay. Home from Howard for an internship in the mayor's office. I saw her today. Sort of an ambush visit, but I think it meant a lot to her. It did to me. I don't know if this all will ever be sorted out—for me, at least. But I can try to be a presence in her life somehow. While I was gone, a friend of mine stepped in to be the support for her."

"Very nice. Would that be Dorrie or maybe Lissy?" he asked. "I'm guessing Dorrie would be a better bet as a mentor. Lissy's more the muscle. Right?"

Frederica raised her eyebrows, but didn't take her eyes from the road. "You're good. Dorrie."

She pulled over by the side of the road, got out of the car and took the picnic cooler and a blanket from the back seat. Handing the cooler to Abe, she gestured to a spot under a shady grove of dogwood trees.

On the other side of the dogwood stand, nearby but not entirely out of earshot, sat a young mother having a sippy cup and cutup hot dog picnic with a small boy. The woman smiled and waved. Freddie

waved back.

Abe cocked his head, obviously wondering about the privacy of their conversation. "She can't hear us, Abe. Besides, she's busy." She looked over to see the young mother chasing the boy who was, in turn, running after a bird.

"Yeah." Abe shrugged.

Without speaking, Freddie spread out a large "Maine—the Pine Tree State" blanket with images of pine trees, mountains, and a couple of moose. Abe took in the blanket and nodded.

She sat cross-legged and leaned over to the picnic cooler. "So, you will have some questions."

"Oh yeah, I'd say so."

'Before we start talking, we need a decent lunch while you ask questions, listen and learn. Help me set some of this stuff up and then get ready for the ride."

"We don't have a lot of time, Freddie."

"Oh yes, we do. For this we do."

She brought out a bottle of San Pelligrino and two glasses followed by a couple of caprese paninis and a tortellini salad. Even a thermos of coffee with two mugs, and some Baileys Irish Cream chocolates.

Abe couldn't restrain himself. "Very, very nice, but talk to me." He waved his hand over the picnic blanket. "You've been in Maine this whole time? Three weeks? What the hell?"

"Presque Isle."

"You're kidding."

"Even climbed Katahdin. Your beautiful mountain. It was you who gave me the idea."

He couldn't help giving her an affectionate smile, though he clearly didn't want to.

"I'm glad you listen to me on some things. Why did you go?"

"Complicated. Here's to complications." Frederica raised her glass to Abe and settled back. "Well, all the *recent* complications started here when I got an email announcement from the chamber about New You Gym CEO Alex Massey coming to town and speaking at the CEO Breakfast."

She took a sip of her water. "I knew that was trouble for me. I'm not usually really visible around town. "

"Maybe kind of," Abe interjected.

"Okay, I am known a little around town. Anyway, wouldn't you know that he'd be coming just as the Roundtable was putting up these damned banners all over the city with my face plastered on them to advertise the Mover and Shaker Award?"

"Great timing."

Frederica threw her arm up for emphasis. "It's not as if I could have avoided him at all, but that was really bad timing. So, then it got serious. He sent me a message."

"What kind of message?"

"An ugly message – threatening. I sent it to one of my cells and saved it."

"One of your cells?"

Frederica took out a cell phone, put it on the blanket and pressed play. Then, she stood and walked over the dogwood tree while Abe listened to Skip Massey's voicemail.

"Goddamn." Frederica started back to the blanket when she heard Abe's reaction. Before she got there, Abe stood and took her in his arms. "Oh, baby, baby."

"Oh no, don't be understanding and comforting. Don't. Don't. I'll cry. I don't want to cry."

"Shut up, Freddie."

And then she cried.

47

THE MARIPOSA CIRCLE –
BUTTERFLY GIRLS GROWN UP

Frederica and Abe settled again on the blanket. Freddie sat next to Abe and leaned against him.

"Butterflies?" he asked.

"The Butterfly Girls all grew up." Frederica pulled the neck of her black T shirt to the side to show him the shadow of a delicate butterfly tattoo still on her shoulder.

Abe smiled. "I remember."

She pulled up her T shirt and returned the smile.

"We all went to get tattoos together to show we were family— or some kind of family, since most of us didn't have anything like real families. Skip was furious at first."

"Why?"

"He always said tattoos made people look cheap. And it was really important to him that we didn't look cheap." She gave a sad laugh. "Pimped us out but didn't want us to look *cheap*. Go figure. He didn't notice them at first – until we wore our sleeveless jerseys in a volley ball game with another team. He couldn't restrain himself and had an outburst, though he really tried hard not to because there was a team from another gym there and he didn't want to look bad in front of their manager. He had kind of a crush on her." She turned to Abe. "Even though we were pretty sure that he didn't girls in that way – or boys, for that matter."

Abe raised his eyebrows. "Okay."

Frederica shook her head. "So weird. Anyway, he had an outburst, but this lady changed his mind fast. He did a one eighty when she said our tats were cool and then showed him the rose tattoo on her arm. After that, he was quiet about it and then actually said that he thought the butterflies were pretty and we were his butterflies, his girls."

"His girls."

"Oh yes, his little stable of girls."

"Jesus, Freddie."

"I know." After some moments, Frederica continued.

"That night we got the tattoos was a big one for us. It even gave little Aggie some spine." Frederica studied the light through the tree branches overhead. "We were getting older. I was on a schedule to graduate early from Pitt. Skip didn't know I'd been taking extra classes on my scholarship to pile up the credits."

Freddie took a deep breath, remembering their journey. "Dorrie had graduated. In her senior year, she took IT courses at the community college too, prepping herself to earn a living. Lissy had been held back a year or two when she was young, so she was the last to graduate, but she had taken over some operations at Skip's gym and had good experience to bring to another gym.

So, we were poised to leave, though we never talked about that with Skip and he acted like we would be there forever – working for him. In his mind, he had me managing the business, Dorrie in IT support, and Lissy in gym operations."

She shifted and took a deep breath. "He wanted to expand. He'd brought a couple of younger girls in and was starting to work them. Kind of damaged girls from backgrounds like ours." She stared off to the distance for a moment before saying, "Yeah, they were just like us. That's when we started to feel bad. Really bad."

Frederica was quiet for a while. "But it was Aggie that put us over the top." Her voice broke and she covered her eyes.

"I know about Aggie."

"You do?"

He nodded.

"Poor, sweet Aggie. He just used her up—rented her out to that jerk who got her hooked and then shared her with his pusher. It killed her—Skip might as well as put a knife through her heart. He murdered her."

They could hear the drone of traffic on Memorial Drive and Mount Auburn Street and the faint chatter of the small child on the other side of the dogwoods. Dogs barked in the nearby neighborhood. A brilliant cardinal settled in the trees nearby, and a cool

breeze ruffled the fringe of the Maine blanket.

"We started to make plans after Aggie died."

"What kind of plans?"

"Plans to build real lives for ourselves and plans to undermine at least some of the other Skips of the world."

"Like how?"

"First, we needed a plan to get the three of us the hell out of there. We'd all leave at the same time, but we'd go to different places to set up new lives for ourselves."

She ran her fingers through her hair, closed her eyes, and took a deep breath before continuing. "The prep only happened over the space of a few weeks, but still the hardest thing was to keep quiet. Skip is – was—pretty sharp. I'm surprised he didn't feel something changing in the air. Some days, it felt electric. I guess he was so preoccupied with expansion."

"And you just took off?"

"We did—in all different directions. All three of us were ready with cash, small bags and our documents. There was a big fire at the gym that gave us our opportunity."

"Yes, the big fire. How did that happen, Freddie?"

Frederica shifted on her blanket. "He'd gotten loans from some bad people."

"That's all you know about it?"

She looked at him directly. "That's all I can tell you about it."

Abe did not respond. Frederica looked down at the blanket, and traced the outline of a pine tree with her forefinger. "And then— when the flames started and we heard the fire engines—we took off. I said goodbye to the old me, Vickie Czinski, took a cab to the air-port and boarded a flight to Boston as Frederica Strauss. I'd already changed my legal name, gotten myself a job here and rented an apartment in Brookline."

"And the Mariposa Circle?"

"Where to start?" She let out a deep breath. "We had decided that once we were settled, we would find a way to help as many trafficked girls as we could. Because we were outside the system ourselves, we decided to work outside the system, but build links

into the system. The way it should have been for us.

The rough plan was to get the lay of the land in the cities where we had moved and identify girls we knew were in danger, maybe even girls who were already being moved from city to city. It would be a long process but if we could get a girl to trust us, and she was ready – not too far into drugs or whatever—we knew how to persuade her to move. Because we had all been there."

She stopped and said again as she looked at Abe. "Because we had all been there."

She took a few moments. "We called ourselves the Mariposa Circle. For the butterfly."

"I know from butterflies, Freddie."

She smiled. "Of course, you do."

"How did you set up the system?"

"We recruited volunteers who would take the girls for a few days or weeks once the girls were able to get away from their handlers and until they moved to the next stop—maybe a residential program and then into the foster system. That was Jenna Conway's role. She's that kind of volunteer. Sort of like the Underground Railroad."

"How many girls did you move through this system?"

"Maybe thirty or forty so far among all of us."

"Impressive. You have issues with girls who use?"

"If they are too far in, we can't handle them right now. Too complicated and we don't have the expertise or systems set up yet to help them. That really reduces the number of girls we can help since these guys also usually run drugs or are pushers too."

"And the handlers, the pimps?"

"Yeah. Those guys." She turned to face Abe again. "We've been able to manage up till now. It's not as if a small-time operator in Turner's Falls, say, would have the wherewithal or attention span to go after a girl who left, and he probably feels he can replace her by targeting some other troubled high school kid. But a larger operation is different. It's starting to feel like those guys understand more and more that there is this underground movement working against them. It's a small one, but one that will probably grow. Now, they're getting mad and ugly—or even madder and uglier."

48

MURDER WASN'T IN OUR PLAN

On a nearby road through the cemetery, a funeral hearse crept along, followed by several black cars. The hearse stopped at an open grave. Mourners waited for the coffin to be carried to the grave and funeral flowers to be arranged. Then, the mourners climbed out of their cars slowly without speaking and gathered at the grave site. The only sound was that of a nearby wood thrush singing its fluting hymn.

When the ceremony began, Abe made the sign of the cross. Frederica gave him a questioning look. "Just respect—a habit from my mother. I'm not practicing."

She nodded. "Want me to keep going?" she asked.

"Please," Abe responded.

Frederica lowered her voice, looking over at the nearby ritual. "Having a conversation feels a little disrespectful right now."

"No more than eating paninis in a cemetery. Keep your voice low."

Frederica ran her fingers through her newly short hair and watched the cardinal in a nearby tree peck at the berries. "After I got the voicemail, I thought maybe somehow I could reason with him, work something out. Make a deal—I wouldn't out him if he did the same for me, but . . . well, I knew I couldn't trust him and, besides, he was too angry. I know that tone of voice. I figured it was only a matter of time before I was in a fatal accident of some kind or maybe a suicide off a bridge into the Charles. I'd count myself lucky if it was quick and clean."

She sat up, stretched and reached for the last of her panini. Telling the backstory hadn't ruined Frederica's appetite. Abe's own sandwich sat untouched.

"So, I thought about it and finally decided we had to out him. I

169

did consider arranging his own fatal accident, but that was just emotion." She looked at Abe. "Did you think it was me that did him?"

"Crossed my mind. I couldn't see you actually doing it hands-on, but I could see one of your friends. I could see Johnny. I could see Alyssa. And I didn't want to, but I could see you involved."

"That's hard for me to hear, Abe."

He shrugged. "It's hard for me to think, Freddie, but it's an awful story. You were all abused and used so callously. Would make me want to do him, if he wasn't done already."

The birds rustled in the trees. The sky was becoming overcast and the air a little damp. Frederica looked at the graying sky. "I started working out the details of how to reveal his past and ours. Just get it all out there at once. I had to be careful because of the Mariposa work we did moving these trafficked girls around, although we never crossed state lines and we passed them into the system. But I decided we were going to be open about that too."

Frederica offered Abe a Baileys Irish Cream chocolate, which he declined, though he did take a cup of hot coffee with a touch of Jameson.

"In the end," Frederica continued, "I decided to go to the *Globe* investigative reporting team. They were the best ones to handle it— and making everything public was the best protection we could think of, for us and for the girls we were helping. Let the chips fall where they may."

"Who did you go to at the *Globe*?"

"One of the reporters on the Spotlight team. I had a phone conversation with him from Presque Isle."

"You're not going to tell me the name."

"You can figure it out—it's a small group. Anyway, next thing I knew, Skip—or Alex Massey—was murdered at the Boston Harbor Hotel garage. I told the guy at the Globe that I'd be in touch and give him what he needed for the overall story, but things were too complicated to talk now."

"You going back to him?'

"He's leaving all kinds of messages and I know he's approached the *Pittsburgh Post-Gazette* for a joint investigative series. I told

him I would work with the group soon, just not yet. I need my mind to calm down a little before I go into that history. Right now everything's too messy and complicated. But soon."

"Well, when you start work with him again, there's a retired reporter in Pittsburgh who's a gold mine of information about this story."

"Oh yeah?"

"Later."

"So, someone heard from the security guard who found Skip that he had a butterfly on his mouth. Is that true?"

"Tried to keep that information out of the press."

"I figured you would." She smiled. "But it will always come out."

"Yeah." Abe grimaced. "You warn the security guard to keep quiet about it. He keeps his mouth shut for a while but, finally, he has to tell his best buddy over a beer or maybe his wife late at night in bed. And it's gone."

Frederica shrugged. "Things just leak out. You know that."

She was pensive for a moment before turning and giving Abe a wry smile. "That's how I would have done it too. The butterfly, I mean. But I'm not into stabbing. Maybe just a gun. Or, a bad accident." She shook her head. "Of course, the jerk bought himself a top-of-the-line beemer."

"Christ, who are you that you would think about those possibilities. Freddie?"

She laughed. "Oh, I might think about it, Abe, but I wouldn't *do*."

Frederica studied Abe. He was still clearly confused and trying to come to terms with this side of her and what he'd heard.

"You know," she said, "This murder was similar to one that Skip did before. But you knew that, right? Roger Coombs—he was a dry cleaner from Oakmont outside Pittsburgh who got Aggie hitched on drugs—that other butterfly murder in Pittsburgh?"

"Yeah, yeah. We heard about it when we were down there. Weapons were different, and there was some over-the-top brutality in that one. But there was the butterfly."

"I heard you were visiting."

"Christ. Our control over the information flow around here is for shit." Abe threw his head back and surveyed the clouds. "So, if you and the Circle didn't do Skip Massey, who did?"

Frederica took a long drink of her coffee and stared into space before responding.

"My original bet was on Tommy."

"Tommy who?"

"Aggie's brother Tommy. Tomaz Janek Urbanowski. Johnny Thomas.

"Right. Detective Compagnone in Pittsburgh identified him. But, yeah, Johnny's out. He's got his alibi. He was walking Jenna to work at the time of the murder."

"I was so relieved to hear that. I love Tommy. The same way I loved Aggie."

Abe nodded. And leaned forward. "Alyssa involved, Freddie?"

Frederica hesitated. "Yeah. She's an original Mariposa, but she has the same alibi as Tommy for the time Massey was killed – she was with Tommy, keeping Jenna company on the way to work."

"She's Lissy, right?" A long Abe Leone sigh. "No one seems to be who you think they are."

Frederica gave him a sad smile. "Yes, Alyssa is Lissy Kelly— the first Liberty Avenue girl that got swept in and pimped out." Frederica's hand ran around the rim of her coffee cup. "Big, too loud, funny, friendly kid then." She looked away before adding in a matter-of-fact tone. "He killed that part of Lissy."

A red ball came bouncing through the dogwoods and landed on their blanket. "Sorry!" called the young mother who stood up to retrieve the ball.

"Stay there," Frederica called as she picked up the ball and snapped it toward the woman.

"Nice throw," Abe commented.

"Played a little softball at Pitt. That was fun." Frederica smiled. "Now, where was I?"

"Johnny and Alyssa became a couple?"

"Yeah. After the fire, Lissy went to be with Aggie's brother,

Tommy, in Buffalo. She knew him through Aggie and knew he would be in tough shape. One thing led to another and they became a couple. Tommy decided to use the English version of Janek— John—as his first name and changed his last name to Thomas. They came to Boston to help me with the Mariposa work."

Abe and Frederica both looked over to see the mourners from the funeral clustered into groups—consoling each other, quietly talking, perhaps confirming arrangements for the funeral luncheon before getting into their cars and slowly leaving the cemetery.

Frederica glanced up at the sky, getting a little grayer now, and went on. "I didn't want to think it. I did think they might have done Skip."

She traced the design on her Maine blanket, her long finger tracing the outline of a pine tree. "When I told Alyssa that Skip was in Boston now under another name, she got real quiet. I know her and I know that kind of quiet. I knew she and Tommy were a team and I knew how much they hated Skip. I didn't want to believe they'd killed him but I was uneasy when I thought about it. As for Coombs, the dry cleaner guy, I wouldn't have been surprised if they were tempted to do him. But they swear they didn't and I believe them. We all think it was Skip Massey who did Coombs but we have no proof."

The red ball rolled past their blanket again. Frederica deftly reached behind her with one hand and tossed the ball back. The young mother in turn rolled it to her little boy. "David—roll the ball over this way" she told him. She rolled the ball in the opposite direction of Frederica and Abe's blanket, and apologized again.

"No problem," Frederica called before turning back to Abe. She gave a wry smile when she saw his face. "Not a pretty picture, I know."

"It's not."

"Want me to go on or do you need some time?"

"No, no, go on."

"After the break-in at Jenna's, the short-term plan was for Jenna to stay at my place until we figured out something better. That's when Lissy and Johnny agreed to stay in Charlestown for a while

and take care of the Jenna situation."

They were both quiet. The little boy on the next blanket was starting to melt down—something about wanting a strawberry squeegee—not a blueberry one. Inconsolable, he howled as his mother explained that they didn't bring a strawberry one and started to pack up their things to make a quick getaway.

"So." Abe stood, running his hand over his bald head. "Now, we have to head back to Tremont Street and the Station, Ms. Czinski. You have a formal statement to make." He brushed his slacks and added. "I'll have to recuse myself from the investigation—hand it over to someone else." He looked at her. "Since I'm involved with one of the key witnesses and . . ." He didn't finish the sentence, which might have ended with "the suspect".

Frederica closed her eyes. She sat very still for a few moments before she gathering her things. "Let's go, Abe."

"You going back to your place now? No more backwoods Maine?"

"Nope. I'm back."

"Bye," called the little boy over his mother's shoulder—a sunny smile through his tears as he gave an energetic, chubby-handed wave.

49

"THOUGHT I'D TRY THE CADDY THIS TIME" – DR PEPPER MAN IN CHARLESTOWN

Frederica was home in Charlestown after giving a full statement to the police, and after her Presque Isle neighbors in the multi-family had confirmed she'd been there at the time of Skip Massey's murder.

While she was glad to be home, life was still beyond complicated. The high-powered lawyer she contracted for Johnny gave her reason for optimism as to how Johnny's case would roll out, given the circumstances of an attempted kidnapping and the victim's knife attack. She chose to have faith in the lawyer's opinion and the system.

She had no clue what would happen to her career. She remained on leave from the investment firm while everything was being worked out, but had no sense how the firm would deal with this series of events, her history, or the media attention to both. She'd given a public statement to the press about the Mariposa Circle and her own background. The press was having a field day. The city couldn't get enough of this stunning real-life story of one of their own—a respected woman financial executive and community leader. Not to mention the true identity of the high-profile CEO and murder victim Alex Massey.

She craved the routine of ordinary routines and tasks. One particular morning, she decided to figure out how she could take a simple walk down to the market in the Bunker Hill Mall. A sunny day. A short shopping list, some cheese and maybe some flowers for the table. Perfect for stretching her legs and trying to clear her head. This first little excursion would settle her mind and, God knows, her mind needed settling. The walk would get her blood flowing if she could make a smooth escape.

Looking out the parlor window, she was not surprised to see a cable news van set up outside. After some thought, Frederica walked

down the cellar stairs and slipped out a small bulkhead exit. The rest of the plan required squeezing through a wooden fence to another yard, and emerging on a small side street out of view.

And it worked. Excellent. Such a pleasure to just walk on the street without being chased by reporters. She hoped another story would soon catch the media's attention and she would be old news. But today she was not yet old news.

She had to admit too that even when that day came, when the media was focused on another person, another story, it would be hard to find peace. So much jostling in her own mind—so many thoughts and memories competing for attention. On top of it all, it was painful to know that Abe had been sidelined from the Massey Harbor Hotel murder case because he was "involved" with a key witness. That witness being . . . herself.

She knew Abe was now occupied with an urgent case of two shootings near a public high school in Dorchester. But the Massey Harbor Hotel case was higher profile and would have been much more important to his career. She was affecting that career and not in a good way. One of the last people in the world that she wanted to hurt was Abe Leone and here she was repaying him with a professional setback.

Frederica had always known that Abe Leone was a jewel, a unique man. Now, somehow, he was holding her blameless for her complicated history and for a professional opportunity lost. Those facts, and his kindness to her during this challenging time, sealed the deal for her. When this was all over—if it ever was—Abe would be moving into the sage green house on Winthrop Street.

At the rate the Cronin Brothers were going with the renovation, Frederica knew she and Abe would probably have the Cronin's crew as company most days—maybe forever. Of course, one member of the Cronin crew, Conor O'Leary, would be happy to stay working on Frederica's house indefinitely as long as Jenna Conway was in residence.

She was glad too, for now, to host the recuperating Jenna's daytime caregivers, her old neighbor George Hennessy and his dyspep-

tic apricot poodle Princess, who made the trek to and from Cambridgeport to Charlestown every day. When Jenna was well enough to go back to her little yellow house, all three would decamp back to Cambridgeport – where Jenna let it be known that Conor O'Leary would be welcome to visit anytime.

Freddie also knew that one occupant of the house would be very glad to see Princess the poodle leave. Archie had taken to sulking on his bed in the corner of the kitchen, turning away when Princess walked through the room.

Alyssa and Johnny were still staying at the house while Johnny was out on bail and hoped to clear the system. Afterward, he and Alyssa would move back to their own house in Dorchester.

And then perhaps things would start getting back to some semblance of normal. Just Abe, Archie and her. That would be nice.

* * * *

Frederica entered the busy market and walked down to the back of Aisle Six. Whoa. She'd forgotten that the cheese selection at the store was so enormous.

So many choices and everything looked good. These days, she was not great at decisions, even little decisions. She wanted to fill her basket with Gouda, cheddar, brie, crumbled blue cheese, or maybe feta, even though she'd only come for some Havarti and Dubliner.

Frederica was suddenly paralyzed with random thoughts and indecision. Why was she having such a hard time with decisions now? Even about what kind of cheese to buy?

Overload, she guessed. She had certainly been in overload before, but this was different. This was overload around fundamentals—like, for instance, who she was. Maybe if things straightened out in her life, even a little, she'd go see someone for help. She just didn't know how she could ever begin to put together her story for any professional counselor.

Breathing deeply several times, she cleared her mind and reached into the cheese case. She was picking up a nice block of Havarti with dill when a large hand with a pinky ring stopped her hand and guided it to put the cheese back in the case.

"You can put it back, Vickie. We're going for a ride." A gentle, affectionate and possessive voice from her past.

He looked older, but attractively so. A little gray in the dark hair, lines around the eyes and the mouth, and deeper lines in his neck. Still the same presentation. A cashmere sweater under a well-cut sports jacket. Dr Pepper Man. Prestige Investments. Skip's loan shark.

"What are you doing here?"

"We'll talk about that on our ride. Let's go."

"I'm not getting in a car with you."

He laughed. "I remember you said that to me once before." He appraised her. "So gorgeous and spunky."

A woman reached between them for some cheddar. "Sorry."

He gave the woman a charming smile. "No problem, honey."

Startled, the woman turned to look at him and returned the smile—if somewhat tentatively. Clearly taken and intrigued. Perhaps not the kind of man one usually encounters in her neighborhood market . . . but interesting. She pushed her cart away and turned to look at him over her shoulder once or twice.

He shifted his gaze back to Frederica. "You haven't changed. That's good. Except for the hair. I'm not crazy about that cut. Hope you can fix that."

Then there was that look she remembered from him. Amused, a soft smile, almost loving. To her annoyance, she found herself responding to that smile again. Just like when she was young on Liberty Avenue in Pittsburgh.

"Anyway, this time you're getting in the car, sweetheart."

He pulled his jacket aside to reveal the handle of a small gun.

"You don't want to get anyone else hurt." He looked to the end of the cheese case where a young mother with an infant in a jumper on her chest was comforting a tired toddler in the shopping cart's child seat.

"What do you want?"

"We'll talk. Get moving."

And so they did. Through the prepared takeout cases, down the natural beauty products aisle, through the flower department, lush

with Peruvian and Asiatic lilies, tulips, daisies. Out the exit, across the parking lot and into a black Cadillac Escalade SUV.

He ushered her into the passenger seat and locked the car with his fob. "Child lock." He smiled. "Be smart, Vickie. Don't make trouble. Too many other people can get hurt."

He walked around the car, unlocked his door again and slid into the driver's seat. "Decided to try the Caddy this time, as long as I was renting." He clipped his seatbelt. "Put your seatbelt on, Vickie."

She stared at him. So unreal.

"Hurry up."

She clicked the seat belt fastener.

"But, you know, I just like the Rover. I'm glad I tried the Caddy, but I guess I'm more of a Rover guy. I think it handles better, especially with the hills in the Burgh. Different terrain, right?"

He drove out of the parking lot and took a left into the heart of Charlestown.

"These are pretty good hills, though." He took a steep side street up to Bunker Hill Street and drove slowly past Saint Francis de Sales Church with its triumphant statue of Saint Michael vanquishing the devil.

"I don't think he's a saint anymore. Didn't they decide he was . . ." He thought for a few moments. "Like a fairy tale?"

Frederica didn't answer.

"Course, I think they're all fairy tales." He paused for a moment and pursed his lips. "Except for Francis. He was a real saint."

Frederica stared at this man, this loan shark, this brutal assaulter of borrowers behind in their payments, this arsonist and probably worse. She was trying to imagine his saying the Franciscan Prayer of Peace when she heard him muse, "Of course, in the real world, we can't all be Saint Francis. We have to be practical."

He slowed for some children crossing the street near the Boys and Girls Club. "My mother is big for Saint Anthony." He laughed. "Every time she can't find something in the kitchen like a favorite spoon or bowl, I can hear her praying to Saint Anthony." He turned to her briefly. "You know he's the patron saint of lost things, right?"

Dazed, Frederica nodded.

"Every once in a while, she says she was not sure if she should pray to Saint Anthony for me since she thinks I'm lost, or maybe she should pray to Saint Jude because he's the one that does hopeless cases." He roared with laughter, leaning over the steering wheel. "She says, 'You're just a hopeless case—but no one loves you like I do.'"

He wiped laughter tears from his eye and then said softly, "And she's right. Nobody loves me like my ma does."

Then, he resumed his comments. "A guy at Zume's the other day . . ." He grinned when she looked at him in disbelief that he was at her neighborhood coffee shop. How long had he been here? How many times had she walked by him? "Had to get my bearings for a couple of days, Vickie. Anyway, a guy was telling me they are talking about the Saint Catherine of Siena Church being sold as a Dollar Store now." He shook his head. "Now, that would be a crime."

50

"YOU DON'T GET AN A ON THIS ONE, VICKIE"

He pulled in across the street from the old Bunker Hill Burying Ground. "Always seems to end in cemeteries, huh?"

Frederica gave him a confused look.

"Well, you look confused, Vickie. That surprises me. You know where Saint Peter's Cemetery in Arlington – down in Pittsburgh—is?"

She nodded, remembering Roger Coombs and his gruesome end in Saint Peter's Cemetery.

"You send me a message, Vickie?"

"No, what for? Why would I do that? I don't even know how to reach you."

"You knew how to reach me when we decided to burn down Massey's Gym."

"You did that. I didn't"

"Oh, I beg to differ, Vickie. You *colluded*—isn't that the new word of the hour? You propped the door open."

She shook her head. "Oh, no . . ."

"Never mind. Who cares?" he said impatiently. "You didn't send me a message?"

"What message? What did it say?"

"Just these words. *You did Coombs and I'm going to give you up.*"

"I didn't know you did Coombs and why would I give you up if I did?"

"Well, see, here's the thing." He leaned against the window and faced her. "Everybody's snooping around suddenly down in the Burgh. Looking into old cases, like your friend Abe and his partner talking to a cop named Compagnone and that crazy old reporter named Murdoch, about the murder in Saint Peter's Cemetery—that Coombs guy."

"I don't get it—that was horrible. What's that got to do with me?"

181

"Oh, cut it out," he snapped. "All this is going on in Pittsburgh and I suddenly get a text from an unknown cell saying *I'm going to give you up.*" He smiled. "And the ping comes from a cell tower in Boston. Well, well. Now, who could that be?"

"Not me. How did you know where I was?"

"I've always known where you are, sweetheart. Give me some credit for smarts. I bet that jackass Massey must have gone into a tizzy when he moved here and saw that banner. Oh, look who else is here? His old favorite and then mortal enemy—Vickie Czinski."

"So, what does this have to do with you?"

He looked amused. "Who do you think did the deed back there at Saint Peter's Cemetery?"

"Skip."

"Shit. That's as far as you got?" He stared at her. "I gave you too much credit."

He looked out the window at a young tree near the car. "They're planting a lot of these—I think they're chestnuts. Maybe kind of a city chestnut because they can survive big city life." He turned to her. "Some species, some people don't—right?"

"Don't what?"

"Don't survive." He inhaled. "Like Roger Coombs. Boy, did he get in over his head."

"He took Aggie Urbanowski with him." Frederica couldn't help herself.

He nodded. "She was like a puppy. Cute little puppy. Used and abused and dropped like a dead puppy in a church alley on Polish Hill."

"Stop it."

"You know Coombs shared her with his dealer? To try and pay his bill? That's how she got in such bad shape the night she gave it up—Coombs's dealer was rough with women. And, of course, he fed her too much stuff."

"That's enough." Frederica closed her eyes.

He continued as if she hadn't spoken. "Coombs was in for big money with me and he offered the kid to me as partial payment too. I

told him that's not how I do business. Cash is how I do business. Besides, she wasn't my style and I don't need to get mine that way." He gave Frederica a lingering look. "You're more my style, Vickie."

She looked out the side window, shaking her head. Lips trembling, eyes red.

"You and me. We could have been something if things weren't so mixed up. I have another side, you know, Vickie. I'm good to my women." He was quiet for a moment. "I could have been interested in you."

Frederica continued to look out the side window.

"But enough of that." He inhaled deeply. "Look at me, Vickie." She continued to look at the sidewalk.

"Look at me," he said softly again, but with more hardness in his voice.

She did.

"Skip seem like the kind of guy that broke legs and fingers one by one before he offs somebody? That his style?"

She stared at him, not really seeing him, her mind reaching back. "No, no, it wasn't."

She almost wasn't afraid of him now, just thinking, thinking. "I don't think he would even know how to do that."

He chuckled proudly. "No, he wouldn't. Special skill set. Right?" She searched his face.

"Well. Look what a dumbbell I am." He threw his head back and laughed a long, rich laugh. "Oh, Jesus." He wiped his eyes. "All this time, I thought you knew. I flew all the way up here when I heard some detectives were down nosing around and I got that message. I thought you'd been doing some talking about things you shouldn't have. And you knew nothing." He slammed his palm on the dashboard. "Nothing."

"But the butterfly on Roger Coombs's body?"

"Oh, I didn't say Skip wasn't involved or that he didn't do the final deed. Skip brought Coombs to me, at my request, after he told him some shit story about why we were meeting. Skip did that because he owed me. He was there as part of a deal, but he was there because he wanted to get Coombs too. He never forgave Coombs for

that little Polish girl."

Frederica looked out at the row houses beside them as he went on.

"So, I took care of the early part—the bones part, the payback, the message to the rest of my clients that you don't fool around. In this business, you have to keep everyone in line, Vickie. People get out of line, they disrespect you, they don't pay, then you come down hard. No exceptions. Sends a message to everyone else. You pay one way or the other." He was giving Frederica avuncular advice—professional to professional. A mentor.

"Massey had to leave when things got too interesting. My work . . . well, we have to say, can be brutal. Just the way it is. Massey didn't have a lot of stomach for the hard stuff." He shrugged. "But he came back with the gun to finish off whatever was left of Coombs, and afterward, he took that damned cheap paper butterfly out of his pocket."

"Aggie," Frederica whispered.

"Yeah, I figured. I didn't know her name at the time. Heard it later. Massey had a soft side. Kind of a flaw in our business." He looked across at her. "I sort of have one too, Vickie, but I don't let it get in the way of things that need to be done."

She was sure he didn't.

"I wasn't going to let him leave the butterfly. I figured it might screw up the message I wanted to send to my clients—the butterfly was Massey's message, not mine. And, you know," he paused, "it was a little decorative. So girly, you know. Not me. I could see the headlines." He waved his hand in the air in front of him. *"The Butterfly Murder"*. And, sure enough, that's just how they wrote the headline."

He shrugged again. "But you know, I was tired and I was hungry. It takes a lot of physical energy, that kind of job." He turned to her. "I work out every day. Have to."

He looked down at his hands. "So, anyway, I just let him leave the frigging butterfly and then I went out for pasta at Tambellini's and home for a nap."

"That's why I thought it was just Skip."

"The butterfly? Right. But I'm disappointed you didn't think about whether that was his style. You've got to think these things through, Vickie." He smiled. "I'm not giving you an A on this one, Vick."

"Did you . . . Skip?"

"Kill Massey?" He laughed. "With all those wounds and that frigging butterfly again?" He looked out the window before turning back to her. "Please. I thought you knew me. I don't do ornate. A few broken bones and then a bullet as necessary. *That*," he emphasized, "that piece of work—that hit at the Harbor Hotel—was not a clean job. That was theater." He snorted in disdain.

"What are you going to do now?"

"Well, you know a lot—about the fire in the gym, and now that I'm such a big mouth, about the Coombs guy." He gave her that look again. "You know I like you. See what you've made of yourself since you got out from under Massey? I knew you were a star."

He nodded to himself for emphasis. "I heard a guy say once that some people have bigger dreams than where they were planted. I think he was right. You know what I mean, Vickie?"

She didn't respond. "You're one of those, Vickie. A star."

He took her left hand and stroked it softly, separating her long, slim fingers with his own. He lifted her hand to his mouth as if to kiss it.

And then he snapped her ring finger like a chicken bone.

Frederica gasped and jerked her hand back to her mouth. The pain was so intense she couldn't speak. Her eyes watered.

"I'm sorry, honey. I could do more. I usually do more, but you know I like you. A lot." He looked at her with a kindly smile. "Just a reminder to keep your mouth shut. Every time it rains and that finger hurts, just remember what it felt like and keep your mouth shut. About everything."

She nodded.

"You're a rightie?"

She nodded again.

"That's what I thought. Shouldn't be too bad, then. Just a memento."

She looked at him before unlocking her seatbelt and reaching for the door handle.

"Okay," he gave her permission. "And, if you ever want another line of work or a business opportunity, just call me. You never knew my name, did you?"

She stared at him.

"It's Eddie. Wish we'd gotten to know each other better, Vickie." He looked at her. "Say my name."

"Eddie."

"Say 'Bye, Eddie.'"

"Bye, Eddie."

"Bye, Vickie. Now get out of the car. You have a good new life. Go live it."

51

LIVE BY THE SWORD

S he started to open the door when the Escalade suddenly jolted forward and shuddered.

"What the hell?" Eddie looked behind him to see a dark car backing up to hit the rear of the Escalade again—hard. Frederica's head hit the dashboard.

Eddie opened the car door, pulled a gun from his jacket pocket and leapt out onto the street, shielding himself partially with the back car door. "Get down, Vickie."

She never heard shots. Just a fast *thwack thwack*—like a nail gun. Eddie fell to the street in an instant.

A big man jumped into the black car behind them and pulled out onto Bunker Hill Street, turned down Armory Street and was long gone.

Her head pounding from hitting the Caddy's dashboard, Frederica struggled to get out of the car. Minutes later, she was leaning against the cemetery's iron gates assisted by a woman from a neighboring house who'd come down to see what was happening. Patrol cars and an ambulance came flying up Bunker Hill Street—blue and red lights flashing and sirens swirling.

A young officer hopped out of the second patrol car. "You okay, ma'am?"

"I'd like to talk to Sergeant Janelle Mahoney, please. At the Tremont Street Station." She had started to say that she wanted to talk to Abe, but remembered that he was off the case.

"With all respect, ma'am, you don't get to choose the officer you want to discuss an incident with."

"This incident is connected to the Harbor Hotel Alex Massey murder."

"Got it. Give me some details on this—what you saw and how it happened. Your name and contact information and then we'll take

you down." The officer picked up his phone. "I'll let them know you're coming." He looked at her hand. "Let's get a splint on that finger first."

He waved an EMT over and asked, "Guy dead?"

"Oh yeah, he's gone."

"Fix her finger up and look at that bump on her forehead. If she checks out okay, she's headed down to Tremont Street after I talk to her."

52

COFFEE AND AN UPDATE AT DUNKIN'

Janelle slipped into the seat across from Abe at the Dunkin Donuts in the Bunker Hill Mall.

"You're not supposed to be talking to me." He continued to scroll through messages on his cell phone.

"Right." Janelle was surprised to see how red and weary Abe's eyes looked when he raised his face. "How's Freddie?"

"Exhausted. She was smart enough to follow the doctor's advice and take a sleeping pill. Out cold. Alyssa's with her now."

"She talk to you at all?"

"Just the bare bones. What you probably already know from her."

"Maybe. Doesn't hurt to go over it again."

"Yeah," Abe blew out a long breath. "Guy was Massey's loan shark. Messina. Eddie Messina."

"Did she tell you why she was in the car with him?"

"He ambushed her at the supermarket, the one at the Bunker Hill Mall. Knew we had been asking questions down in Pittsburgh, and got spooked. He thought she knew more than she did on the Coombs murder."

"So, he wanted to lean on her to stay quiet." Janelle said. "Lucky he only broke one of her fingers. He's got a real bad history, you know."

"Yeah."

"That's all pretty consistent with what she told us."

"I just don't know how much more there is to come out. I'm worried for her."

Janelle reached across the small table to put her hand on his. "She's a good person, Abe. We have to see how this all shakes out, but she's a good person."

He nodded without replying or looking up.

189

"She say anything more about the assailant's car?" Janelle asked.

"She said it all happened too fast. Just that it was a black, blocky car."

"Yeah, well. We're pretty sure it's the black Toyota Rav 4 that got dumped in the Quincy Quarry that night."

"Thought those gates were locked. They have CCTV cameras there, right?"

"Our guy got through the gates. We have his image—not that it's going to help a lot—looks like a big black bear in a dark hoodie pulled up around his head and a ski mask on his face."

"Figures. He knows what he's doing."

Janelle took a sip of her coffee. "Hey, I need some good news. How's it going with the shootings near the school?"

"Got 'em yesterday."

"Congratulations. Gang?"

"Yeah, with drugs and a fight over a girl thrown in."

"Never changes."

"Yeah."

"Guess what?"

The tenor of her voice made Abe look up. "What?"

"We matched the fingerprints—you were right to make us stay on them. They were the key."

"You mean those *smudges*. The ones nobody would be able to identify."

"Don't rub it in. Grace in victory, Abe."

"Next time, listen to your elders without giving guff, Mahoney." Abe cocked his head. "But whatever. What'd you find?"

"Daniel Coombs."

"The son? You're kidding me. I thought he was in the Middle East."

"Got out late last year. Great record, decorated, highly thought of. Just started working at a veterans recovery center over near the Navy Yard." She pulled her carry bag close to her and pulled out a folder.

"His fingerprint was on file in Pittsburgh and with the new software—okay, okay, you were right."

"Didn't say anything."

"Didn't have to."

"Anyway, with the new software, they were able to do a match. He'd assaulted Massey—back when Alex Massey was Skip Massey—after the Coombs murder. Massey refused to press charges, but the fingerprints were still on file."

She removed a photo from her folder. "This is the employment photo from the vet center. Been using the name Daniel Halligan—his mother's maiden name—for years, but we tracked him down with the fingerprint." She pushed the picture toward Abe. "Nice job, old man."

Abe looked at the close-cropped hair, the unsmiling square face, the war ink on the sides of the man's thick neck. He tried to find in the picture a beaming young athlete standing beside his parents in a Coombs family photo he'd seen in Pittsburgh. A family photo from long ago in a small western Pennsylvania town. A moment in time when his family was solid, he was a star athlete, and life was good. Abe couldn't find that boy in this picture.

As Abe was studying the photo of Daniel Coombs, Janelle was taking another photo out of the manila folder. She pushed it across the table to Abe. He looked at the image of an attractive blonde woman in a nurse's uniform. Short hair, a certain hardness around the mouth, but compassionate eyes. "Meet Sheila Coombs. Hospice nurse in Wayland."

"Goddamn. Didn't see that coming." He fell back in his seat. "You get 'em?"

"Still working on it, but so far no trace." She glanced at the pictures and met his eyes. "Think they're long gone."

"Got a national search out?"

"Oh yeah." She took a sip of her coffee—now gone cold. "So, what do we have? Two murders—one of a sex trafficker and the other of a violent loan shark. According to Freddie, this Eddie character that picked her up and broke her finger admitted he did the

bodily damage to Roger Coombs in Saint Peter's Cemetery in Pittsburgh before Skip Massey shot him."

"Did the damage?"

"The ugly punishments part." She raised her eyebrows "To send a message to his other clients, he said." She took another sip of her coffee. "But Massey actually pulled the trigger and left the butterfly."

"For the girl."

"Yeah, for Aggie."

Abe raised his eyebrows. "I'm surprised. I didn't think Massey was a sentimental guy."

"It's complicated, as they say."

"Like he didn't have any part of pimping her out."

"Yeah." Janelle looked down at her hands, searching for words. "This sounds strange, I know, but I believe that Massey did have strong feelings for those girls. He was so damaged himself that he didn't know what love was."

"Don't make excuses for the jerk, Janelle."

"No way." Janelle gave a sigh almost like her boss's. "But no one should get away with murder, even the murder of lowlifes like these. We'll all do our job." She put the pictures back into her folder. "Don't quote me and you know I'm going to work my ass off on this case, but I'm not going to lose any sleep if they don't find the Coombs brother and sister."

Abe nodded.

They both rose from their seats and Abe walked Janelle out to her car.

"One more thing?" Abe asked.

"Yeah?"

"Can you call this Josh Brown in Pittsburgh again for one more detail?"

"Like what?"

"See if they had a big round maple table and captain's chairs in their kitchen when he was growing up."

"That's a weird question." Janelle dropped her hands by her side. "Kind of strange to ask."

"Yes, kind of strange, but not weird. It's a nice story. A scared,

lonely, ambitious girl who made up a fantasy life from someone else's good fortune." He inhaled deeply. "And Josh Brown probably never fully understood what his great good fortune in his family and his home meant to her and how it drove her. But that's another story."

"I get it." Janelle opened the driver's door of the care. "You want a ride?"

"Naw, thanks. It's a good day to walk. Let everything fall into place."

53

THE AVENGERS

Later that week, before heading up to the third floor of Freddie's house to continue the renovation work there, Matty Cronin dropped the *Boston Globe* and the *Herald* on the green granite counter in the kitchen as Abe was leaving for work. "Well, Abe, social media, TV news, and the papers are having a hell of a day with all this."

Abe looked at the newspapers on the counter. "The Avengers!" read the breathless *Boston Herald* tabloid headline with past and present pictures of Daniel Coombs and his sister, Sheila.

The more subdued *Boston Globe* headline featured a statement from the Suffolk County District Attorney's office—a district attorney, for the record, running for reelection the next year. "These people will be brought to justice. Ours is not a vigilante society. This is a society of laws."

"Don't hold your breath, huh, Abe?" commented Matty. "They did a pimp and a loan shark."

"It's still a murder, Matty. The Boston Police Department is a professional organization. They'll do their job."

"Right. Well, for my money, I'd say those two are on a sunny beach somewhere and we'll never see them again."

Abe didn't respond.

Matty Cronin shifted his feet and rubbed the back of his neck. "Johnny going to be okay, Abe? I thought he'd just plead self-defense and that would be the end of it, but now somebody said they might tag him with second degree murder. Would they do that?"

"I can't say, Matty. He still has another hearing while they figure it all out. But the guy came at Johnny with a knife and he tried to kidnap Jenna. That's before you consider his trafficking history. Not a pretty picture. I have to believe that Johnny will be just fine."

"Yeah, sometimes the system can work. Hope this is one of those times."

54

DORRIE AND VICKIE ON A BENCH BY THE CHARLES

Frederica and Dorinda La Pierre—the long ago Pittsburgh twosome of Vickie and Dorrie—sat quietly on a bench in the Cambridge side of the Charles River, looking back on the Boston skyline.

The traffic behind them on Memorial Drive was light, the evening commute long since passed. The pedestrian traffic now largely consisted of MIT students and faculty going in and out of the buildings behind them. A steady stream of joggers pounded the pavement along the river.

"Nice city," commented Dorrie.

"Yeah, I've been happy here."

"You will again, Vickie. This is salvageable."

"Looks like it." Frederica pulled out a thermos from a knapsack. "More coffee?"

"Yeah, but hold the shot."

"Got it." Frederica poured coffee into Dorrie's travel mug and her own.

"Lose the funky cut," Dorrie said, glancing at Frederica's hair.

"Well, pardon me."

"Just sayin'." Dorrie sipped her coffee and inhaled deeply before asking. "So, what's the Johnny situation? Is he going down for second degree or are they going to give him the keys to the city?"

"Don't know. He's all over the papers. The mayor loves him. I think it will be hard to prosecute him in this city."

"And you?"

"Oh, Christ, Dorrie. And me. Well, it's a mess. Nothing to charge me with, but Abe is still off the case. Too close to a key witness."

"That would be you."

"Yep."

"All the publicity about your bad girl past doesn't seem to have hurt."

"I'm really surprised about that. I'm like a media star now. Not as big as Johnny, but people seem to love a complicated back story." Frederica laughed. "And I sure have one."

"Are all the Mariposas going to be in trouble legally now—you, us, the volunteers?"

"We'll see. We got the girls into the state systems as fast as we could and we never moved them across state lines." Frederica threw her head back, stretched her arms and smiled. "We've got a line of lawyers from here to Stockbridge, including the three biggest legal firms in Boston, who want to work for us pro bono. Abe says he thinks that in the end this case will be tried in the media, in the public arena, and not the courts. And the public is behind us. I'm told we'll come out okay. We'll see."

"We really have to protect the volunteers, like Jenna Conway."

"Couldn't agree more." Frederica took a deep breath. "I'm going to trust the system and the universe to do the right thing on this one. And, you know, I think the case will stimulate some new initiatives around the sex trafficking of young girls. So, whatever happens, that's a good thing."

Dorrie stretched her long legs out and inhaled the fresh evening breeze off the river. "How's Jenna?"

"She's doing fine. But still a little shaky. Got a pretty good concussion when her head hit the door of that van."

"And you got one too from hitting your head on the dashboard in Dr Pepper Man's car."

Frederica stared at Dorrie, remembering the big man who had gunned down Dr Pepper Man. Dorrie let out a long breath and turned to look at the river.

"Yeah, I did," Frederica said, turning away from Dorrie. "But a minor one—not like Jenna's. Hers was really rough. She's still kind of off-balance and gets headaches. She's taking a short-term leave from work and staying with me. Her old neighbor George comes over every day to keep her company. He's very sweet, actually. And, I have to say, he was quite a hero, considering his age, when she was

almost kidnapped."

Frederica gave a wry laugh. "And, of course, that Cronin crew is still there—coming up with new jobs and soaking me to keep my house standing. One of them – cute guy – Conor O'Leary – has a thing for Jenna. The feelings are apparently mutual and I think it will be a long-term thing."

"You have a full-service safe house – even match-making." Dorrie chuckled. "You have to be the world's best caretaker, Vickie Czinski."

"I don't know about that—Jenna got her house ransacked, almost got kidnapped by a murderous pimp, and suffered a concussion. Johnny's dealing with a possible second-degree murder charge. Abe was taken off a prime career-building homicide case because of his relationship with me. And I was ambushed and held by a big guy who loaned money and broke legs for a living and then got murdered in front of me. It seems to me that all hell is breaking loose around me lately."

"I'm sorry, Vicki. I'm really sorry."

"I know you are."

A lighted boat full of passengers cruised by on the river. "Nice night for that," Dorrie commented. She put her head on Frederica's shoulder. "Unbreakable."

"Yeah."

"Police ask you about the fire?"

"Not too much," Frederica answered uneasily, then added "I didn't set it, you know."

"No, you didn't actually *set* it." Dorrie smiled at Frederica.

"Right. There you are."

It was getting dark. The city skyline, a mix of old and new, festooned with lights like stars, was peaceful and the friends were content.

55

DEED DONE AND AWAY

"You realize that I figured it out a while ago, Dorrie." Frederica picked a speck of lint from her sleeve.

"I thought you might have."

"Well, you were so elusive about where you were staying and who with that it got me thinking."

"Yeah."

"Are you all going to leave together?"

"They're gone. We'll meet up there."

"Did you know they were going to do Massey and Dr Pepper Man?"

"Not specifically, but I wasn't surprised."

"You have anything to do with it?"

"Nope. Just came here to see if I could help while you sorted things out on your end."

"When did Dan and Sheila Coombs arrive in town?"

"As soon as the announcement came out about the New You women's fitness chain moving its headquarters and Massey being based here as CEO. They've been tracking him for years, but they had to wait for the timing to be right. Daniel was still deployed and all that." Dorrie closed her eyes and leaned back on the bench. "They're both sharp. Got jobs here pretty fast." She paused. "I don't think they planned to make the move right away but then I told them about his threat to you and the opportunity presented itself. That sealed it."

Frederica nodded. She couldn't see her friend's face in the dark. "You're pretty serious about him, Dorrie?"

"Oh yeah. You know we've been involved for a long time. He's been on my screen ever since I was on Liberty Avenue and looked him up on the internet when his jerk dad was hooked on Aggie."

"I remember that night. Love at first sight when you saw his picture."

198

"You got that right." Dorrie smiled. "Fell in love with an image on the computer screen and never looked back."

Neither spoke for a while before Dorrie broke the silence. "I think about Aggie every day."

"We all do."

"I'm glad they all got what was coming to them."

"I just wish it could have happened differently."

"Well, it didn't. So somebody had to take care of it and now it's done."

"Yeah." Frederica inhaled deeply. "What's the plan?" She stopped and held her hand up. "Never mind. Don't tell me. I can't know."

Dorrie poked Frederica in the side. "Right. You can't, but it's far away. They've been busy. Already got the new us lined up with passports and work visas."

"Forever place if things work out?"

"That's the plan. Dan has ideas about a private recovery center. Sheila will help with the medical support. I can do my IT consultancy from anywhere."

"Settling down?"

"Yep. Dan and I are starting a family. Sheila will be a terrific aunt. The three of us are a family unit."

"That's nice. I hope it works out, Dorrie."

The deepening night softened their voices. "There's a darkness there, Dorrie. Skip was guilty in so many ways and God knows Eddie Messina was too, but they were murdered. Violently murdered. It was wrong. This is hard to accept."

A pair of joggers trotted by.

"We all have a lot of darkness, Vickie. Maybe in Dan more than others because he saw so much when he was deployed. But there's justice too—and justice needs to be served. I'm not saying this is the right way and I never would have done it that way."

She inhaled deeply. "I liked your plan about going to the Globe. Everything about the past out in the open. We never had things out in the open, Vickie. The timing was not right. These are different days and the timing is right now to bring all that out."

"All of it?" Vicki asked.

Dorrie cocked her head and said softly, "Maybe not all of it, Vickie."

Frederica blew a breath out softly. "No, not all of it."

Dorrie turned to her friend. "You have to believe me, Vickie. I thought Dan agreed with us, but I guess in the end he and Sheila couldn't handle not taking revenge themselves." She looked out on the river again. "I blame Dan's time in the war. Killing became too easy for him. He said it was an honor thing."

"Do you think it could happen again? I worry about you."

"No, he's done. It's over. Or, as over as it's ever going to be. Skip and the loan shark . . ."

"Eddie. We did some work with Eddie ourselves, Dorrie. We're not clean."

Dorrie gave Frederica a long look before turning to the water again. "You're right. Now, they're all gone. It's not easy but I can live with knowing what Dan and Sheila did. They'll be a lifetime dealing with it. But we will find peace together. That will be our life's work."

"Take care of yourself and stay in touch, Dorrie. Love you."

"Oh yeah, love you back, Vickie." Dorrie hugged Frederica. "Okay, got to get a move on. I left my luggage at the airport. The flight leaves in a few hours."

Dorrie checked the time on her cell phone and looked down Memorial Drive. "Uber should be here in a few minutes. I told them to pick me up near the boathouse. I think this is him now."

She stood, gave Frederica a lingering, tight hug and walked to the car. She turned. "Stay safe. Love you, Vickie." And then she was gone.

56

AN UNEXPECTED AND SPARKLING BEQUEST

Frederica was still on a leave of absence from her job at the investment firm. She had been pretty sure the firm would want her to resign what with all the legal complications and the publicity around her and her background. But, to her surprise, the firm asked her to think about staying. Maybe do her Mariposa work pro bono. Frederica was stunned the firm wanted to keep her after all her secrets had rolled out—well, maybe not all her secrets, but most of them. In any case, she was a new Boston heroine. A survivor, a warrior for vulnerable young girls. This was truly a new era.

Some weeks later, she got a call from the administrator in her office. A package had arrived for her from a law firm in Pittsburgh. Her administrator had signed for it and was sending it over to her house by courier. They didn't know if it might be important.

Frederica was curious but had almost forgotten about the package until her doorbell rang. She accepted the delivery after signing for it. Walking back into the kitchen, turning the package over in her hands to get some hint of what it might be, she inspected the return address for a law firm in downtown Pittsburgh—a law firm she was not familiar with. She took a knife out of the kitchen drawer to break the seal on the small brown package and found a letter wrapped around another, smaller packet inside bubble wrap.

Frederica unfolded the letter carefully.

Dear Ms. Strauss,

Our firm represents the estate of Mr. Edward Messina, late of Pittsburgh. In his will, Mr. Messina stated that, upon his death, he wished this letter and packet to be given to Ms. Vickie Czinski, now known as Ms. Frederica Strauss, of Boston, Massachusetts.

If you have questions about the arrangements or, for any reason, you choose not to accept the bequeathal, please contact our

201

offices at the above phone number.
Best regards.

Why in the world would Eddie Messina—who gratuitously broke her finger—want to leave her anything? But Mr. Messina—aka Eddie—answered her question by writing a note on an expensive blue bond, under the heading Prestige Investments of Pittsburgh. Dr Pepper Man from the grave. Dr Pepper Man who met his end on Bunker Hill Avenue—far from his neighborhoods in Steeler City. The content of the note was brief and, Frederica thought, graceful and articulate for a professional loan shark and hit man. The penmanship was classic parochial school Palmer method, and perfect.

Always plan ahead, Vickie.

You won't remember me as Edward Messina. Think of me as Dr Pepper Man or Eddie from Pittsburgh.

I always had a soft spot for you. Maybe you figured that out. I've followed your career since I saw you in a restaurant on Hanover Street years ago when I was visiting other alternative finance colleagues in Boston. The waitress was persuaded to give me the name off your credit card.

Since then—after I learned where you landed—I've checked to see what you were doing and felt as proud of you as anybody could when I read about your successes. Maybe if life had been different, I would have gotten a fancy degree and been in finance too. I think I would have been good at it.

I see myself as kind of a venture capitalist myself, but not like the ones you read about in the Wall Street Journal. *Still, you know when I hear about those guys, they don't seem a lot different than me. They don't actually break bones, but there are some times they might as well.*

All the same, except for maybe missing an opportunity with you, I don't regret the choices I made in life. I know my days aren't going to end well. One way or the other, I'm not going to die in my bed. So, I'm planning ahead here—just like you advise your clients to.

My ma's taken care of. I left money to the shrine for Saint Francis in Loretto—he's my favorite—and I want you to have my pinky ring. I'm told it's worth pretty good money. A guy over in the North Hills was in arrears and gave it to me. Don't usually do that in my business, as you know, but I took a liking to the ring and it's brought me luck—mostly.

I figure the ring might have some bad memories for you, even if your meeting me got you your breakout opportunity from Massey and his creepy gym. So, I wouldn't be hurt if maybe you'd like to sell the ring for the Butterfly rescue thing you and your friends run for girls. That seems right.

I don't know how it will all have ended for me when you get this. Probably won't be peaceful. Live by the sword and die by the sword.

Have a good life, Vickie.

Love from wherever I end up. Maybe Saint Francis will put in a good word for me.

Your friend Eddie

Frederica sat in the parlor for some time, the small box on her lap. Then, she called to Abe in the kitchen. "I have to run to the jeweler's building downtown."

"What for?"

"I have something to sell. I'll explain later. I'd like to get rid of it right away."

Abe stood in the doorway and considered her. "Okay. I can't go today but I'd like you come down there with me while I do some other business tomorrow."

"What's that?"

"I'm having a ring re-sized there."

"You don't wear rings."

"No, I don't. It's Maureen's—my mother's."

"Your mother's."

"Maybe you'd like to try it on."

They stared at each other across the room. Freddie's voice broke slightly. "Maybe." And then with a smile. "Yeah, maybe, maybe."

57

MISSIVE FROM A SMALL, SUNNY COUNTRY

Two weeks later, Frederica was trying to find a place for Abe's battered green plaid recliner in her parlor—stopping occasionally to admire the late Maureen Conneely Leone's emerald ring on her left hand. The jeweler had to re-size the ring because Frederica's broken ring finger had healed with a noticeable bump—her forever memory of terrifying and long minutes with Eddie, Dr Pepper Man, parked near the Bunker Hill Burying Ground.

She wanted to get the plaid recliner out of the hallway this morning before she and Abe drove up to the Emerson Inn, not too far from Halibut Point on Cape Ann. They still had a few arrangements to make for their wedding ceremony there—small, with just a few friends and family, an over-the-moon Antoinette as the maid of honor, good food and the ocean air. She couldn't believe it all and still felt cautious about being too confident, too happy. But it was nice. Very nice.

She heard the mailman drop the day's post in her hallway. "Thanks," she called as she walked to get it, still ruminating on how she could position Abe's ancient and tattered recliner among the high-end furniture in her parlor. Perhaps a unique, patterned throw that might blend with the other colors. No, it was hopeless. He would quietly and firmly disappear the throw.

Through the front door window, she saw the mailman raise his hand in response to her thank you. Sitting on the hall floor, Frederica quickly went through the small pile of mail, separating out those destined for recycling and the mail she might actually want to read.

A small padded envelope sat in the middle of the piles. Frederica recognized the handwriting but not the brightly colored stamps. Then, she looked more closely and saw that the stamps were from a small, sunny country. She smiled as she thought about this small, sunny country that, as she could recall, had no extradition treaty with

the United States or maybe that it was a country that reserved the right to decide when it felt like honoring such treaty.

Vickie sat on Abe's recliner and savored the opening of the envelope. She knew who it was from and hoped she knew roughly what might be in it. She separated the tissue paper inside to see a tiny pink knitted baby bootie and a picture of a rainforest butterfly. On the reverse of the butterfly picture was this: *Agnes Vickie 8 lbs. 2 oz. 21 inches. Unbreakable. For Aggie and Vickie.*

The End

AN APPRECIATION

MARIPOSA CIRCLE was long in the making.

Begun shortly before the pandemic and before my late husband Bill descended deeply into Alzheimer's, MARIPOSA benefited early from the steady, helpful and foundational editorial support of author Sara Henry.

I was also blessed at the time with a number of a number of supportive beta readers who forged through early drafts. My longtime friend book club members - Sandra King, Brigid Menzi, Jody Newman, Marcia Smith, Jean Vnenchak and Fiddle Walton. The volunteers from the Fowler Library Mystery Book Club in Concord, MA - Enid Hart Boasberg, Valerie Maser-Flanagan, Suzanne Knight, Darshana Merchant and Pat Pluskal. The manuscript was rougher then, but they gamely read through – making suggestions and comments, all of which had an impact on the final product.

My sister Jane Compagnone, to whom MARIPOSA is dedicated, was my Pittsburgh guide. Over days of driving rain on one memorable trip, we explored the city's neighborhoods, the bars and coffee shops around Pitt, churches, cemeteries and tea rooms. It's fun to remember those excursions – a time when the shape of the MARIPOSA back story, characters and scenes emerged.

Jane read over drafts of the book, as did her friend Mickey Gatto, also of Pittsburgh. Neither Jane nor Mickey, who were both so helpful, is responsible for any errors in my grasp of Pittsburgh. Special thanks to Mickey Gatto (again) and Jack McGinley of Pittsburgh, who helped make sure that the Pittsburgh skyline on the book cover fit the timeframe. Pittsburgh is an interesting city, rich in history – different from my own hometown of Boston, but rich in its own right. I enjoyed getting to know it further.

One of the Pittsburgh Police Department detectives in the book is named Toto Compagnone, after Jane's late husband Ralph. I could hear Ralph's voice in the dialogue, which was kind of fun and brought him back in a small way.

When we envisioned a book partially set in Pittsburgh, I don't think either of us anticipated the complicated and sometimes tough story it would be. It was, in the end, the plot that came to me and wouldn't go away. I felt compelled to run with it. It's a story, a plot that could be set in any major city.

Then, the pandemic expanded and my husband Bill's decline accelerated. We cared for Bill at home, a challenge made increasingly complicated by the deepening pandemic. It soon became difficult to focus on anything other than caretaking. Out of necessity, I put the various MARIPOSA drafts, the background research, the editorial input from Sara Henry and the suggestions from beta readers into a brown box behind a sofa in the parlor. All away for another day.

That day didn't come for a year or two and the start was halting. I wasn't sure of the market for a story like this and it didn't help that the small independent press that had published my first two books had closed shop. But I took the manuscript out of its box and waded in again.

It felt good to revisit and rework the book. Again, a difficult story at times, but I thought a rich one with overarching themes of personal agency and redemption. And, of course, I fell in love with the characters all over again.

I thought joining the Novel Critique II class at the Gotham Writers Workshop in New York City would serve me well in getting a jump start on MARIPOSA again. I was so right. Teacher extraordinaire and author Susan Breen led a lively, candid and constructive group of writers who critiqued and improved each other's work, including my own.

Sisters in Crime New England, Penn Writers and the Mary Roberts Rhinehart Chapter of Sisters in Crime in Pittsburgh were all great resources for ongoing support and skills enhancement.

Thanks to friends and authors Edith Maxwell and Susan Oleksiw for their support and to Susan who volunteered to wade in with light copy-editing on the book, saving me from multiple embarrassments. It's always a source of wonder to me how we can read over our own prose multiple times, gliding serenely over errors and omissions.

Jim Rada, a fellow member of Penn Writers, offered helpful independent publishing suggestions and also formatted MARIPOSA manuscript for publication

Finally, thanks, as always, to my wonderful family, who make me proud every day and enrich my life beyond measure. Special gratitude to my artist daughter Maggie for her work on the production of MARIPOSA and the creation of the cover. And, of course, to our West Highland White Terrier Archie, my faithful and comforting sidekick through it all.

Writing this book has been a long journey. Unfinished business from a challenging time when we all did the best we could, including my husband, Bill. I'm grateful to everyone who helped bring it to completion.

April 2025, Concord, MA

ABOUT MARIAN McMAHON STANLEY

Marian McMahon Stanley is a writer of mystery novels as well as a number of short stories and essays. Before turning to writing mysteries, Marian had two different long and satisfying careers – the first in a Fortune 500 corporation with significant international responsibilities and the second in a senior role for a large urban university. Marian lives and writes in a small historic town west of Boston near her extended family. Just as in her mysteries, she has a faithful Westie canine companion named Archie.

MORE FROM MARIAN MCMAHON STANLEY

The Immaculate
Buried Troubles

WWW.MARIANMCMAHONSTANLEY.COM

ROSARIA O'REILLY MYSTERIES
BY MARIAN MCMAHON STANLEY

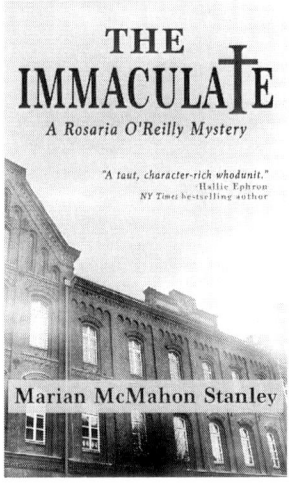

THE IMMACULATE - An elderly nun, Sister Mary Aurelius, widely beloved as she is feared, is murdered just as the clerical abuse scandal in the Boston Archdiocese is coming to light. Her former student Rosaria O'Reilly is determined to find those responsible.

BURIED TROUBLES - Long memories link Irish communities across the Atlantic. A young Galway journalism student is murdered in Boston as he unearths a dark secret there tied to the West of Ireland and the never-ending Troubles in Northern Ireland. Rosaria O'Reilly decamps to Connemara to find the answers.

WWW.MARIANMCMAHONSTANLEY.COM

Printed in the USA
CPSIA information can be obtained
at www.ICGtesting.com
LVHW090847181223
766490LV00058B/1197